3/74

Moorestown Library
3 2030 00095 2621
NJML 973.3448 Van
1973 c1943
Van Doren, Carl,
Mutiny in January:the story of

D1777586

96543

973.
3448   Van Doren, Carl
Van   Clinton
           Mutiny in
        January

Moorestown Free Library
Moorestown, New Jersey
08057

Viking Reprint Editions

MUTINY IN JANUARY

*The Story
of a Crisis in the Continental Army
now for the first time fully told from many
hitherto unknown or neglected sources
both American and British*

BY

CARL VAN DOREN

AUGUSTUS M. KELLEY • PUBLISHERS
CLIFTON 1973

First Published 1943
(New York: The Viking Press, Inc.)
Copyright 1943 by Carl Van Doren

RE-ISSUED 1973 BY
AUGUSTUS M. KELLEY · PUBLISHERS
Clifton New Jersey 07012
By Arrangement with THE VIKING PRESS

Library of Congress Cataloging in Publication Data

```
Van Doren, Carl Clinton, 1885-1950.
   Mutiny in January.

   (Viking reprint editions)
   Bibliography: p.
   1. United States--History--Revolution--Regimental
histories--Pennsylvania.  2. United States. Army--
History--Revolution.  I. Title.
E255.V26 1973        973.3'44'8           76-122061
ISBN 0-678-03175-4
```

973.3448
Van

PRINTED IN THE UNITED STATES OF AMERICA
by SENTRY PRESS, NEW YORK, N. Y. 10013

PREFACE

THE soldiers of the Continental Army have become legendary men, about whom it is known what great deeds they did but not what they ate or drank, how they were clothed or housed or paid, why they acted, when they grieved or grumbled. They are here, so far as possible, set forth as they actually were and as they thought of themselves, during a dangerous and crucial month. It turns out they were not vague figures of romance but tough, warm flesh and blood, in whom nothing is hard to understand except their patience and endurance—which are the incredible qualities in the whole indestructible race of man.

Though the story to some readers may seem unexpectedly full of intrigue, they have only to remember that in January 1781 the United States was an occupied country, with traitors, double-dealers, informers, and spies of all the kinds which recent events have made familiar throughout the world. Stealthy agents were everywhere in New York and New Jersey in the fifth year of the Revolution, on either side of the conflict and sometimes on both sides. There was no battle of armed forces, but a continual skirmishing between the secret services. The story sounds like plays or novels, but it is history.

It sounds, too, like news from all democratic countries, where men in the face of threat or temptation from the enemy can without treason still contend for justice among themselves. To Americans it will sound natural, and yet somehow encouraging, that so many native and foreign-born American soldiers, at a time when there was hardly yet an American nation at all, instinctively took it for granted that they should ask and receive redress of their wrongs in what has come to be called an American way.

CONTENTS

	PREFACE	5
1	ALARM	13
2	ROADS TO MUTINY	15
3	HARDSHIPS AT MOUNT KEMBLE	27
4	NEW YEAR'S DAY AND NIGHT	41
5	MARCH TO PRINCETON	53
6	NEWS AT NEW WINDSOR AND NEW YORK	62
7	THURSDAY AT PRINCETON AND TRENTON	72
8	EMISSARIES FROM THE ENEMY	82
9	OFFICERS AND OFFICIALS FROM PHILADELPHIA	96
10	PRELIMINARIES ON SATURDAY	104
11	SATURDAY NIGHT AND SUNDAY MORNING	115
12	NEGOTIATIONS ON SUNDAY	125
13	SUNDAY ELSEWHERE	133
14	AGREEMENT ON MONDAY	142
15	TRENTON, MASON, OGDEN	150
16	CONFUSION AMONG EMISSARIES	160
17	COUNTERACTION	180
18	TROUBLED SETTLEMENT	194
19	MORE MUTINY	204
20	SUPPRESSION AT POMPTON	215
21	CONCLUSIONS	228
	APPENDIX	241
	Oliver De Lancey's Journal of the Pennsylvania Mutiny	
	Note on the After-Mutiny at York	
	ACKNOWLEDGMENTS AND SOURCES	258
	INDEX	271

ILLUSTRATIONS

	Page
MOUNT KEMBLE	28

Plan of the Camp at Mount Kemble to accompany General Wayne's Diagram of December 10, 1780. Based on notes furnished by the Staff of the Morristown National Historical Park.

	Facing page
ANTHONY WAYNE	28

Facsimile of Wayne's unpublished Diagram of the camp at Mount Kemble, sent in a letter to Washington, December 10, 1780, here supplemented by a more detailed Plan newly drawn. *Reproduced with the permission of the Library of Congress.*

ALEXANDRE BERTHIER   60

Facsimile of an unpublished plan of Princeton drawn in August 1781 by a cartographer with the Comte de Rochambeau on his march to Yorktown. The camp site of the French troops here indicated is the same as that occupied by the Pennsylvania mutineers the previous January. *Reproduced from the Alexandre Berthier Papers with the permission of the Princeton University Library.*

ANDREW GAUTIER TO OLIVER DE LANCEY   94

Facsimile of an unpublished cipher letter sent by Gautier to De Lancey, January 5, 1781, under cover to Daniel Gautier, and of a contemporary transcription. *Reproduced with the permission of the William L. Clements Library, University of Michigan.*

WILLIAM BOWZAR TO ANTHONY WAYNE   104

Facsimile of an unpublished letter to Wayne from the Secretary of the Board of Sergeants, January 6, 1781. *Reproduced with the permission of the Historical Society of Pennsylvania.*

ALEXANDRE BERTHIER   152

Facsimile of an unpublished plan of Trenton, indicating the camp site of Rochambeau's troops in September 1781 in the field beside the Delaware near the Trenton ferry where the Pennsylvania mutineers had camped the previous January. *Reproduced from the Alexandre Berthier Papers with the permission of the Princeton University Library.*

SIR HENRY CLINTON   176

Facsimile of an unpublished List of Proposals Sent out and by Whom Carried, in Clinton's handwriting, January 9, 1781. *Reproduced with the permission of the William L. Clements Library, University of Michigan.*

GOULD TO ELIAS DAYTON   192

Facsimile of an unpublished letter from Gould, a British spy, to Dayton of the American Secret Service, February 22, 1781. Some of the information sent about "Poor Benedict" (Arnold) seems to have been deliberately misleading. *Reproduced with the permission of the Library of Congress.*

ILLUSTRATIONS

Facing page

ELIAS DAYTON TO ROBERT HOWE   224
    Facsimile of an unpublished letter from Dayton, January 27, 1781, announcing that British emissaries had been sent to the New Jersey mutineers. *Reproduced with the permission of the Library of Congress.*

MAP OF THE MUTINY COUNTRY   240
    Drawn specially for *Mutiny in January* by Margaret Van Doren.

MUTINY IN JANUARY

Alarm

AT HALF-PAST four on the moonless morning of January 2, 1781 Brigadier General Anthony Wayne, commanding the Pennsylvania troops then in winter quarters near Morristown, New Jersey, wrote a hurried letter to George Washington, who was at the Headquarters of the Continental Army at New Windsor six miles above West Point on the Hudson.

"It's with inexpressible pain that I now inform your Excellency of the general mutiny and defection which suddenly took place in the Pennsylvania Line, between the hours of nine and ten o'clock last evening. Every possible exertion was made by the officers to suppress it in its rise, but the torrent was too potent to be stemmed. Captain Bettin has fallen a victim to his zeal and duty. Captain Tolbert and Lieutenant White are reported mortally wounded. A very considerable number of the field and other officers are much injured by strokes from muskets, bayonets, and stones. Nor have the revolters escaped with impunity. Many of their bodies lay under our horses' feet, and others will retain with existence the traces of our swords and espontoons.

"They finally moved from the ground about eleven o'clock at night, scouring the grand parade with round and grape shot from four fieldpieces, the troops advancing in a solid column with fixed bayonets, producing a diffusive fire of musketry in front, flank, and rear.

"During this horrid scene a few officers with myself were carried by the tide to the fork of the roads at Mount Kemble.

But placing ourselves on that leading to Elizabethtown and producing a conviction to the soldiery that they could not advance upon that route but over our dead bodies, they fortunately turned towards Princeton.

"I have been induced to issue the enclosed order, from the ideas advanced last evening by many of the noncommissioned officers and privates, and hope it may have a happy effect.

"Colonels Butler and Stewart, to whose spirited exertions I am much indebted, will accompany me to Vealtown where the troops now are. We had our escapes last night. Should we not be equally fortunate today our friends will have this consolation: that we did not commit the honor of the United States or our own on this unfortunate occasion.

"Adieu, my dear General, and believe me yours most sincerely. . . .

"N. B. I am happy to inform your Excellency that every officer was present and exerted themselves to the utmost to prevent the extreme of mutiny. Major Fishbourne will be able *viva voce* to give you a more full account."

This letter (with the enclosed order) was not sent, and Fishbourne with another did not set out till after nine o'clock. Things moved fast in the first hot hours of a mutiny that for a week threatened the Americans with the violent collapse of their whole Army and the loss of their prospects of independence. A long story had come to a climax that might be its end.

2

Roads to Mutiny

THE threat of mutiny had hung over the Continental forces for two years. Even at Valley Forge, during the heroic winter of 1777–78, there was a mutinous unrest that troubled Washington profoundly. Two days before Christmas a field return showed that 2898 men were unfit for duty because they were "barefoot and otherwise naked." Few had more than one shirt, some had half a shirt, others had no shirt at all. Hundreds had to sit up at night by their fires, "instead of taking comfortable rest in a natural and common way." Hardly expecting more of the ration due them than their daily pound of beef and pound of hard bread, they had sometimes to go three days without bread (or flour to make it) and as much as a week without meat. These privations lasted through February. Most armies, Washington said, would have mutinied and dispersed under such treatment. He could not "enough admire the incomparable patience and fidelity" of his soldiers who held out. Yet, as he well knew, there had been "strong symptoms" of discontent, controlled only by the most active efforts of the officers and the powerful presence of Washington himself.

The spring after Valley Forge, which brought relief from cold and hunger, brought also a rapid decline in the value of the Continental currency in which the soldiers were paid. A private's monthly pay was six and two-thirds dollars, which in the first year of the war had been the equivalent of forty Pennsylvania shillings. In January 1778 this was worth about four and a half dollars in specie (silver). In July it was worth only about three, and in December only one. There were still soldiers in the Army who could remember being told, in General Orders for October 31, 1775, that they were to receive "higher pay than private soldiers ever yet met with in any war"; and perhaps could remember comparing their forty shillings a month with the British soldier's shilling a day. But in 1778 the British soldier still got his pay and got it regularly, in specie, while the American soldier might have to wait for weeks for his depreciated paper dollars.

The men of the Pennsylvania Line—the regiments enlisted and supplied by Pennsylvania for the Continental Army—were at a special disadvantage. Whereas soldiers from some of the other States had enlisted for a year at a time or less, and on their discharge might take what leave they chose and then get handsome bounties for re-enlisting, the Pennsylvanians had many of them enlisted "for three years or during the war" and so must continue serving, without free leave or compensatory bounty, for pay that steadily fell off in actual value. Those who had enlisted before February 1778 had received only the fixed Continental bounty of twenty dollars. After that month Pennsylvania gave each new recruit a hundred dollars in addition. But as depreciation went rapidly on in 1779, with New Jersey paying a bounty of 250 dollars for enlistment and Virginia 750, and certain towns in New England even larger sums for shorter terms, there was increased resentment and grumbling in the Pennsylvania Line.

They "never wished," Colonel Walter Stewart of the 2nd Pennsylvania wrote this year to the President of the State, "to be placed superior to any other troops. But from their situation, and the length of time they have endured the fatigues of a camp, they look upon themselves as entitled to an equal attention. . . . It is distressing to officers and hurtful to soldiers to see a man come to the same Army enlisted for nine months, eleven hundred dollars in his pocket and a new suit of clothes on his back. He will go to his State commissary to purchase his rum at 30 shillings per gallon, coffee 2/6 per pound, sugar 2/6, and every other article in like proportions. This I assert to be the case in numberless instances amongst the Eastern troops. While the Pennsylvanian, who has been in the service since the commencement of the war and enlisted during the same, and has but twenty dollars' bounty, is obliged when he wants a little liquor to pay the exorbitant price of 4 dollars per quart; his coffee will cost him 15 shillings per pound, sugar 15 shillings." Each Continental soldier was supposed to have a gill of rum or whisky a day in rainy weather or when on fatigue or guard duty, and also "occasionally" when there was a supply on hand. The Pennsylvanians were hard drinkers and, if they had money, bought liquor where they could find it.

Washington pointed out to Major General John Sullivan in February that falling money and rising prices were evils felt by almost everybody more than by the common soldier, who got—or was supposed to get—food and clothing, whatever they cost the public. But the difficulty of recruiting was so great in 1779 that Congress on January 23 voted a bounty of two hundred dollars (worth then about twenty-five in silver) to each man engaged in the service for a limited term who would now re-enlist for the war. This was of no benefit to Pennsylvanians who were enlisted for the full term already. Chiefly on their account Washington in June suggested and Congress allowed a gratuity of a hundred dollars to all soldiers enlisted for the war before January 23. Because of the "great uneasiness prevailing among many of the Pennsylvania troops, and frequent desertions," in July he paid their gratuities first, at the risk of causing dissatisfaction elsewhere in the Army.

There was a good deal of justice in their complaints, and these were veteran regiments such as Washington depended on.

During the summer campaign of 1779 the Pennsylvanians, naturally better behaved in the field than in winter quarters, gave little trouble. Two regiments of infantry and one of artillery were detached from the Line to go under Sullivan in the joint expedition against the Six Nations of the Iroquois. In the spectacular capture of Stony Point on the Hudson by picked men from the whole Army on the night of July 16, Wayne was in command and in person led the right wing; Colonel Richard Butler of the 5th Pennsylvania led the left; Lieutenant James Gibbons of the 6th and Lieutenant George Knox of the 9th led the advance called the Forlorn Hopes and both won the brevet of captain for conspicuous gallantry; and Sergeant Donlop of the 9th got a prize of a hundred dollars for being the fifth man to enter the enemy works. "Our officers and men," Wayne reported to Washington, "behaved like men who are determined to be free." But that winter, when the Army retired to quarters at the grand camp near Morristown under Washington's command, there were again hardships even worse than those at classic Valley Forge, and again dangerous unrest.

Though this was the coldest winter of the entire war, with deep snow, the soldiers had to sleep in tents or in the open air till they could build log huts, which were not finished at the end of December. At times they were "five or six days without bread, at other times as many days without meat, and once or twice two or three days without either.... At one time the soldiers eat every kind of horse food but hay." At the end of the first week in January 1780 they could no longer be restrained "from obeying the dictates of their sufferings," as Washington put it, and had begun to plunder in the neighborhood. On the 8th he took matters into his own hands, laid requisitions on the counties of New Jersey through their magistrates, and sent officers out to collect supplies, leaving certificates in payment at the market price, without too much concern for the feelings of the owners. "For the honor of the magistrates and good disposition of the people," he wrote to Philip Schuyler on the 30th, "I must add that my requisitions were punctually complied with, and in many counties exceeded." As to the Army, "they bore it with a most heroic patience; but sufferings like these, accompanied by the want of clothing, blankets, etc., will produce frequent desertions in all armies. And so it happened with us, though it did not excite a single mutiny."

The soldiers, Washington knew, were patient, and he believed the people were willing. The officials whose business and duty it was to keep the Army supplied were sometimes incompetent and sluggish, always at the mercy of State governments that were afraid to tax their constituents in the amounts needed. "We have," he wrote his brother, "no system, and seem determined not to profit by experience. We are, during the winter, dreaming of independence and peace, without using the means to become so. In the spring, when our recruits should be with the Army and in training, we have just discovered the necessity of calling for them. And by the fall, after a distressed and inglorious campaign for want of them, we begin to get a few men in just time to eat our provisions and consume our stores without rendering any service. Thus it is, one year year rolls over another, and without some change we are hastening to our ruin."

II

The Pennsylvanians, quieted by their gratuities in July 1779, in the following February had begun "to revive their former dissatisfactions" and to desert in serious numbers, as they heard of this year's bounties of 300 dollars paid new recruits by Connecticut and Rhode Island and 1000 by New Jersey. But the mutinies of 1780 were not in the Pennsylvania Line.

On January 1 about a hundred Massachusetts men of the garrison at West Point declared—not all of them accurately—that their enlistments for three years had expired, and marched off in a body intending to go home. They were forcibly brought back, some of them punished, most of them pardoned. Early in June thirty-one men of the 1st New York Regiment, garrisoned at Fort Schuyler on the Mohawk, for "want of pay and the necessary clothing, particularly shirts," left with their arms, to go—it was said—to the British at Oswegatchie (now Ogdensburg) on the St. Lawrence. Lieutenant Abraham Hardenbergh pursued them with a party of friendly Oneida Indians, overtook them when fifteen had just got across a river, and in a sudden gunfight shot thirteen of the others. This is perhaps the only time in the history of the American Army when an officer used Indians to kill white soldiers.

At Morristown the worst trouble came late in May. Strict discipline and frequent punishments had been necessary during the delaying months before the troops were ready to take the field for the summer's campaign. On May 25 General Orders announced that the "criminals now under sentence of death are to be executed tomorrow morning; eleven o'clock near the grand parade; fifty men properly officered from each brigade to attend. The camp color men from the Pennsylvania, Connecticut, and York Lines under the direction of a sergeant from each to dig the graves this afternoon." There were eleven of these criminals, all deserters but one: three from New Jersey regiments, three from New York, five from

Pennsylvania. Corporal Thomas Clark of the 4th Pennsylvania, Joseph Infelt and John Earhart of the 10th, and Thomas Calvin of the 11th had been convicted of attempting to desert to the enemy; James Coleman of the 11th, of "repeated desertion, forgery, and disposing of his arms and accouterments."

The Army was too familiar with capital sentences and last minute reprieves to expect that all these men would be put to death. But nobody could be sure who would be pardoned, or whether the occasion might not be more severe than usual. It was the first time this year so many executions had been ordered at once, as if, possibly, to set an unforgettable example. Nerves were tense in camp the afternoon and evening of the 25th.

Moreover, the British at New York had recently managed, by means of undetected spies, to drop printed handbills among the Americans full of sympathy with their distresses and tempting offers to them if they would desert. "The time is at length arrived," the handbills said, "when all the artifices and falsehoods of the Congress and of your commanders can no longer conceal from you the misery of your situation. You are neither clothed, fed, nor paid. Your numbers are wasting away by sickness, famine, nakedness," and expiring enlistments. "This is then the moment to fly from slavery and fraud." Those among the soldiers who had been born in the British Isles ought to know that the difficulties in Ireland were now settled, and Ireland firmly united with Great Britain "as well from interest as from affection." Native Americans need not be told that they had been "cheated and abused." All of them must realize that "in order to procure your liberty you must quit your leaders and join your real friends, who scorn to impose upon you and will receive you with open arms, kindly forgiving all your errors. . . . Associate then together, make use of your firelocks, and join the British Army, where you will be permitted to dispose of yourselves as you please."

Remembering the hardships they had endured so long, looking forward to the grim disciplinary measures to be taken the next day, some of them perhaps wondering whether flight to the British might not give them relief, the soldiers at Morristown were close to mutiny, which might break out anywhere in a sudden explosion of angry temper in either officers or privates. It came that evening, in the Connecticut Line.

Certainly few, and possibly none, of the Connecticut soldiers meant to desert to the British. But their Line had been five months without pay, in any currency, and had had no meat for several days after some weeks during which they had had only a half, a fourth, an eighth of "this essential article." They believed, too, that they had been discriminated against by the commissary. Two of the regiments about dusk got under arms, beat drums, systematically assembled on their parade ground, and prepared to leave camp in search of provisions, wherever that might lead.

Colonel Return Jonathan Meigs of the 6th Connecticut, then acting as brigade commander, was struck by one of the men in a scuffle, but no weapons seem to have been used. All was protest and expostulation, in which the Connecticut officers had the help of two Pennsylvania colonels. The mutineers were "reasoned with," as Washington reported the episode to Congress, "and every argument used that these gentlemen and Colonel Meigs could devise, either to interest their pride or their passions. They were reminded of their past good conduct, of the late assurances of Congress, of the objects for which they were contending; but their answer was, their sufferings were too great, that they wanted present relief and some present substantial recompense for their service." The final argument was an armed brigade of Pennsylvanians, as hungry as the Connecticut men but still not disaffected, who moved against the mutineers and secured their leaders. Most of the malcontents went back to their huts. A few who "nevertheless turned out again with their packs" were arrested and confined. The whole affair was soon over and afterwards disregarded.

What had happened did not interefere with the executions set for the 26th. The ceremonies were designed to bring home to the Army both the gravity of the offense of desertion and the mercy shown the offenders. Three had been sentenced to be shot, eight to be hanged. The eleven were brought in carts from their prison to the gallows, preceded by a "band of music" (fifteen or more drums and fifes) and attended by the Reverend William Rogers, a Baptist chaplain of one of the Pennsylvania brigades.

At the scaffold the chaplain, according to an eyewitness, "addressed them in a very pathetic manner," but loudly enough to be heard by all the soldiers drawn up in a hushed square under the May sun, and by more distant spectators; "impressing on their minds the heinousness of their crimes, the justice of their sentence, and the high importance of a preparation for death." With the men sentenced to be shot standing by to see the others hanged, the eight were placed side by side on ladders leaning against the crossbar of the tall scaffold, "with halters round their necks, their coffins before their eyes, their graves open to their view, and thousands of spectators bemoaning their awful doom. . . .

"At this awful moment," still according to Dr. James Thacher of a Massachusetts regiment, "while their fervent prayers are ascending to heaven, an officer comes forward and reads a reprieve for seven of them by the Commander-in-Chief"—and also for the three waiting to die on the ground. "The trembling criminals are now divested of the implements of death, and their bleeding hearts leap for joy. How exquisitely rapturous must be the transition, when snatched from the agonizing horrors of a cruel death, and mercifully restored to the enjoyment of a life that had been forfeited! No pen can describe the emotions which must have agitated their souls. They were scarcely able to remove from the scaffold without assistance. The chaplain"—who had probably known in advance that some or most of the men were to be pardoned—"reminded them of the gratitude they owed the Commander-in-Chief for his clemency towards them, and that the only return in their power to make was a life devoted to the faithful discharge of their duty."

The eighth man under sentence to be hanged was James Coleman of the 11th Pennsylvania, who had to hear ten names read off, and no one of them his. He had forged "a number of discharges by which he and more than a hundred soldiers had left the Army. He appeared to be penitent and behaved with uncommon fortitude and resolution." His fortitude and resolution might have been expected. On Sullivan's expedition the past September Coleman and another soldier of the tough 11th had somehow got separated from their regiment at Lake Canandaigua and had spent seven days catching up with it, with nothing to eat but the hearts and livers of two dead horses left behind by the troops.

Coleman's behavior on the scaffold was in the form his century almost demanded of actors on that final stage. "He addressed the soldiers, desired them to be faithful to their country and obedient to their officers." Being Coleman, he also "advised the officers to be punctual in their engagements to the soldiers and give them no cause to desert. He examined the halter and told the hangman the knot was not made right, and that the rope was not strong enough, as he was a heavy man. Having adjusted the knot and fixed it round his own neck, he was swung off instantly. The rope broke and he fell to the ground, by which he was very much bruised. He calmly ascended the ladder and said: 'I told you the rope was not strong enough. Do get a stronger one.' Another being procured, he was launched into eternity."

News of the Morristown mutiny and desertions reached New York and seemed to the British and loyalists there to mean that the rebel army was at last ready to break up. For weeks deserters had been coming in from the American camp, tired of the hardships they had borne, ready to change sides for the sake of better treatment, and pleased with the guinea each of them got when he came. If desertion were made easier for them, more might desert. In June the British landed an expedition in New Jersey in force much superior to all that Washington had to oppose them with. Though both Continental soldiers and Jersey militiamen fought, as Washington wrote, "with a spirit equal to anything I have seen in the course of the war," instead of deserting, they could hardly have withstood the British and German troops if the invasion had been pressed. Washington never understood why it was not.

The reason was ironical. The invading army that had come to encourage mutiny and desertion among the American soldiers was checked by the secret treason of an American major general. While the British were in New Jersey Benedict Arnold arrived at Headquarters at Morristown on June 12 and dined with Washington. Told in confidence that a French fleet and army were due at Rhode Island in two or three weeks, Arnold stealthily sent the information to British Headquarters in New York. Sir Henry Clinton, unwilling to move too far away for fear the French might attack New York in his absence, withdrew from the mainland to his fortified islands.

The Connecticut regiments, peacefully brigaded for a time with the Pennsylvanians, were sent late in June to West Point, and the Pennsylvanians were hurried after them late in September when Arnold's treason came to light and a possible British advance up the Hudson had to be guarded against. Both Lines seemed willing and eager to defend their country, whatever their own grievances. There were no grave signs of unrest in either Line, and few anywhere in the Army, till the troops went back to the dullness and hardships of winter quarters.

3

Hardships at Mount Kemble

THE Pennsylvanians were returned to the main Army at Totowa on the Passaic in October. Wayne at once was busy with the problem of winter clothing. "The weather begins to pinch," he wrote on the 17th. They planned to cut off the tails of the soldiers' coats "to repair the elbows and other defective parts," if they could be supplied with thread and needles. On the 25th, he reported, they had found they could make three decent infantry caps out of "one tolerable and two very ordinary hats" and thought they could make "three short coats out of three tattered long ones. I must acknowledge they would answer much better for the spring than fall, but without something done in this way we shall be naked in the course of the next two or three weeks, nor will even this expedient answer longer than Christmas."

Every Continental soldier enlisted for the war had been supposed, since September 1777, to have an annual suit of clothes consisting of one regimental coat, one jacket without sleeves, one pair of buckskin and two pairs of linen or woolen breeches, one hat or leather cap, two shirts, one hunting shirt, two pairs of overalls (trousers), two pairs of stockings, two pairs of shoes, and one blanket. The Pennsylvanians in October 1780 might have no more than a mended coat apiece, a bad shirt, a worse pair of trousers, any kind of shoes, and a share in a blanket. Almost no cloth was then made in the United States. The ten thousand

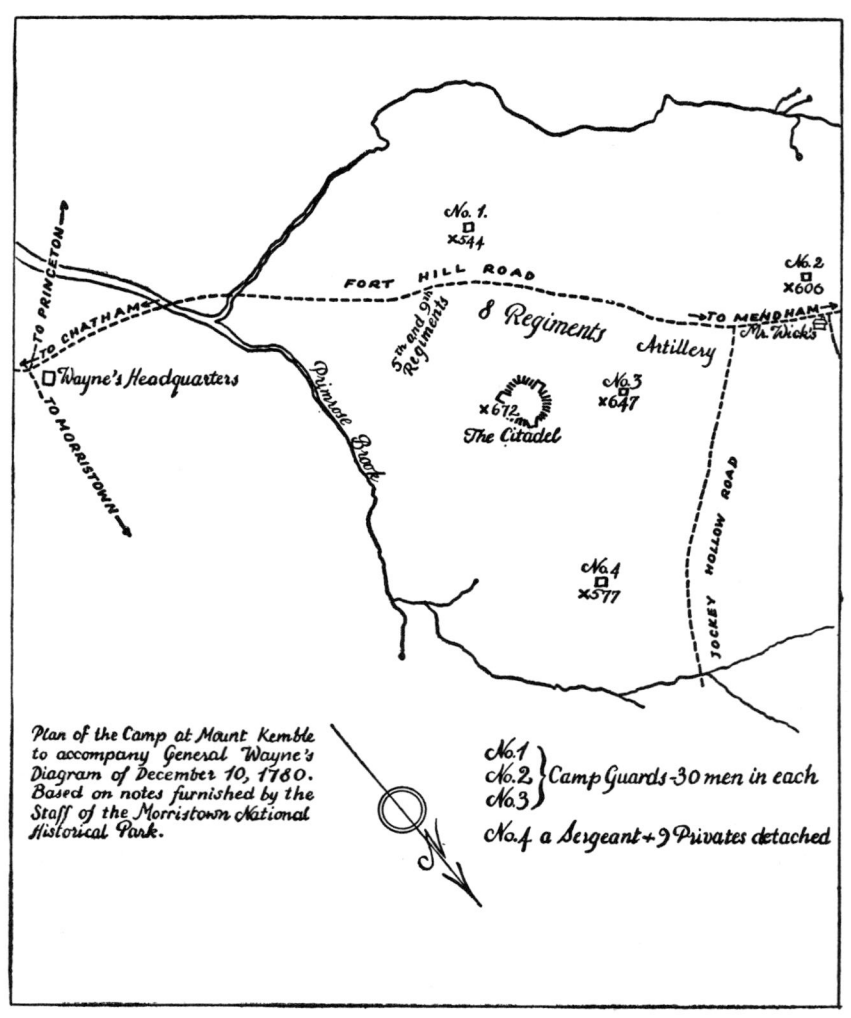

MOUNT KEMBLE

ANTHONY WAYNE

Facsimile of Wayne's unpublished Diagram of the Camp at Mount Kemble, sent in a letter to Washington, December 10, 1780, here supplemented by a more detailed Plan newly drawn.

suits expected from France that year had not come. The ladies of Philadelphia had subscribed money to buy shirts for their troops, but the shirts were still being made. Pennsylvania in July had sent an agent to Europe to borrow money on the credit of the State and had authorized him to make visionary purchases: 12,000 hats, 20,000 blankets, 30,000 yards of blue cloth for greatcoats for privates, 15,000 yards of blue and 15,000 yards of white broadcloth for ordinary coats, 24,000 pairs of white yarn stockings, 24,000 pairs of strong shoes, 70,000 yards of linen for soldiers' shirts, 6000 pairs of woolen mittens, 40,000 yards of coarse drilling for overalls, to say nothing of buttons, thread, linings, buckles, finer materials for officers' clothing, 1000 razors, and 10,000 "ivory small teeth combs." Pennsylvania had no credit in France or Holland, and none of these supplies came in 1780, or ever.

In November Washington, dividing the Army for winter quarters, assigned only the "bad clothed men of Pennsylvania" to Morristown. They arrived there, from Totowa, on the evening of the 29th and pitched their tents in the woods. The camp was about four miles southwest of the town along the Jockey Hollow road, and was known as Mount Kemble from the highest of several hills within the grand camp limits. Colonel Thomas Craig of the 3rd, who had gone ahead with two hundred men two weeks before to put the Pennsylvania huts in order, had found many of them demolished, though the Army hospital had preserved some officers' huts for the use of the sick.

On December 1 the officers met and settled the plan of hutting. The 5th and 9th regiments were to repair as many huts as they needed of those occupied the year before by the Connecticut Line. These, facing southeast, lay at right angles to the Army road leading eastward past Fort Hill out of the camp to the highway, where Wayne had his headquarters at the cross-roads. The other eight regiments of infantry and Colonel Thomas Proctor's artillery would take over the huts in which Brigadier General Edward Hand's mixed brigade had been quartered, adding to them some or all of last year's Maryland huts moved into line with Hand's. All these huts, facing southwest, lay along the Fort Hill road, with the artillery at the extreme right. There was a magazine for ammunition and for the Line's six fieldpieces close to the Jockey Hollow road, apparently beyond it in Thomas Wick's orchard. The camp made up, roughly, two sides of a rectangle, the huts facing outwards. Behind each line of huts the ground rose to the top of Fort Hill from which a central citadel could command the whole. There were—or were to be—outlying guard posts beyond the camp on the north, east, south, and west. The land was irregular and had been heavily wooded, but had of course been cleared for its earlier use as winter quarters.

The huts now repaired were built and laid out according to regulations issued at Valley Forge and followed with varying changes every winter of the war. Each hut was about sixteen feet long by fourteen wide, the side walls six and a half or seven feet to the eaves. The walls were logs notched and crossed at the corners and made tight with clay or mud, and the roofs were smaller logs sloping down from the ridgepole, or split slabs, or large shingles. In the side of the house facing the company street was a door, of slabs or boards hung on wooden hinges. In the center of the other side or at one end was a fireplace built also of logs, but plastered with clay supposed to be eighteen inches thick. There was ordinarily a window, or two, but in cold weather this was not always insisted on. The windows were merely holes sawed through the side walls, with wooden shutters hinged like the doors, without glass but sometimes with oiled paper pasted over the openings. The huts of the noncommissioned officers and privates were one room each, where ten or twelve men slept in bunks one above another against the wall, with straw and blankets for bedding. Most of the huts had only packed dirt for floors. In the rear of the men's huts were the officers' huts, not always uniform but commonly two rooms each, occupied by three or four officers who composed a mess. Back of these were the kitchens. Each regimental hutment was laid out in straight lines like a compact village with a front of three hundred feet on the parade, and a depth of a thousand. The parade was free of trees and stumps and swept reasonably clean every morning for roll call.

Many of the men lived in camp much as they would have lived at home: in log houses they had built themselves. The huts were more soundly built than most pioneer cabins, and the camp better kept than most remote villages. Chimneys had to be at least two feet higher than the roofs as a precaution against fire. The men were forbidden to sink their huts part way in the ground or cover them with earth for the sake of warmth, at the expense of dryness and ventilation. Careful attention was paid to draining the camp ground, keeping the streets and parade free of trash, and constructing proper necessary houses (latrines).

With the soldiers at Mount Kemble this winter were about a hundred women and children. Most of the women seem to have been the wives of noncommissioned officers or privates and to have lived in the huts. Women and children were allowed rations along with the men, who had no other homes for their families and who would, Washington knew, desert if they were not provided for. The women, besides looking out for their men, were usually laundresses for the officers, sometimes nurses in the hospitals, and now and then unofficial sutlers selling liquor or other commodities. Occasional orders during the war saying that women must not throw soap suds or refuse on the parade, and that women and children must use the necessary houses, indicate that they were slovenly. Persistent orders against permitting the women to ride in baggage wagons on a march make it fairly plain that they did ride.

Of the children in camp with the Pennsylvanians this winter nothing appears to be known. Some of the soldiers themselves were hardly more than children. Jeremiah Levering, fourteen or fifteen, had been for three years enlisted in the artillery, "but not taught to beat the drum or blow the fife, and being of small stature and weakly habits." He was perhaps a waif picked up by the soldiers and put through the form of enlistment so he might be fed and clothed. David Hamilton Morris, of the 3rd regiment, had been enlisted for a year, but was still only twelve. His widowed mother, who lived near Morristown, had put him in charge of Captain James Chrystie, to whom the boy acted as waiter (servant). Others boys, enlisted as soldiers, served other officers in the same capacity.

By December 7 the men were generally comfortable in their huts, and there were no complaints with regard to housing. But Wayne's letters throughout the month insisted on the dangerous shortage of clothes and rations.

The troops had had, he wrote on the 7th, no spirituous liquor for sixty days except half a gill of rum a man about two weeks before. In cold weather rum was "an article as necessary in the eye of a soldier as provisions or clothing." On the 16th Wayne wrote to Joseph Reed, President of the Supreme Executive Council of Pennsylvania, in something close to desperation. In the past forty-six weeks, he said, the Pennsylvania Line had not been adequately served a third of the time. "We are reduced to dry bread and beef for our food, and to cold water for our drink. . . . This, together with the old worn-out coats and tattered linen overalls and what was once a poor substitute for a blanket (now divided among three soldiers), is but very wretched living and shelter against the winter's piercing cold, drifting snows, and chilling sleets.

"Our soldiery are not devoid of reasoning faculties, nor are they callous to the first feelings of nature. They have now served their country for near five years, poorly clothed, badly fed, and worse paid. Of the last article, trifling as it is, they have not seen a paper dollar in the way of pay for near twelve months." Pennsylvania should not only feed and clothe its soldiers but should also make up to them for their losses in pay by the depreciation of the currency. They had been promised, on enlistment, that each noncommissioned officer and private would be rewarded with a hundred acres of land at the end of the war. This should be made more than a promise. "Give your soldiery a landed property, make their interest and the interest of America reciprocal, and I will answer for their bleeding to death, drop by drop, to establish the independency of the country. On the contrary, should we neglect rewarding their past services and not do justice to their more than Roman virtue, have we nothing to apprehend from their defection? Believe me, my dear sir, that if something is not immediately done to give them a local attachment to this country, and to quiet their minds, we have not yet seen the worst side of the picture.

"The officers in general, as well as myself, find it necessary to stand for hours every day, exposed to wind and weather, among the poor naked fellows while they are working at their huts and redoubts, often assisting with our own hands in order to produce a conviction to their minds that we share and more than share every vicissitude in common with them, sometimes asking to participate of their bread and water. The good effect this conduct has is very conspicuous, and prevents them murmuring in public; but the delicate mind and humanity are hurt, very much hurt, at their visible distress and private complainings."

Besides the usual troubles over clothes and rations, there was a crucial discontent over pay and enlistment. Congress in October has voted a new arrangement of the whole Continental Army to take effect the first day of the next year. This would reduce the eleven Pennsylvania regiments of infantry to six, "deranging" many of the officers but retaining all the noncommissioned officers and privates. There was confusion among the deranged officers, numbers of whom had no prospects outside the Army which gave them at least quarters and rations. The soldiers who were to be held saw no prospects in the Army for them. The Continental currency in which they were still paid had by December sunk in value till the ratio to specie was 75 to 1: that is, a soldier's paper pay for an entire year was worth only about a dollar in silver. If they must continue to be soldiers, enough of the men thought, they were no better off than slaves.

In the circumstances they kept remembering that some Pennsylvania enlistments had been "for three years or during the war." Many privates could not read. Many had paid little attention to the papers they signed or made their mark on, often when they were drunk. But in this hard December it was easy for a soldier to persuade himself that he had understood, and had been told, he was enlisting for the war only in case it should end before three years, and for three years at the most. Before the arrangement of January 1 was

HARDSHIPS AT MOUNT KEMBLE

made final, the soldiers argued, men who had served three years ought to be given their choice either to leave the Army or else to re-enlist explicitly for the duration of the war, for the new bounties paid by Pennsylvania since July. These were three half-johanneses (three Portuguese gold coins worth about twenty-seven dollars in silver) and the promise of two hundred acres of land after the war. Prisoners in the Philadelphia jail were being pardoned if they would enlist, and being sent to Morristown with sums of money that made them rich among the destitute veterans—though as it turned out even these favored recruits did not always get the full bounty due them.

The veterans, resentful at what seemed a fresh injustice added to their long hardships, clamored to their officers about their enlistments. The officers declared that most of the men were enlisted for the war, without the three-years' alternative, but did not have the papers on hand to prove it. There was more bad blood among the men than the officers were generally aware of.

Wayne was afraid that January 1 might see the smoldering animosities blaze up. "I sincerely wish," he wrote on December 16 to his old school friend Francis Johnston who was colonel of the 5th Regiment, "the Ides of January was come and past. I am not superstitious, but can't help cherishing disagreeable ideas about that period." His presence in camp, he believed, was "absolutely necessary." Never had there been such need as now for Pennsylvania to "adopt some effectual mode and immediate plan to alleviate the distress of the troops and to conciliate their minds and sweeten their tempers, which are much soured by neglect."

II

According to the return of December 11 there were 2473 officers and men of the Pennsylvania Line at Morristown: ten of the Line's eleven regiments of foot and its regiment of artillery. Besides these, Pennsylvania had another regiment (the 8th, commanded by Colonel Daniel Brodhead) at Pittsburgh, guarding the frontier against Indian attacks; Colonel Stephen Moylan's light dragoons quartered at Lancaster; and Colonel Benjamin Flower's artillery artificers, permanently established at Carlisle. Five companies of German soldiers were expected to come to Morristown on January 1, when the German Regiment, raised in Pennsylvania and Maryland, would be done away with and the men returned to the Lines of their separate States. Wayne on the 16th believed the total number of officers and men supported by Pennsylvania was "not far short of 3500."

This, even with the considerable force of militia also maintained by Pennsylvania, was not a large total for a State that then had a population of 300,000 or more. But the Pennsylvania authorities had always hesitated to lay sufficient taxes for the support of a Revolution which many of the people had not favored in the beginning and of which others had grown tired. The Quakers and the German quietists in the State were opposed to war on principle. There were many conservatives who, while not outwardly loyal to the former British government, were at least not devoted to the new American administration. Pennsylvania was divided by two intensely antagonistic political parties, quarreling over the State constitution and every act of the Assembly and Council. Because Philadelphia was the seat of the Continental Congress, Pennsylvania had sometimes been called upon for emergency money and supplies and had come to feel that it had done more than its share while distant States had done less. And of course Pennsylvania suffered with all the States from the steady, recently headlong, depreciation of the Continental currency.

In March 1780 Congress had discontinued the old currency and had undertaken to replace it with money issued by the States, with a guarantee by Congress. But public faith was lacking, and the new issues at once began to depreciate. Pennsylvania might be, as Washington said, full of flour, but had no money to buy it with; might have wagons, but had no money to hire them for the use of the Army. The ladies of Philadelphia headed by Esther Reed, wife of the President, worked hard during the summer and raised 300,634 dollars by subscription. These were Continental dollars and bought only 2005 shirts, none of which reached Morristown till after the mutiny. The shortage of money was responsible for many delays, and some dishonesty. In August Lieutenant John Bigham of the 5th Pennsylvania was sent by the Council from Philadelphia with 14,068 dollars to pay bounties due recruits in the Line, but never arrived with it. When he was afterwards cashiered he frivolously claimed he had spent the money for necessary charges on the road to camp. This money had so little value there was as much temptation to squander it as to save it.

How little it was worth appears from three bills allowed by the Council in September: £259 for spirits and bell-ringers on the birthday of His Most Christian Majesty of France; 27,733½ dollars for ten head of cattle; 5000 dollars for two Indian scalps taken by Pennsylvanians, "agreeable to the late proclamation of this board."

Wayne's desperate letter of December 16 asked particularly for hard money to pay recruits. The treasury was empty, but efforts were made to raise funds by subscription among the citizens. On the 27th Brigadier General James Potter of the Pennsylvania militia, a member of the Council, was instructed to go to Morristown with all the money that had come in. It amounted to £484 2 shillings, made up of the bewildering varieties of money then used in a country that had no coinage of its own: $80\frac{1}{2}$ English guineas, 3 French guineas (louis d'or), $5\frac{1}{4}$ moidores, 5 Spanish pistoles, 4 ducats, 1 half-caroline, $99\frac{5}{8}$ half-johannesses, $43\frac{1}{2}$ Spanish dollars, and $3\frac{1}{2}$ English shillings.

The bankrupts in the capital were sending money to the paupers at camp. As Washington had on the 10th written to Gouverneur Morris, "it would be well for the troops if, like chameleons, they could live upon air, or, like the bear, suck their paws for sustenance during the rigor of the approaching season."

III

The hungry, shivering soldiers had heard of civilians living luxuriously at Philadelphia, in fine houses, with warm clothes, delicious food, all sorts of wines and spirits, and money to spend. They had heard of extravagance and peculation. Accustomed as they were to hard work and plain fare, they would not have grumbled too much at occasional shortages such as the whole country had to endure. But, no matter how patriotic the soldiers were, they could not live on patriotism. They must have food and clothing, as well as arms, if they were to fight. They worked for wages like other men, and should be paid, particularly since they were not free to leave their work for other livelihoods.

There was a chance they might have to fight that winter. News came of much activity in the waters round New York.

This might mean that the British intended a landing in New Jersey, or an expedition sailing for some Southern port. If they should land, and advance as far as Morristown, Wayne's camp might be attacked. If they went south, Mount Kemble would be safe, but the men would still be uneasy. Wayne was sure that, in any case, it was better to keep the men working at camp defenses than to let them brood in their huts. On December 10 he wrote to Washington that the citadel on Fort Hill was to consist of "three small redoubts, the whole joined by a stockade. But if this embarkation"—to the southward—"actually takes place, I believe I shall content myself with some strong huts surrounded by a good abatis, in the nature of blockhouses, for our camp guards. Their position is such as to give great strength and security to the camp," of which Wayne sent a diagram he himself had drawn.

The British expedition turned out to be Benedict Arnold's raid to Virginia, which sailed on the 21st. But Wayne could not be sure of this. "The accounts from New York are so complicated and contradictory," he wrote to Washington on Christmas Day, "that very little credit is to be given to anything we hear. The present, or *late,* embarkation (for it is yet a moot point)" might be only a trick of the British to throw the Americans off guard, "in order to mask the grand operation." He could not give up work on his citadel, but kept at least a hundred men busy there. He stationed a sergeant and nine privates at the guard post south of the camp, with thirty men at each of the other three.

The December days were short. At nightfall the men had to huddle in their crowded huts, after an unsatisfying monotonous meal without rum or coffee, to sit on the floor or sprawl in their chilly, dirty bunks, muttering about the lack of bread and meat, of clothes and blankets, of—probably—soap and candles, of—certainly—pay or prospects of pay. It naturally came about that their resentments were specially acute towards their immediate officers, who had personally to exercise repressive discipline over the embittered men.

This was the time for the British to send fresh officers. A few more handbills found their way into camp. There is nothing to show that these had any real effect, or that the mutiny owed anything to British instigation. Neither is there any evidence that the movement towards mutiny was fully concerted in advance or that all the men were prepared for an outbreak at a specified hour.

About the 29th Potter arrived from Philadelphia, expected to have money to pay bounties to new recruits or to men whose terms were definitely expiring and who would re-enlist for the war. It then came out that the money sent earlier by Bigham had never reached the camp and that some of the men had been defrauded. Potter had less than was required, and some short-term recruits had to be allowed to leave the service. Those who remained had lost the last hope that anything would be done for them. Three days more, and then the new arrangement. Unwilling noncommissioned officers and privates would be bound by it once and for all.

Here was a general grievance overshadowing any particular one. Yet Wayne mentioned only one in his letter to Colonel John Moylan, assistant clothier general, on December 30. "The distressed condition of the soldiery for clothing beggars all description. For God's sake send us our dividend of uniforms, overalls, blankets."

4

New Year's Day and Night

ANTHONY WAYNE, not yet known as Mad Anthony, was thirty-six on New Year's Day. Born at Waynesborough, Pennsylvania, he had inherited a prosperous tannery from his father and was not dependent on his Continental pay as brigadier general, which would not have bought a month's oats for his horse. Ever since he joined the Army in January 1776 Wayne had been thought a man who could "fight as well as brag" with vigor and enthusiasm. Washington later—perhaps already—looked on him as "more active and enterprising than judicious and cautious . . . open to flattery, vain, easily imposed upon, and liable to be drawn into scrapes." Nobody ever questioned Wayne's bravery or loyalty. He was muscular and energetic, with dark eyes in an animated face, wore handsome uniforms of blue and white, and spoke and wrote dramatically. "I know that I have the hearts of the soldiery," he had written on December 16, one of his most discouraged recent days.

He did not like Major General Arthur St. Clair, who outranked Wayne in the Line; but St. Clair was just then absent in Philadelphia and Wayne was in command at Mount Kemble. He had his headquarters at Peter Kemble's house at the forks of the main road east of the camp. Kemble was a loyalist of the firmest principles, formerly a member of the royal Council of New Jersey, with a son who was a lieutenant colonel in the British Army and a daughter married to Thomas Gage, who had been British commander-in-chief in North America when the war broke out. Kemble was related also, at least by marriage, to such New York patriot families as the Bayards, the Schuylers, the Stuyvesants, the Van Cortlands, and the Van Rensselaers, as well as to the loyalist De Lanceys; and Kemble was considerately treated even by the Americans who occupied a large part of his "plantation" with their camp.

Wayne had been invited to dine on New Year's Day at Beverwyck, where Lucas Beverholt (van Beverhoudt), a Dutchman from the West Indies, lived in some state near Whippany five miles northeast of Morristown. If Wayne had gone he might have stayed convivially late, or all night, and so have been absent from camp at a time of crisis. Fortunately he declined the invitation, with the excuse that he must be busy on the 1st with the new arrangement of the Line.

That Monday was fresh and bright, not very cold. The German soldiers marched in from Suffern, New York, and were assigned to temporary quarters. Wayne and the field officers "met to settle the arrangement," Captain Joseph McClellan of the 9th noted in his diary. "The day spent in quietness." Possibly the 9th and the 5th, in the former Connecticut huts and separated from the other regiments, may have been quieter than the rest of the camp. The officers of the 10th, according to Lieutenant Enos Reeves, had an "elegant regimental dinner and entertainment" to celebrate what they supposed would be their last day together, and "spent the day very pleasantly." As for the men, every one of them was issued a half-pint of liquor, and those who had money bought more liquor in the neighborhood. When about eight o'clock at night, according to Captain McClellan, "a number of men in the 11th Regiment began

NEW YEAR'S DAY AND NIGHT 43

to huzza . . . it was generally thought it only proceeded from the men drinking. . . . A number of officers collected in order to quiet the men, which was done in a great measure."

It is by no means certain that the tumult in Lieutenant Colonel Adam Hubley's 11th was altogether intended as mutiny from the first, but this was one of the more unruly regiments, with an unusually mixed personnel. Of its 25 sergeants, 7 had been born in Ireland, 7 in England, 1 in Scotland, 4 in America, and 6 in countries not specified; of 22 corporals, 2 in Ireland, 3 in England, 2 in Scotland, 5 in America, and 10 not specified. Out of a rank and file (not all present that day) of 194 whose birthplaces were set down, Ireland had furnished 87, England 37, Scotland 6, Germany 8, and America 56. Since the 11th had been originally raised in the western counties of the State, where Scotch-Irish Presbyterians were numerous, it naturally had more men born in Ireland than some other Pennsylvania regiments had. It was like all the regiments in having foreign-born soldiers, on account of the heavy emigration to Pennsylvania in the decade or two preceding the Revolution.

The soldiers of the 11th had done many kinds of work in civilian life. Out of 57 in two companies whose trades were listed, there were 7 farmers, 7 laborers, 5 weavers, 5 shoemakers, 4 carpenters, 3 saddlers, 3 hatters, 3 barbers, 2 tailors, 2 blacksmiths, and 1 bookbinder, butcher, cabinetmaker, cooper, distiller, millwright, potter, ropemaker, silk-dyer, silversmith, soap-boiler, staymaker, tinker, tobacconist, vintner, and watchmaker. Out of 59 men in these same companies whose heights were recorded, there were only 7 over five feet nine inches, and 17 under five feet five.

Something like these varieties was typical of the whole Line. The mutiny was carried out, not alone by rustic

Pennsylvanians, but by native and foreign town-bred men as well, skilled at trades; men alert, angry, hungry, dressed in shabby odds and ends; a good many small furious men who felt bullied; men at or near a bursting point, and some of them with stubborn plans for a settlement, no matter what it might cost.

The shouting in the 11th died down. By nine o'clock all the men in camp were in their huts or properly accounted for. But, whatever designs and agreements they had, there was still a general excitement that had not been quieted. About an hour later another "disturbance began on the right of the division" near the Jockey Hollow road and was answered from the left. Lieutenant Reeves "went on the parade and found numbers in small groups whispering and busily running up and down in the Line." Muskets were fired and a skyrocket sent up. As if this were a signal, soldiers everywhere came "running out with their arms, accouterments, and knapsacks"—which Continental soldiers kept with them in their huts. "The officers in general exerted themselves to keep the men quiet, and keep them from turning out. We each applied himself to his own company, endeavored to keep them in their huts and lay by their arms, which they would do while we were present, but the moment we left one hut to go to another, they would be out again. Their excuse was they thought it was an alarm and the enemy coming on."

In spite of all the officers could do, the mutinous soldiers—at that time much less than half of the Line—got to their own parades fronting on the Fort Hill road and moved in regimental groups towards the right, which seemed to be an appointed rendezvous. Lieutenant Francis White of the 10th, trying to stop such a group, was shot through the thigh. Captain Samuel Tolbert of the 2nd had an encounter with a soldier of his company, Absalom Evans, who later deserted to the British and told his own story. He was, he said, "one of the first that revolted; and immediately after, Captain Tolbert run him into the thigh with a sword, on which (for he was loading at the time) he shot Captain Tolbert through the belly." (Both White and Tolbert recovered.)

The firing of muskets became so general that the officers could only withdraw and let the men have their way. Lieutenant Reeves heard "a confused noise to the right, between the line of huts and Mrs. Wick's." He crept through the orchard in the dark, mixed unnoticed in the crowd, "and found they had broken open the magazine and were preparing to take off the cannon." Four of the fieldpieces were dragged into the Fort Hill road. There was dispute over firing the pieces, "one party alleging that it would arouse the timid soldiery; the other objected that it would alarm the inhabitants. For a while I expected the dispute would be decided by the bayonet, but the gunner in the meantime slipped up to the piece and put a match to it, which ended the affair." Several shots were fired, to be followed by louder shouting and the discharging of more muskets.

In the mêlée one of the soldiers was killed. The mutineers, seizing the magazine, had forced the sentinel from his post and replaced him by one of their own number. Another mutineer, unaware of this and not recognizing the new sentinel, officiously ordered him away, "received a ball through the head, and died instantly." Other men are said to have been wounded, and perhaps some killed, by accidental musket bullets, but there are no trustworthy records.

"About this time," still according to Reeves, "General Wayne and several field officers (mounted) arrived. General Wayne and Colonel Richard Butler spoke to them for a considerable time, but it had no effect. Their answer was, they had been wronged and were determined to see themselves righted. He replied that he would right them as far as in his power. They rejoined, it was out of his power, their business was not with the officers, but with Congress and the Governor and Council of the State. . . . With that, several platoons fired over the General's head. The general called out: 'If you mean to kill me, shoot me at once, here's my breast,' opening his coat. They replied that it was not their intention to hurt or disturb an officer of the Line, two or three individuals excepted."

One of the soldiers a few days later gave another version of this passage between Wayne and the mutineers. "General Wayne entreated them to desist, and opened his breast, offering it to anyone who had any resentment against him. One Irishman said he had, and was going to kill him, but was stopped by the others."

The majority of the men seem to have been still indisposed to mutiny, or undecided whether or not to fall in with the active minority. Colonel Walter Stewart's regiment (the 2nd) had to be forced to join or else be bayoneted. Captain Thomas Campbell of the 4th paraded a part of his regiment and led them in an incompleted charge to recapture the fieldpieces. They advanced a little, then dispersed and left the officers alone. A soldier from the mob attacked Lieutenant Colonel William Butler of the 4th, "who was obliged to retreat between the huts to save his life. He went around one hut and the soldier, around another to head him, met Captain Bettin [Adam Bettin of the same regiment] who was coming down the alley, who seeing a man coming towards him in a charge, charged his espontoon to oppose him, when the fellow fired his piece and shot

NEW YEAR'S DAY AND NIGHT

the Captain through the body, and he died two hours later." (What is said to be Bettin's grave is still shown under what is called the Bettin Oak on the Jockey Hollow road.)

The mutinous men moved along the parade towards the left, protected by the cannon on the Fort Hill road, gathering numbers as they went. "As they came down the line, they turned the soldiers out of every hut, and those who would not go with them were obliged to hide till they were gone." When the 1st, 2nd, 3rd, 4th, 6th, 7th, 10th, and 11th regiments reached the Connecticut huts they found the 5th (commanded by Francis Johnston) and the 9th (by Richard Butler) drawn up on their parades. They were kept in order till they were threatened with the cannon, which fired over their heads. Then "the greater part of them mixed in with the other regiments" and moved with them along the Fort Hill road and across Primrose brook towards the forks near Wayne's headquarters. About half the Line had now joined the mutiny.

While all this went on, there were systematic mutineers taking possession of horses, wagons, ammunition, tents and baggage, provisions, and preparing for a march.

A hundred officers could not subdue a thousand or so armed men, especially when the men had many of the sergeants on their side. The pistols, swords, and spontoons (half-pikes) of the officers were of little use against muskets and fieldpieces. However mounted, officers could not ride down a column of bayonets. Wayne himself was forced to the cross-roads, where he and a few officers made their last determined stand.

If the men took the road either to their left or straight ahead they could go to Chatham and Elizabethtown, and then on to the British if they wished. So far as Wayne knew, this might be a general defection, engineered by secret agents of the enemy and supported by an enemy expedition already landed or landing from New York. He was willing to risk his life in an effort to turn the mutineers to the other road, which could lead them, by way of Princeton, towards Philadelphia. Given time to cool off and reflect, they might be persuaded to make peaceable and reasonable terms with Congress and the Pennsylvania Council, no matter what the British might offer them.

The mass of the soldiers had no desire to go to the British, and perhaps wondered at Wayne for suspecting them so strongly. "They declared it was not their intention, and that they would hang any man who would attempt it." Wayne pleaded with them not to desert their country's cause. They answered they were not deserting it, only demanding what their country had long owed them. They would fight fast enough, and under Wayne, if the enemy were to come out. Until their wrongs were righted they would not take further orders even from him. There must be a settlement in which the soldiers could meet on equal terms with officers or officials. For that they must first get away to some place where they could be on their own ground and insist on being heard.

The column took the road to the right and marched off in regular platoons under command of the sergeants: an advanced party, then artillerymen with two of the fieldpieces, wagons, the regiments in order, and two more fieldpieces covered by a rear guard, with drums and fifes playing in the disturbed night. "They went off very civilly," Reeves observed, "to what might have been expected from such a mob." The camp was left in turmoil that lasted most of Tuesday. Mutineers kept coming back and coaxing or forcing undecided men to join the revolt till most of the Line had gone from Mount Kemble.

NEW YEAR'S DAY AND NIGHT 49

(An incident that may actually have taken place on Tuesday gave rise to one of the few legends of the mutiny still surviving in Morristown. Temperance Wick, the legend says, a young girl who lived with her recently widowed mother in the farmhouse near the magazine, was riding along the Jockey Hollow road when two soldiers tried to take her white horse from her, saying they would use him only to go to their homes in Bucks County and then would send him back to her. She talked the mild, and perhaps embarrassed, mutineers into letting her ride to her own home first, where they might come and have her horse. But before they arrived she had hidden him in a small back bedroom, which is still shown to visitors, and kept him there till they had given up the search and gone.)

At some time before half-past four Tuesday morning Wayne wrote out what he called an order but what was a request and a promise: "Agreeably to the proposition of a very large proportion of the worthy soldiery last evening, General Wayne hereby desires the noncommissioned officers and privates to appoint one man from each regiment, to represent their grievances to the General, who on the sacred honor of a gentleman and a soldier does hereby solemnly promise to exert every power to obtain immediate redress of those grievances; and he further plights that honor that no man shall receive the least injury on account of the part they have taken on the occasion. And that the persons of those who may be appointed to settle the affair shall be held sacred and inviolate." In this Wayne credited the "worthy soldiery" with first suggesting a committee to represent them, and admitted that they had grievances. He closed with a pleasant reference to the outbreak, as if it had been a kind of night's outing. "The General hopes soon to return to camp with all his brother soldiers who took a little tour last evening." This he may have sent after them, or may have held till he could confer with them again.

When Wayne wrote his conciliatory order he had lost half his command and could not hope to put down the mutiny by force. But the mutineers had not gone towards the enemy, and had not seemed to expect the enemy to come to them. Surely if they had expected that they would have taken the other road in spite of him, alive or dead. There was some comfort in this thought.

It did not last long. Eastward from Mount Kemble beacons began to flame against the black horizon. Wayne knew that there was a line of beacons—log pens rising each in a rough pyramid and filled with tar and dry fuel—on hilltops all the way from Morristown to the Jersey shore. He could guess that watchful militiamen, hearing the cannon fired by the mutineers, had sent up their signals. But he could not be certain from what direction the alarm had come. The flaring beacons might indicate that the British were on their way westward, and that it was Wayne who was being warned.

For the present, Wayne decided, New Jersey would have to defend itself. He sent an order to the Continental brigade at Pompton to hurry to Chatham, where the militia would assemble. His own first duty was to get control of the mutineers, if that was possible, and at any rate not to leave them alone with their resentments. If he went after them, they might kill him. But he might hold them together, keep them from joining the British, and persuade them to negotiate with the civil authorities. The possible gains seemed worth the probable risks.

For this dangerous errand he chose Richard Butler and Walter Stewart, his brigade commanders, to go with him. Butler, born in Ireland, was a gallant and popular officer, whose brother William was commandant of the 4th Regiment, and who had three younger brothers who were officers in the Pennsylvania Line. Stewart, of Irish descent though born in Pennsylvania, was one of the youngest colonels and reputed to be the handsomest man in the Army. Wayne had no Irish blood in him, but he always remembered that his English grandfather had lived in Ireland for a time before coming to America, and he himself was an ardent member of the Friendly Sons of St. Patrick. The Irish soldiers among the mutineers might look favorably on Irish officers.

News of the outbreak must be sent to the Continental Congress and to the Pennsylvania Council, informing them of what had happened, warning them that the mutineers might reach Philadelphia in a destructive mood. It might be prudent, Wayne thought, for Congress to leave town for the time being. General Potter, who had just come from the Council, and Wayne's friend Colonel Johnston had both witnessed the insurrection. They could furnish a fuller account of it than Wayne could write. They left early on Tuesday, and if they passed the mutineers on the road they were not halted long.

About nine o'clock Wayne wrote another letter to Washington to take the place of the one he had written at half-past four. There was now more information, but no mention of the order Wayne had issued. "I am this moment, with Colonels Butler and Stewart, taking horse to try to halt those on their march to Princeton. As a last resort, I am advised to collect them and move slowly on towards Philadelphia. . . . Their general cry is, to be discharged, and that they will again enlist and fight for America, a few excepted." In this second letter Wayne was simpler in his forebodings than he had been in the first. He called himself not "yours most sincerely" but "yours most affectionately." Benjamin Fishbourne, chosen to convey what had been written and to tell more, was one of Wayne's aides who had helped carry their wounded general into the captured fortress at Stony Point.

5

March to Princeton

THE mutineers did not keep minutes of their proceedings. No private letters written by any of the men during the mutiny have been found, nor any later reminiscences of those who took part in it. Samuel Dewees of the 10th, the only soldier in the Line at the time who is known ever to have published a book (sixty-three years afterwards), was not, as he said, "of the mutiny party." The story of the mutinous men has to be looked for in accounts by the American officers and officials who worked to defeat the uprising, or in scraps of news sent by spies and informers to the British who hoped to encourage it. And even in those incidental records the men were seldom mentioned by their names. It seemed precise enough to refer to a soldier as a sergeant or a private of this or that regiment.

The midnight march of the mutiny party made its first halt four miles from camp, at Vealtown (Bernardsville) where the Virginia troops had the year before cut timber for huts that were never completed, but where there would now be plenty of firewood. There the main body waited for some hours till group after group caught up with them, each headed by a sergeant who had—in effect—gone recruiting for mutineers. One group brought with them nearly a hundred live cattle that had just arrived at camp. (Some of the cattle were left behind for the officers.) Before the march was taken up again the mutiny had grown to fifteen hundred men or more, accompanied by their women and children.

They left Vealtown early on Tuesday morning. Cornelius Tyger, a loyalist who was at Pluckemin about eight miles away, "stood and saw them all march by. . . . They were in very high spirits. They marched in the most perfect order and seemed as if under military discipline." They had what he thought a "vast number of wagons."

Behind the disciplined column was a long line of stragglers. Wayne, Butler, and Stewart, who expected to catch up with the troops before they reached Pluckemin, passed numerous small parties "who would not generally attend to anything which was said to them," as Dr. Henry Latimer next day wrote the story for Washington. At Van Veghten's bridge over the north branch of the Raritan "some honest fellows advised the General not to go to the main body, many being intoxicated and very ill-disposed. The advanced guard were at this time arrived at their old huts"—their winter quarters of 1778-79 at Middlebrook —"where they were all to halt for the night.

"As it was evening the General considered it most eligible not to go on to them, but request a sergeant or man from each regiment to be sent to his quarters to represent the complaints of the soldiery." Wayne's quarters were probably at the house of Derrick Van Veghten, a patriot farmer who two years before had refused payment for many acres of his timber cut down to build huts for the Continental quartermaster's corps. The sergeants came, "and among these the sergeant whom they appointed to command. The grievances were pointed out, and modes of redress proposed, of the justice and propriety of which they were fully satisfied." The sergeants then returned to the troops "with a determination to prepare the minds of their fellow-soldiers to attend calmly and dispassionately to such modes for the redress of their grievances as the General would offer to them" the next morning.

Wayne was ordered a guard of a sergeant and twelve men. The mutineers treated the officers "with as much complaisance and respect as they can consistent with their principal design." But the officers could not be sure whether the guard was an honor or a precaution, whether they were guests or prisoners. They would have to depend on their courage, their wits, and whatever was left them of their rank.

The sergeants exerted "every influence they possessed" with the soldiers, "but to very little effect; for they took up their line of march" on Wednesday "very early, not waiting for the General, in contradiction to the solicitations of the commanding and other sergeants. However, by the influence of these, the column was turned off into a field, formed a circle, where the General and the Colonels Butler and Stewart had an opportunity of addressing them; which had not the wished-for influence. The majority or the most clamorous were not to be swerved from their design. They again marched on. Those who were willing to return were directed to proceed with the refractory, supposing they might be capable of convincing some of them of the propriety of the propositions offered and the fatal tendency of persisting in their present conduct."

Anger and alcohol made the men headstrong. They had set out for Philadelphia and meant to go there. The sergeants, more reasonable, desired to halt at Princeton for further negotiations. Wayne and the colonels, noting the conflict between the sergeants and the men, began to be "sanguine in their expectations of effecting a disunion among them." The men of Stewart's 2nd Regiment were said to be in favor of halting at Princeton, and perhaps the 5th and 9th also. If these regiments could be separated from the column, still others might follow them. The Somerset and Middlesex militia were assembling at Rocky Hill near Princeton. Wayne found means to send an order to the officers of the Line still at Mount Kemble. They were to arm themselves, press horses, and proceed by Bound Brook to Rocky Hill, where they might be called upon if the mutineers were willing to receive them, or might join with the militia if force should prove necessary. Wayne had decided to make a last proposal to the mutineers at Princeton, and to make every effort to keep them from all going on to Philadelphia in their present frame of mind.

Dr. Latimer, physician and surgeon at the military hospital at Mount Kemble, may have accompanied Wayne, may have met him on the road. At noon, when they were at Van Nest's mill, between Middlebrook and Somerset Court House (now Millstone), Latimer left for Morristown, with Wayne's instructions to write to Washington. The rest of the march to Princeton was without a narrator.

II

An admiring spy reported to the British that "the Pennsylvanians observe the greatest order, and if a man takes a fowl from an inhabitant he is severely punished." The behavior of the troops on the march was so good that the people of the district, who had suffered from the marauding of British, Hessian, loyalist, and rebel soldiers, at once felt friendly and sympathetic toward these honest mutineers.

Their good order was a special concern of the Board of Sergeants who, first thought of as spokesmen for the regiments, became the managers of the mutiny. Contemporary reports said the mutineers raised a sergeant major to the rank of major general and created other officers for a division. While some such staff existed, it was no more than a military convenience and was always subordinate to the Board.

Of these governing sergeants only two are known certainly by name, with a few other names to be guessed at. Daniel Connell of the 11th signed one of the Board's letters. Except for that he is merely a name on the regiment's muster-roll, without even the date of his enlistment. Not much more is given about William Bowzar, secretary to the Board, who had enlisted in the 10th in May 1777, been appointed sergeant the following September, and become quartermaster sergeant in August 1778. Unsupported gossip says that George Goznall of the 2nd was a member; and that there was another member known as Macaroni Jack, who may have been an Englishman named John Maloney, who may have been a sergeant in the artillery. The sergeants seem to have avoided putting their names on paper, and nobody else did it for them. They were simply experienced, capable soldiers who got ten dollars a month and could read.

The sergeants from the ten infantry regiments and one from the artillery chose for a twelfth, to be president of the Board, a soldier who was early a leader in the uprising. The documents of the mutiny preserve only his surname, which was Williams. There was at least one Williams in every regiment of the Pennsylvania Line. But since the Williams of the Board is known to have been a deserter from the British, and seems to be the only Williams in the Line who was, he may fairly be identified as John Williams of the 2nd.

A British spy reported that the Williams who led the mutiny was a Pennsylvanian of some property who was captured in the first year of the war, got out of prison by enlisting in a loyalist corps, and then deserted back to the Americans. This would mean that before being reinstated in his American regiment he must be tried by court martial for his original desertion. Washington's General Orders for July 13, 1780 announced that John Williams of the 2nd had been tried the day before on the charge of deserting to the enemy and bearing arms in their service. He pleaded guilty of this capital offense. The court sentenced him "to suffer death (more than two-thirds agreeing thereto)" but "from his youth and former good character" recommended him for mercy. Washington, approving the sentence, accepted the recommendation, pardoned the prisoner, and set him at liberty. He was forgiven for his desertion because he had returned to his duty.

These facts are meager and throw no light on the qualities and activities which between July and January raised Williams to leadership. He may have been appointed sergeant because of merits his officers found in him. He may have led the men into mutiny by his eloquence, but no words certainly of his have been preserved. He never signed his name during the negotiations. Colorless and dim, so far as the records show, Williams seems to have been merely a leader thrown up in an emergency, perhaps by chance.

But the mutineers had, in the Board of Sergeants, a committee. This was what Americans of the age were used to. Committees had been formed to direct the people ever since the first resistance to British rule began. If it was natural for the mutineers to rise in rebellion against bad treatment, it was no less natural for them to choose representative leaders and then let them have authority.

At some time on Wednesday, either during a halt in the afternoon or that evening after they got to Princeton, "a sergeant from each regiment" met Wayne and the two colonels and "mentioned" their grievances, without putting anything in writing. Many men, the sergeants claimed, had been kept in the service after the expiration of their enlistments. They had all suffered "every privation for want of money and clothing." They had not received the pay due them, nor money to make up for what they had lost by depreciation. Though they had been furnished or promised depreciation certificates, they were not free to dispose of them as they pleased. (The officers, aware that the soldiers would sell promises to pay for almost any amount of cash in hand, had tried to prevent or regulate such sales, sometimes apparently by withholding the certificates.) This, the sergeants said, was "very hurtful to the feelings of the soldiery."

Wayne, Butler, and Stewart agreed that whenever there was a dispute over any enlistment a "disinterested sergeant or private from each regiment" should meet with the commanding officer of the corps to "determine in the case." Each regiment might appoint a sergeant "to carry an address to Congress, backed by the general and field officers." This was as far as the three officers could go in the matter of enlistments. They knew the men had grounds for complaint about pay, clothing, and food. They were silent as to the disposing of certificates, which did not figure in the later negotiations. The most important result of the meeting was the stated plan to send a committee to Congress—not go there in a body. This might, the officers thought, make the men forget the British, and would at least for a time keep their attention fixed on lawful redress, without any danger to Philadelphia.

In the late afternoon or evening the mutineers arrived at Princeton. It had in 1781 about seventy houses, one church, and two or three inns, most of them lying along the post road from New York to Philadelphia. The whole was dominated by Nassau Hall which stood in grounds that then were almost treeless. With the president's house (now the dean's) and a few outbuildings the Hall made up the College of New Jersey, not yet known as Princeton. Ever since the British occupied Nassau Hall as stable and barracks in the winter of 1776–77, it had been a massive ruin, though the ground floor had been partially restored and used as a hospital by the Americans after the British left. A few students lived there, others in the town. Most of the rooms of the upper stories were cold and empty caves which had been stripped of all wood, even floors, to make fires with.

The Board of Sergeants took Nassau Hall for their quarters. The main camp was on Colonel George Morgan's farm, already called Prospect, south of the College. If the mutineers had brought along enough tents to conform to Army regulations, there was one tent for the noncommissioned officers of each company, and one for every six privates "including the drums and fifes." The mutineers had slept in tents on worse nights than these in a mild January. Picket lines were drawn round the town and vigilant sentries posted.

Wayne and the colonels were probably quartered at one of the taverns across the road from Nassau Hall. The Hudibras was kept by a militia colonel named Jacob Hyer, a talkative man of county prominence; the Sign of the Col-

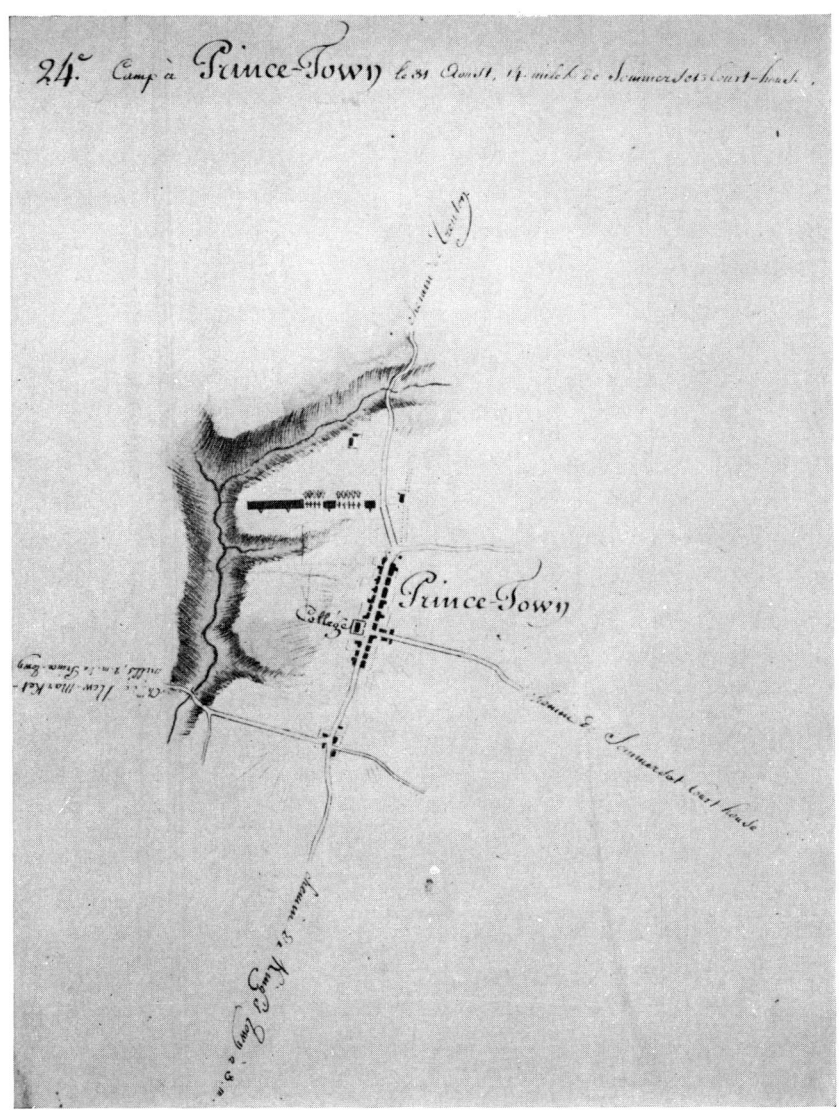

ALEXANDRE BERTHIER

Facsimile of an unpublished plan of Princeton drawn in August 1781 by a cartographer with the Comte de Rochambeau on his march to Yorktown. The camp site of the French troops here indicated is the same as that occupied by the Pennsylvania mutineers the previous January.

lege by hospitable Cornelius Beekman and his wife Grace Otis. At either of these inns the officers could have been easy and happy if it had not been for the appalling business that brought them there.

6

News at New Windsor and New York

WASHINGTON, who had settled his Headquarters at New Windsor three weeks before, was as near to discouragement as he ever came during the whole course of the Revolution. The fall of Charleston the past May and the rout of the Americans at Camden in August might forecast—as the British and loyalists were sure they must —the loss of the Southern States to the enemy for good. The treason and desertion of Arnold in September had seemed to stiffen the Army rather than shake it; but if a general as trusted as Arnold could be a traitor, there might be others as unsuspected and yet as guilty in their intentions. The winter's hardships had begun again. New soldiers coming in had to be turned away because there were no provisions or clothing for them. For want of forage most of the Army horses were sent off, with barely enough left for orderly duty and a few express riders. On December 10 Washington had not been able to "obtain a farthing of public money for the support of my table for near two months"—though this, he said, was "a matter of trivial concern because it is of a personal nature." He took no pay for his services and was used to advancing his own money for the expenses allowed him.

Congress and the country, he declared, could not expect the Army "to rub through" a campaign in 1781 more effective than that of 1780. "It would be as unreasonable as to suppose that because a man had rolled a snowball till it had acquired the size of a horse that he might do so till it was large as a house." Before going into winter quarters Washington had, in an "earnest desire" to close the year's operations "with some degree of éclat," let his wishes for a time get the better of his judgment and had planned an attack on the British posts at the upper end of York (Manhattan) Island. At the last moment he gave up the venture because of British armed vessels in the Hudson. In December he undertook nothing but a raid by a small party with the bold design of capturing the commander-in-chief of the Hessian or the British forces.

There was nothing new in such a scheme. The British throughout the war laid frequent plans to capture Washington. Arnold just before the discovery of his treason sent them a hint as to where this might be done. Washington in March 1778 worked out details for a projected attempt on Clinton, and in October 1780 for one on Arnold, then living next door to Clinton's Headquarters at 1 Broadway. Now, on Christmas Day, four officers, two guides, and twenty or thirty enlisted men slipped down the river from Nyack in a barge and two whaleboats, with axes and crowbars and orders not to fire their muskets. The expedition was in charge of Lieutenant Colonel David Humphreys, the tall young poet from Connecticut who was one of Washington's devoted aides.

Humphreys was authorized by his instructions to "surprise and bring off General Knyphausen from Morris's house"—later known as the Jumel Mansion—"on York Island or Sir Henry Clinton from Kennedy's house in the city; if from the tide, weather, and other circumstances you shall judge the enterprise to be practicable." But in the night a strong wind blew up from the north and made it impossible to land anywhere with any prospect of success. The boats were driven past the Battery, one of them into Staten Island, one almost to Sandy Hook. Unable to row back against the wind, the party made its way up the Raritan to Brunswick and traveled back by land. Humphreys arrived with the news of his disappointment on New Year's Day. The year had ended with another failure.

About noon on the 3rd Major Fishbourne brought the far worse news that the Pennsylvanians had mutinied and were marching towards Philadelphia.

Washington at once sent to inquire about the New England soldiers at or near West Point. Though they had not mutinied, they were resentful and restless. They might be ready to follow the calamitous lead of the Pennsylvanians into what could become a general revolt of the whole Army. In the widespread discontent it would be hard to confine an uprising to a single Line. This was the most ominous mutiny that had taken place: not of a few men among many who were loyal, but of eleven regiments with artillery, desperate and organized, moving through the country at their own will for purposes not yet made clear. There was not force enough in the New Jersey Line to subdue them. Washington's Continental forces in the Highlands would not be enough if his men were to sympathize with the mutineers.

While he waited at New Windsor to hear what his officers could learn about his men, he gave orders for "a small escort of horse" to set out with him the next morning for Philadelphia, which he supposed the mutineers might reach ahead of him. Waiting, he wrote to Wayne, asking him to remain with the mutinous troops if they would permit it. When their "first transports of passion" had worn

NEWS AT NEW WINDSOR AND NEW YORK 65

off they might be more placable. For the present it seemed dangerous to oppose them, either with Pennsylvania militia drawn up at the Delaware or with Jersey militia collected to bar the mutineers' way to New York. This would only anger them and "tempt them to turn about and go in a body to the enemy, who by their emissaries will use every argument and mean in their power to persuade them that it is their only asylum." It would be better, Washington thought, for Wayne to cross the Delaware with the mutineers, find out their principal grievances, and promise to represent them faithfully to Congress and the Pennsylvania Council. "If they could be stopped at Bristol or Germantown, the better. I look upon it, that if you can bring them to a negotiation matters may afterwards be accommodated; but that an attempt to reduce them by force will either drive them to the enemy or dissipate them in such a manner that they will never be recovered."

Washington here recommended what Wayne was already trying to carry out. But Washington could not approve of Wayne's warning advice to Congress "to go out of the way to avoid the first burst of the storm." Such an action, besides being undignified, "might have a very unhappy influence. The mutineers, finding the body before whom they were determined to lay their grievances fled, might take a new turn and wreak their vengeance upon the persons and properties of the citizens; and in a town the size of Philadelphia there are numbers who would join them in such a business. I would therefore wish you, if you have time, to recall that advice and rather recommend it to them to stay and hear what propositions the soldiers have to make."

No further news came from Wayne during the day, but there were disturbing reports from West Point about the "temper of the troops and distress of the garrison for want of flour, clothing, and in short everything." At seven o'clock the next morning Washington had changed his mind about going to Philadelphia. The affair might be settled one way or the other before he could arrive. In any case, he was needed where he was. Whatever might happen elsewhere, he must do all he could to hold a part of the Army together. Fishbourne went off with the letter to Wayne, who for the present would have to manage his mutineers alone.

II

Word of the mutiny seems to have reached Clinton in New York before it reached Washington at New Windsor.

A spy named Gould, whose first name does not appear in the secret service papers, was used to going back and forth like a shuttle between British Headquarters and various places in New Jersey, particularly Elizabethtown where the Americans had their advanced post and where Gould probably lived. He was out on Tuesday the 2nd picking up bits of information: among them the erroneous bit that Wayne had recently come to Elizabethtown "to settle a plan of intelligence." As Gould was returning to Staten Island he "saw some smoke rise and heard some cannon fired towards Morristown and Springfield." At first he did not know what this meant. But on Staten Island he met a man who came in after him with a story that the Pennsylvania troops had mutinied. It was the kind of news it would be profitable to carry to Clinton. Gould fretted at being detained on Staten Island till the next morning, but he got to Headquarters before confirming reports came in from Newark later in the day.

Gould's news was partly guesswork. The Newark informers were not positive whether the furor at Mount Kemble had been a "drunken frolic" or an outright mutiny. Clinton thought it was necessary to know more before taking steps to encourage and support the mutineers. He sent Gould back at once, to find out what he could for himself, and to bring a letter from a correspondent in New Jersey whom the British secret service thought particularly reliable.

The correspondent was Andrew Gautier, possibly the elder of that name, but almost certainly his son. The father had for years been a notable cabinetmaker—especially a maker of Windsor chairs—in New York and an alderman of the Dock ward. Like the De Lanceys he was of Huguenot stock, like them he was a loyalist who had welcomed the British occupation of New York in September 1776. He retired about that time from the dangerous town to a house at Acquackanonck (now Passaic). If he was there in January 1781 he was too far away to serve the British during the mutiny. But his two sons, Daniel and Andrew, were closer at hand and in positions that made it easy for them to be secretly of use yet little suspected by the Americans.

Daniel Gautier in New York was known to be a loyalist. Andrew Gautier, Jr., in New Jersey was supposed to be a patriot. After a year or so at King's (now Columbia) College in the class of 1773 which had as many future loyalists as future patriots in it, he had been married at seventeen to an heiress whose father Captain Thomas Brown lived in considerable opulence, derived from the slave trade, in a stone house near Paulus Hook on the Hudson opposite New York. The younger Gautier and his wife lived with or near his father-in-law, who was on the patriot side. Though in June 1776 Gautier had been charged with refusing to accept Continental currency for tea he sold in New York, he had then cleared himself by his declaration "that he hath always been a steady and warm friend to the American cause, and that he is determined to support the same at the risk of his life." He may have been discreet then, or he may have changed his sympathies as the war dragged on.

However that was, Gautier in January 1781 was in stealthy communication with the British by means of letters sent in addressed on the cover to Daniel Gautier. Now Gould was hurried off to Andrew Gautier, and a letter came from him the next day in the cipher that he used for all his letters about the Pennsylvania revolt. Here was no errand-running spy like Gould. Gautier was a gentleman of property and credibility.

Clinton on the 3rd knew less than Washington about the mutiny, but more about his own troops. He could confidently send orders to "the British Grenadiers, British Light Infantry, 42nd, 37th regiments, Hessian Grenadiers, and Hessian Yagers to hold themselves in readiness to march at a moment's notice." They were quartered on Long Island and could cross in boats to Staten Island and from there to New Jersey at almost any point from Elizabeth Point to South Amboy. Clinton, unlike Washington, could act as soon as he was convinced there was enough of a mutiny to warrant it.

His position was a sound one. Almost perfectly safe on his islands from any American attack, he had also a strong British garrison across the Hudson at Paulus Hook and a loyalist post called Fort De Lancey on Bergen Neck. These gave Clinton, though not command of the Jersey shore, at least points of entry and communication. No matter how closely the Americans watched the long water line, it was possible for secret agents to travel back and forth between New York and Paulus Hook or Fort De Lancey in British boats under the protection of British ships of war. From

Paulus Hook they could creep into New Jersey, to carry messages and bring others back. The loyalists on Bergen Neck, commanded by Captain Thomas Ward of the irregular Loyal Refugee Volunteers, were also useful in communications. But they had taken their post primarily for revenge against the patriots who had confiscated loyalist property and taken loyalist lives. From Fort De Lancey, which was only a blockhouse and stockade, they could raid the neighborhood for provisions to send into crowded New York, damage patriot goods which could not be carried away, and keep up a fierce guerrilla warfare between the lines of the opposing armies.

This was a war of raids and retaliations. Loyalist refugees on Staten Island, with Cornelius Hatfield of Elizabethtown as guide, regularly stole across the narrow Kill to New Jersey, to spy on the rebels, to plunder and kidnap. Denying that the rebel government had any right to take action against loyal subjects of the king, the loyalists felt that they were fighting outlaws. If loyalist property could be confiscated, rebel property could be burned. If loyalists could be imprisoned, rebels could be seized and carried off to the Sugar House prison in New York. Retaliation led to counter-retaliation, and was continued in brutality and blood. Patriot bands raided Staten Island, burning and pilfering. Clinton and Washington alike made efforts to stop these lawless little wars which dishonored both sides in the conflict and almost ruined whole communities.

There was bitter division in near-by New Jersey—son against father, brother against brother, almost any cousin sure to have a cousin who was his enemy—which was of great value to the British. They could count on loyalists for reports of whatever the rebels did or planned. The British secret service was managed by Major Oliver De Lancey who had succeeded John André as adjutant general after André lost his life the past October in the affair of Benedict Arnold. De Lancey was more systematic than André had been, not quite so much given to melodrama. A considerable part of the business of the adjutant general's office was questioning deserters; sending out loyalist spies to get hold of rebel secrets; trying to detect rebel spies who came in to get British secrets; maintaining corespondence with disaffected Americans outside the British line. De Lancey used spies to carry propaganda to enemy soldiers, urging them to give up their criminal and unhappy lives under the rebel usurpers and come to refuge among the British. The effort had so far seemed to have small success. But it might at last have piled up conviction in the Pennsylvanians, so that another generous and skillful offer would bring them in.

Sir Henry Clinton was not too sanguine. Arnold had promised to draw half the Continental Army after him to the British, but in weeks of vigorous recruiting he had been able to get only a handful of men for his Legion. The mutineers might not be eager to join another service. Perhaps they only wanted to go home, as many soldiers do most of the time, even when they are well treated. Clinton's first judgment was the same as Washington's: the mutineers must be given time to make up their minds. If the British were to march hastily against them in force they might fight as hard as ever, on the side they were accustomed to. It was never Clinton's plan to try to destroy the mutineers, as so many American soldiers, without caring what their state of mind was. The most he intended was to move his regiments into New Jersey to receive and protect the mutineers if they listened to the emissaries whom, as Washington had had no doubt, Clinton would be prompt to send with enticing proposals. And even that intention would have to wait on the further report of Gould and the expected letter from Gautier.

Clinton and De Lancey did not know there was an American spy in New York that day, who found out that the news of the mutiny had reached the British about noon. "Nothing could possibly have given them so much pleasure," he reported at Elizabethtown at five o'clock the next morning. "Every preparation is making among them to come out and make a descent on Jersey. I think South Amboy is their object. They expect those in mutiny will immediately join them. . . . If they come out it will be with considerable force, and may be expected within twenty-four hours from this time."

7

Thursday at Princeton and Trenton

ON THURSDAY the 4th Princeton and its approaches were so strictly guarded that the mutineers could say who should come in and—more or less—what news go out. The forenoon was given up to negotiations with Wayne, Butler, and Stewart. The sergeants and the officers may have remained in their separate quarters and exchanged communications across the street, or they may have met all together at what Wayne called his headquarters. He did not go to the committee.

The Board's Proposals, in writing but without any secretary's name, were really demands. The men who had enlisted in 1776 and 1777 with the Continental bounty of twenty dollars were to be "without any delay discharged; and all arrears of pay and depreciation of pay be paid to the said men, without any fraud, clothing included." Men enlisted in 1778 or since, with the Pennsylvania bounty of a hundred dollars in addition, were to be "entitled to their discharge at the expiration of three years from the said enlistment, and their full depreciation of pay and all arrears of clothing." Recent recruits, admittedly enlisted for the duration of the war, were to have the pay, bounty, and clothing they had been promised but not yet supplied in full, and then to return to their regiments; "and no aspersion be cast and no grievances to be repeated to the said men."

All the men discharged and furnished their arrears were to do what they liked about re-enlisting. They "shall not

THURSDAY AT PRINCETON AND TRENTON 73

be compelled to stay by any former officers commanding any longer time than what is agreeable to their own pleasure and disposition." Any who might choose to remain "for a small term as volunteers" were to be "at their own disposal and pleasure."

"As we now depend and rely upon you, General Wayne," the Proposals concluded, "for to represent and repeat our grievances, we do agree in conjunction, from this date, January 4, in six days for to complete and settle every such demand." And the whole Line was "agreed and determined" to support the Board.

Although the Proposals possibly asked for more than the Board expected, they seemed to the officers to point to nothing short of the dissolution of the Pennsylvania Line. Only the few late recruits would be left. The older soldiers would be, according to the Proposals, free to go after their discharge, but also free to insist on arrears of pay and clothing that Pennsylvania could not then provide. The original terms of enlistment seemed to mean nothing. The officers of the Line had contended that these were generally for the war; the men, that they were for three years, or for the war. Now the mutineers, without concern for the periods of service fixed upon before the present year's enlistments, took nothing into account but the size of the bounties paid. There was nothing here to show that the men, if satisfied, would "again enlist and fight for America," as they had said when they left Mount Kemble.

Having no authority over enlistments and payments, Wayne had in his answer to imply that these were for Congress and the Pennsylvania Assembly to decide upon. But he so far committed them as to promise that "all such non-commissioned officers and soldiers as are justly entitled to their discharges shall be immediately settled with, their accounts properly adjusted, and certificates for their pay and arrearages of pay and clothing given them . . . and be discharged from the service of the United States." Men not entitled to discharge should "be also settled with": given certificates for what was already due them, present pay in hard money, and "comfortable warm clothing." They would then be expected to return "to their duty as worthy, faithful soldiers."

Wayne concluded with admonishment: "These propositions are founded in principles of justice and honor, between the United States and the soldiery, which is all that reasonable men can expect, or that a general can promise consistent with his station and duty, and the mutual benefit of their country and the Line which he has had so long the honor of commanding. If the soldiers are determined not to let reason and justice govern on this occasion, he has only to lament the total and unfortunate situation to which they will reduce themselves and their country."

These exchanges were tentative, not bad-tempered. At noon there seemed to be some chance that a compromise might be reached. For one thing, the mutiny party had enough to eat. Colonel Charles Stewart, commissary general of issues for the Army, was permitted to enter the lines; and he ordered the troops "well fed on purpose they might have no excuse to maraud." They had beef with them for three or four days. Flour could be obtained from Trenton. Throughout the negotiations the mutineers, not being hungry, appeared to forget they ever had been. Colonel Stephen Moylan of the Pennsylvania cavalry, who happened to be somewhere in the neighborhood of Princeton, joined the three officers with the permission of the mutineers. He, like Butler, had been born in Ireland.

But about noon or shortly after, two officers of the Line

rode up to "the borders of Princeton" to bring Wayne word that eighty armed officers, headed by Colonel Craig, were on their way by the Middlebush road to Cranberry (now Cranbury), ready to take a position and wait for the settlement of the mutiny. The messengers were "stopped by a guard, treated with a great deal of insolence, and turned back." (The officers went on from Cranberry to Allentown for the night.) Also that day, probably in the afternoon, some members of the New Jersey legislature came from Trenton to confer with the mutineers, "but were not permitted." The Board of Sergeants and the rank and file were suspicious of interfering officers and officials. This affair was directly with Congress and the Pennsylvania Council. The mutineers could not help hearing that the Jersey militia were being collected between them and New York, between them and the Delaware. Nor could they help dreading some kind of trap.

After one o'clock a note came to Wayne from the Board, signed by William Bowzar as secretary. "We would be glad you would inform us who these men are that you mean, that are entitled to their discharges. As we jointly think that you don't deem the men enlisted for the bounty of twenty dollars to be entitled to their discharges, therefore, sir, be punctual what you say or do, as we reasonably think it is our due." The Board did not write clearly, but they clearly saw that Wayne had avoided giving an opinion on one of their most emphatic points: the immediate and unconditional discharge of the men who had been longest in the service.

Wayne had no more authority to consent to a general discharge of the twenty-dollar men than he had had before, and again he temporized. Yesterday, he reminded the Board, they had been willing to leave disputed enlistments to a committee "of yourselves and the colonel of the regiment." Since there was now "so great a variety of opinions" among them he could not undertake a decision, but would at once send an express to the Pennsylvania Council asking for "a committee of that body to meet the Line at Trenton, or elsewhere, who with myself and Colonels Butler and Stewart will give you a full and explicit answer." Suggesting that the conference might be held at Trenton, Wayne was still hoping that the mutineers could be drawn further from New York.

The reply of the sergeants was involved but threatening. "As we now are upon a principle of honor, justice, and right, we are now as well situated to receive any gentlemen of rank at this post as if we were to march any further, and therefore I would not have you think that we cannot settle these matters by such a formidable body of men as we are." In this the Board—or perhaps Williams as president—plainly declined to go to Trenton. The mutineers were strong enough to ask the Council to come to them. The reply went on with a warning to Wayne. "Therefore [we] should be glad you would be explicit in your expresses, or otherways we must take some measures that will procure our own happiness."

The officers did not even acknowledge the receipt of this warning and threat. If it was unpleasant to overlook the insult of being told they must not represent the mutineers to the Council, it was still more unpleasant to speculate on what the mutineers meant by the measures they might take to gain the happiness they desired.

There could be no doubt as to the implications. During the day a messenger had come in from American headquarters at Elizabethtown with the American spy's report that the British had heard of the revolt, were already taking steps to give it countenance and aid, and expected the mutineers to join them at South Amboy. A sloop of war was lying "in the mouth of the Raritan" with several vessels including barges that might be used as transports. Other intelligence pointed to Perth Amboy as the more likely destination of the British forces. Wherever they were to land, it was assumed this would be "to cover the embarkation of the rioters in case they should take a turn" towards the British lines.

The majority of the mutineers still had no thought of going to the British. But here was a development that strengthened the hands of the negotiating Board of Sergeants. If their own country would not listen to their grievances, this would have to be in the knowledge that the enemy would.

Wayne and the colonels, in the letter they sent express to the Council, did not even mention Trenton as a possible meeting place. They urged that the Council send one or more of its members to Princeton "with all possible dispatch, and with full powers to them and us to treat" on the subject of enlistments, and with information as to "what prospects you have of furnishing an immediate supply of clothing and cash, which will be indispensably necessary to insure success." The mutineers, the officers were saying, must be seriously dealt with.

At the same time, the three officers had "some glimmering of hope" from the mutineers' attitude towards a possible British move into New Jersey. "The troops assured us" that in any such event, they would "act with desperation" against the invaders. "Whether this be their sentiments or not, a few hours will probably determine."

After the express had left for Trenton and Philadelphia the officers wrote a letter to Washington, so candid that they must have expected it would go without being stopped or read by the mutineers. Inclosed were copies of all the "orders, propositions, interrogations, and answers" that had been exchanged in writing. If with the assistance of the Pennsylvania Council "this unhappy business cannot be settled, your presence and influence will be more proper in other quarters, or where you are, than with us." This was a polite hint that Washington would be better employed in holding what was left of the Army than in trying to win the Pennsylvania Line back.

The officers still hoped for the best, the letter said, from the apparent disposition of the men "to fight the common enemy, however they may differ with us in other respects." The conclusion was in Wayne's dramatic language. "Any change must be an alleviation to our present feelings. However, we have one resort left, for which we trust we shall be more envied than pitied."

II

The letter to Washington, a hundred miles away by any route the courier might take, could—and did—not reach him till Saturday afternoon or evening. It was only a dozen miles to Trenton. Charles Stewart left Princeton at one on Thursday. The express rider followed him some hours later. By nightfall Trenton was full of discordant rumors and of perturbed men gathered there on account of the mutiny.

News of the affair, carried by Potter and Johnston, had got to Philadelphia the day before. Congress and the Pennsylvania Council, both meeting in the State House (now known as Independence Hall), were informed at about the same time. Congress at six o'clock appointed a Committee consisting of General Sullivan of New Hampshire, retired from the Army, the Reverend John Witherspoon of New Jersey, president of the College at Princeton, and John Mathews of South Carolina. They were to confer with the Council "on the subject matter of the intelligence received this day." The first and only recorded action of the conferring officials on Wednesday was to arrange that several officers then in Philadelphia should set out for Princeton at four o'clock the next morning.

General St. Clair, ranking commander of the Pennsylvania Line, and Colonel Proctor of the Pennsylvania artillery belonged with the troops. The Marquis de Lafayette and Lieutenant Colonel John Laurens, aide to Washington, were just departing for Washington's Headquarters on another errand and expected to pass through Princeton. These four, with other officers, arrived at Trenton about three o'clock on the afternoon of Thursday.

Most of what they could find out came from Charles Stewart, the only outsider admitted to Princeton that day. He had thought when he left for Trenton that the situation looked promising. But from later reports, largely at second hand, he began to fear that "Arnold's friends and British gold" were working among the mutineers. In this he was mistaken, but he affected others with his uncertainty. Nobody could make up his mind whether the mutineers were likely to go to the British or to stay at Princeton or to come to Trenton; whether they were willing to make terms or bound to run wild. Governor William Livingston of New Jersey thought it might be prudent—and safer for his State—to let them cross the Delaware into Pennsylvania. In that case, a detachment of Jersey militia might follow and join with the Pennsylvania militia in putting the mutiny down. St. Clair thought it encouraging that the mutineers "have as yet done very little injury to the inhabitants and profess that they do not mean any . . . It appears to me that compliance" with the mutineers' demands, could not "well go farther than it has in General Wayne's answer," St. Clair said. He decided that he and Lafayette would go to Maidenhead (now Lawrenceville) that night, "so as to be able to see them in the morning when the effects of the liquor they have most probably kept themselves hot with may be gone off."

Lafayette, who had listened to all the rumors and believed most of them, looked forward to the next day with the grandiose conviction that he might end the mutiny with a triumphant harangue to the troops as a whole. Lafayette had been a major general for three and a half years, but he was only a few months past twenty-three. The letter he wrote, at six o'clock on Thursday to the French minister in Philadelphia, was full of rumor and resolution.

"The insurgents," Lafayette reported, "are more devilish than ever. . . . A deputation was sent to them from Trenton to beseech them not to move to this town. Some persons believe they will come here tomorrow." But the mutineers have said "that they will remain at Princeton as an intermediate point from which, if the militia should show signs of attacking them, they could go to New York, after putting the country to fire and sword without distinction of age and sex. But if they are left at peace, they say they will not turn to the enemy. . . . General Wayne and Colonels Butler and Stewart are with them as hostages of a kind, with a guard at their quarters, but may speak only with a committee of sergeants sent to treat with them. . . . What is worse, the sentries and pickets have orders to let no Continental officer pass; and nobody is permitted to address the soldiers. Everything is done through committees. This last precaution proves that the British emissaries are determined to prevent any effect which influence or eloquence might have" on individual mutineers. Lafayette took it for granted that there were emissaries at Princeton.

Charles Stewart, who had talked "not only with the committee of sergeants but also by chance with a crowd of soldiers who gathered round him," had formed the opinion that they were extremely hostile to almost all American generals. If St. Clair went among them he might be killed; so might Lord Stirling (Major General William Alexander of New Jersey, who claimed a Scottish title). The soldiers had "avowed their friendship only for me," Lafayette wrote, "though they find me too severe in the article of discipline." They would not kill him, but would probably make him prisoner. Yet let the cost be what it might, he was resolved to go among them and deliver his harangue. He was, in fact, just leaving Trenton for Maidenhead from which—"despite its pretty name"—he would go on the next morning. Perhaps with St. Clair and Poctor, perhaps alone, he would venture among these fellows "and see if they can interrupt my passage or my eloquence."

8

Emissaries from the Enemy

NEW YORK did more about the mutiny on Thursday than either New Windsor or Philadelphia. Gould came back some time during the day with a good deal of circumstantial information, most of which was correct except that he had heard the mutineers had gone from Middlebrook to Brunswick (now New Brunswick). He brought a letter from Andrew Gautier, dated at Elizabethtown the day before, who said they were at Princeton. Gautier had been confined to his room with a bad cold when the first news of the mutiny reached Elizabethtown on Tuesday and so had not been able to be the first to report it to the British. But even with his cold he seems to have found out on Wednesday as much as the American headquarters at Elizabethtown then knew. This need not mean that he was treacherously informed; perhaps merely that at a small post in a small town a civilian of Gautier's standing would normally know as much, on a matter everywhere talked about, as the Continental or militia officers stationed there.

Convinced by Gould and Gautier, Clinton at once went ahead with his plans. Another American spy who was in New York that day thought he had never in his life seen the British "exert themselves so much.... Notwithstanding the rain, which poured down like torrents, they did not slacken their proceedings." The British and Hessian troops on Long Island were set in motion with orders to march to Denyce's ferry Friday morning, and be ready to cross to Staten Island. The armed schooner *Neptune* was already in Raritan Bay. The *Vulture*, the sloop of war from which André had gone ashore to his death, was ordered to drop down the Narrows to join the *Neptune*. Barges were hurriedly rounded up. The observant spy thought there were enough to transport four or five thousand men to Amboy, with eighteen or twenty cannon.

Bitter loyalists in New York hoped—and would have demanded if they dared—that Clinton, who had about twelve thousand British, German, and loyalist soldiers fit for duty, would pour them into New Jersey and exterminate the rebels, whether mutinous or faithful, before the militia could be assembled or Washington with his Continental troops arrive from West Point. One of Clinton's officers hinted what he thought a more economical measure. Let a proclamation be issued, "now or immediately on our entering New Jersey," with an offer of full back pay in hard money to the first thousand mutineers who would come in and lay down their arms. "If they all had nine months' pay due to them, it would not amount to £7000"—which would be a trifle in comparison with the cost of a winter campaign.

Clinton had exactly a week before issued a proclamation, in his capacity as commissioner for the peace which he was as ready to make as war. The proclamation announced to "the inhabitants of the British colonies on the Continent of North America now in rebellion, of every rank, order, and denomination (excepting always such persons who, under the usurped forms of trial, have tyrannically and inhumanly been instrumental in executing and putting to death any of his Majesty's loyal subjects)" that "the door is . . . again thrown open (if happily you are disposed to avail yourself of the opportunity it affords) for commencing negotiations which may instantly terminate the miseries of your country."

Any colony or group of colonies, any individual or association of individuals, had only to "declare their abhorrence of the rebellion, separate from its councils, and afterwards demean themselves as dutiful and peaceable subjects of his Majesty's government" in order to be granted "pardon for all past treasons and the full benefits of the king's clemency. . . . If any shall be so hardy and desperate as to contemn the proffered clemency of their sovereign, the liberality of the nation, and the means and mediation we now tender for effecting the mutual reconciliation of countrymen with each other and the equitable adjustment and composure of their differences and ferments, they are hereby warned of the aggravation of such guilt and most earnestly implored to shun the punishment ordained by the laws of their country and which, when [the laws are] restored to their free course, will be inflicted for their treasonable offenses."

It was still too early to expect much response from this declaration, and there was little reason to suppose it would be more effective than earlier offers and warnings of the same official kind. But the British and loyalists in New York believed that the active rebels were losing their hold on the people.

"There are expectations of a revolt and defection in Connecticut," Major Frederick Mackenzie of Clinton's secret service wrote in his diary. "Ethan Allen and the Vermonters appear to be inclined to declare for us, and 'tis reported some of them have joined the King's troops at Ticonderoga. . . . We have the most sanguine hopes that the loyalists in Maryland and the other Southern provinces, on hearing of the mutiny of the Pennsylvania troops, will immediately rise up and declare themselves." Cornwallis had by this time probably conquered the Carolinas, and Benedict Arnold with his raiding forces had probably reached Virginia. "I do not see how the rebellion can possibly exist much longer. The people in general are so much oppressed, and long so earnestly for a return of peace and the re-establishment of their former mild government, that they only wait to see a beginning made, when they will join heartily in overturning the tyrannical and oppressive government under which they now suffer. . . . If Congress are able to satisfy the Pennsylvanians, there can be no doubt but all the rest of the Continental troops in the same situation will make the same demands and expect the like satisfaction, which must embarrass them not a little. Should the insurgents join us, the matter must be at an end. The rebels will find it impossible to raise another army, all strength and confidence will be lost among them, and a general defection must be the consequence."

Others besides Mackenzie at British Headquarters saw the mutiny as a symptom of collapse not only in the Continental Army but also in the civilian population. So did Clinton. But he had had a long experience of the ability of the rebels to persist and recuperate to the dismay of loyalist prophets. In a delicate crisis like this, to invade New Jersey might be to unite the people, of that State and of others, to fresh resistance and prolonged rebellion. Better begin with rebels known to be disaffected, like the mutinous soldiers. They had specific grievances and could understand plain language. Sympathy would soften them, and the promise of good treatment might bring them in of their own free will.

The proposals drafted at Headquarters on Thursday were both sympathetic and generous. They agreed that the Pennsylvania troops "and others" had been "defrauded of their pay, clothing, and provisions" and "after the terms of their enlistments are expired" had been "forcibly detained in the service where they have suffered every kind of misery and oppression." If now they would lay down their arms and return to their true allegiance, they would be welcomed by the British, pardoned for all former offenses, and paid the money due them from Congress, without "expectation of military service except it may be voluntary."

Any commissioners they might send to Amboy would be met by persons empowered to treat with them and pledged to furnish them security. If all the Pennsylvanians should, "for their own safety," cross South River and ask for "a body of British troops" to protect them, these would be sent. "It is needless to point out the inability as well as want of inclination in the Congress to relieve them, or to tell them the severities that would be used towards them by the rebel leaders should they think of returning to their former servitude."

The proposals were of course unsigned, but they promised that the commissioners sent by the Line to Amboy should not be left in doubt as to the authority behind the offer. It was addressed "to the person appointed by the Pennsylvania troops to lead them in the present struggle for their liberties and rights." Gould had reported that the mutineers were led by a sergeant who was a deserter from the British.

II

It was easier to write these proposals than to get them into the hands of the mutineers. The Jersey militia were out and sure to be vigilant along all the roads to Princeton. Any messenger with offers from the enemy would be unquestionably a spy. The Americans, when they took spies, seldom failed to hang them. And it was by no means certain that the mutineers themselves would look favorably on the proposals and safeguard the emissaries. Only a daring man would go on such an errand, and only a discreet man should be trusted with it.

On Thursday evening three copies were prepared, each of them wrapped—apparently rolled up—in a sheet of lead of the sort tea was then shipped in. This would be weatherproof and would not look like a letter if a man were carelessly searched. Two of the copies were given to Gould to take to Gautier, who was to forward them by a messenger of his own choice. A bearer for the third was found in New York, where two weeks before he had been in the military prison called the Provost from which since then he had been enlisted in a loyalist regiment that was being raised for a service likely to be congenial to him.

His name was John Mason. While in prison he had, in pleading memorials to Clinton, told more about himself than is known about any other emissary sent to the Pennsylvanians. Some of this is confirmed from other sources.

Before the war Mason lived in Orange County, New York. In that county's ferocious conflict between Whigs and Tories he was—he told Clinton—"plundered of all his substance by the rebels, and suffered everything but death for his loyalty, being confined in two of their provosts; and consequently would [have] suffered death" had he "not made his escape from the Morristown jail; the bloody Governor Livingston" having eleven indictments against Mason "for high treason against the States." From that time he was "a bitter enemy against them." With a "small party" which included Thomas Ward of Orange County, later of Bergen Neck, he set out to capture Livingston "and pressed him so hard as obliged him to change his quarters every night, and at last fled to Philadelphia." Livingston offered a reward of five thousand dollars in "square money" for Mason dead or alive, so Mason said. He did not say, as a member of his band had confessed, that they hunted Livingston partly for the sake of two hundred guineas offered for his capture by David

Mathews, the royal mayor of New York, to whom the band once gave a gold watch plundered from a rebel woman.

Though Mason and his band on occasion went across the State line into New Jersey, he belonged rather to New York, where he was equally at war with Governor George Clinton. For a time Mason was one of the Tory freebooters led by Claudius Smith of Smith's Clove in Orange County. After Claudius Smith had been captured and hanged in Goshen jail in January 1779, Mason succeeded as leader, with two of Smith's sons in his "little company." They announced that in the future they would hang six Whigs for every Tory sent to the scaffold. One of their victims was John Clark, whom they dragged out of his house and murdered, leaving his body with a warning pinned to his coat.

As Mason told the story to Sir Henry Clinton, this killing took place "in a small skirmish with the rebels where their captain fell (named Clark), a noted committee man and great persecutor of government." It was Mason who "fixed" on Clark's breast a copy of the warning which within eight hours "was conveyed to Mr. Washington's camp at Middlebush. Mr. Livingston, hearing of the affair, offered an additional reward." Possibly Mason was the author of the original document. The revised version which he sent, as evidence of his loyalty, to Sir Henry Clinton in July 1780 was Mason's declaration of war against all rebels (in his own grammar, spelling, and punctuation).

A Warning to Rebels

"You are hereby warn'd at your parels; to Desist; from Executing more friends to Government; as you Served the unfortunate Claudus Smith; and Numbers of Loyalists that fell into Your Merciless hands; for the Blood of those Innocent men; crys aloud for Vengance; Your are Likewise

EMISSARIES FROM THE ENEMY

warn'd; to use the Prisoners well; and ease them of their Irons; that is Confin'd in the Goals of; Poughkeepsie; Goshen; Sussex; and Morristown if you Continue in Your Murders and Cruelties; as you have begun; and is Still determined to give the Refugees no Quarters; we Loyalists do Solemnly Declare, that we will Hang Six for One, which shall be inflicted on your Headmen; and Leaders, and wherever we Loyal Refugees finds Malatiamen; under Arms against us; or against any of his Majesty's Loyal Subjacks; we are fully Determined; to Masacre them on the Spot we Embody not with the British Army; but keeps by our Selves; in full Companys, Chooses our own Officers; men that is well Acquainted; with all your Lurking places where the Authors of Your Tyranny; and Oppressers resorts; we acquaint you; that there is Some Thousands of us; from all the Provinces on the Continent; who have been Banish'd & Robbed of our Estates by your Tyrannical laws; we are now Roused with Spirit of of Resentment; and will be revenged on you, for the Blood of our Friends; and the loss of our Estates; you will find your Selves Surrounded on every Quarter by us and Col. Butlers Army [of loyalists and Indians from Canada] we acquaint you; to prepare for your Sudent doom and Destruction poor Miserable wratches; you will bring your selves into Slavery and Thraldom; You have Rebelled against your Gracious Sovereign; the best of Kings and has Disannuled all Connections; with his Realm; Crown; and Dignity; and held in Contempt his Manifastos; and Proclamations; and has join'd with France as your Good, and Great Ally; who will at last lave you in the Lurch; and will stand a great chance to loose his Crown; for Interfering with you in; your Cursed Rebellion Contrairy to the laws of all Nations; In reguard of the Royal Army; they are to hunt and persue your Racer; and his Runners; I mean your Commander in Chief; and

Army; where they will get such a Whiping; and Spuring up; with the points of Byonnets and Cutlashes; as will Gald their Wind and Consequently must loose the Race; as for your Two titular Governors; (the bloody Neroes) I mean Clinton [George Clinton of New York] and Livingston (a name too Honourable for the former) will meet with their Just Deserts; (one Day or Other) in the same manner that they have serv'd the unfortunate Loyalists that fell into your Merciless hands; for the Blood of those Innocent men; and the crys of the Widows; and Fatherless; will be heard; and be Recompenced with the Almighty's Wrath; and Indignation; for Vengance is mine; and I will repay it Saith the Lord—I therefore shall Conclude; you Bloody Tyrants; and lave you to your Destruction; between God; and your own Black Souls be it; and finishes with the poet

On your Governors
"You Infernal Bloodhounds; now Desist
And in your Murders; no more persist
Unless you Repent, you'll tormented be
With Incarnate Devils; to all Eternity
"Signed in Behalf of the Loyalists

John Mason

"Dated at Rabels Defiance March 27th, AD 1779
"N. B. the above lines is wrote in a low Stile Sutable to your Capacitys."

Mason in March 1779 may have heard of the plans being laid by William Franklin, the royal governor of New Jersey who was now a refugee in New York, to embody loyalists in companies for revenge and retaliatory plunder. But Mason's band was made up of swashbucklers like himself, operating out of the New York islands on minor raids. He brought in, he reminded Sir Henry Clinton, "all useful intelligence he was capable [of] and likewise prisoners" and deserters. In November 1778 he with two of the sons of Claudius Smith captured two important prisoners: Colonel Joseph Ward, commissary general of musters for the Continental Army, and his deputy Captain William Bradford, Jr. For this Clinton rewarded the captors with a hundred guineas. Late in 1779 Mason, "having received an authentic draft of Mr. Wayne's situation from his friends in the country," planned to capture Anthony Wayne from his quarters on the Passaic. But before this could be undertaken, Mason was arrested by the British for—he explained—"inadvertently plundering some invetrite enemies to government on Long Island who carries on a clandestine trade with the rebels in New England, and sends them all the useful intelligence they can obtain from their friends in New York concerning the British Fleet and Army, and has induced many soldiers to desert the royal standard." The court martial that tried Mason did not find him so innocent as he made out. He was confined in the Provost, and two months later his wife was sent to the same prison. They were undoubtedly thieves whose claim that they had robbed rebels only did not convince their judges. British military rule in New York was severe.

In July 1780 Mason appealed desperately to Clinton "to forgive and extricate your memorialist" from the prison in which he was still detained "to the grief of the loyalists and great joy to the rebels. . . . He never shall be guilty of such enormities again and shall endeavor, with all the emulation in his soul, to retrieve his former character." His "poor unhappy wife" was in a "languishing state of health . . . and has had the small pox to a shocking degree, and never had no hearing nor trial since she was committed. . . . Your memorialist . . . humbles himself at your Excellency's feet for mercy and clemency (which has never been implored by the unhappy in vain), praying that the God of all mercy may further crown your Excellency's victorious arms with success, triumph, and laurels."

In December Mason had an interview in the Provost with Captain John Stapleton, one of De Lancey's assistants in the secret service. Stapleton said that if some gentleman would be security for Mason's loyalty and future good behavior, he might be "employed from Headquarters." Mason wrote a letter to Mayor Mathews, but got no reply. On the 21st, ten days before the mutiny, he sent a memorial to Stapleton. "My long confinement, with my wife's," he declared, "and living on short allowance shall never make me derogate from my allegiance, but has exasperated me to desperation against the rebels, they being the instigation of all my misfortunes. And should it, Sir, ever be in my power I shall endeavor to retaliate the murder of brave Major André; and should his Excellency most graciously please to receive me into mercy and extricate me from my confinement, I am willing to serve his Excellency in the capacity of a spy."

He knew the colonies so well, Mason said, that he could carry messages to any of General Arnold's friends and bring intelligence back. During his confinement he had found out many rebel schemes from fellow-prisoners: among them, a scheme to destroy New York by fire that winter. From now on he would never offend again. If he should, he was willing to undergo "the cruelest tortures and ignominious death. . . . Your Honor may be fully assured I shall run all risks and strain every nerve to retrieve my former character."

Relief came unexpectedly to Mason from the West Indies. Major William Odell of Jamaica had been sent by the governor of the island to New York, the past July, to raise a corps of adventurers willing to go on an expedition against the Spaniards in Nicaragua. Rich prospects of plunder on the fabulous Spanish Main were held out to possible recruits. It was hoped that this might be bait to draw deserters in from the rebel Army. By October the Loyal American Rangers had enlisted 38 men with 5 women; by November 166 men with 10 women and 2 children: scarcely any of them from the rebels. Clinton, obliged to give Arnold first pick of American deserters after he joined the British, cut off this source of supply to Odell and sent him to the prisons for recruits. He got, according to Major Mackenzie, "a set of the greatest villains that were ever collected," about thirty of them men who had been sentenced to death or corporal punishment and who now won pardons by enlisting. And he got John Mason, who was made a sergeant.

Almost at once Mason was given another opportunity, this time for immediate service. Stapleton, when the need of an emissary to the Pennsylvania mutineers came up, naturally remembered Mason, who had volunteered to serve as a spy. The first shipload of Loyal American Rangers had sailed for Jamaica. One of the later recruits could be spared for a few days. The swaggering Mason, exasperated and no doubt destitute after his confinement, was selected by De Lancey and released by Odell, to take one copy of the proposals to Princeton.

III

It was arranged that Gould, with the two copies for Gautier, and Mason should both go down to the *Neptune* in Raritan Bay, from which they could be put ashore while it was dark. Gould, used to such trips and having no special preparations to make, got to the *Neptune* in the rain that night and was landed at daybreak at Elizabeth Point. He had only two miles or so to go to Elizabethtown and Gautier.

With Mason it was different. He had to be furnished for a journey of two or three days at least. Since the roads would probably be guarded, he would need guides familiar with every foot of the country. Before he landed he must know what men could be confided in and where they lived. Various things delayed him so that he did not get to the *Neptune* till eight that Friday morning, when it was too late for him to land with any safety. Captain Stewart Ross of the *Neptune*, unwilling to wait for night and so waste a day, pressed two horses somewhere and sent them with Mason to the *Philadelphia* armed galley, with instructions to proceed up the Raritan River and land Mason where he chose during the afternoon. This was carried out, though it is not known where Mason went on shore. It was probably not far from South Amboy, for John Rattoon of that town, who had been a valued messenger between New York and Philadelphia during the Arnold negotiations, found the guide who was to conduct Mason on the first stage of his journey, to South River. The night's rain and the forenoon's fog had passed by now, and Mason with his guide set out on their horses about dusk in a fresh west wind.

Three proposals were not enough. On the same day three more copies were sent out "and a verbal message to the same import," according to De Lancey's Journal of the mutiny. Nothing is known about the oral message or the messenger. Of the written copies, one went to Cornelius Hatfield on Staten Island, one to Thomas Ward on Bergen Neck, both to be forwarded. The third was carried by a man named Blank (or Blanck) who has not been identified. Besides these men with proposals, Joseph Clark went off towards Morristown your letter with the two addresses came safe, which I have forwarded, by a faithful friend express to prince town, where the ~~British~~ Insylvanian Troops make a stand, you are expected, over to Amboy and all the Rebel militia of New Jersey are order'd out, the New Jersey Troops have from Prompton to Morist: and Genl. Washington is on his way from West point to see Wayne saturday

ANDREW GAUTIER TO OLIVER DE LANCEY

Facsimiles of an unpublished cipher letter sent by Gautier to De Lancey January 5, 1781, under cover to Daniel Gautier, and of a contemporary transcription.

merely to find out what was happening in that quarter, and Isaac Siscoe towards West Point to learn, if he could, whether mutiny was spreading to the soldiers under Washington's command.

Clinton crossed to Long Island about noon on Friday, and then to Staten Island, where he took quarters near Decker's ferry on the north shore in order to be on hand if encouraging news from the mutineers should warrant rapid movement of the troops. The British regiments were ferried to Staten Island after dark, and the Hessians were to follow the next morning. De Lancey went with Clinton. His two assistants in the secret service, Major Mackenzie and Captain Stapleton, remained at Headquarters in New York.

Late that night, or the next day, a prompt reply from Gautier arrived, though not by Gould. "Your letter with the two addresses came safe," it said, "which I have forwarded by a faithful friend express to Princeton, where the Pennsylvania troops make a stand." The Jersey militia were all ordered out, and Washington was on his way—Gautier incorrectly said—to Wayne.

9

Officers and Officials from Philadelphia

ST. CLAIR and Lafayette, riding towards Princeton Friday forenoon with two or more light horsemen who had escorted them from Philadelphia, met several noncommissioned officers and privates outside the mutineers' lines. The generals asked the stragglers what had caused all this trouble. They replied, Lafayette thought, in embarrassment and shame. This seemed a good sign that the men might not be all of the same mind with their chiefs. When the party came to the lines they were required to halt and identify themselves according to military regulations, and were sent with a guard to the Board of Sergeants in Nassau Hall. The sergeants received the generals very respectfully.

"We talked with them, and they showed us what had been written between General Wayne and themselves. From there we went to General Wayne's quarters, where at various times we saw the chosen leaders."

Lafayette could not decide whether this was a plot with British emissaries behind it, or only a revolt led by men who were pleased with their new power and unwilling to let anybody go over their heads to the rank and file. Whichever was the case, he saw that there was no chance of his haranguing the "multitude." All business had to be transacted through the Board of Sergeants. Organized like a small army, with generals, colonels, and so on, the mutineers could

OFFICIALS FROM PHILADELPHIA 97

not be stampeded into a susceptible audience such as Lafayette had hoped to find. (He could hardly be expected to perceive that this was what would some day be called a well-managed strike.)

It was plain to him, listening to the sergeants, that the troops had grievances, particularly over the terms of their enlistments and the way the protests of many of them had been received by certain of the officers. But it was mutiny, and there was danger that the enemy might take advantage of it. Perhaps Walter Stewart's regiment, which had held out till they were threatened with overwhelming bayonets, could be detached from the Line. Perhaps the majority could be persuaded to move on to Trenton. The Board of Sergeants were resolved to keep the whole Line at Princeton till they had been settled with. They reiterated their promise to fight under Wayne if the British should come out.

During the conference Colonel Laurens arrived to join the visiting officers. At this the troops became suspicious. Too many officers among them might mean mischief. They already had Wayne, Butler, Stewart—and Moylan besides. The sergeants sent a message advising the visitors "to make a prompt retreat for fear of evil consequence. Another message gave us an hour and a half" in which to dine. "My name was not mentioned," Lafayette pointed out. "But since everybody was going, and everybody was agreed as to the impossibility of speaking to the soldiers or of dealing with them except in the manner established between them and General Wayne, we quitted Princeton, leaving the three gentlemen who may be regarded as prisoners." Lafayette was astonished that the others were permitted to go.

St. Clair went on to Morristown, to take charge of the soldiers who had refused to join the mutiny. Lafayette and Laurens accompanied him on their way to New Windsor.

They met many men going to Princeton, and persuaded them to turn back. One party of about thirty was difficult. "But after many effusions of the heart, and fine words, they at last consented to return to their huts. I wish that rum or the influence of their leaders may not change their minds. All these people tell me that they would follow me wherever I might need them . . . that they would die to the last man under my orders; but that I do not know all they have suffered; that they will have justice from their country."

If there were other negotiations between Wayne and the sergeants on Friday, there is at least no record. At three in the afternoon he instructed one of the light horsemen who had come with St. Clair and Lafayette and now were returning to Philadelphia, to "send up the auditors of accounts immediately to settle the pay and depreciation of the Line." This was all Wayne cared to put in writing. But he told the messenger, whose name was John Donaldson, to report to the authorities in Philadelphia that the mutineers were somewhat divided in their aims, though all determined not to have their former officers back, even in a march against the enemy.

II

It was four o'clock when Donaldson left Princeton. At that same hour in Philadelphia, then counted forty miles away, twenty other light horsemen were parading in front of Joseph Reed's house in Market Street.

They belonged to the Philadelphia Light Horse (since famous as the First Troop Philadelphia City Cavalry). The troop was made up of "gentlemen of fortune," in Washington's words, who before the war had hunted foxes in Gloucester County, New Jersey. In the war the sportsmen turned soldiers, with Samuel Morris as captain, and served

OFFICIALS FROM PHILADELPHIA

in special emergencies for short times with what Washington called "a noble example of discipline and subordination, and in several actions ... a spirit of bravery which will ever do honor to them and will ever be gratefully remembered by me." They appeared on all decorative occasions, which they graced with their good horses and horsemanship, fine bearing, and brilliant uniforms: "A dark brown short coat, faced and lined with white; white vest and breeches; high-topped boots; round black hat, bound with silver cord; a buck's tail [worn on the hat as a crest]; housings brown, edged with white, and the letters L. H. worked on them." Their arms were "a carbine, a pair of pistols and holsters, with flounces of brown cloth trimmed with white; a horseman's sword; white belts for the sword and carbine." The silken standard they carried on their campaigns was the earliest American flag made with thirteen stripes. Now, on Friday the 5th, part of the troop had been called out to escort the President of the Supreme Executive Council of Pennsylvania to Princeton, or wherever he might have to go, on the affairs of the Pennsylvania Line.

The Council, having that day received Wayne's Thursday letter asking that somebody be sent to the mutineers, had conferred with the Committee of Congress and had resolved to send President Reed and General Potter at once. A "very good horse" was ordered for Potter, and he was allowed £100 in new State money for expenses. The Committee would follow the next morning, with two new members appointed that day—Samuel John Atlee of Pennsylvania and Theodorick Bland of Virginia—and the rest of the Light Horse.

Joseph Reed, a native of New Jersey and a graduate of the College at Princeton, had studied law in the Middle Temple in London, and come home to practice his profession in Trenton and Philadelphia. Married to an Englishwoman, he had family and political connections with England, but he had early favored independence and had served in the Continental Army as Washington's military secretary, then as adjutant general. In 1777 Reed had been elected a delegate to Congress from Pennsylvania, and in December 1778 President of Pennsylvania. Because in the dark weeks late in 1776 he had temporarily sided with Charles Lee against Washington, Reed was suspected by some patriots of having divided loyalties. In June 1778 he had been offered, by one of the British peace commissioners, what Reed considered a bribe. Though he refused it with indignation, and let the public know about it, there were still people who wondered why he had been singled out for the attempt. As a private citizen, or even as a soldier, he might soon have lived the unjust scandal down. As head of the Council he made political enemies who took pains to keep it alive. All his executive maneuvers were seen as intrigues. And it is true that, while Reed with his sharp and pointed face was perfectly faithful to the American cause, he was sometimes crafty and generally eager for popular applause, like almost any politician.

With Potter and the light horsemen Reed left Philadelphia late in the afternoon and that night rode twenty miles to Bristol. On the way they met a sergeant and two or three other mutineers "going to town to prevent the bad report of their abusing people." Though the leaders of the mutiny insisted on staying tight within their lines at Princeton, they knew that distorted rumors about them might reach Philadelphia and prejudice their case. Reed sent back orders that the deputation of mutineers should be carefully watched, for fear they might work among the garrison or the militia in Philadelphia, but not be ill used, "lest it have a bad effect on their fellows in Jersey."

At Bristol Reed met the light horsemen with Wayne's letter of the afternoon, and learned from Donaldson several things that Wayne had not written. The mutineers had little ammunition except for the artillery, which they guarded with remarkable vigilance. The "country" supplied them with provisions "to prevent being plundered. The men in general have expressed a desire to cross the Delaware, but the sergeants oppose it from a fear that in that case they will disperse to their friends, and their leaders will be exposed to danger"—without the protection of the men in arms.

Reed sent Donaldson on to the Council, himself endorsing Wayne's request to have the auditors of accounts hurried to Princeton. "I think the auditors should come forward," Reed wrote. "It will have a good conciliatory effect." And in a separate letter he made other suggestions. "I think it will be best to send provisions on, but not to unlade it out of the shallop without orders." It would be imprudent to give the mutineers a chance to take the supplies by force instead of having to come to terms for them. "In the meantime, let the clothing be forwarded, and the money prepared. At all events I fear we must make some douceurs in some way or another." Wayne's letter and Donaldson's report had convinced Reed that the mutineers were in a position to insist on more than words.

III

While American officials were on their way towards the mutineers with vague ideas as to what might be done, and British emissaries with secret but definite overtures, New Jersey was making an effort to surround Princeton and control the mutiny if possible. There were battalions of the New Jersey Line at Morristown, Pompton, and Chatham; and bodies of militia at—or gathering at—Brunswick, Elizabethtown, and South Amboy and along the roads to New York, and at Hopewell and Crosswicks near Bordentown. But the New Jersey officers and officials were already troubled by the sympathy which Continentals and militiamen felt and expressed for the mutineers. The Pennsylvanians had outrageous grievances, it was said in every Jersey camp, and were entitled to the redress they had demanded. So long as they behaved themselves with their present decency, and did not join the British, they should be left alone while they negotiated with Congress and their State.

These were local measures. Washington at New Windsor saw the mutiny as a national concern. On Friday he drafted a circular letter to the governors of all the New England States, telling them of the insurrection, its causes, and possible consequences. "At what point this defection will stop, or how extensive it may prove, God only knows. At present the troops at the important posts in this vicinity remain quiet, not being acquainted with this unhappy and alarming affair. But how long they will continue so cannot be ascertained, as they labor under some of the pressing hardships with the troops who have revolted. . . . The circumstances will now point out more forcibly what ought to be done than anything that can possibly be said by me on the subject.

"It is not within the sphere of my duty to make requisitions without the authority of Congress, from individual States. But at such a crisis, and circumstanced as we are, my own heart will acquit me; and Congress and the States eastward of this (whom for the sake of dispatch I address) I am persuaded will excuse me when once for all I give it decidedly as my opinion that it is in vain to think an army can be kept together much longer under such a variety of sufferings as ours has experienced; and that unless some immediate and spirited exertions are adopted to furnish at least three months' pay to the troops, in money that will be of some value to them, and at the same time ways and means are devised to clothe and feed them better (more regularly I mean) than they have been, the worst that can befall us may be expected."

The mutineers at Mount Kemble, thinking only of their own privations, had taken a stand that promised to be of service to the entire Army.

10

Preliminaries on Saturday

BY NOON on Saturday the 6th Reed was at Trenton, where he took quarters at the Trent-Cox house known as Bloomsbury. Colonel John Cox, who then occupied it, was a Philadelphia merchant and Reed's uncle by marriage. A conspicuous patriot, Cox was in such temporary need of money that his wife had not a dollar in the house for expenses.

From the governor and other officials of New Jersey Reed could learn little at first hand about the mutineers. His first move was to write a letter to Wayne inviting him to a conference at Maidenhead, four miles from Princeton, at four o'clock that afternoon. Though the letter is missing, its main points appear in the effects it had. It was not certain that Wayne would be permitted to come out to the meeting. The letter must either assume that he would be or else imply that the mutineers had some kind of right to prevent it. If they did try to prevent it, they would have to show their hands, and might lose credit by seeming to hinder an orderly settlement. Nor could Reed know whether the mutineers would open the letter before turning it over to Wayne, or whether they would turn it over at all. The letter was, as Reed elsewhere wrote, "more calculated for them than for General Wayne." Its meaning for Wayne had to be explicit without compromising him with the men, while at the same time conveying to them what Reed wanted them to know or believe.

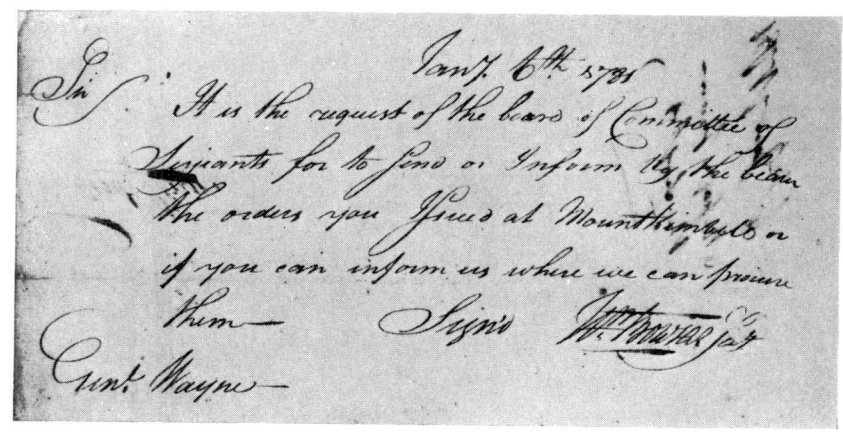

WILLIAM BOWZAR TO ANTHONY WAYNE

Facsimile of an unpublished letter to Wayne from the Secretary of the Board of Sergeants, January 6, 1781. *See page 106.*

In this strategic letter Reed said that the "indignities offered" St. Clair and Lafayette the day before made him now unwilling to go into Princeton. But he was ready to hear the complaints of the soldiers and to promise redress for all reasonable grievances. Their worst necessities should be promptly supplied. He hinted that different groups among the mutineers with different complaints should apply to him through separate agents. (This might serve to divide the men and make them easier to deal with.) And he may have hinted that he would expect them to take their officers back. He certainly let it be understood that the men responsible for the killings on the night of the outbreak could not expect to be included in the general pardon promised by Wayne.

Reed and Potter went as far as Judge Daniel Hunt's house at Maidenhead and sent the letter on to Princeton by Blair McClenachan and Alexander Nesbitt of the Light Horse. The messengers were "civilly treated" by the Board of Sergeants, and allowed to carry the letter to Wayne unopened. Soon afterwards the sergeants sent Wayne a request to come to their quarters. He refused, "upon which they went to him." He let them see the letter and take it away with them, but for no longer than half an hour. Though the plan was to have the letter read to the men, Wayne insisted on reading it himself, and was not willing to have it circulate through the camp. It was agreed that the men should be assembled for parade the next morning and the letter then be read to them in form.

But before Wayne was ready with a reply to the letter there were some exchanges in writing between him and the Board of Sergeants. "Those articles of clothing which you mentioned yesterday to our Board," Bowzar wrote, "would tend to a great pacification if you would procure them as early as possible, as the men in general is in great want and profound necessity for the same, and therefore should be glad how soon you could send us answer in how short time you can procure them." To this Wayne answered: "When General Wayne is assured that the terms offered by him on the 4th instant will be complied with on the part of the noncommissioned officers and privates of the Pennsylvania Line, he will take the proper measures to procure an immediate and full supply of shirts, shoes, socks, and overalls."

This brought from Bowzar his shortest note in the whole mutiny correspondence and the bluntest refusal by the Board. "As you insist that the Line must comply with your proposals of the 4th instant, they cannot agree to them, as the approbation of the whole is quite contrary." Then, as if such bluntness made the sergeants reflect on the possible consequences of their refusing, another short note followed. "It is the request of the Board of Committee of Sergeants for to send or inform by the bearer the orders you issued at Mount Kemble, if you can inform us where we can procure them." The sergeants may have had no copy of the order of the 2nd, and may have been in doubt as to Wayne's precise words: "that no man shall receive the least injury on account of the part they have taken on the occasion." Or they may only have wanted to remind Wayne of his promise to them, and to have it renewed before they turned to negotiations with Reed, who had hinted that some men would not be pardoned for their actions on the first night of the mutiny.

The sergeants seemed "much affected" by Reed's saying he could not put himself in their power after the reception given St. Clair and Lafayette. If those generals had been asked to leave, it was, as the mutineers saw it, because they were indisposed to negotiate piecemeal while waiting for persons with final authority to end the whole dispute. Reed had that authority. The Board drew up a polite letter offering him welcome and safe conduct. "General Wayne having communicated to the Committee of Sergeants convened at his request to represent the grievances of the Pennsylvania Line, the purport of your Excellency's letter of the evening of this instant signifying some doubt of your safety in meeting him in Princeton—but your Excellency need not be in the least afraid or apprehensive of any irregularities or ill treatment, that the whole Line would be very happy how expedient your Excellency would be in settling this unhappy affair."

Bowzar, writing for the Board, did not mention Wayne's going to Maidenhead, but Wayne in a brief note said he would meet Reed there the next morning. Wayne preferred to trust his communications to the light horsemen. "Mr. McClenachan and Mr. Nesbitt will inform you how matters are."

When the two reached Reed at Maidenhead, probably about seven o'clock that evening, they had much to say. The sergeants had been anxious to know whether Reed "entertained any unkind sentiments" regarding them. "Some of the sergeants and men took pains to inform the gentlemen privately that they were not fond of the business." Fresh intelligence had come from Elizabethtown that British and Hessian troops had been ordered extra clothing and provisions as if for an advance into New Jersey; and the enemy had heard on Friday "by a man who went over from Woodbridge, that the new commandant of the Pennsylvania Line would join them if he could have an opportunity." Actually no such message had been received by the British. Wayne could not know that. The mutineers might be secretly committed to the enemy, behind his back, and might be tricking him when they still professed "a good disposition against the enemy." There seemed, however, to be "no signs of British gold or of British emissaries, except a few sergeants who have been imprudently raised from the ranks." The men were "very shabby" and laid particular stress on their want of clothing.

Wayne had suggested, confidentially by the light horsemen, that if Reed felt unsafe at Maidenhead he might spend the night at Pennington, to which the banished officers of the Line had come the day before from Allentown. Reed sensibly guessed that the men would resent his going among the officers, and so instead returned that night to Trenton.

There he conferred with the Committee of Congress who arrived after dark: Sullivan, Witherspoon, Atlee, and Bland (but not Mathews who never left Philadelphia during the affair). Reed could inform the Committee that the people and militia of New Jersey were in sympathy with the mutineers and would not oppose them while they refrained from violence towards civilians and stayed away from the enemy. Potter may have heard already that the Pennsylvania militiamen were likewise reluctant to march against the Line that had suffered so much and so unjustly. With little hope of being able to put the insurgents down by force, and in possible danger of losing them to the British if force were tried, the deliberating officials saw they must make concessions. It was decided that Wayne's promise of total amnesty should be kept without question, and that men enlisted for three years or for the war should be released if they had served three years, and had not re-enlisted. Men who had voluntarily enlisted or re-enlisted for the war were not on any account to be discharged. The negotiations were to be left to Reed, with the Committee of Congress remaining in Trenton for consultation or support if either should be needed. The conference agreed that the men had not yet acted like traitors, unless their refusal to leave Princeton meant that they thought of going to the enemy if their grievances were not redressed on their own terms.

II

It was now five days since the Line revolted. They had left Mount Kemble in tumult, had settled with enthusiasm into good order, and since their arrival in Princeton had won the friendship of the citizens. Some deserters had left the camp, but other soldiers had come late from Morristown to join the mutiny. With their women and children the mutineers claimed to number the two thousand for whom they drew daily rations—though they may, after long hunger, have drawn lavishly. There were perhaps never more than seventeen hundred men at Princeton, if so many. Yet that was a formidable body, as Continental forces went. And it was at present united in a venture as dangerous as a battle, and as instinctive as self-preservation.

A few special discontents seem to have existed in individuals. Some obstinate Presbyterians were angry and sulky over the alliance with Catholic France. The Englishmen and Irishmen in the Line often hated each other. The veterans were jealous of the new recruits. These discontents were slight compared with the fundamental grievances of hunger, cold, and poverty which all the troops had shared. They believed it was unreasonable to expect them to suffer so much, and unjust to compel them to.

They had, it was true, on enlistment bound themselves to conform to the rules and regulations of the Army, under which mutiny or desertion to the enemy was punishable with death. But ever since enlistment they had been entitled to food, clothing, and pay for their services. Any contract between them and the government had in effect been broken by the government, in its failure to supply the soldiers what was due them. The government, through the officers, had been able to force the soldiers to go on fulfilling their part of the one-sided contract. Now it seemed to the soldiers only fair to demand that the government meet its obligations to them, or release them.

The men of the Line, neither lawyers nor philosophers, were common soldiers such as their age bred and employed in its wars. Whether they could read or only listen to orators, they understood that they were fighting for liberty and the rights of man, defending their altars and their fires. But many of them were recent immigrants, wandering landless men with no fires and no altars to speak of, who felt that in the Army they were without liberty or rights. Surely the men who did the actual fighting ought to be provided with the necessaries of life, at least till they died in the service. If independence was worth giving their lives for, it was worth the money the country had agreed to pay its soldiers.

Perhaps some of them remembered what had been said in General Orders on July 17, 1780: "An American soldier, equal in bravery, in capacity equal, superior in patience, fortitude, and patriotism to any other, should scorn to be inferior in anything." But praise was not food and clothing, encouragement was not pay, and there were limits to human strength. The Line thought they had passed the limits before they mutinied.

They still did not blame their sufferings altogether on Congress or Pennsylvania. As if unable to take a long view of their situation, they kept their sharpest resentment fixed on their own field and company officers. Since the original enlistment papers have not survived, it is now impossible to know how far the men were right in their contentions. But they did contend, and were generally convinced, that many of them who had understood they were enlisting for a maximum of three years were entered on the lists for the war. In disputes about terms the word of an officer had almost invariably been accepted over any protest by a soldier. The men recalled that "fine deception" had been practiced on them when the gratuity of 1779 was paid. It was a free gift to veterans and it did not commit them to any added obligations. But some of the officers had taken advantage of ignorant men and had required them on receiving the gratuity to sign new enlistments. Or so the men insisted, with an increasing sense of grievance, imagining that such cases had been more numerous than they were.

Officers charged, whether justly or unjustly, with deception had been short and harsh with the soldiers. It was not enough that high-minded officers like Wayne and Richard Butler and Walter Stewart, and others, had stood hour after hour in the cold among the men and had shared their poor food. It was not enough that efforts had been made to discover and punish officers guilty of misbehavior: such as Captain Lieutenant Theophilus Parke of the artillery artificers who in March 1780 had been convicted of "defrauding his men of their pay and bounty" and for his "scandalous, infamous, and villainous conduct" had been sentenced "to be cashiered with infamy, by having his sword broke over his head on the public parade in front of the regiment to which he belongs by the adjutant of the said regiment." For the men knew that there were officers, neither high-minded like Wayne nor discovered like Parke, who treated the men fraudulently or unfairly, and despised and bullied them. And the men did not always comprehend that the officers too were in wretched straits for clothes and money. A colonel's pay was much less than the wages of an unskilled laborer in civil life. Major

Thomas Church of the 4th Pennsylvania had written on Christmas Day that his retirement in January would leave him without a farthing and had begged Wayne to allow him Army rations till spring. Privation had reduced men and officers to primitive squabbling over the bare means of existence.

This antagonism was largely to blame for the peculiar fury of both officers and men on the night of the outbreak. The men felt unbearably aggrieved, the officers unbearably insulted. Men without thought of mutiny in principle joined in the fight from instinct. After that they left camp in fear as much as in anger. Men who had no share in the violence, and no stomach for it, went along because they were forced to go or because they would rather take a dangerous chance with their friends than stay safely and shamefully behind. And many left, without acting or reasoning one way or the other, in the wild contagion of the general exodus.

Between Tuesday morning and Saturday night the transports of passion, as Washington called them, had cooled as he foresaw they would. Men who had been united in a first rush of impulse found themselves, when they came to take second thought, considerably divided. Some of the 20-dollar men, demanding immediate discharge, were disposed to be satisfied with that, without holding out in sympathy with the 120-dollar men till they should be conceded their right to discharge after three years from enlistment. Some of the 120-dollar men, who might still have to serve a year or more, were not too sure that they should jeopardize their own prospects by insisting that the 20-dollar men be released at once. Neither of these groups could be counted on to sacrifice themselves for the sake of the men enlisted recently and unreservedly for the war.

Besides this division on the matter of demands, there was

also division on the matter of methods. The men were all soldiers and knew that mutiny was a serious affair. Only last May a brigade from the Line had suppressed the Connecticut mutineers. The Connecticut brigades, so far as the Pennsylvanians knew, might be eager to get even with them, and might now be marching, perhaps with the Massachusetts men as well, from West Point towards Princeton. The New Englanders, mostly natives, and the Pennsylvanians, many of them foreign-born, were not congenial and sometimes thought of themselves as belonging to separate countries though at war with a common enemy. The Pennsylvania mutineers seem to have been little apprehensive of the New Jersey Continentals, who amounted to only three regiments, and still less of the Jersey militia, who were not regular soldiers and who, the mutineers had probably heard, thought the mutiny was justifiable so long as it continued to be well ordered. But of course if the New Englanders should come they might be joined by the New Jersey troops in overpowering force.

Though the Pennsylvanians considered themselves, from their long service and training together, to be the flower of the Army, as Reed said, they knew they might suffer heavily in an engagement in which they were outnumbered, and then would still be liable to the severest punishments for their revolt. If they had to fight, it would be for their lives. They naturally felt it an outrage that their brother-soldiers might be used against them, to defeat their righteous claims to justice. Let that be undertaken, and they would as naturally turn from their peaceable aims and means to the savage destruction they had been accused of intending. They might, some of them argued, prevent such bloodshed and damage by making terms and laying down their arms. But they had only Wayne's word for it that what they had already done would be forgotten. Peace might cost them as much as war, and the risks they had run might bring them nothing.

Who then would be the enemy: the Americans denying them their rights or the British more than willing to grant them? Here was a question which desperate men might reasonably ask, but to which the conduct of the mutineers had not yet given any answer. On Saturday night the officers and officials concerned with the mutiny were alert with suspicion that the Line was looking towards New York. There was nothing against this but the facts: that the mutinous party had marched in the other direction, sent no emissaries to the British, resolved to be "regular and chaste" at Princeton, and settled down to wait for redress from the constituted authorities. On Saturday night when they went to quarters they had no assurance as to what they might expect. It might be everything or nothing.

Saturday Night and Sunday Morning

MASON the emissary, put ashore somewhere in the Raritan at dusk on Friday the 5th, had about twenty-five miles ahead of him by the roads he probably took. On a less secret mission he might have gone to Brunswick and there picked up the post road which crossed New Jersey by way of Newark, Elizabethtown, Brunswick, and Princeton to Trenton. But he was sure to encounter militia patrols on that route, and sentinels guarding bridges. It would be safer to travel by Spotswood and Cranberry.

Another spy who landed from the *Vulture* near Cheesequake eleven days later found this course difficult enough. "We immediately proceeded," that spy (Andrew Fürstner) told his story, "on our journey to a certain Mr. Lott about five miles from the shore, where we expected to procure a guide. But a command of about fifty men being posted at his house, the sentry of which hailed us and fired . . . made us retreat and attempt to cross Deep Run bridge. But upon finding another sentinel here, we waded the Run above the bridge and proceeded to South River bridge, where we were again hailed and repulsed. And then we went on to Johnson's bridge, where a sentry fired upon us again and wounded one of my recruits in a finger with a buckshot. This put us under the necessity of retreating again. But daylight appearing, and we not thinking ourselves safe in that neighborhood, we swam South River the 17th in the morning and traveled through the woods wet and cold towards Spotswood. But mistrusting this also to be a dangerous place, we left Spotswood to our left and crossed the road some little distance above it, where we met a battalion of militia marching towards Brunswick, who pursued us and took one of my men prisoner. But the other and myself got into a thick swamp where we lay all day. The night following we proceeded towards Cranberry where we came near another sentinel on the bridge a little before daylight, took to the woods, and proceeded the 18th seven miles further to Mr. Morris's, a friend to government, where we were safe."

On the 5th the country can hardly yet have been so well patrolled, and Mason's ride to Princeton took less time. His first guide, whose name appears to have been Fegany (or Feguny), got Mason to the village of South River without much delay. There or near there he found James Ogden. He was the son of Nathaniel Ogden of Brunswick, had been married the past November to Catharine Pitt, and was probably a farmer living on the land, between South River and Old Bridge, of Benjamin Ogden, who was to administer the small property James Ogden left intestate. These are buried facts about a man who is remembered—when he is remembered—only as Mason's guide to Princeton, where he rose to his four days of fame. Ogden may have been a secret loyalist in his patriotic community. He may have been merely a young man in want of money and ready for adventure, who was willing to lead a plausible daredevil on a hazardous errand.

Mason was no stranger in New Jersey, but if he were recognized he would be at once arrested as a criminal loyalist. He needed a guide acquainted with back roads and short cuts. The best roads were scarcely better than bridle paths through the woods or between clearings. South River (often known as Willettstown) was less than a dozen houses, and Old Bridge was rather a landmark than a settlement. Spotswood, three miles further, and Cranberry, nine miles from Princeton, were somewhat larger, but still only little villages on the undeveloped road from the Amboys to Bordentown. If Mason and Ogden went by this route, they could go softly through the villages in the dark or ride round them through the woods or fields. Nobody seems to have stopped them, and they got to the lines at Princeton late Saturday night or early Sunday morning.

On whatever pretext or with whatever arguments Mason was permitted to go "to the College, where Williams was": this according to the report of another spy. Mason "asked the sentry for the commanding officer and was sent up to his room. He told him he had an express for him. Williams asked him from whence. He says from Elizabethtown. Williams then asked if the enemy were coming, which Mason answered in the negative. He then asked: 'Where do you come from?' The other said from Sir Henry Clinton and produced a piece of square lead enclosing a paper, which when Williams had read he ordered them to be secured, and went with them to a Committee of Sergeants, who agreed to deliver them up to General Wayne, which they did next morning."

The story is continued by Wayne, writing to Washington the day after. "About four o'clock yesterday morning we were waked by two sergeants, who produced a letter from the enemy enclosed in a small piece of tea lead. They also brought under guard two caitiffs"—this was Wayne's favorite word of opprobrium—"who undertook to deliver it to the leaders of the malcontents. One of these culprits says he is a sergeant in Odell's new-raised corps and was promised a considerable reward on bringing back an answer. The soldiery in general affect to spurn at the idea of turning Arnolds (as they express it). We have used every address to inflame them against wretches who would insult them by imagining them traitors; for had they thought them virtuous they would not have carried these overtures." Wayne promised the two sergeants who brought the prisoners fifty guineas in gold apiece in recognition of their loyalty.

In this there was no sign of hesitation on the part of Williams or the Board of Sergeants. They cannot have debated long, or they would have waited longer and not roused Wayne at an hour so early even for a Continental camp. Their prompt and voluntary surrender of the emissaries seemed proof that they had not been in negotiation with the British and that they rejected the British proposals made to them. Once more the sergeants declared that if the enemy should land in New Jersey the revolted men would oppose their advance, as Wayne informed Congress, "at every expense of blood."

Wayne, in an emergency full of doubts and suspicions, dared not be too confident. The sergeants might have brought the proposals to him as evidence that the mutiny had strong friends and must not be underrated. It did not matter who had possession of the emissaries at Princeton, since Wayne and the colonels were themselves in the power of the mutineers. And the troops at large, overruling this first move of the sergeants, might insist that the proposals be made public, with results not easy to predict. The officers urged the sergeants, and persuaded them, to send Mason and Ogden off under guard along the Trenton road towards Reed, wherever he might be. This would both rid the camp of their possibly disturbing presence and indicate that the Line admitted the right of the Pennsylvania Council to deal with them. Mason, baffled if not amazed, and Ogden, terrified, left early that Sunday morning with a guard chosen by the sergeants before most of the troops learned that emissaries had arrived.

Another emissary may have been already in Princeton when the two were taken, may have heard about them and concluded that he would have no better luck with the mutineers. Whenever the second emissary arrived or however he reasoned about his situation, he dropped his proposals on Sunday night: "among the sergeants" according to Wayne, "before the door where the sergeants met" according to Reed. The next morning the paper was found and carried to Wayne. The emissary got away undetected and remains unidentified. A still more secret agent mysteriously turned up Sunday night at Morristown and delivered his copy of the proposals to St. Clair. As it is hardly likely this man could have reached Princeton, heard about the first two spies, and then made his way so far as to Morristown before night, he seems to have gone there directly, and to have been merely a double-dealer willing to take money from the British for accepting the mission and then to get what credit he could from the Americans for betraying it. He too remains unidentified.

II

Joseph Reed in Trenton, unaware that the British were ahead of him with offers to the mutineers, wrote to Wayne at seven o'clock on Sunday morning. Once more the letter was aimed chiefly at the men, and chiefly with the purpose of drawing them away from Princeton.

"My reasons," he carefully itemized, "are these: First, the commissioners inform me the provisions are nearly exhausted, and the men have hitherto behaved so well to the inhabitants that it would be a pity to drive the troops to the necessity of distressing them, when at this place they may be otherwise supplied"—from the Continental stores at Trenton or from Pennsylvania. "Secondly, they will find this town more convenient to receive the clothing, which is prepared at Philadelphia and will come up by water. Thirdly, they will be nearer to Congress, to whom it may be necessary to apply in the course of the business, as the whole Continental Army will be affected by the measures which may be taken in consequence of this unhappy event. Fourthly, I am persuaded the Pennsylvania Line have the honor of the State too much at heart to request their President to attend them, when convenience and propriety will make it better on all other accounts they should come here, and in this case I should be able to be nearer to them than at present."

Though Reed had received Bowzar's letter of reassurance and safe conduct, he avoided answering it directly. To do that would be tacitly to recognize the Board of Sergeants. Pretending to know less about the Board than he did know, Reed sent his answer through Wayne, thereby stressing the importance of the Line's lawful commander in the negotiations. "I have received a letter from Mr. Bowzar, who signs as secretary but does not say to whom. But as it is probable you can convey my sentiments to him, I would wish you to inform him and the persons with whom he acts in conjunction that it is rather a regard to my own station which prevents my going into Princeton than any distrust of them, either on the score of safety or good treatment. But as it is certain that, however just their complaints may be, the power now assumed is in opposition to the authority of the country, it would, I fear, give offense to the people of the State if I should even pass their guards." Actually Reed thought he was in danger of being killed or held captive by

SATURDAY NIGHT AND SUNDAY MORNING 121

the mutineers, but he preferred to take his stand, in words intended for their eyes, on grounds that would remind them of his dignity and their lack of status.

Delicately snubbing them, he must not alarm them. He had, he said, brought up "only a few" of the Philadelphia Light Horse, "to serve as expresses and for intelligence; but far be it from me, in the last necessity, to ask their service against these our brethren—if they were a more effective force than they are. You know, my dear General, that I have ever been a soldier's friend, that I have used all my influence to procure them comforts of all kinds, and that they really have been more attended to than the troops of any other State, which I am sure they will acknowledge. If we have not done better, it is owing to want of means. We hourly expect great supplies from Europe which would make them easy on the score of clothing, and which I do not think they will ever want again. Though I must lament the unfortunate occasion, I shall with great pleasure hearken to well-founded complaints and concur in any reasonable plan to accommodate matters to general satisfaction."

With this already written, Reed set out from Trenton intending again to go to Maidenhead and, if there were no word from Wayne about a meeting, to send the ingratiating letter to Princeton. On the road between Trenton and Maidenhead he met the guard with Mason and Ogden. There could hardly be, Reed saw, a better proof that the mutineers were acting for themselves, on no previous understanding with the enemy. He sent a trusted messenger—Dr. Hugh Shiell—to inform the Committee of Congress, and himself proceeded to Maidenhead with the spies, who were put in charge of McClenachan and Nesbitt of the Light Horse. Potter was with Reed, but is seldom mentioned in the records.

From Daniel Hunt's house Reed wrote again to Wayne, this time with greater confidence. The mutineers' "honorable and patriotic conduct this morning," he said, "will ever be remembered and suitably rewarded"—but he went on—"if nothing unfavorable to their country should happen." He hoped they would have "too much honor and spirit to tarnish their former good conduct by asking unreasonable things, or those which are impracticable." The proposals they had made on the 4th seemed "to favor a reasonable ground of accommodation," but they had been hastily drawn and might have to be altered at some points. If the State was under contract to make up loss of pay by depreciation, the men who had "freely enlisted" for the war were under contract to complete their term of service. "They certainly will not vindicate a breach of contract" on either side. Some "equitable mode of determining who are so enlisted" could be worked out. Men held to be so enlisted, and not entitled to discharge, might have a gratuity proportioned to the length of time they had already served. "Those who, after being discharged, choose to re-enlist will be kindly received, but they will be at their liberty to do it or not. If they choose to engage again they will be allowed furloughs to see their friends when the circumstances of the Army will admit." The immediate needs of the Line would be taken care of. After this, Reed concluded, if the mutineers were to "take any rash step . . . all the world will condemn them and they will condemn themselves—for America will not be lost if they decline their assistance to save her." Enough strength would be left in the country to punish them.

There was no more need to send the second letter than the first, for before noon Wayne, Butler, Stewart, and Moylan arrived at Maidenhead to confer with Reed. They assured him that the temper of the mutineers was generally fair, that he would be safe among them, and that it would have an excellent effect if he went. There was a particular reason for his going. The men were not yet sure that he (with Potter) was really on the way to them, with power to settle their claims. As Reed wrote to the Committee of Congress at one o'clock: "With the suspicions, usual in ignorant minds, that we are not here, that it is a plan of the officers to protract and forbear giving answers, they begged to be informed if I proposed coming, that they might show me every mark of respect. . . . In such cases some risk is to be run. My personal safety is a small consideration. . . . Besides, their behavior this morning seems to warrant a confidence that would not have been justifiable yesterday." Or as he wrote to the Pennsylvania Council: "The consequences of their [possible] defection to the enemy are so great and alarming that I think nothing ought to be left unattempted to improve a good disposition. I have but one life, and my country has the first claim for it."

Wayne sent a message back to Princeton with the announcement that Reed would be there that afternoon. But just as the party was leaving Maidenhead two sergeants with a guard checked them with a disturbing letter from Bowzar in behalf of the Board, addressed to McClenachan and Nesbitt. "It is the request of the Board, on account of the rumor of the Line, that you will send them two strangers who brought that letter from New York, by the bearers, two sergeants of the Committee, as you may depend they shall be brought forth at the request of Governor Reed or any other gentleman when called on, as we shall lodge them in security at our quarters."

Reed could readily suppose that "the rumor of the Line" was only the suspicion among the men as to the actual proximity of the Council members. This was confirmed by the address of the letter. The mutineers had seen McClenachan and Nesbitt, liked them, and put faith in them. They, not Reed, were asked to return the spies to Princeton and were given the promise that they would be securely kept till called for, by Reed. But Reed could not be sure what lay behind this apparent change of mind, or whether it had been forced upon the Board by the men after they had heard of the coming and going of the emissaries. It at least meant that the mutineers were not yet committed to a single course. It might mean that they thought they could drive a better bargain if they held their prisoners. It could even mean that they now looked with favor on the British proposals.

Since Wayne and Butler had given their word that the spies would be returned to the sergeants on request, there could be no thought of refusing. But some members of the party at Maidenhead considered this request "so unfavorable a symptom" that they advised Reed not to keep his engagement. He had made it, "did not choose to run the risk of disappointing them, and accordingly went into Princeton at three o'clock."

12

Negotiations on Sunday

WHEN Reed reached the picket, probably at the bridge over Stony Brook, the guards turned out and saluted his party. As he advanced along the post road to the College he found the whole Line drawn up under arms with the artillery ready to fire in his honor. This he or Wayne managed to prevent, for fear of alarming the country. The men stood smartly, if shabbily, at attention, the sergeants in the place of the officers and saluting. Reed, "though much against my inclination," returned the salute as if all were in proper military order. "We did not apprehend," he later explained to Washington, "in an affair of such consequence that, having gone within their lines, it would be prudent or politic to risk anything on account of ceremony. Their demonstrations of civility we should gladly have excused, but the officers who had been with them seemed to consider it an evidence of a good temper which ought to be encouraged rather than repressed. Their opinions on such points were conclusive to us, and as we were then fully in the power of the mutineers, it did not seem prudent to give cause of offense on unessential points." For all his rank and their condition, Reed was as courteous as the mutineers.

Dismounting, presumably at whatever tavern was Wayne's headquarters, Reed was met by a number of sergeants who crowded up ostensibly to find out when he would receive them. Their real purpose was to make sure of his identity so that some of the sergeants who knew him by sight could convince the suspicious soldiers that they were not being duped. An hour was set for the meeting, when Reed and Potter could be ready. They intended in the meantime to talk with various inhabitants of Princeton, to whom the mutineers might have said things they did not care to say to Wayne and the colonels.

"But in a few minutes Sergeant Williams returned with several others, bringing the two spies, whom they had paraded through the lines." Though the spies had left Maidenhead before Reed, they had possibly been forced to travel on foot—since on horseback they would have a better chance to escape—and had got to Princeton after him. They were manifestly shown to the rank and file of the mutineers to assure them that they had not been cheated out of the emissaries. Mason and Ogden had become merely a strong point in the negotiations.

In the presence of the two, Wayne vigorously urged that they be put to death by the sergeants. This would slam the door on the enemy, and be a conciliatory "peace offering to the country." If the Board was not prepared to sign the warrant for the execution, Wayne would do it for them. Most of the sergeants were willing, but Williams and another deserter from the British opposed them with such insistence that they wavered. For some reason, Williams preferred sending the spies back "with a taunting message to Sir Harry Clinton." Reed would not agree to this, because he thought such a message, "stripped of its tone of merriment," would have "a very different import from discouragement."

If the two deserters, or any other of the sergeants or soldiers, wanted to go to the British, they did not dare, in the prevailing sentiment of the camp, to press their scheme or even to discuss it openly. The majority of the mutineers on the Board or outside it still thought there was no disloyalty or treason in their demands for justice. They had given up the spies without waiting to see what terms were likely to be made, and had promised to give them up again. But the position of the insurgents was perilous and uncertain. Force still might be attempted against them. They might have to withdraw some of their claims—even to a general pardon—in order to get others granted. They might be trading for their lives. Reed and the officers were plainly much afraid that the British would land and the mutineers either join them, or refuse to fight, or try to drive some bargain before they fought. In the circumstances the Board of Sergeants, with the backing of the men, felt obliged to hold to the advantage given them by their possession of the emissaries while their fate was being settled. So long as they were alive the American officials and officers would not be too rigid or downright in their dealings with the Line.

When it became evident that Wayne could not win the Board over, Reed proposed "a middle way." Let the spies be securely kept, as the mutineers had promised, "till we should consider further." Reed reminded the sergeants of their promise to hold the spies subject to his call. "They took them away undetermined; and there were great debates at the Board: the result of which was that my advice should take place, and they were accordingly put under guard till further orders."

While both sides were waiting for the conference about terms that evening, Major Fishbourne arrived from New Windsor with Washington's reply to Wayne. Its advice—to remain with the men, make no trial of force, and lead them if possible to the Delaware or beyond—amounted to approval of what Wayne and the colonels had already done, and virtually to instructions as to what to do next. Reed had, besides, been asked by the Committee of Congress "to bring the matter to as speedy, safe, and honorable an issue as possible." Here was full authority to yield what must be yielded. And there was fresh news of the movements of enemy troops on Staten Island and of enemy boats in and about Raritan Bay.

II

The sergeants also came in an accommodating spirit to the conference: ragged, defiant, unschooled men at a table with the President of Pennsylvania and the commanding officer of the Line. The original proposals of the Board were now reduced to one, concerned with the oldest veterans, who made up the strongest party in the camp. "That all and every such men as was enlisted in the years 1776 and 1777 and received the bounty of twenty dollars, shall be without any delay discharged and all the arrears of pay and clothing to be paid unto them immediately when discharged; with respect to the depreciation of pay the State to give them sufficient certificates and security for such sums as they shall become due."

Reed declared this could not be allowed, since it called for a general release without any reference to the different terms of enlistment entered into by different men. The sergeants replied, in a burst of long-held grievances which were new to Reed and probably something of a surprise to Wayne, that the enlistment papers did not tell all the truth of what had happened. Some of the men had been arbitrarily detained beyond their terms. Some of them had been compelled "by military severity" to re-enlist and take new bounties, even though they had tried to refuse. Some had been required, when given their gratuity in 1779, to sign a receipt which was "framed so as to convey an acknowledgment of being enlisted for the war." Protests had done them no good. "Rigorous severity" had been "frequently exercised, especially when they requested an inquiry into the terms of their enlistment, and corporal punishment inflicted without court martial or inquiry." Nor had they always received the bounties due them, or the whole amount due. The sergeants hinted, not too outspokenly before Wayne and the colonels, that in the distribution of "State stores and occasional clothing the proportions due to the men" had not been "equitably observed."

Though the sergeants could not furnish proofs in support of their claims, Reed found himself unable to doubt any longer that "some undue methods have been taken to engage many in the service. I therefore took up that ground of justice which appeared most likely to serve the country and conciliate them, viz: that all those whose times were expired, and who had not freely entered again knowing the duration of the service, should be discharged; holding firm the principle that where a man had taken a bounty for the war freely and voluntarily, he ought not to be discharged."

In the renewed arguments that followed, one of the sergeants speciously contended that in 1776-77 both Congress and the country at large had favored temporary enlistments, and that the Pennsylvanians should therefore now be treated as if they had enlisted on those terms. Much variety of opinion appeared among the sergeants on all the points of negotiation except one: they were unanimous in their resolution to keep together in a body till they had been heard and answered. Williams appeared to be ignorant or illiterate, or perhaps drunk, and showed little skill in unifying the demands of the Board or presenting them to the best advantage.

"After some time we brought them to acknowledge that the principle contended for by the twenty-dollar men was not just, but they expressed much doubt of convincing the men." Reed feared that this doubt might be only pretended, for the sake of delay. And delay was what he could least afford. He was unwilling to leave Princeton without arriving at a compromise, if not a settlement. Since the sergeants had not agreed on their own proposals, he would draft a set for them. Dismissing the Board, he wrote out a document which promised as much as he thought he could perform and as little as he thought the men would accept. He made no mention of Wayne's former proposals, which had been carefully vague, nor of the Committee of Congress: "we did not think it advisable to bring the supreme authority of the country into view till inferiors had failed." Reed's proposals "were shown to General Wayne and the colonels present and with some small alterations made by the former [were] delivered to one of the sergeants."

Reed, and Potter signing with him, proposed that no soldier should be held beyond the time "for which he freely and voluntarily engaged." If it should appear that he had been "in any respect compelled to enter or sign," the enlistment should be "deemed void, and the soldier discharged." Disputes over terms were to be investigated and decided by three persons whom the Council should appoint.

So far, this was substantially what the mutineers had agreed to at the conference. But there was a question whether, since the Line's records were in Philadelphia or scattered among the regiments, and possibly in confusion, the original enlistments could be produced at once. When any one of them could not be, the soldier concerned had only to take an oath as to "time and terms of enlistment" and would have to offer no proof besides his oath that he was entitled to discharge. Here was a concession that put an extraordinary burden on the soldier. He might have to choose between binding himself to further service by swearing the truth or gaining his freedom by committing perjury. Trouble was sure to come from such an arrangement.

For the rest, men enlisted for three years or during the war were to be discharged if they had not re-enlisted "voluntarily and freely"; the gratuity of 1779 was "not to be reckoned as a bounty"; the auditors of the Line were to "attend as soon as possible" to adjust losses by depreciation; arrears of pay were to be made up "as soon as circumstances will admit." Shoes, overalls, and shirts were already purchased and in a few days would be at Trenton, where the commissioners appointed by the Council would settle with all the regiments in their order. Reed would recommend that "favorable notice" be taken of men who now enlisted for the war. He hoped no soldier would "break his bargain or go from the contract made with the public. . . .

"Pursuant to General Wayne's orders of the 2nd instant, no man to be brought to any trial or censure for what has happened on or since New Year's Day, but all matters to be buried in oblivion."

As it was now near midnight, the sergeants could not reply to these proposals, and could promise only that they would be submitted to the men at troop beating (roll call) on Monday morning. No objection was made to Reed's leaving for Maidenhead.

Wayne and the colonels were much dissatisfied. It would be better to disband the Line altogether than to let some soldiers go and keep others on the terms to which Reed had committed the State and its officers. The officers, accused by the men of compelling or falsifying enlistments, had now been discredited and their word treated as less trustworthy than the men's. Reed's proposals, Wayne and the colonels believed, would be rejected. The conference in that case would have accomplished nothing but a highly undesirable delay of the march away from the enemy. Though Wayne had explicitly asked the Council to send members to Princeton, he now felt that he had been "counteracted" in his efforts to lead the men to "the banks of the Delaware." Reed had taken charge of the negotiations, thinking less of what the officers of the Line might like than of what Pennsylvania would probably support him in undertaking. There was another conflict between Reed, who thought Wayne should leave the mutineers without any further benefit from his presence, and Wayne, who had Washington's instructions to keep with the troops and who was sure that he and the colonels had had "a very happy effect in preventing a revolt to the enemy." The clash of Wayne with Reed is veiled in all their correspondence, but it was there.

They agreed, however, on what ought to be done with Mason and Ogden. Reed, afraid the mutineers might dismiss them or let them escape, approved of "such measures as I trust will hasten their journey to a different place than New York." Wayne declared that the spies might "yet meet with a reward from the soldiery they wished to debauch, but of a more sanguinary nature than they hoped to experience" from the British. Mason had not, apparently, been recognized as a Tory with a price on his head for past offenses. It was enough that he had come with Ogden to entice the Line from their allegiance. The character of their fate would be the measure of the answer sent back to the enemy.

What that was to be still depended on the answer of the mutineers to Reed's proposals.

13

Sunday Elsewhere

THE banished officers of the Line fretted at Pennington nine miles west of Princeton. Forbidden to have any share in the settlement, they knew little of what was going on. Most of them favored the use of force against the mutiny, at any cost. As military men they thought this the only solution, and as officers they felt intense anger towards the soldiers for their violent disobedience at the first uprising. Many of the officers had been unaware of the deep resentment in the camp at Mount Kemble, and were genuinely shocked at learning how much they were hated. Some of them had been tyrannical, some inconsiderate, some merely condescending; some driven by patriotic zeal or personal ambition to recruiting soldiers or holding them by trickery or even fraud. The just and humane majority had still been gentlemen who took the rank and file for granted without too much concern for them as men. The Pennsylvania Line was less democratic than the Lines of New England, and nearer to being professional soldiers. There had been something almost professional in the conduct of the mutiny. This, with its initial successes, made it particularly infuriating to the Pennsylvania officers.

They were in distress for money. At Mount Kemble they would have had rations and quarters. At Pennington they had to pay for food and lodging, and had nothing to pay with. The inhabitants, siding with the mutineers in the controversy, grudged the supplies they were expected to furnish the officers on credit. The officers were not sure that Wayne, Butler, and Stewart had been wise in going with the insurgents, nor sure that their lives were safe at Princeton. Major Thomas Moore had managed to convey Wayne's baggage to the house of Dr. Ebenezer Blachly near Mendham and to send word of this to Wayne. But it was difficult to get letters through in either direction. The Pennington officers had to content themselves with keeping up a patrol on the roads between the towns, on the watch for stragglers or information.

At Morristown, St. Clair, Lafayette, and John Laurens, rejected by the mutineers on Friday, favored force. Laurens on Sunday wrote to Washington urging coercion as the only possible means. St. Clair attempted a ruse which he thought might have some effect. Sunday he sent off a letter addressed to Wayne but aimed at the mutineers, into whose hands it was expected to fall.

Though Washington had not yet arrived, St. Clair wrote, he was looked for at any moment. "He will certainly be very desirous to meet you and the other gentlemen who have been with the troops, to hear your report, and have you convey to them his comments. They must be convinced, from the knowledge they have of his character and his friendship for the soldiers, that every redress of real grievances within his power will be granted to them." In this St. Clair was not only hoping that the great name of Washington would awe the mutineers, but also assuming that the affair would be settled by the military, and hinting that Wayne should come to Morristown. That same day St. Clair wrote to Reed that the mutineers were "impatient to see your Excellency or some of the Council of Pennsylvania. But their demands are so extravagant, and they got on so smoothly hitherto, that I have no hopes of anything but force reducing them to reason."

St. Clair, bluntly dismissed by the soldiers, had few left under his command at Morristown. A good many men must simply have gone home. There had been about 2400 in camp early in December; under 2000 had marched to Princeton or straggled there afterwards. A party leaving the 6th had gone off "with less noise and more impertinence than the first." St. Clair on Sunday understood that only "perhaps a hundred" were left in the Mount Kemble huts, and he wondered if they could be held. "It is certain that British emissaries have set this matter a-going," he mistakenly told Reed; "and many of them [the men] have told us that it was proposed to them to lead them all there. This, however, they nobly refused." But he had just heard that the mutineers at Princeton had "sent some person to bring off the remaining few . . . and all the stores." How this was to be prevented St. Clair did not know. A detachment from the New Jersey Line had been brought from Pompton to Morristown, but had themselves at once shown "appearances of similar disposition," and had been marched to Chatham, away from the scene of the mutiny. Without soldiers to command, St. Clair could only send word to the men in the huts, as he informed Washington that day, that they would be "considered principally in whatever may be done for the Line at large."

In four letters written on Sunday Lafayette set forth his plans and his opinions. To Walter Stewart at Princeton he said that the men chosen from the Pennsylvania Line the past summer to serve in the Continental light infantry corps commanded by Lafayette must still have their former sentiments "for one whom they must know to be their friend."

Lafayette wished that he might, through Stewart, reach these men and appeal to their honor, in the confidence that if he could they would return to their duty. To Sullivan, chairman of the Committee of Congress, Lafayette wrote that he thought it necessary "for the States of Pennsylvania and New Jersey to provide for the extremities to which they will, I fear, be obliged to come. I am sorry to find that the people, sensible of the sufferings of the Army, have not a proper idea of the method these mutinous people have taken to obtain redress."

To Washington Lafayette was briefer than usual. "I impatiently wait for your arrival which has been announced by Major Fishbourne on his going through this place." Fishbourne, on his way from Washington to Wayne, had at Morristown either misrepresented Washington's plans or else been misunderstood about them; and going from there down to Princeton he had missed St. Clair, Lafayette, and Laurens on their way up. (Such mishaps and delays in communication, which now seem paralyzing, were normal then.) "Nothing," Lafayette assured Washington, "is to be hoped but from force or such a division among them [the mutineers] as would produce a partial dissolution. The militia don't seem very willing to fight them. General Wayne was in hopes that they would be divided, but how far he may succeed I do not know. Your going there would be extremely imprudent, and the possibility of success is not by far such as to justify your exposing yourself to any danger of the kind, the less so as the possession of your person would be an inducement to their joining the enemy."

It was to the Chevalier de La Luzerne, minister from France to the United States and an acute and responsible observer, that Lafayette wrote at greatest length. He told in detail the story of his mission to Princeton and his rejection by the mutineers. He ascribed the uneasiness among the New Jersey troops at Morristown to some English and Irish soldiers; "but the others made them hold their tongues." He had heard that a Connecticut brigade was coming, but they could be joined, Lafayette estimated, by only about 200 scattered Pennsylvanians, in or about Morristown, 300 New Jersey Continentals, and 300 Jersey militiamen, against the whole desperate force of the mutineers and perhaps also the enemy—though the enemy had not yet landed. He was worried about the hesitation of the militia to attack the mutineers while they remained quietly at Princeton, and by the appearance at Morristown of "one of their leaders sent for munitions and the remaining men. General St. Clair felt obliged to arrest him, and we can neither hold nor release him without eminent danger." Once more Lafayette regretted that he had had no chance to try his eloquence on the mutineers. If he had gone alone to Princeton, he might have been permitted to stay. If now he must fight, he hoped it would be against the enemy, not against soldiers he had once commanded.

Without repeating what he had written at Trenton three days before, Lafayette still believed that La Luzerne should not send news of the affair to France before it could be settled. That might give the French a wrong impression of American soldiers. Lafayette persisted in thinking that the mutiny had been caused chiefly by the foreigners in the Pennsylvania Line, less loyal than the natives. He seems not to have reflected that this distinction might be no more true of the soldiers than of the officers, who were all conspicuously loyal. Yet St. Clair had been born in Scotland; of the three brigadier generals of the Line, Edward Hand and William Irvine had been born in Ireland, and only Wayne in America. Of the eleven regimental commanders involved in the mutiny, at least three had been born in Ireland and one in England. Some of the mutineers thought that Lafayette was a foreigner himself.

II

The Committee of Congress waiting at Trenton for Reed to carry out his negotiations did nothing on Sunday but write a few letters. One of them, from Sullivan to Washington, told him of the surrender of the British emissaries to Reed, though not of their then unreported recall by the mutineers. This letter took Washington his earliest news of this encouraging "earnest of their sincerity and intentions," but it did not reach him for three days.

On Saturday the 6th the soldiers at West Point had been informed of the mutiny. While they did not follow the Pennsylvanians into revolt, they were reminded of their own sufferings and showed no inclination to rush off to suppress the mutineers. Washington wrote to Congress that "although the other troops, who are more generally composed of natives and may therefore have attachments of a stronger nature, may bear their distresses somewhat longer than the Pennsylvanians, yet . . . it will be dangerous to put their patience further to the test. They may, for what I know, be only wanting to see the effects of the Pennsylvania insurrection; and it will be therefore far better to meet them with a part of their just dues than to put them to the necessity of demanding them in a manner disreputable and prejudicial to the service and the cause, and totally subversive of all military discipline." He still supposed that the mutiny at Princeton might be cured by just redress of grievances, and a further mutiny at West Point prevented by the same means.

On Sunday Brigadier General Henry Knox, chief of artillery, set out with Washington's circular letter to the governors of Connecticut, Rhode Island, Massachusetts (which then included Maine), and New Hampshire. (Vermont claimed to be a separate State, but had not yet been recognized by Congress.) Washington's instructions to Knox told him to lay special emphasis on the immediate need of three months' pay and a complete suit of clothes for every Continental soldier, whether a veteran or one of the new recruits coming in before spring. It was not much to ask for men who had many of them not been paid for two or three times that long, and who though regularly promised clothes were usually as ragged as beggars.

"You will," Washington instructed Knox, "generally represent to the supreme executive powers of the States through which you pass, and to gentlemen of influence in them, the alarming crisis to which our affairs have arrived by a too long neglect of measures essential to the existence of an army. . . . You will press upon the governors the necessity of a speedy adoption of the measures recommended at this time, and inform them"—this a warning not to delay—"that you will call upon them in your way back to the Army to learn what has been done in consequence of your application.

"I wish you a more pleasant journey than can be hoped for at this season of the year."

III

For Sunday Oliver De Lancey, impatient on Staten Island, wrote this in his Journal of the mutiny: "On the 7th received information from General Skinner that the Pennsylvanians continued their march towards Brunswick and that Wayne was detained a prisoner among them; that Colonel

Dayton with the Jersey brigade was at Morristown, but, hearing the riflemen and some light horse had joined the insurgents, he halted fearing a defection among his own troops; and that he heard a man sent with proposals was seen safe within a mile of the revolters on Friday evening. Information by New York that they were at Rocky Hill near Princeton."

There could hardly have been more errors in so few words. The information concerning Rocky Hill came from Lieutenant General James Robertson of the British Army, who had been appointed royal governor of New York but had little to do while the State was for the most part held by the rebels and the islands were under military rule. He was a fluttering old soldier, notorious among the loyalists for his senile susceptibility to "little misses," and at Headquarters for his inability to keep a secret. His news that the mutineers were at Rocky Hill put them at any rate closer to Princeton, where Gautier said they were, than Brunswick, towards which more optimistic news said they were marching.

The rest of the day's intelligence came from the distinguished New Jersey loyalist, Brigadier General Cortlandt Skinner of the loyalist New Jersey Volunteers. He had been misinformed concerning the whereabouts of the mutineers; of Colonel Dayton, who was then at Chatham; of the New Jersey brigade (actually only a detachment) at Morristown, which had already left, and was commanded by Lieutenant Colonel Francis Barber. Some man sent with proposals might possibly have been seen within a mile of Brunswick on Friday evening, though not within a mile of the revolters. And there was a part of Skinner's Sunday letter to De Lancey which was not even entered in the Journal: "They are commanded by one Box, a sergeant of the 43rd [British] Regiment, who deserted at Boston. I have sent a man to New Jersey who will this night bring me every particular."

Information from New Jersey had already become hard to get, and harder to rely on. The landing places were watched by militiamen, the roads patrolled. Clinton still thought that any attempt to land in force would rouse the country and turn the mutineers against him. Nor had he yet tried landing small forces to capture rebel pickets, as he did later, and question them. He continued to trust to his secret service and to the prospect of winning the mutineers without fighting.

On Saturday two more proposals had gone out: one the copy given to Thomas Ward of Bergen Neck and carried by a spy named McFarlan; another a copy carried by Caleb Bruen of Newark. Nathan Frink, who had served in both armies and had recently become one of Benedict Arnold's captains, claimed to be acquainted "in the most intimate manner with the person who is said to be at the head of the present revolt in New Jersey." Nobody in New York yet knew who actually was at the head of the revolt, and Frink was not sent. He hoped he might be chosen to raise a similar commotion in his native Connecticut.

On Saturday Uzal Woodruff of Elizabethtown was put ashore by a boat from the *Neptune* on some secret errand, and came back the same day. Gould was expected, but did not turn up, that day or the day after. These were only local journeys, not to the mutineers. Sunday evening two "trusty men" were carried over to Paulus Hook, to go as close to West Point as they could, and report as soon as possible.

14

Agreement on Monday

THERE was, according to a spy's report, a sergeant among the mutineers who before he deserted from the British had taken part in a mutiny at Gibraltar (presumably that of 1760). "The whole garrison mutinied," he now told his associates. "Government granted whatever they demanded, but took care to hang forty of them immediately after. It was hard trusting."

Whether or not this was true, and whether or not the sergeant said it on Monday the 8th, it voiced a suspicion and fear that was deep-rooted in many soldiers of the Line. So long as they kept together in arms they would be, they felt, reasonably secure. But once they accepted the terms offered them, and began to work out the details of the settlement, they would have exchanged a strong though dangerous position for another possibly as dangerous and certainly weaker. At best they would receive, on Reed's terms, much less than they had asked for. The veterans would not get their unconditional release. Releases would still depend on enlistment papers written by the officers, and so distrusted by the men. Though they were promised pay and clothing, they had been promised both before, again and again, and yet not supplied. And any negotiated settlement, even if agreed to by the soldiers, would be a disappointment to those who for a few days had tasted liberty and dreaded the return to a hard service.

The Board of Sergeants, divided among themselves, knew

that the compromise proposals which were to be submitted to the men might be rejected by them. Since the sergeants genuinely desired a settlement, they were concerned over the possibility that they might be roughly overidden and disavowed, with the work of reconcilation still to be carried out in an increasing—even a hopeless—confusion. Strict as the mutiny discipline had been so far, it might not outlast an uproar of disapproval at troop beating.

Not a syllable in the record gives any account of what happened when the men, drawn up at the ordinary hour of eight o'clock for roll call, heard what was the best their committee had been able to obtain for them. Though Wayne and the colonels had made every effort to win the confidence of a few mutineers who might privately report the doings of the camp, this had met with no success. The mutineers kept their secrets. In the morning Reed's proposals were announced. That afternoon the sergeants brought Wayne their answer. The intervening protests, arguments, debates, angers, threats, resistances, compliances must be guessed at.

II

But Joseph Reed on Monday was active and profuse. He had spent the night at Maidenhead. In the morning he wrote a long letter to the Committee of Congress about the negotiation of the day before. "If it does not take effect, I fear we shall be obliged, on some principle or perhaps no principle, to dismiss them; but I shall endeavor to have this done at Trenton. I am glad to find so little reason to think that they have prejudices with respect to Congress. Their prejudices are most certainly against the officers, and they look to Congress and the State for redress and help. There is, therefore, no occasion for the Committee to take any other quarters than are convenient and suitable to their rank." He thought it better and safer for the Committee to remain at Trenton. "Upon the whole, I think the terms I have offered reasonable. If they are refused, or if the men refuse to march to Trenton, it must be evident that they do not mean sincerely; and I should hope the militia of Jersey might be brought to act against them." He still suspected the sergeants of not always communicating freely to the men, and suggested that his proposals might be printed, in the name of Congress or Pennsylvania, and distributed among the mutineers.

Shortly after noon the Committee, having received Reed's letter with a copy of his proposals, sent him "the result of their deliberations upon the terms which they are of opinion ought to be held out to the soldiers of the Pennsylvania Line." It was in the form of a resolution which Reed would never have dared present to the men, since it blunderingly regarded the gratuity of 1779 as a bounty. The Committee of Congress seemed to have forgotten the true nature of Congress's gift to veteran soldiers, and to have overlooked one of the Line's principal grievances. But the Committee made a stipulation which Reed had not ventured to put forth himself and which he would be happy to represent to the men as coming from Congress. This was that a "free and general pardon" would follow "upon the soldiers of the Pennsylvania Line delivering up the British emissaries sent to corrupt them." The mutineers, well disposed towards Congress, could hardly hold out on this undecided point against so high an authority.

Up to half-past two Reed had had no direct accounts from Princeton; "but from straggling soldiers and indirect intelligence I understand that my proposal has been generally acceptable. . . . I understand they give up the 20-dollar men, and that it now seems agreed to march to Trenton tomorrow morning, if ordered. . . . They drew rations yesterday for 2000 men, but they have not more than 1500; I doubt whether so many. . . . They keep the spies of yesterday in close prison, but have not settled their fate. . . . At present we have no accounts of the enemy of any kind; but the weather is very favorable" to a British attempt on New Jersey.

Till about three the officers at Princeton knew little more than Reed about the mutiny situation. Wayne, Butler, and Stewart in letters to Congress, Washington, and their fellow-officers at Pennington, hinted their dissatisfaction with Reed's terms and doubts of their chances with the mutineers. But at three the answer came, in Bowzar's wandering language with a touch of the heroic. Wayne sent it off to Reed with a curt note: "Mr. McClenachan will carry the answer of the Board. I wish you to prepare the hard cash promised" to the sergeants who had brought Wayne the spies. "We must keep faith with these people. I shall try to prevail on them to advance to Trenton."

What Bowzar wrote and Reed read was partly an agreement, partly a counter-proposal.

"His Excellency's proposals being communicated to the different regiments at troop beating this morning, January 8, 1781:

"They do voluntarily agree in conjunction that all soldiers that were enlisted for the term of three years or during the war, excepting those whose terms of enlistments are not expired, ought to be discharged immediately with as little delay as circumstances will allow, except such soldiers who have voluntarily re-enlisted. In case that any soldier should dispute his enlistment, it is to be settled by a committee, and the soldier's oath. The remainder of His Excellency's and the Honorable Board of Committee's proposal is founded upon honor and justice; but in regard to the Honorable Board setting forth that there will be appointed three persons to sit as a committee to redress our grievances, it is therefore the general demand of the Line and the Board of Sergeants that we shall appoint as many persons as of the opposite to sit as a committee to determine justly upon our unhappy affairs, as the path we tread is justice and our footsteps founded upon honor.

"Therefore we unanimously do agree that there should be something done towards a speedy address of our present circumstances."

Reed in his reply, again addressed to Wayne not to Bowzar, showed himself pleased with the mutineers' agreement, but did not yield on the new demand that the soldiers should appoint three persons to sit with the Council's three commissioners on disputed enlistments. Speaking as for the Council he said: "This implies such a distrust of the authority of the State, which has ever been attentive to the wants of the Army, that the impropriety of it must be evident; but any soldier will have liberty to bring before the commissioners any person as his friend to represent his case." As to the spies, Reed invoked the authority of the Committee of Congress. When they had been "delivered up as soon as convenient," Congress would proclaim "a general oblivion of all matters since the 31st December, provided the terms offered last evening are closed with, and the troops remain no longer in their present state."

In his own suggestions to the Line Reed was less authoritative. "It is my clear opinion that they should march in the morning to Trenton, where the stores are, their clothing expected if not by this time arrived, by which I mean overalls and some blankets. I hope they will come to a speedy determination. . . . As I have the promise of the Board of Sergeants in writing that the emissaries shall be forthcoming to me, I doubt not they will honorably perform it, and therefore expect an answer from them on this point."

Before Reed's reply reached Princeton Wayne got the mutineers to promise what Reed asked for. "We sent for the sergeants at half after four o'clock this evening and insisted upon their marching to Trenton in the morning, or that we would leave them to act as they pleased and to abide the fatal effects of their own folly. In consequence of which" they came "to a resolution of moving for that place in the morning and bringing along the two caitiffs." Wayne had interposed not only to hasten the decision but also to deprive Reed of some of the credit for the settlement. The commanding officer of the Line must keep up such prestige as he could among his men. Their resolve to march to Trenton might seem something like obedience to his commands.

III

Reed at seven, just before he heard from Wayne, still wondered whether the rank and file could be counted on. "Confusion in their claims, and want of all order except military order, has taken place. From their conversation, there is little probability that they will agree to what their sergeants determine. . . . General Wayne's staying, in my opinion, is no longer of any benefit, but otherwise. He promised to come away this evening. What has prevented I do not know; but they certainly take countenance and spirit from having him among them."

Perhaps they did. They had long liked and respected him,

did not hold him to blame for the conduct of the unpopular officers, and believed that he would fairly represent the Line's grievances to Congress and the Pennsylvania Council. In their unsettled state they felt the need of an arbiter of Wayne's standing, whether between the mutineers as a whole and the officials from Philadelphia, or between the sergeants and the men, or between groups of men with conflicting claims. And since the insurgents had all along promised that if the British came out they would fight them under Wayne's command, his being at Princeton might be taken as evidence that the promise was sincere.

The mutineers, suspicious and suspected, had been remarkably faithful to their announced intentions. All they had asked was release from contracts with the public which the public on its part had not fulfilled, and redress of grievances that could be redressed. Now, almost exactly a week after the outbreak, they were still disciplined in behavior yet willing to agree to a considerable reduction of their first demands. The veterans of 1776 and 1777 would not be discharged outright. Disputed enlistments would be subject to examination by commissioners whom the men had not chosen. It was still to be seen whether pay and clothing awaited them at Trenton. Once there, they might have to put up with delays and postponements. They might have to take back the officers they hated. If they disbanded the mutiny they might find themselves at a serious disadvantage, even though they were all pardoned for their recent offenses. Certainly their advance to Trenton would end anything they may have gained, during the negotiations, by staying within reach of the British.

With all these uncertainties in their minds the mutineers resolved to accept Reed's proposals and go on to Trenton. Taking the spies with them was not refusing to give them up to Reed. He would presumably be in Trenton by the time the troops arrived. But taking the spies further from New York was an unequivocal rejection of the British offers.

15

Trenton, Mason, Ogden

AT EIGHT o'clock on the morning of Tuesday the 9th the mutineers paraded in good order, if in less jubilant spirits than they had displayed a week before. By nine or so they had begun their march. Wayne, apparently free of the escort hitherto assigned to him, may have ridden with the column or in a separate party with the colonels, and with General Irvine who had joined them at Princeton on Monday. Reed at Maidenhead, four miles away, at ten heard that the troops had set out. He may have gone ahead to Trenton with his own party, or may have ridden with Wayne's.

Already that morning Reed had finished a letter to the Committee of Congress. "Quarters must be provided for at least 1500 men, though I will endeavor to detach 1000 at least at Bordentown and Burlington tomorrow. At Trenton I expect they will receive their officers; and that is my greatest concern at present, as they appear so deeply to resent the conduct of the troops to them personally. Had General Wayne not given a promise of general pardon the 2nd January, and confirmed it on the 7th, I should have excepted the men who insulted their officers, if they could have been discovered. . . . I beg leave to offer it as my opinion that, for the sake of conveniency as well as dignity, the Committee retire a little distance from them until the officers have taken their places and order is restored; for they are so ignorant and capricious that I would not be within their guards myself for any time, lest some wicked rascals, of whom they have too many, should suggest mischief."

The Army horses were in bad condition from scanty feeding, and even the post roads in New Jersey, a spy reported to the British, were "almost uncapable for a carriage." Unable to go faster than the wagons, the head of the column was five hours in marching ten miles to a point on the outskirts of Trenton where Reed and Potter waited for them.

Reed understood that the men "had expressed some expectation at Princeton of being addressed in a body." Ready with a speech, he was disturbed when the sergeants refused to give the order to halt. This could mean only that they were still in power and the soldiers still inaccessible to outside influence. He discovered, then or later in the afternoon, that "the mutineers were much alarmed with apprehension of being deceived or entrapped."

The column marched through the town, probably along Queen (now Broad) Street, across the stone bridge over the Assunpinck creek, and by the Bordentown road till at the road (now Ferry Street) leading to the Trenton ferry they turned to the right and proceeded to a field beside the Delaware where they pitched their tents on a site used by Pennsylvania recruits the past summer. The ground was cleared, and there were some accommodations for a camp. There the mutineers doubled their guard and freely expressed strong threats, in the hearing of the inhabitants, against any authorities or civilians who might have hostile or treacherous designs. Trenton was half again as large as Princeton, less rural, and possibly less friendly, the mutineers seem to have thought. If the negotiations should now fall through, and the Jersey militia be brought against the revolted men, they would find themselves with the wide river at their backs and it might be with the Pennsylvania militia on the other side. That would be a trap into which they had come in good faith, with no telling what consequences to their claims and to themselves. They might be—as they were—much less ignorant and capricious than Reed called them, and yet naturally feel warranted in every precaution against surprise.

The Board of Sergeants took quarters at Jonathan Richmond's tavern near the Assunpinck bridge. Reed returned to Bloomsbury, accompanied by Wayne. The Committee of Congress, on Reed's advice, crossed the Delaware to Thomas Barclay's house called Summer Seat, in Morrisville, Pennsylvania.

That evening the Committee and the Council members had a long and full conference. To be commissioners "for hearing and determining the claims of the soldiers without delay" they chose Colonel Atlee of the Committee, General Potter of the Council, and Captain Samuel Morris and Blair McClenachan of the Light Horse. The mutineers would expect Congress and the Council to be represented on the commission, and would be pleased with the captain of the light horsemen and the popular McClenachan. The conference also resolved to make a peremptory demand for the spies who were still in the custody of the mutineers.

On Wednesday morning Reed summoned the sergeants and told them that his proposals, which they had accepted, would now go forward into execution, but that the mutineers must first, "as a proof of the sincerity of their professions to the country," give up the spies. The sergeants countered with a condition of their own: that the Line should "remain together in arms until the whole were settled with." Otherwise, they implied, they would be without the power to back

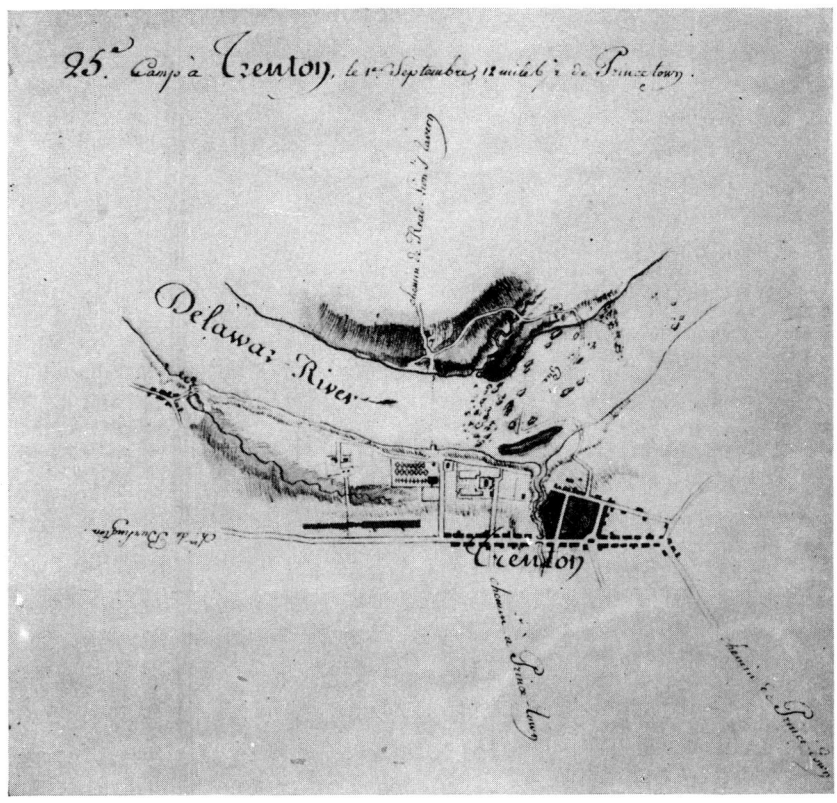

ALEXANDRE BERTHIER

Facsimile of an unpublished plan of Trenton, indicating the camp site of Rochambeau's troops in September 1781 in the field beside the Delaware where the Pennsylvania mutineers had camped the previous January.

their demands and might find they had been deceived with slippery promises.

Reed sharply told them that this was "inadmissible" and "desired they would go together and consider both the points, and send me an answer in two hours." Within that time they brought him the result of their discussions. "Pursuant to your Excellency's demand concerning the two emissaries from the British, the Board of Committee resolved that those men should be delivered up to the supreme authority; and, in order to show that we would remove every doubt of suspicion and jealousy, also that the men may disperse upon being discharged, they delivering up their arms, etc." This came "Signed by the Board in the absence of the President, Daniel Connell, Member." Williams, the president of the Board, and Bowzar, the secretary, may have been actually absent from the meeting, or may have been unwilling to sign a paper which frankly conceded everything the mutineers had withheld.

On the 4th the Line had agreed "in six days for to complete and settle every such demand." This was the 10th, and they had kept their promise to the day.

Some time afterwards the spies, who by agreement had been under Reed's orders, were brought to Reed and Wayne at Bloomsbury. They explained that the prisoners were to be surrendered to the Committee of Congress, now the "supreme authority" in the matter. Mason and Ogden were taken away. Considerably later, probably after dark, an apologetic note came from Bowzar. "As it was a misunderstanding in regard to sending the prisoners to your quarters, we hope you'll excuse. However, they are gone under a proper guard to the Committee of Congress's quarters over the river. However, if you are desirous now to see them, we shall bring them to your quarters."

All but indispensable and authorized boats had been removed to the Pennsylvania side of the Delaware for fear the mutineers might undertake to cross it. Though Reed observed that "they keep up an astonishing regularity and discipline, and have so far on all occasions behaved very respectfully to me," he still believed there was danger they might go on and plunder Philadelphia. They seem never to have threatened anything of the kind. Washington, at the first news of the uprising, had thought such violence might lead to any extremity, even to the plundering of the capital. Reed, who had watched the orderly conduct of the insurgents for several days, trusted his own observation less than the early, remote foreboding of Washington. The New Jersey officials shared Reed's belief. The Delaware had been turned into a barrier.

In a boat ordered for the purpose a strong guard that night crossed the river with the doomed emissaries.

II

There was the less hope for them because other emissaries had followed the mutineers from Princeton and some time on Wednesday had dropped additional copies of Clinton's offer in the new camp. Saving themselves, they gave strength to the argument that detected messengers from the enemy to the mutineers must not be tolerated or forgiven.

Even before the spies had been delivered to the Committee, Lord Stirling, the only major general then at Trenton, had ordered "a court of inquiry to set this afternoon at four o'clock at Summer Seat, State of Pennsylvania, to hear and report their opinion, whether John Mason, late of New York, and James Ogden, of South River, State of New Jersey, were found within the lines of the American

Army in the character of spies; and if the said court find the charge, then to give their determination thereon." Wayne was to preside, with General Irvine, Colonels Richard Butler and Walter Stewart, and Major Fishbourne as members of the court. Since the accused men came later than had been expected, the inquiry was postponed. But at eight o'clock Sullivan, for the Committee, wrote Washington that the spies were "now in this house under a guard of the Philadelphia Light Horse, and a court . . . at this moment determining their fate."

Their trial could not last long. Mason and Ogden were unquestionably spies. They had been sent by the British to corrupt American soldiers and had been seen in possession of the written offers which were in evidence. Probably Williams and other sergeants testified about Mason's coming and tendering the proposals. Possibly Ogden insisted that he had been innocent or comparatively innocent in the mission. Certainly Mason tried to win consideration for himself by revealing a plot which he said had been laid by certain loyalists for capturing Washington.

As Wayne the next day reported the plot to Washington, he was to be waylaid when riding out, with his customary small escort, by Thomas Ward "and thirty more desperadoes." Some such plan was not unlikely. Ward and Mason had done their best to capture Governor Livingston of New Jersey; and "fifty determined refugees" may already have formed the plan which Clinton a few months later would not authorize because they "appeared determined to put him [Washington] to death if they could not bring him off alive." But Mason's warning at his trial was not enough to save him in the circumstances.

The court, having heard "the evidences and allegations of the parties concerned," were "decidedly of opinion that the said John Mason and James Ogden came clearly within the description of spies and that according to the rules and customs of nations at war they ought to be hung by the neck until they are dead." Stirling confirmed the sentence and fixed the time of execution at nine o'clock the following morning, "at the cross-roads from the upper ferry from Trenton to Philadelphia, at the four lanes' ends." Since the inspector general of the Pennsylvania Line was absent, Fishbourne was to be in charge.

Ogden, according to David H. Conyngham of the Light Horse who spent the night with the condemned men, was "much agitated and overcome upon hearing his sentence," but could not believe he would be put to death. He had probably not foreseen that his errand could have a mortal outcome. He had only been a guide for an emissary who had, after all, failed to corrupt the rebels. No harm had been done by Clinton's offer. The rebels surely would not punish an incidental agent so horribly and irrevocably. Ogden was young and he had left a bride of two months at home in South River.

Mason, older and more hardened to the risks of war, "seemed to feel his situation, but declared . . . that if they hung him, he was in fault, but that he would die a true and loyal subject of George III." During the night he joined with Ogden in begging Conyngham to find out if there was any hope for them. "I went and spoke to General Wayne, who decidedly told me nothing could save them, unless we let them escape, which would involve us in trouble. I then procured a Bible from Mr. Barclay and passed the night in reading it to them. Mason was devout, but Ogden was in terror and distress. I got them something to eat, and in the morning Mason slept a little."

After that the spies had the best breakfast Conyngham

could procure. The rest of the Light Horse, who had been camped in Trenton, this Thursday morning crossed the river to perform the last duty of their seven days' service. Mason and Ogden were brought out, their sentence read to them again, and their hands bound.

The Light Horse took the spies a half-mile from Barclay's Summer Seat to where four lanes came together at the place appointed: one from the north and one from the south along the Delaware, one by the cross-country route from Philadelphia, one from the riverside where the Trenton ferry landed. Back of Patrick Colvin's ferry house was a tree which would have to do for a gallows. Colvin's wagon and Negro slave were "pressed to hang them. Upon their being brought in the wagon to the tree, a difficulty occurred." There was no rope for the hanging. Lieutenant James Budden of the troop saw a new rope collar on the horse on which Conyngham's servant had "just arrived with clothes, etc. from Philadelphia." The horse's collar was unwound to make the hangman's rope while the spies waited.

There were spectators, but they are not mentioned; neither is there a surviving word about Ogden's final conduct. Mason "expressed great anxiety" to see Wayne "before he died," Wayne wrote to Washington, "and again repeated the plan for taking or surprising your Excellency. I did not see him, but it was his last injunction to inform me that the intelligence he mentioned the previous evening was literally true." A British informer in Philadelphia, who had probably talked with some light horseman, reported to New York that Mason "behaved with great bravery. He told them he had but one favor to ask, which was that General Clinton might be informed that he had done everything in his power to execute his trust, that he had been unfortunate, and died like a brave man."

In the bare words of Conyngham, "the business was soon finished, and before nine, having orders to return home, we galloped off and left them hanging, and we reached home that evening after a severe week in cold weather." The dead bodies, as warning and deterrent, swung in the January wind for five days and possibly longer.

III

There still remained the matter of the hundred guineas Wayne had promised the sergeants for bringing the spies to him. This was now in Reed's hands. Wayne on the morning of the execution went to confer with the officers of the Line at Pennington, and if possible to relieve their acute necessities. Reed approved, but cautioned Wayne against raising excessive expectations in the officers. "I think your going to Pennington may be of service, if it was only to inculcate prudence and patience. I cannot authorize you to make the promises you mention, because the treasury will not admit, and I think the sum too large. Our finances, my dear General, do not admit of such large promises, and I am sure we shall both be blamed, you for promising and I for confirming them."

Talk about prudence and patience might not fare so well with the sergeants. But Reed thought, with the Council, that Wayne had been "too fast in promising so large a reward." Perhaps the money might somehow be saved without any apparent breach of faith. Reed summoned the two sergeants and explained that with Wayne away he himself was not quite clear about the understanding, "and did not like to give up so much money without farther light," though the promise was of course still good. For the present he would talk about patriotism. He talked so well that he got the same day a letter from the sergeants which was their last official word in the affair of the mutiny.

"Agreeable to the information of two sergeants of our Board who waited on your Excellency," Bowzar wrote, "that in consideration of the two spies being delivered up, they informed the remainder of the Board that your Excellency has been pleased to offer a sum of gold as a compensation for our fidelity, but as it has not been for the sake or through any expectation of receiving a reward, but for the zeal and love of our country that we sent them immediately to General Wayne, we therefore do not consider ourselves entitled to any other reward but the love of our country, and do jointly agree that we shall accept of no other."

Forwarding the sergeants' honorable letter to the Council, Reed said they would see that "by a little address"—that is, cleverness—he had "saved the hundred guineas and our credit." Writing to Washington, Reed put it differently. "A large reward having been offered to the sergeants for their fidelity in this respect, they declined it in a very disinterested manner and in terms that would have done credit to persons of more elevated stations in life."

16

Confusion among Emissaries

FOR thirteen days after Mason was taken into custody by the mutineers on Sunday the 7th the British in New York could get no unquestionable news as to how his mission had been received or what had become of the other emissaries. Spies went out or came back every day, but brought in nothing that was certain. Informers, who arrived in person or sent letters, furnished more rumor than fact, and their rumors were often contradictory and mystifying. Clinton, uninformed, misinformed, hesitated to act. His inaction bewildered the Americans, who found it hard to believe that he knew no more than he did. They themselves did not know that their own watchfulness cut him off from all but random intelligence.

For instance, a party from the *Vulture* landed at South Amboy on Monday under cover of a flag of truce and there had a chance for private conversation—in violation of the flag—with Rattoon "and inhabitants." They reported that the mutineers had gone to Trenton to cross the Delaware, but had found all the boats on the other side; and that on Friday two men with proposals from the Pennsylvanians to Clinton had been captured at Quibbletown (now New Market). The men were not named in the report, but it seemed to mean that a responsive answer may have been sent, and might be repeated by more fortunate messengers.

Gould, who had gone out on Friday morning with copies of the proposals for Gautier to forward, did not for some unknown reason get back till about noon on Tuesday. He brought a letter from Gautier written the night before. "The person I sent to Princeton," Gautier said, "is just returned, which place he left this morning." This was the "faithful friend" by whom four days earlier Gautier had forwarded "two addresses." Now he said: "Your address he delivered Saturday evening. The same night two persons arrived with like addresses. They were both detained."

Here were further confusions. The British had no way of knowing who the two persons with addresses—actually only Mason with a guide and one copy of the proposals—were, or what had become of the faithful friend's second copy, or whether the delivery of the first had had any effect. Nor could they yet know what the detention of two emissaries signified. The mutineers might be weighing Clinton's offer.

Gautier on the authority of his messenger said that Reed and Wayne had made proposals to the Line on Sunday— as they had—but that their proposals had been rejected—as they had not. "Your offers are now known throughout the Army and will have great influence over the majority of them. The most sensible people and officers here [at Elizabethtown] think they will yet join you, as interest and policy ought to lead them to it. I am fully satisfied that Congress cannot nor will not give them redress. In this case they will come over to you. They may be in doubt of protection, as you are not in New Jersey. I am therefore of opinion you ought immediately to take post at Amboy, which will favor their design and secure them in a quick march from Princeton. General Washington is gone to Congress on this business. May all their endeavors be in vain and defeated. Come on, and I trust the lads will join you, as they are amazingly dissatisfied with their officers and Congress." When Gautier wrote, the mutineers had already accepted

Reed's proposals and resolved to march to Trenton the next day.

De Lancey sent Gautier's letter to Clinton, telling him not only that Gautier was the most reliable of their correspondents but also that the other emissaries were expected to come in soon. "The revolters who have detained them"—De Lancey did not yet know who had been detained—"declare they shall be sent back safe." Gautier had not written this, and De Lancey must have had it from some other source, possibly from Gould.

Also on Tuesday the 9th the spy who had been sent to Morristown brought in information of no essential value to Clinton and De Lancey. There was at least amusement in a communication from an unnamed loyalist living somewhere between West Point and Albany, who could not come to join the British till next summer, he said, but had already written loyal verses and hung them on fences along the road for passing rebels to read.

> To the Officers and Soldiers
> of the Continental Army
>
> Shake off the Congress and despise
> Them with their France and Spain allies;
> Their paper money trust no more.
> We have all been cheated enough before;
> Fight for Great George, make no delay,
> For Britain's sons will gain the day.

He added a postscript: "You must not trust the ladies anywhere, for they often come and tell bad news in the country."

Information was harder and harder to get, Major General William Phillips, commanding the British troops on Staten Island, wrote to De Lancey on Tuesday. During the night an armed party of thirty men from the *Vulture* had landed at Perth Amboy and "surprised a picket of rebel volunteers of a very violent disposition." By these men under questioning, or by more amenable informants in the town, it was reported that the mutineers were agreed to fight the British if they moved into New Jersey; and that two men taken with proposals from Clinton—not the other way round —were to be hanged "this day."

Phillips was disposed to credit the reports. He thought the Pennsylvanians would not join the British unless "forced to it by some violent act of Congress or Washington; and I imagine any move of ours would facilitate a reconciliation. I therefore suppose we shall not make any unless we are to treat them as enemies, and that depends on a combination of circumstances which no one but the Commander-in-Chief knows." Clinton had no intention of treating the mutineers as enemies. Otherwise he was so nearly in agreement with his friend Phillips that in a letter three days later he echoed him. "I am apprehensive that these people have no intention of joining us unless some violent act of Washington or Congress should force them to it. And as I fear any move of ours might facilitate a reconciliation, it is in my opinion better to wait for events in our present situation."

On the 10th no news came in that could be trusted. That day General Robertson, royal governor of New York, talked with William Smith, royal chief justice. They were both members of Clinton's council and, while not fully informed, took an intense interest in the secret service. Robertson told Smith, who entered it in his Journal, that "of the six men sent out, one is come back from the mutineers. The rest got safe to them. . . . The five men shall be safely returned, as occasion may require, with messages. . . . General Robertson adds that there are many Arnolds who have sent in their intentions, but desiring to stipulate against serving under Arnold. I asked if any of rank or consequence. He replied:

'Many, many.'" This was the day the mutineers finally gave up Mason and Ogden, and the last of the emissaries dropped their proposals in Trenton and scuttled to safety.

On Thursday the 11th Cornelius Tyger, coming in with his account of the mutineers as he had seen them at Pluckemin on the march to Princeton, reported also that, according to what he had been told by the Pluckemin tavern-keeper, the mutineers had "sent letters to the troops above"—at West Point—"that they intended rising New Year's Day." This—though in fact not true—seemed to the British to confirm the report of Ezekiel Yeomans, back on Thursday from the neighborhood of West Point with the story—also untrue—that the troops above had risen on January 1 in concert with the Pennsylvanians. They had been overpowered and several of them confined. Washington, Yeomans said, "was much cast down." At once De Lancey was willing to pay a hundred guineas to anybody who would carry proposals to the West Point garrison. Chief Justice William Smith, who had helped Benedict Arnold write his self-vindications after his treason, was asked to compose an address, telling the rebels up the river that if they would come down the British would "discharge in solid coin the pay and wages withheld from you by the fraud and injustice of your tyrants." This was the day Mason and Ogden were hanged.

Smith's address to the soldiers at West Point seems never to have gone to them, but the British made plans to send a force in their direction if it should be warranted. On the 11th Robertson informed Clinton that Admiral Marriot Arbuthnot was ready to assist the Army with ships and boats capable of transporting eight thousand men. The ships "have got their sails to their yards and all have either proceeded to, or are proceeding to, the North [Hudson] River." They were

CONFUSION AMONG EMISSARIES 165

prepared to land Clinton's troops speedily in New Jersey, or to land some of them there in support of the mutiny and to carry others north against Washington.

On the 12th the British were still not sure of the name of the leader of the Pennsylvania mutineers, and dispatched a note to Gautier asking him to furnish it by the bearer. "If you can send anybody to Princeton, tell them they will be supported if they come to South Amboy. They should send an officer to us." That day a boat from the *Neptune* put Woodruff ashore, probably near Elizabeth Point, for another of his flying errands. "They were met," Captain Stewart Ross of the *Neptune* wrote to De Lancey, by the person with whom Woodruff lived. This person "desired him to acquaint" De Lancey with the news that "eight hundred of the revolters had absolutely refused to come to any terms; and that on Thursday morning they were supplied with three wagon loads of arms and ammunition, and the whole body to march for Trenton, and supposed to be there now." The officers of the New Jersey Line had had to take ammunition away from their men "for fear of them joining the revolters." Ross would, he said, keep a boat out patrolling "the Bay and along the meadows all night and tomorrow to cover any person wanting to come over." He felt sure some emissary or other must soon return.

That night "a gentleman who came in and can be depended upon," but whose name is not certain, brought intelligence that was thought worth writing out at unusual length. "On the 9th some of the Pennsylvanians going to the body of the revolters told Mr. Parkin [or Perkins] the reason of their being without arms was that the others had taken them from them, as they would not join; but that they had changed their minds and were going to them. That a sergeant major of the 4th Infantry, one Williamson, commands them. They were at Princeton. They said they had not the least apprehension from the Jersey troops, as they were of the same opinion as they themselves."

The mutineers declared that even if their demands were met they would "not serve under their late officers. In case of reconciliation they insist upon the officers they have named being continued, and have in their proposals stipulated a pardon for all the ringleaders of the revolt. . . . One deserter from the [British] 7th said the men depend on us; that if Congress did not redress them they knew what course to take. . . .

"It was reported that we were going to South Amboy to cover them. . . . Wayne is kept among them as a hostage. They say Lafayette was let pay a visit to Wayne but sent away in an hour, as they would not allow any French officers among them. Numbers declare they will not serve Congress at any rate. They have taken two men, one with proposals, the other a guide; the name of the first, Oglethorpe."

Since the British had not sent an emissary of that name, and at the time may not yet have known that Ogden (his name possibly mistaken for Oglethorpe) had guided Mason from South River, this news about the detained men had little meaning. Nor was there much more certainty in several reports that came in on the 15th.

William Boyce from Philadelphia could testify that the mutineers were at Trenton when he crossed the Delaware on the day of the hanging, but he had there heard only, "at the house he stopped at, that the troops had taken two men who came in with proposals to them and delivered them to the Committee of Congress." Not till he got to Elizabethtown had he heard that they were hanged on Friday. Isaac Ruggles said he had seen two men still hanging at the Trenton ferry on Saturday, and had been told they were spies,

CONFUSION AMONG EMISSARIES 167

but did not know who they were. The Reverend Jonathan Odell, active intermediary in the Benedict Arnold negotiations, had been told by Rattoon of South Amboy that one of the men hanged was the guide, Ogden, the other an emissary named "Haynes alias Murphy." Fegany, "the man employed by Rattoon to conduct Haynes to South River," was afraid he might be suspected of treachery in the affair. Another report said the man hanged with Ogden was Hynds, a British sergeant. But Woodruff, who had got to Kingston and talked with a deserter from the mutineers, again brought in the story that the men taken up were two Pennsylvania soldiers, coming to Clinton with proposals but stopped near Brunswick.

Though Woodruff's story was only second-hand, it might throw some light on the names Oglethorpe, Murphy, Haynes, Hynds. What if the two men caught were some mutineer and Ogden, acting as guide on a return journey with an answer to Clinton? In the secret service anything could happen. Gautier and other correspondents from New Jersey still persisted in doubting that the affair was settled or that the reported rejection of Clinton's offers was necessarily the mutineers' final words. But Clinton, whose declining hopes were not strong enough to keep him any longer on Staten Island, returned on the 15th to more congenial quarters in New York.

II

That day Major Mackenzie commented in his diary on the lack of information about the Pennsylvanians. "Many persons have been sent out, but none have returned of late. There are several persons in different parts of Jersey who give very good intelligence at other times, but they are so extremely cautious on this occasion, and dread detection so much, that they dare not be seen near Princeton, so that the accounts we have are little more than hearsay."

Mackenzie, like other officers at Headquarters, was unaware that the British were hampered not only by the vigilance of the rebels, but also by the untrustworthiness of the emissaries.

There was the unidentified friend sent by Gautier to Princeton. Gautier paid him eight guineas for going, and gave him "particular instructions" what to do in case of trouble. Though on his return to Elizabethtown he told Gautier—or at least so Gautier wrote De Lancey—that he had got to Princeton on the evening (afternoon) of Saturday the 6th, before Mason and Ogden, and had delivered his proposals, there is nothing in the American records to show that he was telling the truth. The only trace of him is the copy of the proposals dropped Sunday night, after the arrest of the two spies, and turned over to Wayne the next morning. It does not seem credible that one emissary was permitted to deliver his proposals and go away, but that a few hours later another was instantly seized. It is, all things considered, much more credible that Gautier's agent, on or after arriving at Princeton, learned about Mason's reception, and so risked nothing of the sort himself. In dropping his proposals he may have been following the instructions he had been given for an emergency. Then on his return to Elizabethtown he could with a spy's usual facility lie about what he had done. No one was in a position to contradict him, and eight guineas were eight guineas.

And there was the other emissary who on that fateful Sunday arrived at Morristown instead of Princeton. He carried his proposals straight to St. Clair, and obligingly agreed to join in an intrigue that St. Clair proposed, with the knowledge—if not on the suggestion—of Lafayette. "As we are wholly unacquainted with your Excellency's intentions or what measures you mean to take upon this occasion," St. Clair wrote the next morning to Washington, "we are at a loss what use to make of this intelligence"—of Clinton's offers to the mutineers; "but as the person is acquainted with the contents of the letter, we have determined to detain him until night, in hopes your Excellency may arrive. And if not, some measures must be taken to send him back so as to deceive Sir Henry." For the present, St. Clair said, he was sending orders to Brunswick that all roads leading to Princeton were to be closely watched and all persons going in or coming out carefully searched, "to prevent any intercourse between that place and the enemy." He understood from the emissary that "numbers" of emissaries had been sent out.

Not having heard from Washington, St. Clair on Tuesday, after learning about Mason and Ogden, forwarded the converted emissary to Wayne with a letter. "This will be brought to you by a person who has been sent by Sir Henry Clinton with proposals to the discontented troops, and was honest enough to bring them to me. In order that we might be certain of their intentions with respect to the enemy, we have thought it best to suffer him to go on with a message, and he is to return here with the answer. We have heard that they have already detained two who came to them on the same errand. If this person should meet with the same fortune, you will be pleased to have him discharged, if in your power."

St. Clair thought the mutineers might pretend that by holding Clinton's emissaries they were rejecting his proposals and yet might secretly make a more favorable reply through some other channel. If that reply were trusted to the person who had suddenly become St. Clair's agent, it would go no further than to Morristown. Though this counterplot could not succeed unless the double-dealer were now the honest man St. Clair took him for, St. Clair was willing to attempt it. But when the honest man got to Wayne the mutineers had already marched to Trenton and their answer to Clinton had been made clear. This emissary could be of no further use to either side.

Two more emissaries got belatedly to Princeton on the 10th. One of them was called McFarlan (McFarlane), without any first name, in the papers of the British secret service. He may have been the Andrew McFarland who had been captured in a raid on Elizabethtown the past June. If he was, he would by custom have been brought to New York and questioned. Any man who in those circumstances showed himself disposed to make a bargain would be, after a discreet interval, permitted to go home on his promise to pay for his freedom by sending in useful intelligence or by some other good turn. Another man taken at the same time with McFarland had already made that bargain. McFarland may now have done the same thing. And he may have been the McFarlan who is known to have gone out on the 6th.

The McFarlan who did go on the 6th reached Princeton, he later reported, on the 10th, after the mutineers had left. Perhaps wondering what to do next, he "fell in with Caleb Bruen, who he found after a little conversation had come there on the same errand."

Next to Mason, Bruen is the best known of the emissaries. He belonged to a family that had been numerous and prominent in Newark from the town's earliest days. He lived—later if not then—in Broad Street next door to a cabinetmaker's shop which he shared with Matthias Bruen. Caleb Bruen was a second lieutenant in the Essex County Minute Men. Long after the war, when he had come to be known as

Captain Bruen, he often told his story of the errand he performed in January 1781. He had, he said, "somehow" got the confidence of certain British officers and had learned that they desired to send proposals to the mutineers. Eager to serve his country, he said, he himself offered to convey the "treacherous correspondence"—and conveyed it to Washington. Then, returning to the British, he told them he had fallen under suspicion and been obliged to destroy the letter. The British did not believe him and kept him in the Sugar House prison till the war ended. It was a fine story for an old soldier to tell about his daring and suffering in the famous Revolution.

Parts of the story were true. Bruen was undeniably sent out by the British with proposals on the 6th, and after at least two more visits to New York was imprisoned, in late February or early March, for treachery. The £32 3s which he afterwards said had been taken from him by the British in 1781 may have been in part the money he had been paid for his mission to the mutineers—or had not been paid. And Colonel Elias Dayton, of Washington's secret service in New Jersey, undeniably wrote to Washington the following January that it was Bruen, then still in a British prison, who "first gave notice of Sir Harry's correspondence with the Pennsylvania revolters." But Bruen in reality did undertake the mission, did no doubt receive at least part of his pay in advance, and did go all the way to Princeton instead of carrying the proposals at once to some officer closer to New York, such as Colonel Dayton himself at Chatham. The astute Dayton would never have attempted a counterplot such as St. Clair thought of for his emissary. The most reasonable explanation of the complicated business is that Bruen was enough of an adventurer to undertake the mission for a good deal of hard money down and a great deal more if he were successful, but not foolhardy enough to risk his neck for the British if he could save it by telling a patriotic story to the Americans.

The certain facts about Bruen are that he went out on the 6th, by the 10th was in Princeton, there ran into McFarlan, and with him went on to Trenton.

McFarlan, reporting to the British, was not too truthful. At Trenton, he said, "finding that two men had been taken up, they dropped their papers in camp, which were immediately found and carried to Wayne and Mr. Reed; and next morning a reward of one hundred guineas was offered for the person who dropped them." This reward seems to have been McFarlan's invention. "After the papers were found a Colonel Hayes, who knew Bruen, asked him his business there; to which the other not giving a satisfactory answer, he told him he had no business among troops who had revolted. He [Hayes] then went to General Wayne's quarters." Fearing they might be taken up, McFarlan and Bruen "went across the water to Pennsylvania, where they saw the execution of the two men, and . . . when they returned the next day they were still hanging there." Or so McFarlan said.

There is not a word here of how Bruen and McFarlan gave themselves up to Wayne, convinced him they had virtuous intentions, and seemed willing to serve him in plans against the British who had sent them out. Nor do Wayne's letters furnish much about the episode. But at five o'clock in the afternoon of the 10th he wrote a hasty, blotted letter to the Committee of Congress. "The bearers," he said, "are two emissaries from the enemy, but true to their country they have rendered much essential service at different times, and are therefore entitled to some confidence and bounty. With your assistance and advice we may probably employ them to advantage. Shall we take Sir Harry like a woodcock in his own springe? Think of this matter over night. I will explain myself in the morning, should you not take the idea."

The Committee did not fall in with Wayne's scheme for a foolhardy counterplot, concerning which he gave some hints in a letter to Washington the next day. Wayne had, it seems, planned to send Bruen and McFarlan back with a false answer, as from the mutineers, which would decoy Clinton out, only to be surprised by the mutineers under Wayne's command. The Committee, Wayne explained to Washington, was "afraid to trust our boys so near the enemy lest they change their disposition." And Wayne admitted that the trial and execution of Mason and Ogden would "effectually foreclose all further negotiations with Sir Harry, who I wanted to strike."

As to Bruen and McFarlan, Wayne said he knew them "to be rascals, but serviceable to us. They brought new overtures, such as giving the command of the Line to the sergeants, etc." Possibly these "additional proposals of a more advantageous and alluring nature," as the Committee of Congress called them, were no more than something invented by Bruen and McFarlan to make themselves important. There is nothing in the full records of the British secret service to show that such further offers were ever sent from New York.

III

Two documents in Clinton's own hand sum up, in unexpected detail, the record of the emissaries. One is a paper of January 9 endorsed A List of Proposals Sent out and by Whom Carried. In it Clinton, taking stock, scrupulously if not altogether accurately put spies' and informers' names in cipher (here deciphered and set in brackets).

"Gould came in to Staten Island with an answer to my letter to [garbled name in cipher, possibly Major De Lancey?] acknowledging the receipt of two copies of the proposals sent the 4th." (This was muddled, even for Clinton. Gautier had acknowledged the receipt of the two copies three days before. Clinton seems to mean that Gould had brought in—as he had—an answer addressed to De Lancey, saying the two copies had been received at Princeton and the messenger had returned.)

"[Bruen] sent out the 6th with a proposal.

"[Mason] sent out the 4th, landed the 5th in the Raritan, a proposal.

"Hatfield a proposal on the 5th to send out.

"Dr. [Dayton] says they are at Trenton, some dispersed." (This was Dr. Jonathan I. Dayton of Elizabethtown, a kinsman of Colonel Dayton of the American secret service. At some time during the past year Dr. Dayton had been kidnaped and brought into New York, but afterwards permitted to go home on parole. There he had "behaved very civilly to all who visited Elizabethtown" from the British, and "friends coming in." Now he himself had come in, with motives which do not appear. Some of the loyalists in New York distrusted him as much as any of his patriot neighbors could have done. He had at first been a loyalist, then under pressure from the rebels had taken the oath of abjuration and allegiance; and after his capture by the British had given his word to serve them in secret. He was a double-dealer between the lines trying to safeguard his future no matter which side should win the war.)

"[Woodruff], twice over, says at Princeton." (Woodruff, that is, did not agree with Dr. Dayton as to where the mutineers had gone from Morristown. On the day they marched

CONFUSION AMONG EMISSARIES 175

to Trenton the British were still comparing reports on the Line's whereabouts.)

"Mr. A. J. [Mr. Andrew, Jr., meaning Gautier?], at Princeton, in today." (Gould may have said that Gautier was coming, but he did not arrive.)

"General Skinner, at Princeton and at Trenton." (Skinner, supposed to have excellent correspondents in New Jersey, had not made up his mind where the mutineers were.)

"[McFarlane], at Princeton, went out 5th with a proposal given to Ward." (Since McFarlan had not been heard from since he left, this presumably means that before going he had said the Pennsylvanians were at Princeton and he would go to that place.)

"[Blank] sent out 5th."

Clinton in this List named four of his emissaries—Mason, Bruen, McFarlan, and Blank—and referred to the proposals given to Gautier and Cornelius Hatfield to be sent out by two more emissaries. Of the four named, Mason was taken, Bruen and McFarlan went to Wayne, and Blank disappeared from sight so far as the records go. He may have been the double-dealing emissary who went to St. Clair; or Hatfield's messenger may have been. On the whole the emissaries made a bad showing. But probably of any six who might have been chosen, one would have been captured (like Mason), one would have been lost sight of (like Blank or Hatfield's messenger), one would have lied about what he had done (like Gautier's faithful friend), and three would have saved themselves by double-dealing (like Bruen, McFarlan, and the man who went to St. Clair).

The British were under the same handicap as any army of occupation: they could not rely on the agents they used among the people. The honest loyalists were refugees inside the British lines, the honest patriots were citizens inside the American. The doubtful ground between could be traversed only by doubtful persons. Though the British had money to buy them with, the double-dealers had local attachments to their own country. It might be, if they were discovered, in some respects more profitable to join the British openly; but it was almost sure to be, in the long run, more comfortable to stay among their countrymen. Any spy employed by the British was likely to have taken some kind of pains to stand well also with the Americans, if there should be need of it.

On one of the later spy reports among the British secret service papers Clinton wrote an endorsement that gives his conclusions about the matter. "I had sent six spies; the two last [Bruen and McFarlan] were two too many. They [the mutineers] were saved to America by good management, not lost to us by bad management. Had the Americans tried force we should have had them. Their chiefs were inclined to lead them to us, but were afraid to sound them out."

IV

During the period of uncertainty various plans were made for sending further emissaries. There was talk of Nicholas Dietrich Baron de Ottendorf, a German professional soldier who had deserted from the Continental Army to join Arnold's Legion but had, on coming in to New York, been imprisoned for debt. He might go out on parole, on the pretense that he was going only to collect money due him. If Ottendorf, De Lancey wrote to the British commissary of prisoners on the 11th, would "try to get among the revolted troops and bring or send back an answer with their determination, we will reward him very handsomely. . . .

SIR HENRY CLINTON

Facsimile of an unpublished List of Proposals Sent out and by Whom Carried, in Clinton's handwriting, January 9, 1781. *See page 174.*

As his business will lead him to Princeton, he will not be suspected. He may, I should imagine, converse with the leader. And should he be able to bring him to us his recompense shall be unbounded." The commissary of prisoners (the complacent Joshua Loring whose wife had been the mistress of Sir William Howe) thought there need be no suspicion of Ottendorf, "unless it happens from his own imprudence." But Ottendorf was considered "rather a weak man for any capital undertaking," and seems not to have been employed—on a secret errand that would have been in violation of the word of honor he was ready to give.

Another man was willing to go out on parole and violate it. This was Lieutenant Colonel Elisha Lawrence of Monmouth County, New Jersey, a loyalist who had been captured by the Americans and permitted to go to New York, on his oath to do nothing inimical to them while at liberty. The plan with respect to him went as far as written instructions on the 11th: "To go out by Mount Pleasant," near Middletown Point, New Jersey, "from there by Scott's tavern try to get to Princeton; when there to find out if possible the intention of the Pennsylvanians; if they mean to come to us to tell them we have been ready to go into the Jerseys whenever they chose to call upon us. If they have anything to propose we shall be ready to hear anyone they send and will be answerable for their safety." But there is nothing to indicate whether Lawrence made the journey.

Everybody was cautious. George Playter, who called himself Dr. Welding, had come in from the loyalists in the back counties of Pennsylvania to say they were increasingly eager to revolt if Clinton would support them. Playter flatly refused to carry proposals to the mutineers, but on the 11th he was prepared to try a longer shot: not at the soldiers of the Line, but at Brigadier General William Thompson of Pennsylvania, who had been taken prisoner in Canada nearly five years before, and not exchanged till the past October. He was now living at or near Carlisle, and said to be resentful over the long delay in his exchange and his failure to be given another command in the Army.

On the 11th Playter was furnished a letter "From a Real Friend"—actually De Lancey—to Thompson. "I have been taught to look upon you," the letter ran, "as a person attached to the old Constitution and willing to give your assistance to restoring it to the colonies. I have powers to make the most ample recompense to those friends who exert themselves in our favor, both at present and when their efforts for us are crowned with success. If you should choose to undertake so laudable a task, and will make it known by advertising in your own name that you have lost a carnelian seal and offer a reward in the Philadelphia newspaper, a person will meet you and give you every information."

De Lancey can hardly have expected that Thompson, even if he responded to this, would do it in time to be of use in connection with the mutiny. But the secret service, even in the present emergency, must not lose sight of its long-range designs. Playter would either carry the letter or else follow it to Thompson. (In March Playter returned and said Thompson was friendly, but nothing came of it.)

On the 14th De Lancey was still looking for "people of property" to go to the mutineers. "I will give from one to two hundred guineas each provided they will make use of artifice to find out their intentions and return to us. The reward of the person that succeeds shall be unlimited." Nobody of the sort was found. De Lancey had another scheme. Some deserters had just come in from West Point, without coats—in January—but "dressed as light as in the middle

CONFUSION AMONG EMISSARIES 179

of summer." They said there had been no mutiny there, and their officers had told them the Pennsylvania mutiny "was all a story fabricated by the Tories." If any of these deserters would go to the Pennsylvanians, saying they had deserted on purpose to join the mutiny, "and after finding out their exact situation return to us the best way they can with good information," De Lancey would "give them from fifty to one hundred guineas." The shivering soldiers thought as much of their necks as the men of property.

17

Counteraction

THE American secret service records are less circumstantial and revealing than the British. It was partly a matter of geography. Clinton in a fortified town could preserve full reports of the spies who came in, usually with their names, and drafts of the letters or messages that went out to correspondents, with their replies. Washington, perpetually moving from place to place, had to depend on information sent to him from varying distances and in danger of being lost on the way or intercepted by loyalist partisans. The names of spies were seldom put in writing, or more than their pseudonyms, and many of them are still unidentified or imperfectly known.

Though Colonel Dayton of the 3rd New Jersey was generally in charge of the secret service in his State, other officers as well used spies of their own or tried to counteract those sent out by the British. Wayne had done both these things in December, when he was trying to find out whether the British meant to land in New Jersey or send an expedition by water to the south.

On the 22nd John Hendricks of Elizabethtown, an agent through whom various American spies on the New York islands communicated with Dayton, wrote a letter to Wayne's aide, Major Fishbourne. "I have this minute," Hendricks said, "a person from the other side that saw General Arnold go aboard yesterday"—as Arnold had gone, to set out for Virginia. But Hendricks was still disposed to think the apparent expedition was a ruse, and that Arnold or whoever commanded might still land in New Jersey. For Hendricks could not trust his informers. There was another "that formerly had been in our interest, but I believe he is now bought from it, as the bigger part of our spies are."

It was taken for granted that ordinary spies, working for money, would ordinarily do more for the British, who had gold and silver, than for the Americans, who too often had only depreciated paper currency.

Wayne, receiving Hendricks's letter and other intelligence from Elizabethtown, sent Fishbourne to make further inquiries. He came back with the news that "the caitiff Arnold" had gone on board on the morning of the 20th and that twenty transports had fallen down towards Sandy Hook. But there was no certainty they had gone beyond it, Wayne wrote to Washington on Christmas Day. "As I have not yet received any intelligence from Amboy, where a constant lookout is kept, I am at a loss to determine whether they have sailed or not."

Contradictory information had come that "Arnold was certainly in New York on Saturday afternoon" the 23rd. "A person who was present when he [Arnold] enlisted three refugees from Bergen that day at three o'clock, came out the same evening." Since this person's information was false, he had presumably been sent to deceive Wayne; or he may have had some double-dealing scheme of his own. Wayne, talking with him, devised a scheme for counteraction. "I promise myself some advantage," as he explained to Washington, "not from his fidelity or virtue, but from his villainy."

The spy had come "with some queries" to which he was to get answers for the British. Instead of trying to ferret out the answers by secret methods, he seems to have gone to

Wayne, admitted his errand, and pretended that in loyalty to America he would take back misleading reports. Wayne, with no faith in the spy's loyalty, figured that his villainy might operate in either direction. If he were permitted to return to New York with intelligence, he might be partly credited there, and then might come again to Mount Kemble. Let him go back and forth, perhaps telling or giving away some part of the truth to both his employers, and serving each of them by some falsehood to the other.

The spy asked where Washington was and how his Headquarters were protected. Wayne answered that Washington was at New Windsor—which the British would be sure to learn—but represented him as somewhat more strongly "covered with troops" than he was. Asked what number of boats the Americans had on the Hudson, and where they were, Wayne answered only that the boats were secreted. On these points he was more reticent, and less deceptive, than about his own command.

The Pennsylvania troops, near Morristown he told the spy, were about 3600—which exaggerated their number by a half. They had "three redoubts upon a strong commanding ground with a citadel in which are six pieces of cannon, six- and twelve-pounders." In fact the citadel was not yet completed, and the fieldpieces were still in the magazine in the Wick orchard. "Guards and sentries so vigilant as to render it dangerous and difficult to approach. Officers haughty, and men insolent." To the spy's query about what plans the rebels had for joint action with the French, Wayne gave him an answer to take to the British: "The French and rebels have some capital operation in view—but can't determine where."

With this deceiving news the spy was to go to the British,

who might not believe Wayne, but might think the spy had established a promising line of communication, and so might value him accordingly. He was then to repay Wayne by reporting on the British embarkation and the position of their forces left on the islands. By an alternative device the double-dealer was "to try to put the enemy upon attempting the Pennsylvania Line, by giving out that they are remiss in duty, badly clothed and injudiciously posted, discontent, etc. Give notice of their approach, to the end that means may be taken to prevent any possibility of the enemy effecting a retreat."

Here was intricate manipulation, with the slightest chance of success. The revolt on New Year's Day put an end to any further designs Wayne may have had.

But the mutiny did not find the Americans without spies. The spy who was in New York on the 3rd had Fishbourne's permission to go; and the one who was there on the 4th reported to Dayton. Though the American records are too guarded to furnish any certainty, there is more than a little possibility that the two apparent spies were only one man making two trips. And his trips coincide so remarkably with those of Gould that the unnamed American spy may have been Gould, rewarded in New York for telling the British what had happened at Mount Kemble, and rewarded also at Elizabethtown for telling the Americans what the British planned to do about the mutiny. Gautier, writing to De Lancey, later said he mistrusted the person who had brought the proposals to be sent to Princeton. That person was Gould. And Gautier wrote De Lancey: "You may depend on it, Colonel Dayton knew two or three spies was sent out by you before they reached the Pennsylvania troops." While Gautier was wrong in thinking that Dayton knew so much so soon, Dayton does seem to have had some kind of understanding with Gould, who from February 22, as a surviving letter shows, was actually in correspondence with Dayton.

So is it possible that Caleb Bruen of Newark and Uzal Woodruff of Elizabethtown, both of them soon afterwards imprisoned by the British for double-dealing, though Gould was not, may have connived with Dayton in some degree from the first. In a letter to Washington on March 9 Dayton announced that "three persons upon whom I very considerably depended for the discovery of every important movement or transaction of the enemy are apprehended and closely confined in New York, and I am just informed are sentenced to die." Two of the three unnamed persons were almost certainly Bruen and Woodruff, whom Dayton named to Washington on December 27 as having "been very serviceable to us" but "now confined in irons in their dungeons as criminals."

The names of the double-dealers and the dates of their services are a tangle of uncertainties. But it is at least certain that much of what the British tried to do was counteracted by the Americans. De Lancey for the British and Dayton for the Americans played a kind of secret military chess across the Hudson, using spies for pieces.

One episode in the game has left more abundant traces than usual. Captain William Bernard Gifford of the 3rd New Jersey (Dayton's regiment) was an Irishman, born in Cork, who had had a commission in the Continental Army since February 1776. He was taken prisoner at Elizabethtown a year before the mutiny, along with the Andrew McFarland who may have been the spy McFarlan. According to the loyalist *New York Gazette,* Gifford, "having seen his error, and being also sensible that it would neither redound to his honor nor benefit the cause of America to continue longer in the service under the present system of French politics, he wisely embraced the first opportunity of laying down his commission and returning to the allegiance of his rightful and lawful sovereign." This was written after Gifford openly joined the British. There had been secret and less creditable passages in the affair.

Gifford's captivity was not harsh. In May 1780, he was married, at New Utrecht, Long Island, to Nancy Voorhies, "a very amiable young lady with a handsome fortune" and a loyalist. By November Gifford was converted and had made his bargain with the enemy. On the 10th of that month he was ready, as he wrote from New Utrecht to De Lancey, to go back to the Americans on parole to settle his exchange. While he was about it, on his word of honor, he would "send or bring in such intelligence as may be of service. I can know how many brigades and their numbers nearly, also their situation and where they may be attacked to advantage. I can know where the [artillery] park will be stationed and the number of pieces of artillery, also G. W.'s quarters, and the quarters of the different general officers. I can know where the magazines of provisions, stores, laboratory, etc. are, and also many other things that don't occur to me at present. . . . I wish for an opportunity to convince the Commander-in-Chief [Clinton] and the world that I am a friend to King George and his government. The sooner I go out the better. You know, Sir, my situation as to cash. If you can procure me a little, I shall esteem it a most particular favor, and will pay you when I return."

On the 28th Gifford had been at Trenton and had dined with Governor Livingston and several members of the Council and Assembly, who thought they were learning from Gifford something about the British. He reported to De Lancey that though the States were all busy raising an army for the next year's campaign, they were not likely to get one because of the falling currency and the public's dissatisfaction with Congress. "The cry of the country is that Congress with their money has distressed 'em more than Sir Henry Clinton with the whole British Army. . . . I shall set off for West Point tomorrow. I am fearful from the divided state of the Army I shall not be able to give you that particular account I could wish."

His fears were justified. On his way north he met the New Jersey brigade marching to winter quarters at Pompton and could have no excuse not to accompany them. His exchange took less time than he had counted on, and he found that in the new arrangement of January 1 it was planned to drop all officers who had been prisoners among the British. Gifford could consequently not remain in the American Army and send its secrets to the enemy as he had expected to do. "I mean in a few days to go to the regiment and resign," he wrote De Lancey on December 7. "After that I shall return as soon as possible to New York, and will abide by the British Army if they should go to the utmost ends of the earth." While he waited, he sent in detailed information, especially about the American forces along the Jersey coast.

But Gifford was suspected by another officer of his regiment, Lieutenant Colonel Francis Barber, who on December 11 wrote to Washington that Gifford had sent in his commission and now seemed less loyal than before. Washington advised Barber not to give Gifford "a discharge from the Army, because he then might go off to the enemy, and we should not have it in our power to treat him as a deserter should he fall into our hands again." Whereas if he should be tried and cashiered, "and then go off, the enemy will not have much to boast of from the acquisition of such a character."

From then on Gifford was so carefully watched that he had no chance to send a letter to New York till after the Pennsylvania mutineers had gone to Trenton and given up the emissaries. Then a note from Cornelius Hatfield of Staten Island, making an appointment with Gifford, somehow fell into American hands. He must have been betrayed by a spy or double-dealer, for Washington said this was testimony against Gifford that could not be used: that is, could not be used without revealing the identity of the person who had turned it over and whose secret must be kept. Gifford could only slip away to the British, who seem to have rewarded him chiefly with brief approbation in a newspaper.

II

At eight o'clock on the evening of Wednesday the 10th, while Mason and Ogden were being tried at Summer Seat, Washington at New Windsor, who had not yet heard even of their arrival and arrest at Princeton, wrote a letter to St. Clair, from whom two letters had come in the course of the day. Washington had, he told St. Clair, directed Major General William Heath at West Point to assemble all the general officers and regimental commanders of the Highlands department, so far as they could be reached, at Heath's quarters the next morning, "where I shall meet them. What I have to propose is of too delicate a nature to commit to paper; neither can I say, until I have had the meeting, whether it will be prudent for me to go down towards Morris." Washington could not be sure where or in what circumstances the letter would find St. Clair, or whether it would ever get to him. It might be stopped by the mutineers.

St. Clair had told of the discreet emissary who brought Clinton's proposals to Morristown and whom St. Clair planned to send back with a deceiving answer. Washington diplomatically advised against the scheme. "I think it appears by the letter which has fallen into your hands that there has not been much, if any, intercourse between the mutineers and Sir H. Clinton. And if the future correspondence can be intercepted"—not answered—"it will embarrass the British and the troops. You"—St. Clair and Wayne—"will have been the best judges of the kind of answer which it would be proper to give to Sir Henry's messenger. But as we had not force sufficient to wish to decoy him out, perhaps it will have been most prudent to answer him in the negative."

That same evening Washington wrote to his friend Philip Schuyler, who had retired from the Army and was at Albany. The mutiny had a "bad aspect," Washington thought, though again he would not say too much "in a letter (liable to miscarriage)." The mutineers were still at Princeton, Washington supposed, where they could weigh the offers of the enemy against the offers of Congress. He must confer with his officers before he could decide what to do. "In five minutes I shall step into the boat for West Point."

Before he sealed the letter he received Sullivan's of the 7th about the detention of the two spies, and added a postscript. "I have this instant received authentic information that the mutineers have delivered up one of Sir Henry Clinton's emissaries (with his guide) charged with written propositions very favorable to the revolted troops—though without any intention, I am persuaded, of fulfilling them." This seemed clear proof that the Pennsylvanians did not intend to go to the enemy.

At ten the next morning Washington met his officers and

read them Sullivan's letter. Since it was their "almost universal opinion that their men might be depended on" to march against the mutineers if they persisted in disorder, he directed that a thousand New England soldiers should be detached from their several Lines and "held in the most perfect readiness to march at the shortest notice, with four days' provisions cooked." He went back to New Windsor in better spirits. But on Friday he learned that after the spies had been given up they had been quickly taken back again, and were held, as Wayne said, "in mortmain": to be put to death if the mutineers were pleased with Reed's offers, otherwise "to be spared and rewarded."

Though Wayne misjudged the mutineers, Washington had no better source of information. He believed the men had risen on account of genuine grievances. They would, he had predicted, at once get tempting offers from the enemy, and in their first anger might respond to them, even turn to New York, if any premature attempt were made to suppress them by force. The surrender of the spies had appeared to mean that the mutineers were attached to the American cause, though in rebellion against American mistreatment. This was to be, it seemed, a domestic matter between the mutineers and their own people. If that was true, and the mutineers had refused help from the British, then they might make some kind of reasonable peace. If, as was always possible in a mutiny, the men should get out of control, then force might have to be used. A thousand resolute disciplined soldiers could subdue a much larger number of rioting mutineers.

On Thursday Washington had felt some assurance that the uprising could be quieted either by a just settlement, which he preferred if possible, or by the usual military methods, which he would employ if necessary. On Friday he was not so sure. The conduct of the insurgents, he wrote to St. Clair, "appears to me in this light: they have made known the propositions offered by Sir Henry Clinton only by way of threat and seem to say: 'If you do not grant our terms we can obtain them elsewhere.'"

Washington saw in this a double threat: possible desertion, certain delay. On the whole, he feared loss by desertion less than the disquieting confusion of an affair dragged out with nothing decisive done. He had the entire Continental Army to consider. If the Pennsylvanians were to desert to the enemy or dissolve, any other Line might try to follow them. If their grievances should be redressed on their terms, all the other Lines with grievances would have demands. Either event must mean the end of the Army as it then was constituted, with no prospects of another with which to carry on the war. To wait for developments was to give confusion a chance to grow, yet to move towards the mutineers with a punitive or preventive force might only accelerate confusion to the point of catastrophe. Nothing could be worse than for the Commander-in-Chief to risk an effort and then find himself unable to make good his authority.

Washington had so little knowledge of what was happening in New Jersey that for two or three days he stopped writing to Wayne, Reed, or Sullivan, for fear his letters would not get through to any of them. "I am extremely embarrassed," he wrote to another correspondent on the 13th, "and waiting with the utmost anxiety for further advices." That same day he heard from Heath that the troops at West Point were in general more discontented than the officers had understood, and in particular the men of the detachment being prepared to march.

Heath had sent a woman of the camp into one regiment to listen to the conversation of the soldiers. She reported that they said they would take no part in putting down the Pennsylvanians. A communicative sergeant reported much the same thing. According to Heath's steward, a good many of the men declared that, though they might march, it would be only after they themselves had been paid and clothed.

Washington disapproved of such measures to sound out the men. Even "the most prudent officers, in the most cautious manner," he wrote to Heath, might cause trouble by appearing to have any doubt of the "fidelity and firmness of the soldiers" or of their obedience. Discipline must be unquestioned if it was to be habitual. "I could wish to have these matters treated with the greatest prudence by the officers, and not conversed upon before their domestics, as I am apprehensive has sometimes incautiously been practiced"—as by Heath, whom Washington was tactfully reproving.

Washington had not credited the gossip of the woman and the sergeant and the steward. Two days later Heath had to admit that they were wrong. And Major General Robert Howe, who on the 15th took command of the detachment, the next day reported circumstantially to Washington.

"I have by every means in my power," Howe wrote, "endeavored to find how far the fears entertained of the disaffection of the Massachusetts troops to the proposed service was well or ill founded; and not content with my own personal efforts, I have desired officers of address and abilities to exert themselves also. It appears to be the opinion of [Colonel Rufus] Putnam, [Captain Thomas] Vose, [Lieutenant Colonel Ebenezer] Sprout, [Lieutenant Colonel John] Brooks, [Major Billy] Porter, [Major Lemuel] Trescott, and many others that a dependence may be had upon the good conduct of the men in any service your Excellency shall require of them. I confess I am of that opinion; and though all human events are uncertain, yet I rely so much upon it that I am ready to take my chance with the detachment if it becomes necessary to proceed with it, and shall do it with confidence.

"The doubts General Heath has suggested to your Excellency were taken up principally upon a report of a sergeant to Colonel [Ezra] Newhall. But when it was inquired into, the giant dwindled into a dwarf. I will relate it. Colonel Newhall was alarmed by a sergeant who told him that the men detached from his regiment had refused to draw the four days' provisions ordered them. And this circumstance has been construed into their dislike of the service. But upon inquiring, their murmurs appear to have arisen from the late hour of the night when they received the order and a dispute which of them should go for the provisions, which was settled by themselves and the provisions instantly sent for. Colonel Putnam formed some pretext to be among them the next day. He inquired strictly if they had cooked their rations agreeable to order and asked many questions which might have led to a discovery had their feelings been much against the service. But not one word like it was expressed, except from one man lately exchanged and arrived from New York, who said he was willing to fight against anything but a brother-soldier. This and a camp girl's mentioning at a sutler's shop that she did not believe the men would fight against the Pennsylvanians is, I believe, the whole basis of this affair.

"The day being very bad yesterday, and I much indisposed, I did not go to General [Samuel Holden] Parsons as I had intended, but sent by express, desiring to be particularly informed of all circumstances respecting the detachment ordered from his [Connecticut] Line. He writes that the men were never ordered on any service which they more

GOULD TO ELIAS DAYTON

Facsimile of an unpublished letter from Gould, a British spy, to Dayton of the American Secret Service, February 22, 1781. Some of the information sent about "Poor Benedict" (Arnold) seems to have been deliberately misleading. *See page 184.*

willingly undertook. All this taken together persuades me there is great reliance to be placed on the good dispositions of the detachment.

"All the officers uniting in opinion that some rum now and then distributed would be attended with good effect, indeed would be exceedingly necessary, I take the liberty to request that your Excellency would be so kind as to give Colonel Blaine"—Ephraim Blaine, commissary general of purchases—"some directions thereupon, who tells me it may be obtained by impressment if no other method can procure it. And the necessity of the case will I think warrant the measure."

Washington was satisfied with this report, and with the news from Trenton that the two emissaries had been put to death. He wrote to Howe that it was probable the detachment would not march, "though I would still have it held in readiness." There might be need for it—as it turned out there was, in another quarter.

18

Troubled Settlement

JOSEPH REED, who after the execution of the spies frugally talked the sergeants out of the reward promised them by Wayne, on that same day—January 11—had another scheme for mollifying the men and thereby saving money. This was, as Reed wrote to the Council, "to take some notice of their women and children by providing some decent clothing, which they have not at present. There are about a hundred of them, and, like ourselves, they have their attachments and affections." Reed imagined that his attitude towards the soldiers and their wives, with their sentiments surprisingly like those of ladies and gentlemen, was generous condescension, which his age thought was a virtue. "A new gown, silk handkerchief, and a pair of shoes, etc., would be but little expense, and I think as a present from the State would have more effect than ten times the same laid out in articles for the men." Reed was willing to contribute to the cost of his scheme. "If it should not be convenient or agreeable to the Council to do this, I will be one of a hundred to provide for one woman each, to be given only to those soldiers' wives who continue in the service. I have not mentioned it, lest I should not be able to effect it; therefore request to hear from you as soon as may be. I verily believe many of the men will do their duty better than ever"—if this should be done for their families.

The petty stratagem was not undertaken. Perhaps it did not seem petty to Reed, in the distracting circumstances that submerged him. He had been able to see no way out of agreeing to terms the mutineers would accept. Yet all the time he knew he was promising money and supplies which Pennsylvania would find it hard to produce, if not impossible to produce while the men's patience lasted. "It will be necessary to forward on the articles promised without delay," he told the Council. "In such a case a breach of faith would ruin us, and expose me to great disgrace, which I hope my fellow-citizens will not do after the risk and fatigue of body and mind which I have gone through."

Much of the food and forage so far consumed by the mutineers and the officials, with their horses, had been purchased from the people of New Jersey. But now they were themselves running short, and "very sore on the subject of supplying us, as the distress is occasioned by our own Line." Pennsylvania must look out for Pennsylvania troops. Reed supposed that there was "a great quantity of salt provisions in town, and very probably cattle in the meadows." Whatever was available should be sent at once, but should stop at Kirkbride's wharf in Bordentown and be held there for further orders. Clothing and rum, which the men were demanding, should by no means come to Trenton. While it was indispensable to feed the men, it was still inadvisable to give them a chance to seize clothing, which was a part of their bargain, or rum, which might make them disorderly while they waited.

There were enough symptoms of disorder already, Reed thought. He had expected that the Board of Sergeants would retire, and the men give up their arms and receive their officers again. But the sergeants, who had said only that the men would disperse "upon being discharged," insisted on continuing in command till matters were settled. The soldiers, after ten days' tension, were growing relaxed and restless, but still as firm as ever against the return of the officers. Wayne, going to Pennington on the 11th, had to tell the officers there of the men's stubborn resentment. The regimental commanders were to come to Trenton for the settlement, and the other officers to stay where they were. Though most of them were unchangeably convinced that the mutiny ought to be put down by force and the worst offenders made an example of, they must stand aside and see the mutineers appeased by the civil authorities.

The Committee of Congress and the Council members at Trenton were without any hope of force sufficient to reduce the mutineers if they should become unruly, or any confidence that they would not become unruly if the settlement were delayed. The officers urged that the Line be dissolved outright, the trouble-makers dismissed the service, and as many men re-enlisted as possible. Both the Committee and the Council members believed that this could not be done without establishing a precedent for the entire Continental Army. Dissolve one Line, and all the Lines might clamor for the same relief. Nobody could tell how many of the soldiers would re-enlist. The Pennsylvania problem must be kept a special case, to be settled on the special terms already proposed and accepted. And the settlement must begin at once.

The men had been promised their arrears of pay only "as soon as circumstances will admit" and the adjustment of their losses by depreciation only "as soon as possible"; and might be reasonable if these were not immediately forthcoming. They would expect clothes without delay. On this point there need be no early difficulty. A shipment arrived from Philadelphia on the 11th: 1200 shirts and pairs of shoes, 2500 overalls, 1000 blankets. Each man continued in the service was to have a pair of shoes and of woolen overalls, a shirt, and a blanket, "unless he have one." There was little money on hand, but each man could soon be provided with fifty Pennsylvania shillings, regarded as the equivalent of a month's pay, and a furlough for sixty days. The money would pay his way home, and the furlough separate him from the embodied mutineers. Men proved to be "freely and voluntarily" enlisted, or now re-enlisted, for the war were to be given six pounds in the new State money and a guinea—counted as nine Pennsylvania pounds all told. There remained the problem of enlistments, on which the commissioners "for hearing and determining the claims of the soldiers" set to work on the 12th.

II

Then followed a week or more of wrangling and dissatisfaction, with the Committee of Congress and Reed gone back to Philadelphia and the commissioners in charge. The regimental records had not yet reached Trenton. The officers demanded that the commissioners wait for the papers. The commissioners refused and went ahead. The soldiers had, according to Reed's proposals, the right to swear as to their "time and terms of enlistment" without any further proof. With no records to confirm or contradict, about a hundred men of the 1st, 2nd, and 3rd regiments freely returned to the service. At least five-sixths of the total took their oaths that they were enlisted for three years or for the war and had not re-enlisted, or that they had been compelled to enlist; and so in either case were entitled to discharge. Some of them in ignorance, more of them in violent unconcern, rushed into perjury.

It is true that numerous soldiers of the 1st, it turned out, had gone as volunteers from Pennsylvania to the siege of

Boston in the first year of the war and had served ever since on "that voluntary plan," without further enlistment. It is probably true that more than a few others in the first three regiments had believed they were enlisting for three years or for the war, but had been carelessly or unscrupulously entered for the war. There were men whose papers showed them enlisted for the war, but who had been tricked or forced into enlisting on those terms. Others had been, it was evident, cheated out of their bounty or gratuity by officers who had since left the Army. Yet there were still many men who dishonestly and insolently swore off, to avoid returning to a present service which they hated more than they feared the future hell-fire which most of them had been taught to believe was the punishment for swearing falsely.

Who was to blame for the precipitate beginning of the commission's inquiry, before the regimental papers could be procured? The officers put the responsibility first on Reed, second on the Committee of Congress. The Committee, while it had technically appointed the commissioners, and regularly conferred with Reed, gave him an almost free rein in the conduct of the affair. And it seems to have been he, more than anybody else, who decided that the inquiry must begin, with or without documents to go by. He put the blame on the "impatience of the troops, discipline every hour declining, and increasing waste of public stores." But Reed had never trusted the mutineers, and even when admitting their good behavior had always expected worse things of them any moment—worse things than had so far appeared. There is no sure evidence that the men would not have waited a few days for their papers to be brought. Certainly when these came, and showed how many men were really enlisted for the war, there was less turmoil than there had been before. And a good part of the turmoil seems to have sprung from the events of the first day, when the officers disputed with the commissioners, and the men of the single company then settled with found they could all swear off if their consciences would let them. Their example spread like fire through the camp.

To the protests of the officers the men responded with infuriating disobedience. "Great indulgences must and ought to be shown to the feelings of the officers in this new and unexpected scene," Reed wrote that day to the Council. "It is a sore trial, and requires no small degree of patience and good sense to submit to it. The men certainly had not those attachments which the officers supposed, and their fears being now at an end, they give loose to many indecencies, which are very provoking to those who have long been accustomed to receive unconditional submission." The men went beyond passive disobedience in the first days of the settlement, and forcibly excluded their officers from camp or from the hearings of the commission. Colonel Francis Johnston of the 5th Regiment, before its hearings began, was so "cavalierly" treated that on the 13th he refused to come again to Trenton unless peremptorily ordered by Wayne. Colonel Craig of the 3rd was threatened by his men with their firelocks. Colonel Proctor of the artillery was not permitted to come forward with his enlistment papers, "my men knowing," he said, "the tenor of their enlistments" was for the war. Colonel James Chambers of the 1st was "very particularly dissatisfied," a spy reported to the British. Walter Stewart of the 2nd warned his men that he would prosecute all who perjured themselves. At some time during this week or the next angry men even "fired on General Wayne's quarters one evening, but happily without any damage."

On the 16th Colonel Atlee, chairman of the commissioners, reported to Reed that the arms of the 1st and 2nd, and the four fieldpieces of the artillery, had been loaded at Bordentown on a schooner which was to remove them to Philadelphia. Some of the soldiers of the 3rd assembled at the wharf to prevent the sailing, and the commissioners were obliged to go and disperse the mob. They sent for the Board of Sergeants, who were "very submissive and wishing to be dissolved." It was the commissioners, not the sergeants, who now thought it best to continue the Board, "for the sake of some order." The sergeants promised to give the rioters up.

The turmoil in Trenton cannot be ascribed wholly, or anything like wholly, to the misbehavior of the soldiers. To say nothing of the grievances which they had for years borne without redress, there was mismanagement on the part of the officials. Philadelphia did not send money enough to give the men their month's pay as fast as they were discharged, and instead of going off they hung about the camp. Nor could they, for want of money, be re-enlisted as a good many of them desired. "The soldiery are full," Wayne wrote to the Council on the 15th, "in the spirit of re-enlisting. Had we money and instructions we could improve it to great effect. On the contrary we shall lose the chief part of them." Wayne had heard that New Jersey officers were in Trenton, ready to "fill up their lines out of our discharged men." And General Irvine on the 17th reported to Washington that "many of the mutineers who are discharged are now pestering us to re-enlist them."

It was not to be expected that the men, so long mistreated and so often put off when they asked for redress, would now speedily re-enlist on the mere promise that they would some time be paid what was due them at once. They had risen in desperation and at great hazard, and were unwilling to throw away what they had contended for and had been newly granted. The perjurers among them deserved no consideration. But something like a third of the total were lawfully entitled to discharge and had sworn the truth or had conscientiously refused to swear at all. Most of these could have been re-enlisted, and the perjurers kept in the service, if the commissioners had waited a little longer to begin their investigation and if the Pennsylvania authorities had furnished the necessary and promised money a little sooner.

Pennsylvania was in distress for funds and apathetic towards the crisis in the Line. In Reed's absence the Council undertook to raise £15,000, or £20,000 if possible, in specie by popular subscription among the merchants and citizens, and encouraged Reed to think some such sum would be available. On his return he found that only £1400 had been actually subscribed. On January 15 he issued a proclamation, reciting the needs of the soldiers and officers and of the public treasury. "If, under these circumstances, those who are reaping the benefit of a protecting army and the security of civil government, and pursuing their own interest, will not assist the public with only a small portion of their stock on this emergency, they must expect and can only blame themselves for the consequences." Unless the subscription were completed, the Council would recommend "a general and total suspension of all foreign trade." This caused such an uproar among the merchants and citizens that the subscription was closed and the treasury left empty. The Council could only turn to the slow and complex business of selling further confiscated loyalist estates for what money could be got out of them.

Matters dragged on at Trenton, the men disappointed, the officers bitter, hitherto dispersed soldiers drifting in for their settlements. To the fifty shillings each man got on his discharge, when he got it, was added "one ration of provisions for every twenty miles" he would have to travel to his home, or "to see his friends." This was confirmed by a resolution of Congress on the 18th. It was intended both to get the discharged men out of the idle camp and to discourage them from going to visit the famous city of Philadelphia—and there possibly reiterate their disappointments and make fresh claims on other officials.

Wayne on the 21st summed up in a letter to Washington. "We have already discharged the chief part of the artillery, 1st, 2nd, 3rd, 4th, and 5th Regiments. I could wish that the commissioners had given time for the officers to produce the enlistments before they made the oath so common. The papers were collected the soonest possible, the enlistments generally and expressly for the war. But the birds were flown. I won't say that it might not be in some degree an act of expediency to get the artillery, spare ammunition, and part of the arms out of the mutineers' hands. These I have taken the precaution to forward by water to Philadelphia. . . .

"From present appearances we shall retain near two-thirds of the remaining regiments, the enlistments being generally come to hand." The retained or re-enlisted men were after their furlough to assemble at various places "on the Ides of March"—each rendezvous within the district from which most of the men of the various regiments had originally enlisted. The new arrangement, set for January 1 but postponed by the mutiny to the 17th, had been completed. Of the six regiments to which the eleven had been reduced, the 1st (Colonel Daniel Brodhead) and 2nd (Walter Stewart) would rendezvous at Philadelphia; the 3rd (Thomas Craig) at Reading; the 4th (William Butler) at Carlisle; the 5th (Richard Butler) at York; the 6th (Richard Humpton) at Lancaster.

"The recruiting service will commence in a few days under proper officers with very pointed instructions to guard against British deserters, etc. etc. and to lodge duplicates of the respective attestations in proper officers, to which appeals may be made should the portentous events of war or frequent removal of baggage occasion the loss of papers as heretofore.

"I am now fully convinced that there is no situation in life but what admits of some consolation. Ours at one period appeared very gloomy indeed. But more lucid and pleasing prospects begin to dawn. The soldiery are as impatient of liberty as they were of service, and are as importunate to be re-enlisted as they were to be discharged. Money is fast collecting for the purpose"—Wayne was too sanguine—"and I trust that a few weeks will put it into my power to announce to your Excellency a reclaimed and formidable Line.

"I shall not take up your Excellency's time, or hurt your feelings, by a picture of our situation, fatigue, and difficulty for these last twenty tedious days and nights. I shall only mention that we have not rolled in luxury or slept on beds of down." Reed, again at Trenton, was still irritating to the officers, though Wayne was not explicit. "An imprudent zeal yesterday from a certain quarter has not added to our repose or security. However, the storm is now abated, but not without some address attended with difficulty and danger. About five days more will put an end to this fatiguing business."

More Mutiny

GENERAL KNOX, going with Washington's circular letter to the New England officials, found them in distress for funds but anxiously aware that steps ought to be taken without delay to quiet the temper of their own Lines and prevent them from rising over grievances too much like those of the Pennsylvanians. The Connecticut legislature was not in session, and Governor Jonathan Trumbull hesitated to call it together for fear of disturbing the whole State. He thought a gratuity of twenty-four dollars would have a better effect on the soldiers than the three months' pay proposed by Washington. "The Governor," Knox reported to Washington, "pledged himself to exert his utmost interest to have the gratuity and deficiency of clothing given to the troops immediately; and requested me to impress on the governors and official gentlemen in the other States the necessity and propriety of New England adopting similar measures." Though the Rhode Island legislature also was not in session, that governor convened it for the 18th.

Both the Massachusetts and New Hampshire assemblies, then sitting, were so convinced by Washington's letter and Knox's arguments that Massachusetts on the 16th voted the gratuity and coats for noncommissioned officers and privates, and New Hampshire three days later made a like present to its soldiers "for their good services and the sufferings they have been unavoidably exposed to." Rhode Island chose somewhat different arrangements, but conformed in the amount of its gratuity. Connecticut alone of the four States put off action till the emergency was past, then voted only one "frock" (coat), two pairs of overalls, two linen shirts, two pairs of white cotton stockings, and two pairs of shoes to each man enlisted for three years or for the war.

Before any word of the New England measures could reach West Point, where most of the New England troops were quartered, twenty-two Massachusetts sergeants on the 17th submitted a memorial to Lieutenant Colonel Ebenezer Sprout respecting their privations and hardships.

"Honoured Sir: We the subscribers, of 2nd Massachusetts Regiment, being engaged in the service of the United States during the present war with Great Britain, being confident of the righteousness of the cause we are engaged in, would be very sorry to do or speak anything that might be detrimental to the same, or what might not contribute to our and our country's advancement; but would humbly beg leave to lay before your Honour the present grievances we labor under in this servitude, hoping for an address [redress].

"First: Our State bounty we have not as yet received, though been lawfully required and demanded;

"Secondly: Our wages we have been kept out of beyond all reason;

"Thirdly: Our clothing has certainly been kept from us (which is our due) either by disaffected men, or neglect of others. Be it as it will, we suffer for the same;

"Fourthly: Our provision is certainly extremely short, by what means we are unable to say; but this we know, it is inconsistent with human reason to think men can live on such allowances.

"We say no more than to humbly desire your Honour to have us righted in those points as far as in your power lies; and if your Honour pleases, would be glad of an answer to this.

"We beg leave to subscribe ourselves your obedient soldiers and humble servants, Jonathan Farnam, Sergeant Major," and the Sergeants Israel Gillitt, Nathaniel Frost, Silvanus Bardham, Moses Bolland, Elisha Bates, Thomas Doty, Jacob Leonard, Theodore Perkins, Joseph Lincoln, Timothy Mitchell, Reuben Mitchell, Ithamar Johnson, Daniel Lawrence, Ebenezer Richardson, Ephraim Pratt, Theodore Sprague, Moses Buck, John Dewey, James Bailey, Simeon Hayward, George Eliot.

There was no hint of mutiny in the petition, "conceived in decent terms and presented with respect," as Washington observed; and nothing to show that these sergeants would be unwilling to march against the mutineers. But Washington, in the uncertain times, thought "everything that looks like combination ought to be discountenanced." The memorial was forwarded to him on the 21st, the day on which news came that the New Jersey Continental troops had followed the Pennsylvania Line into mutiny.

II

To tell the story of the origin and progress and outbreak of the New Jersey discontents would be largely to repeat the Pennsylvania story on a smaller scale. In the first year of the war New Jersey battalions went with the expedition to Canada. New Jersey regiments newly organized in 1777 fought at Brandywine and Germantown, lived through the hard months at Valley Forge, fought again at Monmouth, served with Sullivan against the Iroquois in 1779, spent the next winter at Morristown, distinguished themselves against the enemy incursion of June, and thereafter remained generally in New Jersey, facing the British across the water in New York. During most of their history there were three regiments, after 1780 reduced to two. About five hundred New Jersey soldiers settled into winter quarters at Pompton at the end of November 1780, with a detachment at Suffern to guard the line of communications between Washington's forces at West Point and the rest of his Army. Since there was no general officer at Pompton, the post was subject to Wayne's command.

In personnel the New Jersey troops were much like those of Pennsylvania, with more foreign-born enlisted men than were common in New England regiments. Invading and defending armies had tramped back and forth across New Jersey so long and often that its fighting men chose when possible to serve in the militia for the defense of their homes. The State had been able to keep up something like its Continental quota only by paying high bounties and enrolling soldiers of mixed types and nationalities. By reason of the heavy damage done by the war to the people of New Jersey, they found it doubly hard to support their Continental troops, either officers or men, who by the time of the Pennsylvania mutiny had accumulated many real grievances.

The Jersey brigade was by turns lively and sullen. On May Day after Valley Forge they had taken a hilarious part in the ceremonies in honor of St. Tammany. "The day was spent," according to Ensign George Ewing of the 3rd New Jersey, "in mirth and jollity, the soldiers parading with fife and drum and huzzaing as they passed the [May] poles, their hats adorned with white blossoms. The following was the procession of the 3rd Regiment on the aforesaid day: first, one sergeant dressed in an Indian habit representing King Tammany; second, thirteen sergeants dressed in white, each with a bow in his left hand and thirteen arrows in his right; thirdly, thirteen drums and fifes; fourthly, the privates in thirteen platoons, thirteen men each." All this, and even "a drink of whisky which a generous contribution of their officers had procured for them," was "carried out without any accident happening the whole day, the whole being carried on with the greatest regularity."

But now in winter quarters at Pompton the men were resentful and muttering. Though like the Pennsylvanians they made no complaints about their huts, some of these had been built outside the lines of the camp and were scenes of disorder. The women were said to be badly behaved, persistent in selling liquor to the men, who somehow contrived to find money for that. The food was as unsatisfactory as at Mount Kemble, the clothing nearly as deficient. While the ladies of Philadelphia were making shirts for Pennsylvania soldiers, the ladies of Trenton were knitting stockings for New Jersey soldiers. Mary Dagworthy on December 29 wrote Washington that 380 pairs of stockings were on their way. The Trenton stockings like the Philadelphia shirts arrived too late.

At Pompton there were the same complaints as at Mount Kemble about lack of pay and loss by depreciation, more or less the same dispute over enlistments. Some of the papers were in such confusion that an officer might produce what seemed positive proof that a soldier was enlisted for the war, the soldier produce proof as positive that he was enlisted for three years. The officers themselves were so disgruntled over lack of pay as to be near to resignation if not rebellion. The tone at Pompton was bad and threatening.

Yet there is no particular reason to think mutiny would have come to Pompton without the example of the Pennsylvanians. The news of the outbreak could not be kept from the New Jersey Line. Detachments were on Wayne's orders marched at once to Chatham, to try to prevent any movement of the Pennsylvania mutineers towards the British; and to

Mount Kemble, to keep order among the Pennsylvania troops left behind. The detachment at Mount Kemble, too restless to be trusted there, had to be moved to Chatham to join the larger and quieter body commanded by the very able Colonel Dayton of the 3rd, who looked like Washington and who Washington wished might be made a brigadier general. At Pompton Colonel Israel Shreve of the 2nd was in command: immensely fat, discouraged over the dreary progress of the war and the poverty to which he had been brought by his long service. There was no possible question as to his loyalty. Neither was there, in Washington's mind, any question as to Shreve's incompetence. "Here I drop the curtain," Washington had written in December, over the prospect that Shreve might have to be promoted.

The New Jersey legislature, in session at Trenton when the Pennsylvania mutineers came so ominously close, passed hurried acts to satisfy the New Jersey Line by making up the men's depreciation losses and by fixing a new bounty for recruiting volunteers. Lord Stirling, in a letter to Washington on January 7, hoped this legislation would "keep that body of men in such good humor as will be of use in quelling the mutineers of the Pennsylvania Line." But it was soon evident that the New Jersey soldiers were sympathetic towards the mutiny and could not be safely ordered to suppress it. And when they heard of the terms of settlement at Princeton and Trenton they were roused to a mood of emulation. Paid the first part of their depreciation money between the 15th and 20th, a good many promptly "disguised" themselves with liquor.

Reports on their state of mind went steadily by spies to New York. An unknown correspondent wrote on the 8th that "the Jersey brigade have stuck up libels [handbills] at their officers' quarters intimating their intention of pursuing the same steps as the Pennsylvanians. The flame is general. For Heaven's sake, keep it alive." On the 15th Woodruff came in with the news that he had been at Chatham when Dayton read an order to his men promising them forty pounds in new State money to make up their losses. "A very few obeyed his order to shoulder. . . . He was very much disconcerted and did not know what to do. They are naked and barefooted." Cornelius Hatfield that same day brought further news from Chatham: "Colonel Dayton had spread a report that the Pennsylvanians had made up matters, on which his own people of the Jersey brigade made the same demands. He was obliged to contradict the report to quiet them." Captain Gifford on the 18th wrote: "The detachment at Chatham is much dissatisfied, also the rest of them at Pompton. Parson Caldwell," by whom Gifford meant the Reverend James Caldwell of Elizabethtown whom the legislature had sent to Chatham to begin redressing the Line's grievances, "is now paying twenty dollars of this new trash to each officer, and five to each private. This is a present from the State."

The actual outbreak came at Pompton, after Colonel Frederick Frelinghuysen of the Jersey militia had gone there as commissioner. Late in the afternoon of Saturday the 20th a woman of the camp went to Colonel Shreve and told him that the men were rising and intended to leave their huts. He "immediately ordered all the men off duty to be paraded, with the design to detach them in different parties for the night; but found very few that would turn out." There was no violence, and nobody was hurt, either officer or soldier. But they could not be stopped. When they marched off, Shreve understood they were going to Trenton and feared the troops at Chatham would accompany them. He followed the disorderly march to Chatham.

The ranking leader of the Pompton revolt was Sergeant Major George Grant of what before the new arrangement had been the 3rd New Jersey. His part in the business is obscure. Though he was at the time called a deserter from the British, he had been a soldier of the Line for at least four years, and a sergeant major as early as 1779. On Sullivan's expedition against the Iroquois Grant kept a valuable journal. His remark about "a fine cataract, as handsome as I ever saw in Europe," may mean that he was not American-born and had formerly served in the British Army. He wrote his journal entries like a good soldier and closed with a patriotic tribute in verse to Sullivan, Brigadier General James Clinton, and even to Wayne, who had not gone with the others but whose name furnished a useful rhyme.

> Here ends the glorious and noble campaign
> Which gave honor to Sullivan, Clinton, and Wayne;
> That they be always crowned with merit
> To lead their men on with undaunted spirit.

Nothing in Grant's record makes him sound like a disaffected instigator of the mutiny. It later came out that he had been compelled by the men to assume command and had done his best to restore them to order. It is even possible that there was some understanding in advance between Grant and Colonel Shreve. And there may have been some understanding between Shreve and Sergeant Jonathan Nichols of the 1st and Sergeant Major John Minthorn, also of the 1st, reported in New York to be second and third in command.

Dayton at Chatham heard that the Pompton mutineers were coming and at once got as many of his own men out of camp as he could send away on detail or furlough on such short notice. The men from Pompton arrived on Sunday and were joined by some of the Chatham men. For two days there was turbulence. On the 23rd Dayton and the commissioners from the legislature collected the revolters, told them what measures had been taken for their relief, and promised that as soon as they stopped their mutinous behavior they would be settled with. The mutineers insisted that their oaths be taken as proof of their enlistments, as with the Pennsylvanians. This was refused, "and they finally gave it up." The sergeants drew up a petition for a general pardon. Dayton, with the agreement of the commissioners, offered a form of pardon which the men might take or leave. Since they had risen before they knew what was being done to meet their demands, and since on learning of this they had consented to become orderly again, and since they had "neither shed blood nor done violence to any officer or inhabitant; he hereby promises a pardon to all such as immediately without hesitation shall return to their duty and conduct themselves in a soldierly manner. Those who shall, notwithstanding this unmerited proffer of clemency, refuse obedience, must expect the reward due to such obstinate villainy."

When the form of pardon was read to the revolted men they gave three cheers and seemed to be satisfied. The next day they set out, under Shreve's command, for their huts at Pompton, promising to accept the other officers who had remained there. Not many of the Chatham troops appear to have joined the mutineers, nor all of them to have returned to Pompton with the two hundred who went.

III

The first news of the New Jersey mutiny reached New York after McFarlan on the 20th and Caleb Bruen on the 21st returned by roundabout ways from Trenton with a convincing report that Mason and Ogden had been hanged. If the Pennsylvanians had made peace, there was little chance that the less numerous Jersey mutineers would hold out. But Gould and Woodruff, both coming in on the 22nd, brought circumstantial accounts that could not be altogether overlooked. Gould had, he said, talked with some of the mutineers, who said they intended to come to Elizabethtown. Woodruff said that Nichols, a leader in the uprising, was "a cousin of his." Though Clinton took little interest in the Jersey revolt, he permitted Robertson to go to Staten Island, and De Lancey to accompany Robertson and resume the operations of the secret service.

Again De Lancey's information was belated and inaccurate. On the 25th, the day after the more or less pacified mutineers left Chatham for Pompton, word came that they were "in a state of mutiny still at Chatham." De Lancey drew up two communications, one to "the person commanding the Jersey troops," one to "the Jersey brigade."

"If you wish to join the British troops with the brigade under your command," the first letter said, "we promise to pay you what is due by Congress besides an ample recompense to you individually for the active part you have taken. Should you accept our offer we recommend it to you to take post as soon as possible at Elizabethtown, where people properly authorized shall treat with you and settle the terms you may think necessary; and whenever you call for it a body of British troops shall be sent to support you." It is not certain that this was ever sent.

"Whatever the Jersey troops mean to do, it had better be soon," the second letter said. "If they will put themselves under the protection of the British government they shall receive in hard money the arrears of pay due to them by Congress and pardon for all former offenses without expectation of military service except it may be voluntary. If they choose to accept these liberal offers they had better take post at Elizabethtown, where we will treat with whoever they shall appoint for that purpose; and whenever they ask it they shall be supported by a body of British troops.

"The disappointment of the Pennsylvanians is a sufficient proof the Congress is unwilling as well as unable to redress them, and that in all this time they have only amused [misled] them in hopes of an opportunity to overpower them.

"This comes from sufficient authority to insure the performance of the above proposals."

"I sent out two copies of the inclosed proposals," De Lancey wrote from Staten Island to Sir Henry Clinton, "and shall send out some more, though without much hopes of success." One copy went by Woodruff, another by the unidentified Blank.

20

Suppression at Pompton

AT NEW WINDSOR, to which news of the Jersey outbreak came about ten o'clock on the evening of Sunday the 21st, there was no hesitation or fumbling. Washington "determined at all hazards to put a stop to such proceedings, which must otherwise prove the inevitable dissolution of the Army." General Heath at West Point was ordered to detach "five or six hundred of the most robust and best clothed men, properly officered and provided" for a march to New Jersey. To Shreve at Pompton, or wherever he might be when the letter reached him, Washington wrote that he was immediately sending soldiers to quell the mutiny. "I am to desire you will endeavor to collect all those of your regiments who have had virtue enough to resist the pernicious example of their associates. If the revolt has not become general, and if you have force enough to do it, I wish you to compel the mutineers to unconditional submission. The more decisively you are able to act the better."

Washington urged Colonel Frelinghuysen, commissioner at Pompton, "to employ all your influence to inspire the militia with a disposition to cooperate with us, by representing the fatal consequences of the present temper of the soldiery, not only to military subordination but to civil liberty. In reality both are fundamentally struck at by their undertaking in arms to dictate terms to their country." Here Washington addressed himself to Frelinghuysen as a militia officer rather than as a legislative official, but the letter made it plain that the civil authorities were asked to leave the settlement to the military. The point was explicit in Washington's letter to John Sullivan, of the Committee of Congress appointed to deal with the Pennsylvanians. For all Washington knew, the Committee might again be assigned to mutiny affairs. Briefly announcing the measures he meant to take against the insurgents, he concluded: "I beg leave strongly to recommend that no terms may be made with them."

This second mutiny was in several respects different from the first. The Pennsylvanians at the outset had been superior to any force that could be brought against them, and had since then been settled with and pardoned. The New Jersey mutineers were weaker both in numbers and in grievances. Instead of rising spontaneously, they had waited to see how the Pennsylvania experiment would turn out, and then had imitated it—but not till after the New Jersey legislature had taken steps to meet their own demands. The men at Princeton had come to terms. The men at Pompton, even before they fully knew what their terms were to be, had broken off preliminary negotiations and resorted to arms. They were not likely, in the circumstances, to have the sympathy of the public. But there was a chance that their contumacious example—added to the Pennsylvanians'—might have an even worse influence. To prevent that, Washington believed he must strike hard and instantly. "It is difficult to say what part the troops sent to quell the revolt will act," he wrote to Congress, "but I thought it indispensable to bring the matter to an issue and risk all extremities. Unless this dangerous spirit can be suppressed by force there is an end to all subordination in the Army, and indeed to the Army itself."

On the morning of the 22nd he went to West Point to complete and expedite his plans. The Massachusetts troops under Lieutenant Colonel Sprout were to march from their huts back of West Point, by way of the Forest of Dean and The Clove to Ringwood. There was already a detachment of a hundred Connecticut troops guarding the Ringwood magazine in command of Major Benjamin Throop, who would be joined by other men of his Line from the east side of the Hudson. The New Hampshire detachment under Major Amos Morrill would go, like the Connecticut re-enforcements, down to King's Ferry, there cross the river to Stony Point, and proceed to Ringwood by Suffern. Three fieldpieces from the artillery park at Murderer's Creek near New Windsor would follow as rapidly as possible. The assembled force would act under orders from General Robert Howe, to whom Washington gave stern instructions.

"You are to take command of the detachment which has been ordered to march from this post against the mutineers of the Jersey Line. You will rendezvous the whole of your command at Ringwood or Pompton as you find best from circumstances. The object of your detachment is to compel the mutineers to unconditional submission, and I am to desire you will grant no terms while they are with arms in their hands in a state of resistance. The manner of executing this I leave in your discretion according to circumstances. If you succeed in compelling the revolted troops to a surrender, you will instantly execute a few of the most active and most incendiary leaders."

Small as the detachment was, there were such delays in obtaining the needed horses, wagons, tents, axes, and entrenching tools that only the Massachusetts men were ready on Tuesday the 23rd, after a night of heavy snow.

That day they got to the Forest of Dean, "and at night

crowded into houses and barns," according to Dr. James Thacher. "A body of snow about two feet deep, without any track, rendered the march extremely difficult. Having no horse, I experienced inexpressible fatigue and was obliged several times to sit down on the snow. 24th, marched over the mountains and reached Carle's tavern in Smith's Clove, halted for two hours, then proceeded thirteen miles and quartered our men in the scattering houses and barns. 25th, marched nine miles and reached Ringwood. General Howe and all the field officers took lodgings at the house of Mrs. [Robert] Erskine, the amiable widow of the late respectable geographer of our Army"—who had died the past October. "We were entertained with an elegant supper and excellent wine. Mrs. Erskine is a sensible and accomplished woman, lives in a style of affluence and fashion; everything indicates wealth, taste, and splendor; and she takes pleasure in entertaining the friends of her late husband with generous hospitality." The men were quartered in the houses and barns of the village and of the neighboring farms.

Waiting for artillery and re-enforcements to catch up with him, Howe that evening reported to Washington, who still knew no more about the mutiny than that the Jersey troops had left Pompton saying they would go to Trenton. Howe had learned "with certainty" that they had halted at Chatham, "and from thence are said to be returning to their huts" at Pompton, "where they mean to negotiate; for though they profess to be inclined to open a treaty, they have by no means adopted those subordinate ideas which alone can give existence to military discipline or atone for offenses incapable of exaggeration. I have sent officers to Colonels Shreve"—now at Pompton—"and Dayton"—still at Chatham —"requesting them to suspend all kinds of negotiation farther than to amuse": that is, to let the men think they were negotiating while in fact uncompromising measures to suppress them were being put in readiness.

Some time that evening or night an officer came from Shreve, and Howe at seven the next morning added a postscript to his letter. "The mutineers have so far returned to duty as to permit their officers to take command of them and came to their huts last night; but with this condition, that a committee is to sit on Tuesday"—the 30th—"for the purpose of inquiring into their grievances and to discharge those men who can prove they were enlisted for a less time than during the war. In short, though I cannot properly understand the terms proposed, I understand enough to think that it is but little better than the second part of the Pennsylvania tune, which I by no means am inclined to dance to. And unless you should forbid my taking measures to act . . . in conformity with the orders given me at parting, I persuade myself I shall bring this matter to a conclusion in a manner more consistent with your Excellency's wishes and the principles of service than the committee can do, and that in my opinion without much trouble or bloodshed."

When Howe wrote his postscript Washington was already setting out for New Windsor in a sleigh, with his guard and a few officers including Lafayette. Still unaware of what had happened since the uprising at Pompton, and full of perturbation over the crisis in the Army, Washington had decided to go to Ringwood in order to be "convenient" with advice and command if special difficulties should arise. Lafayette accompanied him in the belief that the British might be coming out and some kind of force have to be organized against them. By midnight Washington was at Ringwood and had conferred with Howe before the detachment, an hour later, moved off through the dark towards the Pompton huts eight miles away.

II

There was no need to stiffen Howe in his determination. He had positive instructions and he detested military disorder. He had been unable to consult with Dayton, whom illness kept at Chatham, or with Shreve, who stayed out of sight during the entire episode but sent Lieutenant Colonel Barber with as much information as Howe required. Barber, at Chatham when the mutineers were there, had information of his own, and was an officer of force and judgment. The mutineers had been promised pardon, by Dayton, if they would immediately "return to their duty and conduct themselves in a soldierly manner." But on their return to Pompton they had become turbulent again. "Though in some respects they would suffer a few particular officers to have influence over them, yet it was by no means the case in general, and what they did do, appeared rather like following advice than obeying command. . . . They condescended once to parade when ordered, but were no sooner dismissed than several officers were insulted. One had a bayonet put to his breast; and upon the man's being knocked down for his insolence, a musket was fired, which being their alarm signal, most of them paraded in arms."

The Jersey officers seem to have agreed, and to have explained to Howe, that the original leaders, Grant, Nichols, and Minthorn, had not been to blame for the later conduct of the mutineers and should not be punished—though Grant, as their official chief, might in form be listed among the principal offenders. The most incendiary agitators were Sergeant David Gilmore (Gilmour) of the 2nd, and John Tuttle of the 1st.

Howe's detachment, marching silently through the snow

SUPPRESSION AT POMPTON   221

in the night, arrived "in view of the huts of the insurgent soldiers" before daybreak, as Dr. Thacher continued his story. "Here we halted for an hour to make the necessary preparations. Some of our officers suffered much anxiety, lest the soldiers should not prove faithful on this trying occasion. Orders were given to load their arms. It was obeyed with alacrity, and indications were given that they were to be relied on. Being paraded in a line, General Howe harangued them, representing the heinousness of the crime of mutiny, and the absolute necessity of military subordination, adding that the mutineers must be brought to an unconditional submission, no temporizing, no listening to terms of compromise, while in a state of resistance."

Some of the sergeants of the 2nd Massachusetts who had ten days before asked for a redress of their grievances stood there on that raw Saturday morning. The Massachusetts rank and file had lived in tents throughout December, "miserably clad" and "obliged to bring all the wood for themselves and officers, on their backs, from a place a mile distant . . . almost half the time . . . kept on half allowance of bread, and entirely without rum," after "twelve or fourteen months" without any of the pay due them. The Connecticut and New Hampshire men had suffered similar hardships. Now these New England troops were faced with the duty of compelling, even killing, men who had revolted in protest against their sufferings. In the hard conflict between sympathy for their comrades and duty to their country the troops from West Point neither complained nor held back.

Howe divided his force to surround the camp of the mutineers, who were outnumbered three to one, with parties of Massachusetts men on the right (with two fieldpieces), on the left (with another fieldpiece), and in front; with the

Connecticut men in the rear; and with the New Hampshire men posted on the road to Charlottenburg in case any of the revolters should try to escape in that direction.

"Thus was every avenue secured," Howe afterwards reported to Washington, "and in this position the mutineers found us when daylight appeared. Colonel Barber of the Jersey Line was sent to them with orders immediately to parade without arms, and to march to the ground pointed out for them. Some seemed willing to comply, but others exclaimed: 'What! No conditions? Then if we are to die, it is as well to die where we are as anywhere else.' Some hesitation happening among them, Colonel Sprout"—leading the Massachusetts party on the left—"was directed to advance, and only five minutes were given the mutineers to comply with the orders which had been sent to them. This had its effect, and they to a man marched without arms to the ground appointed for them. The Jersey officers gave a list of those whom they thought the most atrocious offenders, upon which I desired them to select three (one of each regiment), which was accordingly done." (Colonel Shreve, who had helped name the offenders, was not present, "as those who suffered might look up to me for to intercede for their pardon." Or so he the next day lamely explained to Washington, who thought Shreve's absence from his post of duty "so extraordinary" as to call for explanation.)

Dr. Thacher, who had described one execution ceremony at Morristown eight months before, now described another. "These unfortunate culprits were tried on the spot, Colonel Sprout being president of the court martial, standing on the snow, and they were sentenced to be immediately shot. Twelve of the most guilty mutineers were next selected to be their executioners. This was a most painful task; being themselves guilty, they were greatly distressed with the duty imposed upon them, and when ordered to load some of them shed tears. The wretched victims, overwhelmed by the terrors of death, had neither time nor power to implore the mercy and forgiveness of their God, and such was their agonizing condition that no heart could refrain from emotions of sympathy and compassion. The first that suffered was a sergeant [Gilmore] and an old offender. He was led a few yards distance and placed on his knees. Six of the executioners, at the signal given by an officer, fired, three aiming at the head and three at the breast, the other six reserving their fire in order to dispatch the victim should the first fire fail. It so happened in this instance. The remaining six then fired, and life was instantly extinguished. The second criminal [Tuttle] was, by the first fire, sent into eternity in an instant. The third being less criminal, by the recommendation of his officers, to his unspeakable joy, received a pardon." This was George Grant, sergeant major, diarist, and versifier, about whom it is tempting to guess that he may have been privately told by Shreve not to worry over the trial and sentence. Grant lived to fight at Yorktown.

"After the execution," according to Howe again, "the officers were ordered to parade the men regimentally, and to divide them into platoons, each officer to take his platoon. In this situation they were directed to make, and they made, proper concessions to their officers, in the face of the troops, and promised by future good conduct to atone for past offenses. I then spoke to them by platoons, representing to them, in the strongest terms I was capable of, the heinousness of their guilt, as well as the folly of it, in the outrage they had offered to that civil authority to which they owed obedience and which it was their incumbent duty to support and maintain. They showed the fullest sense of their guilt and such strong marks of contrition that I think I may venture to pledge myself for their future good conduct."

III

It does not appear that emissaries from the British got to Pompton before the affair was settled. At Chatham they had a chance to learn that the mutineers, according to a contemporary newspaper, had "adopted a solemn resolution to put to death any one who should attempt or even propose to go to the enemy's lines, and hang up without ceremony every Tory who should presume to say a word tending to induce any of them to do so." In the circumstances no emissary would feel it safe to go on with his dangerous papers, or even to keep them on his person. A spy reported to the British that "some papers were dropped in camp and two people suspected for having dropped them: one Blanck and. . . . The contents are kept secret." This was at Chatham on the 27th. And there on that day Uzal Woodruff revealed himself to Colonel Dayton and gave up his proposals.

Woodruff at eighteen, in 1762, had run away from his apprenticeship to a shoemaker in Elizabethtown, and had later served in the Essex County militia and for a time in the short-lived 4th New Jersey. He had a large family connection in or near Elizabethtown and Westfield. A kinsman, Isaac Woodruff, was the patriotic and energetic mayor of Elizabethtown at the time of the mutinies. Uzal Woodruff, who after the war operated a ferry between Elizabeth Point and New York and died in March 1794, during the war made more furtive trips over the same course. On this trip, finding himself suspected at Chatham, he went to Colonel Dayton, an Elizabethtown man, and betrayed the British.

Sir,   Chatham Jan'y 27. 1781.

I have this moment received certain intelligence, that Lieu't General Robinson landed yesterday upon Staten Island with about three thousand troops, he appears determined to land in Jersey, in expectation of great part of our revolters joyning him. I am apprehensive Gen'l Robinson will certainly attempt something, as he publicly condemns General Clinton's conduct in not landing here to support the Pennsylvania mutineers. Several emissarys were sent from New York three times to drop papers in the Jersey Camp containing offers from Gen'l Clinton of large rewards to all soldiers who will repair to the British troops upon their landing at Elizabeth Town.

I have my fears, as things are situated at this time; the enemy may attempt our stores at Morris Town; especially as they express a great desire to burn that place. I should do myself the honor of waiting on you in person would my health permit.

I am sir your most
Humble Serv't
Elias Dayton.

ELIAS DAYTON TO ROBERT HOWE

Facsimile of an unpublished letter from Dayton, January 27, 1781, announcing that British emissaries had been sent to the New Jersey mutineers.

Dayton on the 27th wrote to Howe that several emissaries had been sent out "three days since" and that General Robertson was on Staten Island determined to invade New Jersey instead of missing an opportunity as Clinton had done with the Pennsylvania mutineers. Approved, if not wholly trusted by Dayton, Woodruff for a few weeks played patriot, though he also reported to the British that he was "very intimate with Dayton and several other rebel officers." But Woodruff was found out by the British and joined Caleb Bruen in the Sugar House.

Gautier, to whom Woodruff and Gould carried notes asking for information, reported in considerable detail and with considerable accuracy. "You may be assured the Jersey troops knew of the terms offered to you by the Pennsylvanians, but I don't think they had it in view to come to you. They are so connected by relationship in this country that nothing but a total despair of redress of grievances would induce them to come over to you." Though Gautier had been hindered by the mutiny from going to New Windsor, as he had expected, "to procure a list of the general officers and their families [staffs]," he still supposed that a few weeks would furnish him "with many material matters of intelligence, which I shall faithfully communicate." For the present, he had "particular occasion for twenty-five guineas" which he wished De Lancey would transmit as soon as convenient through Isaac Ogden. Ogden was a Newark refugee who had been greatly excited during the Pennsylvania mutiny and had busied himself in New York with arranging intelligence from New Jersey.

Even after the suppression of the Jersey mutineers and the interception of the British proposals to them, the Americans were for a few days concerned over a possible invasion from Staten Island. "Our troops are quelled completely,"

Barber wrote from Pompton to Dayton on the 28th, "but God knows what effect this movement of the enemy may have upon them." Washington, back at New Windsor on the 28th, the next day requested Howe to leave the New Hampshire men and the artillery in the neighborhood of Pompton, and the Connecticut detachment at Ringwood. "For fear of a revival of the discontents in the Jersey Line, I think it advisable there should remain near them other troops on whose fidelity we can more perfectly rely." Howe, finding his men much fatigued and "out of provision," and imagining that "the enemy upon hearing of the event of the 27th will parade over to York Island again," returned with the Massachusetts troops and the artillery to West Point.

General Orders on the 30th thanked Howe and his detachment for what they had done. It had given Washington "inexpressible pain to have been obliged to employ their arms upon such an occasion," when they must have "felt all the reluctance which former affection to fellow-soldiers could inspire. He considers the patience with which they endured the march through rough and mountainous roads, rendered almost impassable by the depth of the snow, and the cheerfulness with which they performed every part of their duty, as the strongest proof of their fidelity, attachment to the service, sense of subordination, and abhorrence of the principles which actuated the mutineers in so daring a departure from what they owed to their country, to their officers, to their oaths, and to themselves.

"The General is deeply sensible of the sufferings of the Army. He leaves no expedient unessayed to relieve them, and he is persuaded Congress and the several States are doing everything in their power for the same purpose. But while we look to the public for the fulfillment of its engagements, we should do it with proper allowance for the embarrassments of public affairs. We began a contest for liberty and independence ill provided with the means for war, relying on our own patriotism to supply the deficiency. We expected to encounter many wants and distresses; and we should neither shrink from them when they happen nor fly in the face of law and government to procure redress. There is no doubt the public will in the event do ample justice to men fighting and suffering in its defense. But it is our duty to bear present evils with fortitude, looking forward to the period when our country will have it more in its power to reward our services.

"History is full of examples of armies suffering with patience extremities of distress which exceed those we have suffered, and this in the cause of ambition and conquest, not in that of the rights of humanity, of their country, or their families, of themselves. Shall we who aspire to the distinction of a patriot army, who are contending for everything precious in society against everything hateful and degrading in slavery; shall we who call ourselves citizens discover less constancy and military virtue than the mercenary instruments of ambition? Those who in the present instance have stained the honor of the American soldiery and sullied the reputation of patient virtue for which they have been so long eminent, can only atone for the pusillanimous defection by a life devoted to a zealous and exemplary discharge of their duty. Persuaded that the greater part were actuated by the pernicious advice of a few who probably have been paid by the enemy to betray their associates, the General is happy in the lenity shown in the execution of only two of the most guilty after compelling the whole to an unconditional surrender. And he flatters himself no similar instance will hereafter disgrace our military history."

21

Conclusions

ON JANUARY 27 Sir Henry Clinton heard, from a loyalist who had been at Trenton, that the Pennsylvania sergeants were still in authority there with about five hundred of the mutineers who refused to leave. One of the sergeants had asked to be remembered to Clinton, and another had accepted a dollar to drink the King's health, the loyalist said. For a day or so Clinton, though not hopeful about the Jersey revolt, thought the remaining Pennsylvanians might after all join the British, if he could send them word to come to some point on the coast in Monmouth County, "from whence our boats and vessels can easily bring them off." The scheme seems to have gone no further than a brief thought, and on the 29th Clinton made his final report to his government about the four weeks of mutiny.

He had been informed that "upwards of 1300" Pennsylvanians had been discharged and gone home with certificates for the pay due them. From what he knew about the circumstances of the rebels generally, he had expected that other corps would make demands. Now he took pleasure in reporting that he had not been disappointed in his expectations. The New Jersey troops also had revolted and had been promptly granted the same terms. Clinton did not yet know of the suppression at Pompton, and so assumed that "the discharge of the Jersey brigade will be in proportion to that of the Pennsylvania Line."

On the whole this seemed a promising outcome. The mutineers had plainly made up their minds "not to serve again as soldiers; which makes it evident that nothing but coercive measures or gross chicane on the part of Congress could have induced those malcontents to join us. General Washington will lose near two-thirds of the troops that have mutinied. Those who are discharged will probably never re-enlist." Their example, Clinton was sure, would be remembered by all the rebel soldiers. And if there should be delay or failure in the payment of their certificates, "which certainly will happen, it will occasion murmurs and discontents that will naturally incline them to join our numerous friends in the back parts of these provinces."

Clinton was as right about the mutineers' unwillingness to enter the British service as he was wrong about their future inclination to turn instead to the frontier loyalists who represented themselves, in frequent letters to Clinton, as very numerous and more than ready to rise against the tyranny of the rebel government.

Washington that same day wrote to the Comte de Rochambeau, commanding the French allied troops at Newport, that the Jersey matter had been settled. "I believe I may venture to assure your Excellency that the spirit of mutiny is now completely subdued and will not again show itself." But in another letter of the 29th, to the New England governors, Washington did not go so far in his assurances. "I hope this will completely extinguish the spirit of mutiny, if effective measures are taken to prevent its revival by rendering the situation of the soldiery more tolerable than it has heretofore been." Neither civil appeasement, as with the Pennsylvanians, nor military suppression, as with the New Jersey men, could have a lasting effect unless the soldiers were to be fed, clothed, and paid.

Lafayette, writing on the 30th to the French minister of

foreign affairs, regretted the mutinies but insisted that the American Army as a whole was still virtuous and heroic. "The Continental troops have as much courage and true discipline as their opponents. They are more hardened and patient than the Europeans, who are not, in respect of these two qualities, to be compared to them." But money was wanting to "draw out the American resources" and restore the Army to activity for the coming campaign. "The prospect of the American soldier being hunger, cold, nakedness, toil, the certainty of receiving neither pay, clothes, nor necessary food, it must be uninviting enough for the citizens, most of whom live at home in a state of comfort." Though the Pennsylvania troops, "almost entirely composed of foreigners" as Lafayette continued to believe, had mutinied, it was only after their grievances had gone to "extremities which would not be borne in any army." The Jersey mutiny had been put down by "the troops of New England, nearly all nationals, whose cause was at bottom the same. . . . This proves, M. le Comte, that human patience has its limits, but also that the citizen soldiers are much more patient than the foreigners." Most of the American soldiers were these same patient citizens.

II

This story is history, which goes on after crucial episodes, not drama, which ends with them. After the mutinies the soldiers of the Pennsylvania and New Jersey Lines were still men who had to have, and were entitled to, food, clothing, and pay. If the public did not keep its word to them, their grievances could grow again.

The Orderly Book of the Jersey brigade at Pompton let the mutiny days January 20-25 pass without an entry and

CONCLUSIONS 231

then on the 26th took up the record in dim, uncertain ink. After the executions on the morning of the 27th the orders were at once rigorous. "A police officer from each regiment will be appointed in future and strictly attend to their duty. No officer to sleep out of camp on any pretence except such whose circumstances require it. No noncommissioned officer or soldier to be absent except by a written permission from the commanding officer of his regiment. Any woman who shall presume to sell any liquors shall be severely punished. And the brigade sutler will not sell any liquor to any noncommissioned officer or soldier without a written permission from the officers commanding companies." On the 28th: "All those huts that have been built without permission from the commanding officers of regiments are to be brought within the encampment within three days, or they will be used for firewood." On the 30th: "No sutler or other person within two miles of camp shall sell strong liquor or other strong drink during the sitting of the commissioners at camp." On February 5th: "Whereas by representation, some women of the brigade have behaved in the most infamous manner, they may be assured that upon the first complaints made against them, their rations will be stopped and they banished the camp."

The commissioners settled the New Jersey enlistments without the loss of many men. Shreve retired from the Army to his farm. The troops were moved from Pompton to the Pennsylvania huts at Mount Kemble, where during Dayton's illness Barber was temporarily in command. Almost at once the Line was called upon for a detachment to go with troops from West Point in the light corps sent under Lafayette against Arnold in Virginia. Barber led the New Jersey detachment, with a dozen other officers and 148 men. On the second day of the march, at Princeton on February 27 exactly one month after the shootings at Pompton, "the Jersey troops . . . created a small riot with the Eastern troops," Barber reported to Dayton. "The grudge occasioned by the late subduction was the leading motive." Barber's men were "clamorous about their money, meaning the fourth part of their depreciation" which was due March 1, and threatened not to march unless they got it. "From being almost the most orderly and subordinate soldiers in the Army, they are become a set of drunken and unworthy fellows. The situation of an officer among them is rendered more disagreeable than any other calling in life, even the most menial, can possibly be." The resentment against the New England troops persisted, but the New Jersey detachment bore itself well in the field and, like the rest of the New Jersey Line which went south in August, behaved with spirit at the siege of Yorktown.

The course of the Pennsylvania Line to Virginia was delayed and roundabout. On January 29 Wayne reported to Washington that the work of settlement at Trenton was done. About 1250 men had been discharged "out of the aggregate of the infantry, and 67 of the artillery, so that we may count upon nearly 1150 remaining." The noncommissioned officers, "except recruiting sergeants and music," had been sent on furlough along with the men—including the Board of Sergeants. The discharged or furloughed soldiers had not gone off with Army property, as was only too usual in such cases, but had scrupulously turned in their arms and accouterments and taken receipts for them.

The commotion of the first few days, when many men for want of enlistment papers were falsely swearing off, did not continue after the papers came and a much larger number of men from the later regiments were being held. But the Line lost more than half its rank and file, had no money for re-enlistments, and could not be sure whether the furloughed men would return.

The call for light companies to go with Lafayette found Pennsylvania almost without soldiers. Wayne was confident that as soon as the sixty-day furloughs were expired, in March, he would have a thousand men. But on March 19 he had to write to Washington that the prospects "of being able to march a decent detachment to cooperate with the Marquis" were still distant. "The same supineness and torpidity which pervades most of our civil councils have prevented any part of the troops from marching, the Executive Council not having complied with their engagements or made any essay towards it until within a few days. However, I yet hope that in the course of three weeks we may have from 1000 to 1200 men in motion. . . . I have been knocking at every door, from the Council up to Congress, to little purpose. They all present me that Gorgon Head, an empty treasury."

"I fancy he rather overrates the matter," Washington commented upon this hope of Wayne. For Washington knew that Pennsylvania was still in a financial paralysis, afraid as well as unwilling to vote the money needed to pay the troops what was still due them or to supply them for a new campaign. The Council went on selling confiscated loyalist estates and pardoning convicts who would enlist in the Line. In March auditors began to settle the men's depreciation losses, but paid them in State money which was falling in value while Continental currency was finally ceasing to have any value at all. Though there was talk of bringing action against the perjured soldiers, the State did not care to do this while it was failing in its part of the bargain. Men were encouraged to come back if they would re-enlist, with gratuities and bounties in addition to other pay and allowances.

But all these payments too were in State money, which by May was worth only about one-seventh as much as specie. This was "ideal money," the men claimed, not real.

With immense efforts on the part both of Reed and of Wayne, and of many other officials and officers, and with a good deal of patience and faith on the part of the soldiers, what Wayne called a "little well appointed army" of about a thousand men was collected at York in May. Wayne on the 19th went there to assume command, intending to set out for Virginia on the 23rd. He was delayed by bad weather for three days, during which there was a flare-up of the Line's former discontents: a kind of after-mutiny.

This affair at York was imperfectly reported at the time and has since then been distorted by confused recollections into a bloody legend. Wayne, whose own accounts were vague, on the 26th sent Washington "the proceedings of two courts martial held at this post which I thought expedient to confirm. A prompt and exemplary punishment has had a happy effect. Harmony and discipline again pervade the Line. The troops have this morning commenced their march."

The trial records furnish all that is reasonably certain about the mutiny. On the 20th John Fortescue of the artillery was tried for mutinous actions now indecipherable in the manuscript. On the 22nd five men were tried for various offenses: Williams Crofts of the artillery for "drunkenness on the parade and impertinent threats of retaliation to Major [Benjamin] Eustis"; Thomas Wilson and Corporal Samuel Franklin, both of the 1st, for "exciting mutiny"; James Wilson of the 3rd for "exciting mutiny as far as in his power"; Philip Smith of the 2nd for "mutinous expressions such as asserting that if any officer dared to touch him he would shoot him."

CONCLUSIONS

At the trial of Franklin, Major James Hamilton, "being sworn, says that on the evening of the 20th instant, having struck and confined a man for misbehavior, and after passing opposite to the prisoner, heard him say the soldiers ought to be damned for standing still and seeing a soldier beat and treated in such a manner, and ought to go to hell for it." Lieutenant James Frederick McPherson testified that "after Major Hamilton had struck and confined a soldier, he heard the prisoner say that men who would stand by and see a brother soldier beat in such a manner ought to be damned."

James Wilson "pleads that he was so drunk that he knows nothing relative to the charge against him." Captain Joseph McClellan "says that on the evening of the 20th instant, being officer of the day and going the rounds, and after passing the prisoner in such a place as he must have certainly seen him and to know him to be an officer, he heard the prisoner say: 'God damn the officers, the buggers.' Captain McClellan returned and ordered him on before him two or three times to the guard house, which he refused till he had received two or three pricks from a sword. On the way to the guard he swore repeatedly he would never leave this town without his pay."

The courts martial found all six men guilty of acts which were a breach of Article 3rd, Section 2nd of the Articles of War: "Any officer or soldier who shall begin, excite, cause, or join in any mutiny or sedition in the troop, company, or regiment to which he belongs, or in any other troop or company in the service of the United States, or in any part, post, detachment, or guard, on any pretence whatsoever, shall suffer death or such other punishment as by court martial shall be inflicted." But at the execution—on the 22nd, according to a contemporary newspaper—only Fortescue, Thomas Wilson, James Wilson, and Smith were shot, Crofts and Franklin pardoned by Wayne. It does not appear that any of these men had been active in the January mutiny. Wayne, powerless at Mount Kemble, was at York able to deal with the "distemper" in the troops with "a liberal dose of niter"—such as had been administered by Howe at Pompton.

On the 26th Wayne with about eight hundred effectives marched off from York, and on June 10 they joined Lafayette. "We are now at the right of the Marquis's army," Wayne wrote six days later, "and shall produce a conviction that death has no terrors when put in competition with our duty and glory."

In their Southern campaigns, in Virginia, at the siege of Yorktown, and as far south as Georgia, the men of the Pennsylvania Line showed themselves, according to Lieutenant Colonel Henry (Light Horse Harry) Lee, "bold and daring" but "impatient and refractory; and would always prefer an appeal to the bayonet to a toilsome march." They were "restless under the want of food and whisky" and carried more baggage than they needed, Lee thought. In April 1782 there were stubborn complaints over food and clothing in some Pennsylvania regiments then under the command of Major General Nathanael Greene in South Carolina. The men put up placards asking: "Can soldiers do their duty if clad in rags and fed on rice?" Increasing discontent, which threatened to extend to the Maryland Line, led Greene to suspect mutinous if not treasonous designs, for which Sergeant George Goznall of the 2nd Pennsylvania was shot. There is no proof that Goznall, as has been often hinted, was one of the ringleaders of the earlier mutiny. The unrest in South Carolina was the Line's renewed protest against continued grievances. And so was the mutiny at Philadelphia and Lancaster in June 1783, when officers were as much involved as men. The whole Army was then on the verge of rebellion over being sent home without the pay they had so long been expected to wait for.

That summer the men of the Pennsylvania and the New Jersey Lines, like all the Continental soldiers no matter what was owing them, were dismissed with one month's pay in specie and three in certificates. This was the last recompense many of them ever got, except praise, for their years of hardship and privation. Though there were some State pensions—as in Pennsylvania—for disabled veterans, with some assistance from the Federal government, it was not till March 1818 (thirty-five years after the close of the war and eighteen years after the original enlistment papers had been destroyed by a fire in the building where they were housed) that pensions were allowed to men who could prove their service in the Revolution, provided they were in need of assistance from their country for their support.

III

The consequences of the January mutinies were mixed at the time and are still not easy to reduce to plain terms. At the outset the Pennsylvanians had such undeniable grievances, and behaved themselves so well, that for a week or more they seemed justifiable rebels rather than rioting mutineers. The disorder in Trenton and the reckless false swearing gave them a bad reputation, whether or not they were primarily responsible for the hasty beginning of the settlement. Then came the imitative and abortive New Jersey mutiny, which further discredited the Pennsylvania Line. The real fault in the whole affair lay with the public, which had broken its contract with the soldiers of all the Continental Lines by failing to supply and pay them, while they were kept in the service by military discipline. The citizens at large should have been blamed because they would not act. But the insurgent soldiers were blamed because they did.

The immediate effect of the outbreak of mutiny was the effort made by the New England States, on Washington's urging, to quiet at least temporarily the worst grievances of their own troops. While no such effort was uniform throughout the nation, yet on the whole the Army fared somewhat better after January 1781 than before. Word came in May that France had made the United States a free gift of six million francs and guaranteed a loan of ten million more in Holland. American credit rose, trade began to revive. Hard money reached the country from the West Indies and from Europe. About three thousand suits of clothes arrived from Spain in June, about ten thousand from France in September. (The Spanish coats were scarlet, and some American soldiers who hated that color had to fight in it.)

There was a connection, not too remote, between the mutiny and the French aid. John Laurens, who stopped for an hour or so among the mutineers at Princeton, was then on his way to Washington to confer with him before setting out to France on a special mission. The United States was represented in France by the incomparable Franklin. But Laurens was a soldier and could speak with first-hand knowledge of the needs of the American Army. Washington specifically authorized Laurens to tell the French government: "that the patience of the Army from an almost uninterrupted series of complicated distress is now nearly exhausted; their discontents matured to an extremity which has recently had very disagreeable consequences and which demonstrates the absolute need of speedy relief, a relief not within the compass of our means." Laurens, who found in Paris that the French had just made a gift, persuaded them also to underwrite a loan. And in his arguments he was sup-

CONCLUSIONS

ported by eager letters from Lafayette, who also had been at Princeton.

As another consequence of the mutiny Congress on January 15 sent a circular letter to the States pointing out that "an immediate provision for the pay of the Army is indispensably necessary. We need not dwell upon the injustice or the probable effects of a delay. They are obvious and alarming." Members of Congress and officials and citizens of the States were sharply convinced that there ought to be some kind of unified direction of the war, not subject to local jealousy or inertia. As far back as November 1777 Congress had submitted the Articles of Confederation to the several States, and all of them had now ratified except Maryland. In January 1781 Maryland applied to La Luzerne for French aid in defending the Chesapeake Bay against the British Fleet. La Luzerne, who was watching the unrest in the Continental Army with natural anxiety, pointed out to Maryland that if the Confederation should be completed this must be favorable to American unity and so to the interests of allied France. About the end of January Maryland ratified the Articles. Congress set the hour of noon on Monday March 1 for the announcement to the public, when the new Confederation would go immediately into effect. It was a "great event," the *Pennsylvania Packet* said, "which will confound our enemies, fortify us against their arts of seduction, and frustrate their plans of division."

That day in Philadelphia the announcement was made, the *Packet* reported, "under the discharge of the artillery on the land and the cannon of the shipping in the Delaware. The bells were rung and every manifestation of joy shown on this occasion. The *Ariel* frigate, commanded by the gallant Paul Jones, fired a *feu de joie* and was beautifully decorated with a variety of streamers in the day and ornamented with a brilliant appearance of lights in the night. . . . The evening was ushered in by an elegant exhibition of fireworks."

Did any of the late mutineers, watching and listening, suspect that the uprising at Mount Kemble, the negotiations at Princeton, even the disorder at Trenton, had obscurely contributed to the event which was now celebrated as a national triumph? Probably they only looked on with satisfaction, reflecting that Philadelphia was pleasanter if milder than the camps in which they had shivered and starved for their country. Possibly some of them still could not understand why, when they had stood up for their rights as men, they had been accused of being the traitors they had never even thought of being. But more than likely when they were old men they told their grandsons that mutiny was a bad business.

Appendix

OLIVER DE LANCEY'S JOURNAL
OF THE PENNSYLVANIA MUTINY

NOTE ON THE AFTER-MUTINY AT YORK

Oliver De Lancey's Journal of the Pennsylvania Mutiny

The Journal survives in three copies in the Clinton Papers with some variations in the texts. The one here printed is the fullest of the three, though it omits a few details found in the other copies and now restored in square brackets along with identifying names from various sources. A much abbreviated version of the Journal, of which also there is a copy in the Clinton Papers, was sent to Lord George Germain with Clinton's letter of January 25, 1781. This was printed in the *London Gazette* for February 20 and reprinted in Almon's *Remembrancer*, XI, 149-51.

Oliver De Lancey (1749-1822), son of Brigadier General Oliver De Lancey (1718-85) of the Provincial forces in North America, was born in New York but educated in England. Entering the British Army, he became cornet (1766) then lieutenant (1770) of the 14th Dragoons, later captain (1773) and major (1778) of the 17th Dragoons. In October 1780, after the death of Major John André, Clinton's adjutant general, De Lancey was appointed deputy adjutant general. At the time of the Pennsylvania mutiny he was in effect chief of Clinton's secret service, with a junior deputy adjutant general (Major Richard St. George) and two assistant adjutant generals (Major Frederick Mackenzie and Captain Lieutenant John Stapleton). In May 1781 De Lancey was promoted to the post of adjutant general and in October was made lieutenant colonel. After the war he went to England, where he rose to the rank of major general (1794), and general (1812).

JOURNAL

On the third of January in the morning received intelligence by an Emissary [Gould] that the Pensylvanians had Mutinyed in their Camp in Morristown that the alarm Guns had been fired and Beacons lighted. He was immediately dispatched to a Correspondent [Andrew Gautier] in New Jersey.

Orders were sent to the British Grenadiers, British Light Infantry, Forty second, Thirty seventh Regiments, Hessian Grenadiers and Hessian Yagers to hold themselves in readiness to march at a moments notice.

On Thursday the fourth of January received the following Intelligence from a Correspondent [Andrew Gautier] dated the third of January The Pensylvania Troops Commanded by General Wayne Mutinyed on Monday last, there was an universal complaint in the Camp that they had received no Pay, Cloathing, and a Scanty allowance of Provision, that a great number of these Troops were detained longer than they enlisted for, their terms being expired above ten Months, these complaints led them to mutiny to a Man, about 1500 seized on the Military Magazines, provision and Artillery which consisted of four Field pieces, and in a body marched from their Huts the same day to Vealtown, distant about seven Miles General Wayne followed, but they will not listen to any proposals and persist in going to Congress for redress, or to disband, yesterday they Marched to Middlebrook and this Morning towards Princeton—Two Companys of Riflemen detached from the Pensylvanians and posted at Bottle hill Marched off this Morning to join them—Their officers following them.

The Messenger [Gould] sent out as above returned with the following Intelligence

The Pensylvania line have been for some time much dissatisfied, on Monday last they turned out in number about 1200 declaring they would serve no longer unless their grievances were redressed, as they had not received either Pay, Cloathing, or Provisions a Riot had ensued in which an Officer was killed and four wounded The Insurgents had five or six wounded. They collected the Artillery Stores, Waggons, Provisions &c &c Marched out of Camp & passed by Wayne's Quarters who sent out a Message to them requesting them to desist or the consequences would prove fatal, they refused & proceeded on their March 'till evening when they took Post on an advantageous piece of ground and Elected Officers from among themselves, appointing a Sergeant Major who was a British Deserter to Command them with the Rank of Major General—On Tuesday they marched to Middlebrook and yesterday to Brunswick where they now are

On Tuesday morning a Message was sent them by the Officers from Camp, desiring to know their intentions, they refused to receive this Message—A Flag of Truce was sent to the same effect.—some said they had served their three years against their inclinations and would continue no longer on any account, others said they would not return unless their grievances were redressed —The Rebels have removed all their Boats to the other side of the Delawar least the Rioters should cross the River—On their first rising the Artillery refused to join, but, being threatened with the Bayonet they consented—Two Companys of Riflemen posted at Bottle hill near Chatham had marched to join them. the Militia not daring to oppose them.

On Thursday Evening three Copys of the following proposals were sent off to the Revolters, one by the Raritan River [carried by John Mason] the others by Newark and Elizabethtown [sent to Andrew Gautier to be forwarded].

It being reported at New York that the Pensylvania Troops and others having been defrauded of their Pay, Cloathing and Provisions are assembled to redress their grievances, and also that notwithstanding the terms of their inlistments are expired they have been forcibly detained in the service where they have suffered every kind of misery and oppression,

They are now offered to be taken under the protection of the British Government, to have their Rights restored free pardon for all former offences, and that Pay due them from the Congress faithfully paid to them, without any expectation of Military service (except it may be

APPENDIX 245

voluntary) upon laying down their Arms and returning to their allegiance.

For which purpose if they will send Commissioners to Amboy they will there be met by People empowered to treat with them & Faith pledged for their security

It is recommended to them for their own safety to move behind South River and whenever they request it a Body of British Troops shall protect them.

It is needless to point out the inability as well as want of inclination in the Congress to relieve them, or to tell them the severitys that will be used towards them by the Rebel leaders should they think of returning to their former Servitude

It will be proved to the Commissioners they may chuse to send that the Authority from whence this comes is sufficient to insure the performance of the above proposals.

To the person appointed by the Pensylvania Troops to lead them in their present struggle for their Libertys and Rights.

As soon as the above was dispatched, Orders were immediately sent to the two Battallions of Light Infantry, the British Grenadiers, three Battallions Hessian Grenadiers and the Yagers to march immediately to Denyses Ferry, whence they crossed the 5th to Staten Island and Cantoned on the Road to Richmond except the Yagers who lay on the road to Deckers ferry

On the 5th I sent out three copies of the proposals [by Blank, Hatfield's messenger, and possibly another] and a Verbal Message to the same import to the Pennsylvanians.

A number of men were sent out towards West point the Clove and Morristown to watch the movements that way

On the 6th received a letter [from Andrew Gautier] acknowledging the receipt of the proposals sent by Newark, informing me they were forwarded by a faithful friend to Princeton where the Pensylvania Troops had halted, that the Rebel Militia were all ordered out and the Jersey Brigade had moved from Pompton to Morristown that General Washington was on his way from West point to see General Wayne.

On the 7th received Information from General Skinner that the Pensylvanians continued their March towards Brunswick and that Wayne was detained a Prisoner among them.

That Col. Dayton with the Jersey Brigade was at Morristown but, hearing the Riflemen and some Light horse had joined the Insurgents he halted fearing a defection among his own Troops and that he heard a man sent with proposals was seen safe within a Mile of the Revolters on Friday Evening.

Information by New York that they were at Rocky hill near Princetown.

On the 8th a man came over by the Blazing Star [landing across from Staten Island] who said part of them were gone to Trenton.

On the 9th there being an appearance of bad weather the Hessian Grenadiers went back to Long Island.

About twelve o'Clock this day Received a letter from the Jerseys [from Andrew Gautier] of which the following is an Extract dated Monday Night

The Person I sent to Princetown is just returned which place he left this morning, your address he delivered Saturday evening, the same night two persons arrived with like addresses they were both detained.

The Pensylvania Troops are still

at Princetown their number 1700, they keep up order in the Town, no Officer is permitted to come into them but by a Flag of Truce—General Wayne and Governor Reed of Pensylvania had an interview Yesterday and made some proposals, but, they were rejected by the Troops, they require their Pay due in hard money and a discharge

Your offers are now known throughout the Army and will have great influence over the Majority of them, the most sensible people and Officers here think they will yet join you as interest and Policy ought to lead them to it—I am fully satisfied the Congress can not nor will not give them redress, in this case they will come over to you.

The Commander in Chief received Information also this day much to the same purpose as the above letter, dated the 8th at 10 o'clock in the morning.

Received intelligence by New York that came from Morristown [by Joseph Clark] and also from Major General Phillips, all which agree that the Revolters are at Princetown, still insisting on the compliance of the Congress to their Demands.

This day I sent out some people from the Refugee Post at Bergen Point and one from the Armed Vessel.

On the 10th the Reports the same, no person came in that could be confided in.

On the 11th Received intelligence by a man [Cornelius Tyger] who had passed by the Pensylvanians, that they were at Princetown, still persisting in their demands. the man sent out the 9th returned this day, reports the situation of the Pensylvanians the same, says the Guards of Militia along the Coast are so numerous as to prevent any persons geting in.

On the 12th a party went into the Country, the officer who Commanded was informed by a friend that a person who had come from Princetown in the morning, said every thing remained in the same situation we had before heard, they still refuse all the offers that have been made them; the Party was fired upon in three or four places

The man sent out [Uzal Woodruff] was met by a person who informed him the Rebel Colonel Barber came to Elizabeth Town Yesterday and reported that eight hundred of the Revolters had absolutely refused to come to any terms; That on Thursday morning they were supplied with three Waggon loads of Arms and Ammunition that the whole body were to march for Trenton and are supposed to be there now—The Militia had received Orders to follow them—That last night and the night before the Officers of the Jersey Brigade were under the necessity of watching their Camp to prevent their people joining the Pensylvanians.

This night received the following intelligence from a Gentleman who came in and can be depended on. On the 9th some of the Pensylvanians who had differed in opinion from the Revolters, told him they were now going to join them having changed their intention.—That a Sergeant Major of the 4th Battallion Commanded them, they had not the least apprehension of the Jersey Troops as they were of the same sentiments with themselves.—Their demands were for their arrears of Pay and Cloathing, and those that had inlisted for three Years insisted on having their discharges, that the depreciation should be made good to them, and should they be reconciled the Officers they have now appointed from among themselves are to be continued being determined not to serve under their late Officers. —They have also stipulated a pardon particularly for all the principle Revolters. One of them a Deserter from the 7th Regiment said if Congress did not redress their Complaints they knew what course to take—The Militia of the Jerseys say they are only doing themselves Justice. General Wayne is kept among them as an hostage. Numbers declare they will not serve Congress at any rate. They have taken two Men one with proposals, the other served as a Guide. They call themselves 2500 but, he thinks from the best accounts they do not exceed 2000 all the Boats are carried to the West Side of the Delawar and kept Guarded. The Militia are ordered out A friend in the Country [William Bernard Gifford] told him that the reports of their going to Trenton was not true. That two Companys of Riflemen had joined them with one Field piece. some of the insurgents were accidentally killed when they fired upon their Officers, who in general denounce Vengeance against them and declare they will not serve unless an exemplary Punishment is inflicted, it seems the general opinion, that the Jersey Brigade are of the same Sentiments.

On the 13th a man came in from Newark who says they are still at Princetown. The people sent out to them are not yet returned.

On Monday the 15th received the following Intelligence

William Boyce left Philadelphia on Wednesday last, crossed the Delawar on Thursday at Trenton where the Pensylvanians are. he spoke to their out Posts their numbers are said to be from 1500 to 2000—They demand their back Pay, Cloathing, and the discharges of those whose time of enlistment had expired

There was a Committee of Congress at Barclay's Tavern on the West side of the Delawar in order to adjust matters some were for forcing them, others for submitting to all their Demands—on the West side of the River he was told they were not to be paid for ten days: on the East side they told him it was to be done that day, and they were to have their discharges it however was not decided. They had delivered over two Prisoners taken amongst them with proposals, to the Committee of Congress.

General Wayne is among them as a Prisoner Governor Reed was permitted to have an hours Conversation with him and then sent back to the Committee of Congress. They are Commanded by one Williams, who was a Sergeant Major—They left Princetown on Wednesday last, he met small parties of Soldiers all along the road that seemed to have come from other parts of the Army, some with and some without Arms. —At Philadelphia the People seemed much alarmed as it was reported they had no money and were disappointed in the Cloathing expected for the Army as Paul Jones who was to convoy it put back to *L'Orient* his Ships being dismasted and in distress. He did not hear that General Washington was at Philadelphia, on the contrary about two miles on the other side Brunswick, he met two Men going with an Express from him to General Wayne, and a Gentleman who was with him and had spoke to the Men sayd Mr. Washington's presence was necessary with his Army as they apprehended a Revolt would take place there.

The Opinion of the people in general is that the Troops are only doing themselves justice — They have killed a Captn Talbot, Tatton and another whose name he does not know There was a report at first of their intention to come over to us but from their moving to Trenton he does not think it likely At Elizabeth Town he heard the two Men taken up were hanged on friday There is a report that five hundred of the Militia are at and about that place.

General Skinner informs me that the Jersey Troops were in the same State as to their Demands, but, have been quieted by a promise of being satisfied in ten days, six of which are elapsed.

Mr. H. [Cornelius Hatfield] informed me that Col. Dayton spread a Report that the Pensylvanians were satisfied, upon which his own people immediately made the same demands, and he was obliged to contradict his own report to quiet them.

On the 15th received a letter from a correspondent [Andrew Gautier] saying that the Pensylvanians had not paid that attention to the offers made them by us, which he thought Policy and Interest would have led them to, that he did not imagine Congress would grant them relief, but, force them to submission —That General Washington was not gone to Congress, as he had mentioned in his last letter.

A Man [Uzal Woodruff] came in who sayd they had left Princetown, but his Intelligence is not to be relied on, he having received it from a Sergeant, who had deserted them and was going home.

The Pensylvanians moving so far from us, and in no instance shewing a disposition to accept of the offers made them. The Commander in Chief returned to Town

No account coming in that could be depended on and no appearance of the Pensylvanians intending any thing in our favour the Troops were ordered to Long Island the 19th.

The same day I was informed from South Amboy, that the Men taken up were people I had sent out, & from the description, I know one of them [John Mason]—They were hanged on friday opposite Trenton where the Pensylvanians still remained not having determined any thing. The 20th received accounts of their being at Trenton, that they were discharging some of them, they having settled with a Committee of Congress

Same Day the account of their being still at Trenton confirmed. The Committee of Congress consists of Genl. Sullivan, Mr. Mathews, Mr. Witherspoon and Mr. Atley. they sit at T. Barclay's Tavern on the Pensylvania side.

Same day a Man [McFarlan] I sent out the 7th [6th] with a Copy of the proposals got to Princetown on Wednesday where he met a Man [Caleb Bruen], he suspected to be on a similar errand; after some conversation, they found out that their business was the same, they went on together to Trenton to which place the Pensylvanians had Marched. Finding that two Men had been taken up they dropped their Papers, which were carried to Mr. Reed and General Wayne who offered one hundred Guineas reward for the apprehending whoever brought them. One of them being known by a Colonel Hayes and he having intimated to him some suspicions of his designs, they crossed

APPENDIX

the Delaware and went into Pensylvania where they saw the execution of the two men, whom he describes exactly.

They are commanded by a Sergeant Williams who is a Pensylvanian and had some little property, he was taken Prisoner in the Year 1776 at Princetown and enlisted in one of our Provincial Regiments, raised at that time from which he deserted

There was a Committee of a Sergeant of each Regt. to meet the Committee of Congress, the proposals herewith inclos'd were made to them at Princetown the 7th of January & the answer signed by the Secretary of the Committee of Sergeants was given the 8th and their determination respecting the two prisoners January the 10th at Trenton.

This person adds that they do not intend going home untill every Man is discharged and tho' they lay down their Arms as they are settled with yet they do not permit them to be taken away but keep a Centry of their own over them

The Pensylvanian Officers are very much dissatisfied, as the Soldiers are allowed to Swear to any thing and their words Credited before any vouched account, which they choose to say they were obliged to sign

He confirms the account of their having on the first of January killed a Captain and wounded another, with a Lieutenant and Ensign, one Soldier was also killed.

They have four pieces of Cannon, they left one spiked at Morristown, he expects the other Man in, who was with him, every moment.

21st. This day a Captain [William Bernard Gifford] of the 3d Jersey Regiment, who I had corresponded with came over to us he confirms the information of yesterday.

He says they will not stir till they are paid and ask hard Money.

The man who was expected [Caleb Bruen], returned this day his accounts are the same.

He says they have shown no intention of coming to us, but on the contrary declared that should the British interfere, they would take up arms to oppose them as readily as ever.

From all accounts the Country is much alarmed the Militia on the Roads made the Communication more difficult, than at any other time, they having also destroy'd all the Boats Cannoes &c.

Note on the After-Mutiny at York

The account in Chapter 21 of the outbreak and suppression at York in May 1781 is based on the court martial proceedings of the 20th (John Fortescue) and the 22nd (William Crofts, Thomas Wilson, Samuel Franklin, James Wilson, Philip Smith), Wayne's letter to Washington of the 26th, and the report in the *Pennsylvania Packet* for the 29th. They seem to say plainly that one man was tried and sentenced to death on Sunday the 20th and five on Tuesday the 22nd of that week, four of the six executed and two pardoned on Tuesday within what must have been a short time after the second trial. Wayne, writing to Washington on Saturday, mentioned no trials or executions besides those indicated by the "proceedings of two courts martial held at this post which I thought expedient to confirm. A prompt and exemplary punishment has had a happy effect. Harmony and discipline again pervade the Line." And the *Packet* not only put the date of the executions on the 22nd but also represented the soldiers as quiet at least till Friday afternoon, with no further troubles.

"By a gentleman who left York Town Friday evening," the *Packet* account said, "we learn that four of the soldiers of the Pennsylvania Line were shot at that place on Tuesday last for mutiny. Six had been condemned and two of them pardoned by General Wayne.

"These men, each of them, at different times had behaved in a very disorderly and mutinous manner, discovering the most seditious temper and calling upon their fellow-soldiers of the several regiments to join them in their revolt. They found however no support from their comrades. The whole Line were drawn up under arms at the execution and behaved in the most orderly manner. A finer body of men never were collected. They were to have marched from that place on Wednesday, but were obstructed solely by the heavy rains. The men appear cheerful and happy without the least appearance of tumult or discontent."

The gentleman who left York on Friday the 25th could hardly have got to Philadelphia before Sunday. By that day Lieutenant Colonel William Smith Livingston heard at Philadelphia a very different story of the York affair, about which he wrote from Beverwyck, New Jersey, on Monday to Colonel Samuel Blatchey Webb (*Correspondence of Samuel B. Webb*, II, 341, quoted in part in Fitzpatrick's edition of Washington's *Writings*, XXII, 191n).

"There has been a mutiny in the Pennsylvania Line at York Town previous to their marching. Wayne like a good officer quelled it as soon as twelve of the fellows stepped out and persuaded the Line to refuse to march in consequence of the promises made to them not being complied with. Wayne told them of the disgrace they brought on the American arms while in Jersey in general, and themselves in particular. That the feelings of the officers on that occasion were so wounded that they had determined never to experience the like and that he begged they would now fire either on him and them, or on those villains in front. He then called to such a platoon. They presented at the word, fired, and killed six of the villains. One of the others, badly wounded, he ordered to be bayonetted. The soldier on whom he called to do it, recovered his piece and said he could not, for he was his comrade. Wayne then drew his pistol and told him he would kill him. The fellow then advanced and bayonetted him. Wayne then marched the Line by divisions round the dead and the rest of the fellows are ordered to be hanged. The Line marched the next day southward, mute as fish."

The story sounds circumstantial, but it is fantastic: with its six men shot, one bayonetted, and five ordered to be hanged, without a sign of any court martial. Though Wayne did not march till Saturday the 26th, and the news would have had to travel fast to cover the ninety miles from York to Philadelphia in time for Livingston to hear of it and then himself be ninety miles or so away in another direction by Monday when he wrote his letter, the letter has been thought of as fixing the date of the bloody scene on Friday the 25th, as if there had been a second round of killings. Some such rumor did get to New York by June 5 (Frederick Mackenzie's *Diary*, II, 536). But all the witnesses at York, however much they differ in detail, speak of only one execution spectacle. Livingston's story may be only what rumor had made of the news reported in the *Packet*. When the executions of Tuesday occurred it was expected that the march would begin the next day, and Livingston in Philadelphia may have supposed that it did.

Still, the witnesses at York confuse the episode as much as they clarify it. Lieutenant Ebenezer Denny in his *Military Journal* (*Publications of the Historical Society of Pennsylvania*, VII, 237-38) described a single formal execution of men who had been duly tried. But he was not precise as to the date, and he, like Livingston, spoke of seven men actually killed on the occasion, not four as in the court martial records and in the *Packet*.

"A few days spent in equipping, etc., and for the trial of soldiers charged with mutiny. General Wayne, the commanding officer, influenced no doubt by experience of the revolt last winter, expresses a determination to punish, with the utmost rigor, every case of mutiny or disobedience. A general court martial continued sitting several days; twenty-odd prisoners brought before them; seven were sentenced to die. The regiments paraded in the evening earlier than usual; orders passed to the officers of the Line to put instantly to death any man who stirred from his rank. In front of the parade the ground rose and descended again, and at a distance of about a hundred yards, over this rising ground, the prisoners were escorted by a captain's guard. Heard the fire of one platoon, and immediately a smaller one, then the regiments wheeled by companies and marched round by the place of execution. This was an awful exhibition.

The seven objects were seen by the troops just as they had sunk or fell under fire. The sight must have made an impression on the men. It was designed with that view."

If Denny, marching with his company past the dead bodies, saw seven, then there must have been three men put to death besides the four Wayne reported to Washington. If that is true, then Wayne in his report did not bother to let Washington know how many men had been executed, or to send all the court martial records. This is harder to believe than that Denny was in error.

In a letter of June 16 to an unidentified correspondent (Bancroft Transcripts, New York Public Library; quoted in part in Stillé's *Wayne*, p. 265-66, where it is incorrectly dated May 20) Wayne told part of the story he had not told to Washington, though it is no such story as that in the rumor Livingston had heard and repeated.

"The day antecedent to that on which the march was to commence," Wayne wrote, "a few leading mutineers on the right of each regiment called out to pay them in real and not ideal money; they were no longer to be trifled with. Upon this they were ordered to their tents, which being peremptorily refused, the principals were immediately either knocked down or confined by the officers, who were previously prepared for this event. A court martial was ordered on the spot. The commission of the crime, trial, and execution were all included in the course of a few hours in front of the Line paraded under arms. The determined countenances of the officers produced a conviction to the soldiery that the sentence of the court martial would be carried into execution at every risk and consequence. Whether by design or accident, the particular friends and messmates of the culprits were their executioners, and while the tears rolled down their cheeks in showers they silently and faithfully obeyed their orders without a moment's hesitation. Thus was this hideous monster crushed in its birth, however to myself and officers a most painful scene. Harmony and the most perfect discipline again pervade the whole."

Wayne's expression "the day antecedent to that on which the march was to commence" need not refer to the 26th, when the Line did march. Writing this letter three weeks after the event, he may have recalled it as happening on the day before the Line was expected to march, the 23rd, which would put the execution on the 22nd, the day specified by the *Packet*. On that day, certainly, five men were tried for mutinous actions, and all found guilty; three of them were executed at once, along with a man who had already been condemned. But those four men were all charged with acts committed on or before the 22nd, and none of them for open mutiny in front of the whole Line. Either Wayne was speaking in his letter of June 16 about an episode of the execution unmentioned by Denny and unknown to the *Packet* correspondent, or else Wayne was telling the story with a very free hand. He was inexact about the date and said nothing of the number of men killed, but he did say they were all tried by court martial.

The trial proceedings and the *Packet* give the only information about the York affair that is reasonably trustworthy. Livingston, Denny, and Wayne are contradictory and uncertain. No wonder the after-mutiny came to be a hash of memory and melodrama in the story told many years later by a soldier who had been an eyewitness of the executions.

That soldier was Samuel Dewees, who at Mount Kemble was not one of the mutineers, he said. He claimed his discharge along with the others, then re-enlisted, spent some time at Carlisle and Lebanon, and in May was at York as a fifer of—apparently —the 6th Pennsylvania. His narrative of the York mutiny appeared in 1844 in *A History of the Life and Services of Captain Samuel Dewees . . . The whole written (in part from manuscript in the handwriting of Captain Dewees) and compiled by John Smith Hanna* (pp. 228-32). This is the only incident of the Pennsylvania troubles of 1781 that was ever recounted by one of the enlisted men.

"Whilst we lay at Lebanon, a circumstance transpired worthy of notice, and which I here record as a prelude to the horridly great tragical event, of which the individual now bearing a part was one of the number that was made to suffer the awful penalty annexed to their crimes, if crimes they may be said to have committed. A sergeant who was known by the appellation of Macaroney Jack, a very intelligent, active, neat and clever fellow, had committed some trivial offence. He had his wife with him in camp who always kept him very clean and neat in his appearance. She was washerwoman to a number of soldiers, myself among the number. She was a very well behaved and good conditioned woman.

"The officers, for the purpose of making an impression upon him and to better his conduct, ordered him to be brought from the guardhouse; which done, he was tied up and the drummers ordered to give him a certain number of lashes upon his bare back. The intention of the officers was not to chastise him.

"When he was tied up he looked around and addressed the soldiers, exclaiming at the same time: 'Dear brother soldiers, won't you help me!' This in the eyes of the officers savored of mutiny and they called out; "Take him down, take him down!' The order was instantly obeyed and he was taken back to the guardhouse again and handcuffed. At this time there were two deserters confined with him. On the next or second day after this we were ordered on to York, Pennsylvania, where upon our arrival we encamped upon the common below the town. Upon our arrival, our three prisoners were confined in York jail. In a few days after we arrived at York a soldier of the name of Jack Smith, and another soldier whose name I do not now remember, were engaged in playing *long bullets*. Whilst thus engaged, some of the officers were walking along the road where they were throwing the bullets. The bullets passing near to the officers, they used very harsh language to Smith and his comrade, who immediately retorted by using the same kind of indecorous language. A file of men was immediately dispatched with orders to take Smith and his comrade under guard and march them off to York jail.

"In three or four days after these arrests were made, a sergeant of the name of Lilly, who was also a very fine fellow and an excellent scholar, so much so, that much of the regimental writing fell to his lot to do, and for which he received a remuneration in some way; this sergeant, having became intoxicated, had quarreled with one or more of his messmates, and upon some of the officers coming around to enquire what the matter was, found him out of his tent. The officers scolded him and bade him to go into his quarters. Lilly, having been much in favor and knowing his own abilities and the services rendered, was (although intoxicated) very much wounded, and could not bear to be thus harshly dealt with, and used language of an unbecoming kind to his superior officers. The officers immediately ordered him to be taken to York jail.

"On the next day in the morning we beat up the troop. After roll call we were ordered to beat up the troop again. The whole line was again formed, and I think the orders were for every soldier to appear in line with his knapsack on his back. I suppose that at this time there were parts of three regiments, in all 800 or 1000 men laying at York, the whole of which was commanded by Colonel Butler. The whole body (sentinels, invalids, &c, excepted) when formed were marched to the distance of about half a mile from the camp, and there made to stand under arms. Twenty men were then ordered out of the line and formed into marching order and all the musicians placed at their head. After remaining a short time in a marching posture, the order of forward was given. We were then marched direct to the jail door. The prisoners six in number were then brought out and their sentence (which was death) was read to them.

"At this time it was thought that none in the Line save the officers knew for what the provost guard was detached. But it appeared afterwards that previous to the firing which was the means of launching four out of the six into eternity, the matter of rescuing them was whispered among the soldiers; but they did not concert measures in time to prevent the awful catastrophe, which they meditated by an act of insubordination upon their part.

"After the sentence of death was read to the condemned soldiers at the jail door, we then marched them out and down below town, playing the 'dead march' in front of them. We continued our march full half a mile and halted on a piece of ground (common) adjoining a field of rye, which was then in blossom. This was some time in the early part of June 1781. After a halt was made, the prisoners were ordered to kneel down with their backs to the rye-field fence. Their eyes were then bandaged or covered over with silk handkerchiefs. The officer in command then divided his force of twenty men into two platoons. The whole was then ordered to load their pieces. This done, ten were ordered to advance, and at the signal given by the officer (which was the wave of his pocket handkerchief) the first platoon of ten fired at one of the six. Macaroney Jack was the first shot at and was instantly killed. The first platoon was then ordered to retire and reload, and the second platoon of ten ordered to advance. When the signal was again given, Smith shared the same fate, but with an awfulness that would have made even devils to have shrunk back and stood appalled. His head was literally blown in fragments from off his body. The second platoon was then ordered to retire and reload, whilst the first was ordered to advance and at the same signal fired at the third man. The second platoon then advanced and fired to order, at Sergeant Lilly, whose brave and noble soul was instantly on the wing to the presence of that Supreme Judge who has pledged himself he will do that which is right. The arms of each had been tied above their elbows with the cords passing behind their backs. Being tied thus enabled them to have the use of their hands. I ventured near and noticed that Macararoney Jack had his hands clasped together in front of his breast, and had both of his thumbs shot off. The distance that the platoons stood from them at the time they fired could not have been more than ten feet. So near did they stand that the handkerchiefs covering the eyes of some of them that were shot were set on fire. The fence and even the heads of rye for some distance within the field were covered over with blood and brains. After four were shot, we musicians with a portion of the twenty men were ordered to march and were then conducted up to the main line of the army. After our arrival there, the whole Line was thrown into marching order and led to this horrid scene of bloody death. When the troops advanced near to the spot they displayed off into double file and were then marched very near to the dead bodies, as also to those still on their knees waiting the awful death that they had every reason to believe still awaited them. The order was for every man to look upon the bodies as he passed; and in order that the soldiers in the Line might behold them more distinctly in passing, they were ordered to countermarch after they had passed and then marched as close to them upon their return.

"The two deserters that were still in a kneeling posture were reprieved, the bandages taken from their eyes, then untied, and restored to their respective companies.

"A number of men were ordered out to dig a large grave. The bodies of the four dead soldiers were then wrapped up in their blankets and buried together therein. This last sad duty performed, the soldiers were all marched back to their quarters in camp.

"My readers may imagine to what a pitch this sad scene was heightened in sorrow when I state that, on our way from the jail to the place of execution, those sentenced were crying, pleading, and praying aloud, women weeping and sobbing over the unhappy fate of the doomed to death, and the wife of Macaroney Jack screaming and almost distracted. On the way she attempted to run into the line, or provost guard, to where her husband was walking, but was hindered by an officer who felled her to the ground with his sword, he having struck her with the side of it.

"The execution of these men by Colonel Butler and his officers was undoubtedly brought about by a love of liberty, the good of country, and the necessity of keeping proper subordination in the army, in order to insure that good ultimately. Mutiny had shewn itself at many of the military posts within the United States. The conduct of the Pennsylvania and Jersey lines in the revolt at Morristown in Jersey had occurred but the year before, and fresh in the memory of all having knowledge of the operations of the army. Still, the destruction of these men seemed like a wanton destruction of human life. The soldiers at York were afraid to say or to do any thing, for so trivial appeared the offences of these men that were shot that they knew not what in the future was to be made to constitute crime. I recollect for myself that for some considerable time after this, if I found myself meeting an officer when out of camp, I would avoid coming in contact with him if I possibly could do so by slipping a short distance to one side, not that I was afraid of an officer more than of a private, whilst I done my duty, but fearing lest they might construe my conduct in some way or other into an offense.

"All disposition of mutiny was entirely put down by these steps of cruelty. There were no doubt many times during the Revolution that such executions were called for and highly necessary, and perhaps there was an evidence as well as a conviction before the minds of the officers composing the court martial in their case that we know not of, and that demanded the punishment of death. But, to state it in a word, it was a mournful day among the soldiers, and hard and stony indeed were the hearts that were not deeply affected in witnessing this distressing execution of their fellow-soldiers."

In the main outlines of the story —the executions before the Line drawn up, the soldiers marched past the dead bodies—Dewees agreed with Livingston and Denny; in the number of men killed and pardoned he agreed with the court martial records and the *Packet*. But Dewees after sixty-three years had completely forgotten Wayne's part in the suppression, even Wayne's presence at York; and he remembered what appears to be a new set of victims.

Dewees's two unnamed, and pardoned, deserters bore no resemblance to Crofts and Franklin, the pardoned mutineers of the official documents; Dewees's Smith, no resemblance except in name to Philip Smith who had insulted Lieutenant John Hughes. Dewees's Sergeant Lilly may have been the same as a John Lilly who had been listed as a private in Proctor's artillery (*Pennsylvania Archives; Fifth Series,* III, 954-55, 1025), but there was still a gunner named Lilly in the artillery at the time of the mutiny of 1783 (*Journals of the Continental Congress,* XXV, 565-66).

Dewees's sergeant called Macaroney Jack, according to Leonard Dubbs, a drummer of the 6th (*Pennsylvania Archives: Second Series,* X, 292), was Jack Maloney, an Englishman: "one of the sergeants in command of the men at the revolt of the Line, and whom he [Dubbs] believed to be a true man, as he had advised the hanging of the British spies." Maloney, still according to Dubbs, started the difficulty at York. When he "called upon all true soldiers to help him, a man named Smith and two other men rushed from the ranks." But this, acording to Dewees, happened not at York but at Lebanon. Dubbs, who died at Harrisburg in 1840, was another aged veteran when he told his story, and perhaps as forgetful as Dewees. No earlier references to Maloney as a leader of the January mutineers have been found. On the surviving regimental rolls there are a Quartermaster Sergeant John Maloney of the artillery (*Pennsylvania Archives: Fifth Series,* III, 978) and a Sergeant John Meloney who acted as a clerk in the 1st and was still alive in Lancaster County in 1808 (*Pennsylvania Archives: Second Series,* X, 369). There is yet no discovered account of the execution of any Maloney at York except in the reminiscences of Drummer Dubbs and Fifer Dewees—if Dewees's Macaroney Jack was the same as Dubbs's Jack Maloney.

The court martial records, hitherto utterly neglected in all accounts of the York outbreak, have been lost sight of, while Dewees's narrative has persisted with a legend's vitality. It was reprinted as late as 1907 in G. R. Prowell's *History of York County* (I, 217-18) and in 1941 was used as the chief authority for the after-mutiny in Harry Emerson Wildes's *Anthony Wayne* (pp. 241-43).

Acknowledgments and Sources

Acknowledgments are due, and gratefully made, to the following libraries and societies for permission to consult, quote, and reproduce manuscripts and other materials in their collections: in the Library of Congress, the Papers of the Continental Congress and the Washington Papers; in the William L. Clements Library, University of Michigan, the Sir Henry Clinton Papers and the Nathanael Greene Papers; in the Historical Society of Pennsylvania, the Anthony Wayne Papers; in the New York Historical Society, the Joseph Reed Papers and the Walter Stewart Papers; in the New York Public Library, the Bancroft Transcripts, the Loyalist Transcripts, the Orderly Book of the New Jersey Line for 1781, and countless other manuscript and printed sources; in the Princeton University Library, the Alexandre Berthier Papers; in the library of Harvard University, an unpublished letter from Lafayette to Washington in the Sparks Manuscripts; in the New Jersey Historical Society, the unpublished diary of William Pennington at the time of the New Jersey mutiny; in the Historical Museum of the Morristown National Historical Park, materials on Wayne's camp at Mount Kemble; in the Morristown Library, materials on early inhabitants of Morris County.

The work could not have been done at all without the courtesies extended by Randolph G. Adams, Director of the William L. Clements Library, and the consideration shown by Luther H. Evans, Chief Assistant Librarian of the Library of Congress, through whose efforts certain papers put away for safekeeping were made available. Howard Peckham, Curator of Manuscripts at the William L. Clements Library, provided indispensable answers to innumerable questions. Captain Mark Rhoads, U. S. Army, Retired, broke the cipher in which the Andrew Gautier letters were written before any of the contemporary transcriptions were identified. Francis S. Ronalds, National Park Service, aided in the investigation of the camp site at Mount Kemble and of the mutineers' route to Princeton. Melvin J. Weig, National Park Service, contributed details about the topography of the camp and the construction of the huts. Harry J. Podmore gave generous information about Revolutionary Trenton. Howard L. Hughes of the Trenton Free Public Library carried out special inquiries in the archives of the Secretary of State of New Jersey. Maud Honeyman Greene of the New Jersey Historical Society supplied missing facts about the New Jersey mutiny. Julian P. Boyd, Librarian of Princeton University, directed attention to the Berthier plans of Princeton and Trenton. Margaret Van Doren, drawing the map of the mutiny country, had the indefatigable co-operation of Bradford Hood Bevans.

The primary sources for this history are the Washington Papers, the Papers of the Continental Congress, and the Clinton Papers (which include the papers of British Headquarters and of the secret service officers and agents for the period).

The Washington Papers have been calendared: one volume devoted to Washington's *Correspondence . . . with the Continental Congress,* four volumes devoted to his *Correspondence . . . with the Officers.* Fitzpatrick's great edition of Washington's *Writings* (including his General Orders) in 37 vols. is now complete. Various letters to Washington during the course of the mutinies are in *Correspondence of the American Revolution* (4 vols., 1853) edited by Jared Sparks. The Papers of the Continental Congress are cited in the footnotes, under respective dates, to the Hunt-Ford edition of the *Journals.* Edmund C. Burnett's *Letters of Members of the Continental Congress* (8 vols., 1921-36) valuably supplements the *Journals* (and in particular gives the letters, expertly annotated, from the Committee of Congress sent to Trenton at the time of the Pennsylvania mutiny).

Howard Peckham's *Guide to the Manuscript Collections in the William L. Clements Library* (1942) lists the names of most of Clinton's correspondents. Two manuscript volumes which were originally a part of the Clinton Papers are in the New York Public Library. The one called Private Intelligence as to the American Army, running from January 20 to July 19, 1781, has been printed *(Magazine of American History,* X-XII, October 1883-August 1884). The volume called Information of Deserters and Other not included in Private Intelligence, from August 1780 to March 26, 1781, remains unprinted.

The Washington, Continental Congress, and Clinton Papers include numerous documents that have not been hitherto examined in connection with the mutinies. So do the Wayne and the Reed Papers. For though a good many documents relating to the Pennsylvania mutiny, and a few relating to the New Jersey mutiny, have been printed, they are nothing like so many as the unknown or neglected manuscripts which have now been brought to light and which enlarge the story from a minor episode to a major crisis in the history of the Continental Army and of the United States.

This story of the mutiny month of January 1781 is based directly on original sources, manuscript or printed. Pierre Eugène Du Simitière before his death in 1784 made a basic collection of the Pennsylvania documents which are now in the Library Company of Philadelphia and have been calendared in *Descriptive Catalogue of the Du Simitière Papers* (1940), Nos. 49-80. They were printed by Samuel Hazard in his *Register of Pennsylvania,* II (1828), 137-39, 156-60, 164-68, 188-90, 204-06, 218-19. Further documents were printed in the *Bland Papers* (2 vols., 1840) of Theodorick Bland; William B. Reed's *Life and Correspondence of Joseph Reed* (2 vols., 1847); the *St. Clair Papers* (2 vols., 1882) of Arthur St. Clair; Charles J. Stillé's *Major-General Anthony Wayne and the Pennsylvania Line of the Continental Army* (1893); John Sullivan's *Letters and Papers* (3 vols., 1930-39). The Hazard text was reprinted, not too accurately, with some additions in *Pennsylvania Archives: Second Series,* XI (1895), 659-706. Further documents are to be found in *Pennsylvania Archives* (commonly referred to as First Series), VIII-IX; and the minutes of the Supreme Executive Council in *Colonial Records,* XII. There are regimental and company lists (though incomplete) of officers and soldiers of the Pennsylvania Line in *Pennsylvania Archives: Second Series,* X-XI, and in *Pennsylvania Archives: Fifth Series,* II-IV.

In comparison the New Jersey mutiny has been neglected in print. Some of the correspondence about it was collected by Jared Sparks in his edition of Washington's *Writings*, VII, 560-66. A few more letters or parts of letters were added to the record in Leonard Lundin's *Cockpit of the Revolution* (1940). There are contemporary newspaper accounts in *Archives of the State of New Jersey: Second Series*, V, 190-91; and various official records in *The Votes and Proceedings of the General Assembly of the State of New Jersey* for 1781 and *Selections from the Correspondence of the Executive of New Jersey from 1776 to 1786* (1848). Unusually full and accurate lists are given in W. S. Stryker's *Official Register of the Officers and Men of New Jersey in the Revolutionary War* (1872), for which there is a useful *Index* (1941).

There are eye-witness accounts of transactions at Mount Kemble and Pennington in the *Diary* of Joseph McClellan (*Pennsylvania Archives: Second Series*, XI, 612-14, 659-705) and in the *Letter-Books* of Enos Reeves (*Pennsylvania Magazine of History and Biography*, XXI, 72-81). Joseph Reed's invaluable account of the negotiations with the Pennsylvania mutineers is given in an unpublished 17-page report dated February 19, 1781, signed by Reed and James Potter and sent to Washington. The letter is in the Washington Papers, the draft in Reed's handwriting in the Joseph Reed Papers in the New York Historical Society. The unpublished diary of Lieutenant William Pennington of the 2nd Continental Artillery (in the New Jersey Historical Society's collections) contains an account at first-hand of the suppression of the New Jersey mutiny; so does James Thacher's *Military Journal* (ed. 1827, pp. 244-47). Thacher's account of the Pennsylvania mutiny was only hearsay. Lafayette's letters to La Luzerne at the time of the mutinies are printed in the *American Historical Review*, XX, 578-87. William Heath's *Memoirs* (ed. 1901, pp. 248-52) has interesting details about activities at West Point during the mutiny month. Frederick Mackenzie's *Diary* (2 vols., 1930) gives a revealing account of British activities in New York during the same month. The unpublished Journal of William Smith (in the New York Public Library) is of incidental value.

Pierce's Register (1915) lists the names of the men to whom, under the Act of July 4, 1783, money was due for services in the Continental Army. The names and services of the officers are in F. B. Heitman's *Historical Register of the Officers of the Continental Army* (1893, 1914). The record of the nation with respect to that Army may be found in *Resolutions, Laws, and Ordinances relating to the Pay, Half Pay, Bounty Lands, and Other Promises Made by Congress to the Officers and Soldiers of the Revolution; to the Settlement of the Accounts between the Several States; and the Funding the Revolutionary Debt* (1838). There is no satisfactory history of the Continental Army, but there is a good study of *The Administration of the American Revolutionary Army* (1904) by L. C. Hatch. *Lexington to Fallen Timbers 1775-1794* (1942) reproduces several important manuscripts relating to the Continental Army now in the Clements Library.

The sources for particular facts or statements in this history have been arranged in chronological order, with references to chapters and sections in which the facts or statements appear. The collected documents of the Pennsylvania mutiny are accessible and are not here listed except for those which

APPENDIX 261

were incorrectly dated or addressed in the printed records; nor are the letters of Washington, which may be found as dated in the Fitzpatrick *Writings*. Documents heretofore unpublished are marked with *asterisks. For convenience the following abbreviations are employed: AHR=*American Historical Review;* CP=Clinton Papers; FW=Fitzpatrick's *Writings* of Washington; HSP=Historical Society of Pennsylvania; JS:C=Jared Spark's *Correspondence of the American Revolution;* JS:W=Jared Spark's *Writings* of Washington; MAH=*Magazine of American History;* NYHS=New York Historical Society; NYPL=New York Public Library; *PA, PA*2, *PA*5=respectively *Pennsylvania Archives, First, Second,* and *Fifth Series;* PCC=Papers of the Continental Congress; PMHB=*Pennsylvania Magazine of History and Biography;* RP=Reed Papers; WLCL=William L. Clements Library; WP= Washington Papers; WayP=Wayne Papers.

1779

March 27: *A Warning to Rebels, by John Mason. Sent to Sir Henry Clinton July 15, 1780. CP. (Chap. 8, Sec. II)

*Walter Stewart to Joseph Reed, undated. Stewart Papers, NYHS. (Chap. 2, Sec. I)

1780

July 15: *John Mason to Sir Henry Clinton. CP. (Chap. 8, Sec. II). Further information about Mason's earlier career in S. W. Eager's *Outline History of Orange County* (1846-47), pp. 551-62

Oct. 7: Anthony Wayne to Joseph Reed. Reed's *Reed,* II, 315, (Chap. 3, Sec. I)

Oct. 15: *John Dalling to Sir Henry Clinton, about William Odell's mission to New York. CP. (Chap. 8, Sec. II)

Oct. 15: *Edward Barry to William Odell. CP. (Chap. 8, Sec. II)

Oct. 25: Anthony Wayne to Joseph Reed. Reed's *Reed,* II, 270-71. (Chap. 3, Sec. I)

Nov. 6: *Marriage bond of James Ogden and Catherine Pitt, in archives of the Secretary of State of New Jersey. (Chap. 11, Sec. I)

Nov. 10: *William Bernard Gifford to Oliver De Lancey. CP. (Chap. 17, Sec. I)

Nov. 20: *Thomas Craig to Anthony Wayne. WayP. (Chap. 3, Sec. I)

Nov. 20: *William Bernard Gifford to Oliver De Lancey. CP. (Chap. 17, Sec. I)

Nov. 22: *Anthony Wayne to William Irvine. WayP. (Chap. 3, Sec. I)

Dec. 6: *Anthony Wayne to William Irvine. WayP. (Chap. 3, Sec. I)

Dec. 7: *William Bernard Gifford to Oliver De Lancey, with intelligence inclosed. CP. (Chap. 17, Sec. I)

Dec. 7: *Anthony Wayne to Azariah Dunham, about want of rum at Mount Kemble. WayP. (Chap. 3, Sec. I)

Dec. 10: *Anthony Wayne to George Washington, with Diagram of Mount Kemble. WP. (Chap. 3, Sec. III-IV)

Dec. 11: Return of Pennsylvania troops at Mount Kemble. *PA,* VIII, 647. (Chap. 3, Sec. II)

Dec. 12: *William Bernard Gifford to Oliver De Lancey. CP. (Chap. 17, Sec. I)

Dec. 16: Anthony Wayne to Joseph Reed. Reed's *Reed,* II, 315-17. (Chap. 3, Sec. I)

Dec. 16: Anthony Wayne to Francis Johnston. Stillé's *Wayne,* 240-41. (Chap. 3, Sec. I)

Dec. 21: *John Mason to John Stapleton. CP. (Chap. 8, Sec. II)

Dec. 22: *John Hendricks to Benjamin Fishbourne, about renegade spies. WP. (Chap. 17, Sec. I)

Dec. 24: *Sir Henry Clinton to John Dalling, about recruiting by Benedict Arnold and William Odell. CP. (Chap. 8, Sec. II)

Dec. 25: *Anthony Wayne to George Washington, inclosing Queries brought by a spy and Answers given. WP; WayP, with different version of Queries and Answers. (Chap. 17, Sec I)

Dec. 25: *Thomas Church to Anthony Wayne. WayP. (Chap. 10, Sec. I)

Dec. 28: *Anthony Wayne to Lucas Beverholt (van Beverhoudt). WayP. (Chap. 4)

Dec. 29: Proclamation of British Peace Commissioners. CP. (Chap. 8, Sec. I)

Dec. 29: *Mary Dagworthy to George Washington, about stockings for New Jersey troops. WP. (Chap. 19, Sec. II)

Dec. 30: *Anthony Wayne to John Moylan. WayP. (Chap. 3, Sec. III)

1781

Jan. 2: Anthony Wayne to George Washington, 4:30 A. M. Draft in WayP. Stillé's *Wayne*, 242-43, omits paragraph about orders of 2nd. (Chap. 1)

Jan. 2: Anthony Wayne to George Washington, 9 A. M. JS:C, III, 192-93. (Chap. 4)

Jan. 2: Enos Reeves to three unidentified correspondents. *PMHB*, XXI, 72-75. (Chap. 4)

Jan. 3: *Henry Latimer to George Washington. WP. (Chap. 5, Sec. I)

Jan. 3: *Intelligence by Gould. CP. (Chap. 6, Sec. II)

Jan. 3: *Intelligence by Thomas and Abram Ward of Newark. CP. (Chap. 6, Sec. II)

Jan. 3: *Andrew Gautier to Oliver De Lancey. CP. (Chap. 6, Sec. II) Account of Gautier and Continental currency in Force's *American Archives: Fourth Series*, VI, 1335, 1345, 1360-61, 1365. Account of the Gautier family by John Stagg Gautier in C. H. Winfield's *History of the County of Hudson, New Jersey* (1874), pp. 549-55. Members of class of 1773 at King's College in M. H. Thomas's *Columbia University Officers and Students* 1754-1857 (1936), p. 103.

Jan. 4: Charles Stewart to Joseph Reed. *PA*, VIII, 698-99. (Chap. 7, Sec. I, II)

Jan. 4: *Anthony Wayne, Richard Butler, and Walter Stewart to George Washington. WP. (Chap. 7, Sec. I)

Jan. 4: *Arthur St. Clair to the President of Congress. PCC. (Chap. 7, Sec. II)

Jan. 4: Marquis de Lafayette to Chevalier de La Luzerne. *AHR*, XX, 578-79. (Chap. 7, Sec. II)

Jan. 5: *Joseph Reed to the President of Congress. PCC. (Chap. 9, Sec. II)

Jan. 5: Joseph Reed to William Moore. *PA2*, XI, 667, with incomplete address. (Chap. 9, Sec. II)

Jan. 5: Thomas Moore to Anthony Wayne. Stillé's *Wayne*. 254-55. (Chap. 7, Sec. II; Chap. 13, Sec. I)

Jan. 5: *Andrew Gautier to Oliver De Lancey. CP. (Chap. 8, Sec. III). Original of letter digested in De Lancey's Journal for Jan. 6.

Jan. 5: *Frederick Mackenzie to Oliver De Lancey, about sending Joseph Clark and Isaac Siscoe as spies. CP. (Chap. 8, Sec. III)

Jan. 5: *John Stapleton to Oliver De Lancey, on landing of Mason. CP. (Chap. 8, Sec. III)

Jan. 5: *Stewart Ross to Oliver De Lancey. CP. (Chap. 8, Sec. III)

APPENDIX

Jan. 5: *Dr. Welding (George Playter) to Oliver De Lancey, declining to take message to mutineers. CP. (Chap. 16, Sec. IV)

Jan. 6: Joseph Reed to William Moore *PA2*, XI, 673-74, wrongly given as addressed to Wayne

Jan. 6: *William Bowzar to Anthony Wayne, refusing compliance with Wayne's proposals of 4th. PPC. (Chap. 10, Sec. I)

Jan. 6: *William Bowzar to Anthony Wayne, about orders of 2nd. WayP. (Chap. 10, Sec. I)

Jan. 6: Enos Reeves to unidentified correspondent, about affairs at Mount Kemble. *PMHB*, XXI, 75-76. (Chap. 13, Sec. I)

Jan. 6: *William Heath to George Washington, on informing West Point troops of Pennsylvania mutiny. WP. (Chap. 13, Sec. II)

Jan. 6: *Stewart Ross to Oliver De Lancey, about return of Uzal Woodruff and failure of Gould to return. CP. (Chap. 13, Sec. III)

Jan. 7: John Witherspoon to the President of Congress. Burnett, V, 515-16. (Chap. 10, Sec. I; Chap. 11, Sec. II)

Jan. 7: John Sullivan to George Washington, JS:C. III, 194. (Chap. 17, Sec. II)

Jan. 7: Joseph Reed to the Committee of Congress. *PA2*, XI, 695, wrongly dated the 9th. (Chap. 11, Sec. II)

Jan. 7: Joseph Reed to William Moore. *PA2*, XI, 678-79, wrongly addressed to the Committee of Congress. (Chap. 11, Sec. II)

Jan. 7: *Arthur St. Clair to the President of Congress. PCC. (Chap. 13, Sec. I)

Jan. 7: Arthur St. Clair to George Washington. JS:C, III, 195-98. (Chap. 9, Sec. I; Chap. 13, Sec. I)

Jan. 7: Arthur St. Clair to Joseph Reed. *PA*, VIII, 701. (Chap. 13, Sec. I)

Jan. 7: Arthur St. Clair to Anthony Wayne. *St. Clair Papers*, I, 535. (Chap. 13, Sec. I)

Jan. 7: *Lafayette to George Washington. Sparks MSS, Harvard College Library. (Chap. 13, Sec. I)

Jan. 7: Lafayette to John Sullivan. Sullivan's *Letters and Papers*, III, 252. (Chap. 13, Sec. I)

Jan. 7: Lafayette to Walter Stewart. Quoted in part in Louis Gottschalk's *Lafayette and the Close of the American Revolution* (1942), p. 170. (Chap. 13, Sec. I)

Jan. 7: Lafayette to La Luzerne. *AHR*, XX, 579-81. (Chap. 13, Sec. I)

Jan. 7: *John Laurens to George Washington. WP. (Chap. 17, Sec. I)

Jan. 7: *Lord Stirling to George Washington. WP. (Chap. 19, Sec. II)

Jan. 7: *Cortlandt Skinner to Oliver De Lancey. CP. Original of letter partly digested in De Lancey's Journal for the 7th. (Chap. 13, Sec. III)

Jan. 7: *Henry Van Dyck to Oliver De Lancey, introducing Nathan Frink. CP. (Chap. 13, Sec. III)

Jan. 8: John Sullivan to the President of Congress. Burnett, V, 518-19

Jan. 8: Joseph Reed to William Moore. *PA2*, XI, 682-83, wrongly addressed to the Committee of Congress.

Jan. 8: *Joseph Reed to Anthony Wayne. WayP

Jan. 8: *Anthony Wayne to George Washington. WP. In part in JS:W, VII, 459n, and in FW, XXI, 88n (Chap. 11, Sec. I; Chap. 14, Sec. II)

Jan. 8: *Anthony Wayne, Richard Butler, and Walter Stewart to the President of Congress. PCC. (Chap. 11, Sec. I; Chap. 14, Sec. II)

Jan. 8: Anthony Wayne, Richard Butler, and Walter Stewart to the

Pennsylvania officers at Pennington. Stillé's *Wayne*, 255-56. (Chap. 14, Sec. II)

Jan. 8: *Arthur St. Clair to George Washington, about the British emissary at Morristown. WP. (Chap. 11, Sec. I; Chap. 16, Sec. II)

Jan. 8: *Thomas Craig to Anthony Wayne. WayP. (Chap. 13, Sec. I)

Jan. 8: Adam Hubley to Anthony Wayne. Stillé's *Wayne*, 257. (Chap. 13, Sec. I)

Jan. 8: *Andrew Gautier to Oliver De Lancey. CP. Original of letter "dated Monday night" in De Lancey's Journal for the 9th. (Chap. 16, Sec. I)

Jan. 8: *John Stapleton to Oliver De Lancey, about Nathan Frink. CP. (Chap. 13, Sec. III)

Jan. 8: *Charles Sterling to William Phillips, about party from *Vulture*. CP. (Chap. 16, Sec. I)

Jan. 8: *Anonymous correspondent to Peter Dubois, about handbills in Jersey brigade. CP. (Chap. 19, Sec. II)

Jan. 9: John Sullivan to the President of Congress. Burnett, V, 522-23

Jan. 9: John Sullivan to George Washington. Burnett, V, 523

Jan. 9: *Sir Henry Clinton's List of Proposals sent out and by Whom Carried. CP. (Chap. 16, Sec. III)

Jan. 9: *William Phillips to Oliver De Lancey. CP. (Chap. 16, Sec. I)

Jan. 9: *Oliver De Lancey to Sir Henry Clinton, with comment on Gautier's reliability. CP. (Chap. 16, Sec. I)

Jan. 9: *Joshua Loring to Oliver De Lancey, about Baron Ottendorf. CP. (Chap. 16, Sec. IV). Further letters about Ottendorf: *De Lancey to Loring, Jan. 11, and *Loring to De Lancey, Jan. 14, both in CP

Jan. 9: *Intelligence by Joseph Clark. CP. (Chap. 8, Sec. III; Chap. 16, Sec. I)

Jan. 9: *From unknown loyalist to British Headquarters. CP. (Chap. 16, Sec. I)

Jan. 10: John Sullivan to the President of Congress. Burnett, V, 526-27

Jan. 10: *John Sullivan to the President of Congress, second letter of the day, mentioning "additional proposals" from the British. PCC. (Chap. 16, Sec. II)

Jan. 10: John Sullivan to George Washington, mentioning trial of emissaries in progress. JS:C, III, 198-99. (Chap. 15, Sec. II)

Jan. 10: *Anthony Wayne to the Committee of Congress, sending two emissaries (McFarlan and Caleb Bruen). PCC. (Chap. 16, Sec. II)

Jan. 10: *Anthony Wayne to the Supreme Executive Council of Pennsylvania, asking that enlistment papers for the Line be sent at once. WayP

Jan. 10: *Intelligence by Isaac Siscoe. CP. (Chap. 8, Sec. III)

Jan. 11: John Sullivan to the President of Congress. Burnett, V, 528

Jan. 11: *Joseph Reed to Anthony Wayne, about Wayne's going to Pennington. WayP. (Chap. 15, Sec. III)

Jan. 11: *Arthur St. Clair to George Washington. WP

Jan. 11: *Anthony Wayne to George Washington, about Mason's warning. WP. (Chap. 15, Sec. II)

Jan. 11: Diary account by David H. Conyngham of execution of spies at Trenton. *History of the First Troop Philadelphia City Cavalry* (1875), p. 28; reprinted in part, without Conyngham's name, in *PA2*, XI, 702. (Chap. 15, Sec. II)

Jan. 11: *James Robertson to Sir Henry Clinton, about co-operation of British Navy. CP. (Chap. 16, Sec. I)

APPENDIX

Jan. 11: *John Stapleton to Oliver De Lancey, sending Dr. Welding (George Playter) with letter to carry to William Thompson. CP. (Chap. 16, Sec. I)

Jan. 11: *Intelligence by Cornelius Tyger. CP. (Chap. 5, Sec. I; Chap. 16, Sec. I)

Jan. 11: *Intelligence by Ezekiel Yeomans. CP. (Chap. 16, Sec. I)

Jan. 12: *Anthony Wayne to George Washington, repeating Mason's warning. WP; also in Bancroft Transcripts, NYPL; in part in FW, XXI, 92n. (Chap. 15, Sec. II)

Jan. 12: Philemon Dickinson to George Washington, mentioning movements and posts of Jersey militia. JS:C, III, 205-07. (Chap. 9, Sec. III)

Jan. 12: *Sir Henry Clinton to James Robertson. CP. (Chap. 16, Sec. I)

Jan. 12: *Sir Henry Clinton to the Duke of Gloucester, on progress of Pennsylvania mutiny. CP

Jan. 12: *Oliver De Lancey to Andrew Gautier. CP. (Chap. 16, Sec. I)

Jan. 12: *Stewart Ross to Oliver De Lancey. CP. (Chap. 16, Sec. I)

Jan. 12: *Beverley Robinson to Sir Henry Clinton, about address by William Smith to troops at West Point. CP. (Chap. 16, Sec. I)

Jan. 12: *Intelligence at Night, giving the mutineers' line of march (Chap. 4), story of Wayne and Irish soldier (Chap. 4), details in Chap. 16, Sec. I; also reference to Gifford in cipher. CP

Jan. 13: John Sullivan to George Washington. Burnett, V. 529

Jan. 13: John Sullivan to La Luzerne, narrative of Pennsylvania mutiny. Burnett, V, 529-31

Jan. 13: *William Heath to George Washington, about attitude of troops at West Point. WP. Digested in JS:W, VII, 367n. (Chap. 16, Sec. II)

Jan. 13: *Francis Johnston to Anthony Wayne. WayP. (Chap. 18, Sec. II)

Jan. 13: *Daniel Coxe to Oliver De Lancey, warning against Dr. Dayton. CP. (Chap. 16, Sec. III)

Jan. 13: *Isaac Ogden to Oliver De Lancey, warning against Dr. Dayton. CP. (Chap. 16, Sec. III)

Jan. 13: *Samuel Wallis to Daniel Coxe, mentioning conduct of John Mason at execution. CP. (Chap. 15, Sec. II)

Jan. 13: *William Bernard Gifford to Oliver De Lancey. CP. (Chap. 17, Sec. I)

Jan. 13: *Cornelius Hatfield to William Bernard Gifford, making appointment. WP. (Chap. 17, Sec. I)

Jan. 14: *Arthur St. Clair to George Washington. WP

Jan. 14: Lafayette to La Luzerne. *AHR*, XX, 581-83

Jan. 14: Enos Reeves to two unidentified correspondents, with later news from Mount Kemble. *PMHB*, XXI, 77-79

Jan. 14: *Oliver De Lancey to John Stapleton, about deserters from West Point and men of property as emissaries. CP. (Chap. 16, Sec. I)

Jan. 14: *George Beckwith to Oliver De Lancey, proposing Samuel Wallis as emissary to Pennsylvania mutineers. CP. (Chap. 16, Sec. III)

Jan. 15: John Sullivan to George Washington. Burnett, V, 533

Jan. 15: *Anthony Wayne to the Supreme Executive Council of Pennsylvania. WayP. (Chap. 18, Sec. II)

Jan. 15: *Andrew Gautier to Oliver De Lancey, CP. Original of letter digested in De Lancey's Journal for the 15th

Jan. 15: *Intelligence by Uzal Woodruff. CP. (Chap. 16, Sec. I; Chap. 19, Sec. II)

Jan. 15: *Intelligence by Isaac Ruggles. CP. (Chap. 16, Sec. I)

Jan. 15: *Intelligence by Jonathan Odell, mentioning Ogden, Rattoon, Fegany, "Haynes alias Murphy." CP. (Chap. 16, Sec. I)

Jan. 15: *Intelligence by unknown person, giving story of British deserter and Gibraltar mutiny. CP. (Chap. 14, Sec. I)

Jan. 15: *Intelligence by William Boyce. Original of long paper digested in De Lancey's Journal for the 15th. CP. (Chap. 16, Sec. I) A copy of this intelligence has Clinton's endorsement about sending six spies. (Chap. 16, Sec. III)

Jan. 16: *Robert Howe to George Washington. WP. (Chap. 17, Sec. II)

Jan 16: *Samuel John Atlee to Joseph Reed. RP. (Chap. 18, Sec. II)

Jan. 17: *Arthur St. Clair to George Washington. WP

Jan. 17: *Anthony Wayne to George Washington. WP

Jan. 17: *William Irvine to George Washington. WP. (Chap. 18, Sec. II)

Jan. 17: Enos Reeves to an unidentified correspondent, with news from Mount Kemble. *PMHB*, XXI, 79-80

Jan. 17: Account of Pennsylvania mutiny in *New Jersey Gazette.* Reprinted in Frank Moore's *Diary of the American Revolution* (ed. 1860), II, 373-74

Jan. 17: New Arrangement of the Pennsylvania Line. Stillé's *Wayne,* 383-89

Jan. 17: Lafayette to La Luzerne. *AHR,* XX, 583-84

Jan. 17: *Benjamin Lincoln to George Washington, about Massachusetts gratuity to troops. WP. (Chap. 19, Sec. I)

Jan. 17: *Sergeants of the 2nd Massachusetts to Ebenezer Sprout. WP. (Chap. 19, Sec. I)

Jan. 17: *Israel Shreve to George Washington, reporting anxiety over New Jersey Line. WP

Jan. 18: *William Bernard Gifford to Oliver De Lancey, intelligence of New Jersey discontents. CP. (Chap. 19, Sec. II)

Jan. 19: Lewis Farmer to William Moore, on progress of settlement at Trenton. *PA,* VIII, 706

Jan. 19 (?): *Andrew Gautier to Oliver De Lancey. CP. Gautier's illness at first news of Pennsylvania mutiny (Chap. 8, Sec. I); Mason's name given as Hynds (Chap. 16, Sec. I); Elias Dayton's knowledge of emissaries (Chap. 17, Sec. I); distrust of Gould (Chap. 17, Sec. I); instructions given to faithful friend (Chap. 16, Sec. I, II)

Jan. 19-Feb. 5: *Entries in Orderly Book of the New Jersey Line, NYPL. (Chap. 21, Sec. II)

Jan. 20: Meshech Weare to George Washington, about New Hampshire gratuity to troops. JS:C, III, 211-12. (Chap. 19, Sec. I)

Jan. 20: Israel Shreve to George Washington, announcing revolt at Pompton. JS:W, VII, 561. (Chap. 19, Sec. II)

Jan. 20: Intelligence by McFarlan. CP. Original of paper copied with slight changes in Private Intelligence, and in *MAH,* X, 333-35. Source of information about Williams (Chap. 5, Sec. II), arrival of Mason at Princeton (Chap. 11, Sec. I), McFarlan and Bruen at Princeton and Trenton (Chap. 16, Sec. II)

Jan. 20: Intelligence by Potts. CP. Printed in *MAH.* X, 331-32

Jan. 20: *William Bernard Gifford to Oliver De Lancey. CP

Jan. 21: Anthony Wayne to George Washington. WP. In part in JS:W, VII, 387. (Chap. 18, Sec. II)

APPENDIX

Jan. 22: Intelligence by Gould, incorrectly dated the 20th. Original in CP. Printed *MAH*, X, 331. (Chap. 19, Sec. III)

Jan. 22 (?): Intelligence by William Bernard Gifford, incorrectly said to belong to a Massachusetts regiment. Original in CP. Printed with variations in *MAH*, X, 332-33, dated the 20th. Entered in De Lancey's Journal for the 21st. According to *New York Gazette* for January 29, Gifford arrived in New York the 21st.

Jan. 23: Form of pardon for the New Jersey mutineers. JS:W, VII, 562. (Chap. 19, Sec. II)

Jan. 23: Thomas Proctor to Joseph Reed, about his men's enlistments. *PA*, VIII, 710. (Chap. 18, Sec. II)

Jan. 23: Benedict Arnold to Sir Henry Clinton, expecting that Pennsylvania mutineers will join the British. CP. Often printed

Jan. 24: Report of the Committee of Congress on the Pennsylvania Mutiny. *Journals*, XIX, 79-83. Valuable at many points

Jan. 24: *James Potter to Joseph Reed, about progress of settlement at Trenton. RP

Jan. 24: *Pennsylvania Packet*, account of the Pennsylvania mutiny. Reprinted in Hazard's *Register*, II, 137-38. Referred to slightly in Wayne to Washington, Jan. 29, Stillé's *Wayne*, 261

Jan. 24: Elias Dayton to George Washington, about New Jersey mutineers at Chatham. JS:W, VII, 561-62. (Chap. 19, Sec. II)

Jan. 24: *Oliver De Lancey to James Paterson at Paulus Hook, telling him to look out for approach of New Jersey mutineers. CP

Jan. 24: *Intelligence by Cornelius Haskins, and other deserters who had been with Humphreys on his Christmas attempt. CP. (Chap. 6, Sec. I)

Jan. 25: Board of War to the President of Congress, about discharged Pennsylvania soldiers clamoring in Philadelphia. Burnett, V, 544. (Chap. 18, Sec. II)

Jan. 25: *Robert Howe to George Washington. WP. (Chap. 20, Sec. II)

Jan. 25. *Draft of proposals To the Jersey Brigade. CP. (Chap. 19, Sec. III)

Jan. 25: *Draft of Letter to the Person Commanding the Jersey Troops. CP. (Chap. 19, Sec. III)

Jan. 25: Sir Henry Clinton to Lord George Germain, on progress of mutiny to date. Printed in part in *London Gazette*, February 20; in Almon's *Remembrancer*, XI, 148-49

Jan. 25: Samuel Wallis to Daniel Coxe, about effect of mutiny on public opinion. *MAH*, X, 497

Jan. 26: Lafayette to La Luzerne, about expedition to Ringwood. *AHR*, XX, 584-85. (Chap. 20, Sec. I)

Jan. 26: *Oliver De Lancey to Sir Henry Clinton, about two copies of proposals sent to New Jersey mutineers. CP. (Chap. 19, Sec. III)

Jan. 26: Frederick Mackenzie to Oliver De Lancey, with intelligence concerning the New Jersey revolt. *MAH*, X, 337-38

Jan. 26: Unidentified correspondent to Peter Dubois, about New Jersey revolt. *MAH*, X, 378-79

Jan 26 (?): Andrew Fürstner's Report, of his secret mission of Jan. 15-25. CP. Printed *Publisher's Weekly*, with reproduction in facsimile. Nov. 29, 1941. (Chap. 11, Sec. I)

Jan. 27: Robert Howe to George Washington. JS:W, VII, 563-65. (Chap. 20, Sec. II)

Jan. 27: *Elias Dayton to Robert Howe. WP. (Chap. 20, Sec. III)

Jan. 27: Intelligence by Mr. J. (Andrew Gautier). Original in CP. Printed in *MAH*, X, 340

Jan. 28: Intelligence regarding the New Jersey revolt. Original in CP. Printed in *MAH*, X, 341

Jan. 28: Israel Shreve to George Washington, explanation of Shreve's absence from the Pompton suppression. In part in FW, XXI, 150n, with Washington's peremptory note of that day.

Jan. 29: *Robert Howe to George Washington, mentioning surrender of British emissaries to Dayton. WP. (Chap. 20, Sec. III)

Jan. 29: Anthony Wayne to George Washington, Stillé's *Wayne*, 260-61. (Chap. 21, Sec. II)

Jan. 29: *Sir Henry Clinton to Lord George Germain. CP. (Chap. 21, Sec. I)

Jan. 29: Account in *New York Gazette* of William Bernard Gifford's arrival in New York and his reasons for quitting the rebel cause. (Chap. 17, Sec. I)

Jan. 30: Lafayette to Vergennes. *Stevens's Facsimiles*, No. 1632. (Chap. 21, Sec. I)

Jan. 31: Intelligence by Abner Badsby (Badgley?), referring to proposals dropped in the Jersey camp. Original in CP. Printed in *MAH*, X, 410. (Chap. 20, Sec. III)

Feb. 3: Andrew Gautier (as Mr. J. at Elizabethtown) to Oliver De Lancey, about New Jersey suppression. Though by Gautier plainly dated the 3rd, this is dated only as received the 7th in *MAH*, X, 417-19. (Chap. 20, Sec. III)

Feb. 7: Henry Knox to George Washington, on Knox's mission to the Eastern States. JS:C, III, 222-25. (Chap. 19, Sec. I)

Feb. 10: Intelligence by Caleb Bruen. *MAH*, X, 419. Not long after this Bruen appears to have been imprisoned by the British for doubledealing. On March 9 *Dayton to Washington: "Three persons upon whom I very considerably depended for the discovery of every important movement or transaction of the enemy are apprehended and closely confined in New York." On Dec. 27 Dayton to Washington referred to "Pool, Bruin, Woodruff, and Blackledge, all of whom have been very serviceable to us, and are now confined in irons, in their dungeons as criminals." (FW, XXIII, 428n). On January 12, 1782, Dayton to Washington: "Bruin, who first gave notice of Sir Harry's correspondence with the Pennsylvania revolters, and whom they have held in irons since that period in New York, I have got enlarged" (FW, XXIII, 428n). Bruen's own later story of his conduct is in Joseph Atkinson's *History of Newark, New Jersey* (1878), p. 116. At some time after 1782 Bruen was one of sixty property owners of Newark who claimed losses of goods and chattels taken or destroyed by British troops or their adherents. (*Calendar of the State Library Manuscript Collection, Trenton, New Jersey* [1939], No. 492). Bruen claimed to have lost a pair of "match horses" and 2 hogsheads of rum in 1776; a silver watch, silver buckles, and sundry dry goods in 1780; cash to the amount of £32-3-0, an English mare, and fifteen sheep in 1781: a total value of £307-3-0. Later references to Bruen in WP show that he was suspected of illicit trading: *Correspondence . . . with the Officers*, III, 2335, 2339

Feb. 11: Walter Stewart to George Washington, on conflict between Reed and Philadelphia merchants. FW, XXI, 280n. (Chap. 18, Sec. II)

Feb. 19: *Joseph Reed and James

APPENDIX

Potter to George Washington. Letter in WP. Draft in RP.

Feb. 22: Joseph Reed to the Committee of the Pennsylvania Assembly, surveying the mutiny. *PA,* VIII, 737-38

Feb. 22: *Gould to Elias Dayton, double-dealing letter. WP. (Chap. 17, Sec. I)

Feb. 27: Anthony Wayne to George Washington. Stillé's *Wayne,* 262

Feb. 28: Francis Barber to Elias Dayton, about riot of Jersey troops at Princeton. Quoted in Lundin, 444. (Chap. 21, Sec. II)

Feb. 28: Intelligence by McFarlan, of offers from Dayton. *MAH,* X, 501

March 2: Arthur St. Clair to George Washington, against attempt to punish Pennsylvania mutineers for "flagitious manner" of getting discharges by swearing off. *St. Clair Papers,* I, 542-43

March 2: Intelligence by Woodruff, about Lafayette's march against Arnold. *MAH,* X, 498.

March 4: *Intelligence by Dr. Welding (George Playter), about friendly attitude of William Thompson. CP. (Chap. 16, Sec. IV)

March 9: *Elias Dayton to George Washington, about capture of three of Dayton's spies. WP. (Chap. 17, Sec. I). Also Dayton to Washington, Dec. 27 (FW, XXII, 428n), naming captured spies as Pool (Thomas Poole?), Bruin (Caleb Bruen), (Uzal) Woodruff, (John?) Blackledge

March 14: William Irvine to Anthony Wayne, about delay in raising Pennsylvania Line. Reed's *Reed,* II, 356-57

March 19: *Anthony Wayne to George Washington. WayP. (Chap. 21, Sec. II)

March 19: *Intelligence by Absalom Evans, deserter to the British, about shooting Captain Tolbert at Mount Kemble. CP. (Chap. 4)

March 21: *Walter Stewart to George Washington, about soldiers' sense of guilt over false oaths. WP.

March 23: *Power of administration to Benjamin Ogden for James Ogden "who died without a will as far as I know and as I verily believe." Office of Secretary of State of New Jersey. (Chap. 11, Sec. I)

Apr. 4: Intelligence by Uzal Woodruff, claiming to be intimate with Dayton but no longer with "Mr. J—ne"—probably "Jeune" or Andrew Gautier, Junior. *MAH,* XI, 60-61 (Chap. 20, Sec. III). Woodruff some time after this was imprisoned by the British for double-dealing. He was still a prisoner on Dec. 27 (FW, XXIII, 428n.) Woodruff's running away from his apprenticeship and his marriage appear in E. F. Hatfield's *History of Elizabeth, New Jersey* (1868), pp. 390, 626; his later operating a ferry, in Nicholas Murray's *Notes, Historical and Biographical, concerning Elizabethtown* (1844), p. 163; the date of his death, March 22, 1794, in *New England Historical and Genealogical Register,* XLV, 50

Apr. 13: *Anthony Wayne to Joseph Reed, about difficulties in equipping Pennsylvania Line. RP

May 20: *Proceedings of a Brigadier General Court Martial held at Yorktown by Order of Brigadier General Wayne, for trial of John Fortescue. WP. (Chap. 21, Sec. II; Appendix: Note on the After-Mutiny)

May 22: *Proceedings of a General Court Martial held at Yorktown by Order of General Wayne, for trial of William Crofts, Thomas Wilson, Samuel Franklin, James Wilson, Philip Smith. WP. (Chap.

21, Sec. II; Appendix: Note on the After-Mutiny)

May 26: *Anthony Wayne to George Washington, sending proceedings of two courts martial. WP. (Chap. 21, Sec. II; Appendix: Note on the After-Mutiny)

June 16: Anthony Wayne to unidentified correspondent. WayP; Bancroft Transcripts, NYPL; in part in Stillé's *Wayne*, 265-66, incorrectly dated May 20. (Appendix: Note on the After-Mutiny)

July 2: Intelligence by Gould, reporting questions asked by Elias Dayton. *MAH*, XI, 534. (Chap. 17, Sec I)

July 8: Anthony Wayne to George Washington, with reference to good conduct of Pennsylvania troops in Virginia. JS:C, III, 349

1782

Apr. 22: *Nathanael Greene to George Washington, about the discontent in the Southern Army. "In the Pennsylvania Line it appears to have originated, and they have endeavored to spread their contagion throughout the Army with appearance of success. I have been able to prove the fact but upon one person, whom I ordered to be shot this day. He was a sergeant and had much influence in the Line." Greene Papers, WLCL. (Chap. 21, Sec. II)

Index

A. J., Mr., probably Mr. Andrew, Jr., meaning Gautier, on Clinton's List of Proposals, 175
Acquackanonck (Passaic), N. J., 67
Albany, N. Y., 162
Alexander, William. *See* Stirling, Lord
Allen, Ethan, reported ready to join British, 84
Allentown, N. J., 75, 108
Amboy (Perth or South), N. J., 83, 86, 117, 161, 181
American Legion, Arnold's corps in Provincial forces, 70
André, John, 70, 83, 92
Arbuthnot, Marriot, ready to assist Clinton, 164-65
Ariel, frigate commanded by John Paul Jones, 239
Arnold, Benedict, dines with Washington, and betrays secret, 25; treason discovered, 26; raid to Virginia, 39; Wayne uncertain about, 39; 62; suggests capture of Washington by British, 63; Washington's plan to capture, 63; believes American soldiers will follow him to British, 70; his American Legion, 70; rumors that his friends are among Pennsylvania mutineers, 79; supposed to have reached Virginia, 84; 92; given first pick of American deserters, 93; 94; Pennsylvania mutineers refuse to follow example of, 118; 141; deserters unwilling to serve under, 163; 167; uncertainty about his departure for Virginia, 180-81 expects Pennsylvania mutineers to join British, 267
Articles of Confederation, ratification, 239-40
Artillery. *See* Fieldpieces
Artillery artificers, at Carlisle, 36
Assunpinck Creek, Trenton, 151
Atlee, Samuel John, appointed to Committee of Congress, 99; 108; to commission on Pennsylvania mutineers' claims, 152; on disorder at Bordentown, 199-200

Bailey, James, 206
Barber, Francis, 140; suspects Gifford, 186-87; informs Howe about New Jersey mutineers, 220; presents ultimatum, 222; on possibility of British invasion, 226; commands New Jersey detachment sent to Virginia, 231-32
Barclay, Thomas, Committee of Congress quartered at his house Summer Seat, 152; Mason and Ogden tried there, 154-56
Bardham, Silvanus, 206
Bates, Elisha, 206
Battery, New York, 64
Bayard family, 42
Beacons, announce Pennsylvania mutiny, 50, 66
Beekman, Cornelius, keeps Sign of the College at Princeton, 61
Beekman, Grace Otis, 61
Bergen Neck, N. J., refugees' Fort De Lancey at, 68-69, 87, 94, 141, 181
Bernardsville, N. J., 53
Bettin, Adam, killed at Mount Kemble, 13, 46, 47; Bettin Oak, 47
Beverholt (van Beverhoudt), Lucas, invites Wayne to dinner, 42
Beverwyck, N. J., Beverholt estate, 42; W. S. Livingston at, 250
Bigham, John, embezzlement of Pennsylvania funds, 37, 40
Blachly, Ebenezer, Wayne's baggage at his house, 134
Blaine, Ephraim, 193
Bland, Theodorick, appointed to Committee of Congress, 99, 108
Blank (or Blanck), unidentified emissary to Pennsylvania mutineers, 94, on Clinton's List of Proposals, 175; emissary to New Jersey mutineers, 214; drops proposals at Chatham, 224; source, 268

INDEX

Blankets, shortage at Valley Forge, 19; allowance of, 27; at Mount Kemble, 33; 40, 147
Blazing Star, N. J., ferry landing opposite Staten Island, 245
Bloomsbury, Trent-Cox house at Trenton, 104; Reed and Wayne quartered at, 152; Mason and Ogden brought to, 153
Bolland, Moses, 206
Bordentown, N. J., 102, 117, 150, 151, 195; disorder at, 200
Bounties, for enlistments in Continental Army, 16; Pennsylvania added bounty of 1778, 16; bounties by other States in 1779, 16-17; in 1780, 20; Pennsylvania bounty of 1780, 35; 20-dollar and 120-dollar men in Pennsylvania Line, 72; for Pennsylvania recruits, 197
Bowzar, William, secretary of Pennsylvania Board of Sergeants, 57; letters to Wayne, 75, 105-06; invitation to Reed, 107; snubbed by Reed, 120; 123, 145, 146; does not sign note surrendering Mason and Ogden, 153; last note, refusing reward, 159
Box, Sergeant, rumored in New York to be commander of Pennsylvania mutiny, 140-41
Boyce, William, information by, 166
Boys, as officers' waiters (servants), 32
Bradford, William, Jr., captured by Mason's band, 91
Brandywine, battle of, 206
Bristol, Pa., Reed at, 100-01
British offers to Continental soldiers, at Morristown in May 1780, 21-22; 40, 70, 83; to Pennsylvania mutineers, 85-86, 94; by Mason, detained, 115-18; other copies of proposals dropped in Trenton, 154; by unidentified emissary to Morristown, 168-70; supposed additional offers, 173; untrustworthy emissaries, 175-76; further emissaries proposed, 176-79; offers to New Jersey mutineers, 213-14, 224-26; text of offers to Pennsylvania mutineers, 244-45
British peace commissioners, proclamation to persons in rebellion, 83-84; alleged offer of bribe to Reed, 100
British regiments and corps, 37th, 42nd, British Grenadiers, British Light Infantry, 68
Broad Street, Newark, 170
Broad Street, Trenton, 151
Broadway, New York, 63
Brodhead, Daniel, at Pittsburgh, 36; 202
Brooks, John, 191
Brown, Thomas, slave-trader, 67
Bruen, Caleb, of Newark, carries British proposals to Princeton, 141; double-dealing at Princeton and Trenton, 170-73; his later story, 171; on Clinton's List of Proposals, 174; 175, 176; imprisoned by British, 184; return to New York, 212; 225, 248, 249, 264, 266; sources, 268; 269
Bruen, Matthias, 170
Brunswick (New Brunswick), N. J., 64, 82, 102, 115, 116, 139, 140, 169
Buck, Moses, 206
Bucks County, Pa., 49
Budden, James, of Light Horse, 157
Burlington, N. J., 150
Butler, Edward, Percival, Thomas, 51
Butler, John, leader of loyalists and Indians from Canada, 89
Butler, Richard, with Wayne among Pennsylvania mutineers, 14; at Stony Point, 18; speaks to mutineers, 46; 47; character, 50-51; on way to Princeton, 54-56; 73-74, 76, 80, 97; just treatment of soldiers, 111; 118; to Maidenhead, 122; 124, 134, 145, 155, 202
Butler, William, attacked by mutineer, 46-47; 51, 202

Caldwell, James, commissioner from New Jersey legislature, 210
Calvin, Thomas, 21
Camden, battle of, 62
Campbell, Thomas, leads men against Pennsylvania mutineers, 46
Canandaigua, Lake, N. Y., 24
Candles, 40
Carle's tavern, in Smith's Clove, N. Y., 218
Carlisle, Pa., artillery artificers at, 36; 202
Cattle, price of in 1780, 37; with Pennsylvania mutineers on march, 53, 74
Chambers, James, dissatisfied with Pennsylvania settlement, 199
Charleston, S. C., capture of, 62
Charlottenburg, N. J., 222
Chatham, N. J., road to, 28, 47; New Jersey brigade ordered to, 50; 101; New Jersey detachment marched to, 135; 140, 171, 208; discontents at, 209-10; settlement with mutineers at, 211-

INDEX

12; 213, 218, 220; British proposals dropped at, 224
Cheesequake, N. J., British spy lands at, 115
Children, at Mount Kemble, 32
Chrystie, James, 32
Church, Thomas, destitute, 112
Cipher, used by Gautier, 68; facing page 94
Citadel, at Mount Kemble, 28, 30, 39, 182
Clark, John, murdered by loyalist partisans, 88
Clark, Joseph, British spy sent to Morristown, 94-95, 246, 264
Clark, Thomas, 21
Clinton, George, governor of New York, 88, 90
Clinton, Sir Henry, treacherously informed by Arnold, 25; Washington's plans to capture, 63-64; news of Pennsylvania mutiny reaches, 66; further inquiries, 67; strong position on New York islands, 68-69; efforts to prevent partisan warfare, 69; intentions respecting Pennsylvania mutineers, 70; 71; proclamation to persons in rebellion, 83-84; hesitates to invade New Jersey, but drafts proposals to mutineers, 85-86; 87; rewards Mason for capture of American officers, 91; obliged to give Arnold first pick of rebel deserters, 93; to Staten Island, 95; 117, 126; still unwilling to invade New Jersey, 141; 154; Mason sends message to before execution, 157; information slow in reaching, 160-67; no intention of treating mutineers as enemies, 163; from Staten Island to New York, 167; 169, 171; Wayne's counterplot against, 172-73; A List of Proposals Sent out and by Whom Carried, 173-75; his comment on his emissaries, 176, 177, 266; records of his secret service, 180; 185, 186, 188, 190; little interested in New Jersey mutiny, 213, 214; last hope of Pennsylvania mutiny, 228; report on mutinies, 228-29
Clinton, James, tribute in verse to, 211
Clothing, shortage at Valley Forge, 15; at Morristown 1779-80, 19; at Totowa, 27; as specified for Continental soldiers, 27; expected from France, 28-29; shirts bought by ladies of Philadelphia, 29, 37; complaints at Mount Kemble, 32-34, 40; at West Point, 62; promised to Pennsylvania mutineers, 74; Washington on Army's need of, 103, 139; Board of Sergeants insistent about, 105-06; 146-47; part of Pennsylvania bargain, 195; reaches Bordentown, 196; shortage in New Jersey Line, 208; from France and Spain, 238
Clove, The, N. Y., 217
Coffee, price at camp in 1779, 17; want of at Mount Kemble, 39
Coleman, James, sentenced to death for desertion and forgery, 21; execution, 24-25
College of New Jersey (Princeton), occupied by British and Americans, 60; Witherspoon president of, 79; Reed graduate of, 99; 125
Columbia College. See King's College
Colvin, Patrick, his wagon and Negro slave used at execution of Mason and Ogden, 157
Commissioners, to settle Pennsylvania claims, 130, 145-46, 148; members of commission, 152; conflict with officers, 197; responsibility for false oaths, 198; ask Board of Sergeants to continue, 200; 202
Committee of Congress. See Continental Congress, Committee of
Committee of Sergeants. See Sergeants, Board of
Connecticut Line, bounty of 1780, 20; mutiny of two regiments in May 1780, put down by Pennsylvania brigade, 22-23; to West Point, 26; former huts occupied by Pennsylvania troops, 29, 47; resentment against Pennsylvanians, 113; reported on way to New Jersey, 137; temper of, near West Point, 192-93; supplied clothing, 214-15; detachment to Ringwood, 217; aid in suppression of New Jersey mutiny at Pompton, 221-23; 226
Connell, Daniel, member of Board of Sergeants, 57; signs letter, 153
Continental Congress, votes bounty and gratuity of 1779, 17; advised by Wayne to leave Philadelphia, 51; Washington disapproves of this, 65; demands of Pennsylvania mutineers referred to by Wayne, 73; 75; learns of Pennsylvania mutiny and appoints Committee, 78-79; 86, 102; not specially blamed by mutineers, 110; 145, 161, 163, 166; resolution concerning

INDEX

rations, 202; 216, 228, 233; circular letter to States on needs of Army, 239; announces ratification of Articles of Confederation, 239

Continental Congress, Committee of to confer with the Supreme Executive Council of Pennsylvania, appointed, 78-79, 99; resolves to send Reed and Potter to negotiate with mutineers, 99; confers with Reed at Trenton, 108-09; receives news of detention of Mason and Ogden, 121; 123, 127-28, 130, 136, 138; resolution on terms to be offered mutineers, 144; authority invoked by Reed, 146; advised by Reed to leave Trenton, 150; to Summer Seat, 152; appoints commissioners to settle Pennsylvania claims, 152, 198; 155, 166; does not approve of Wayne's proposed counterplot, 173; 196; returns to Philadelphia, 197; asked by Washington not to offer terms to New Jersey mutineers, 216

Continental currency, rapid decline of in 1778, 15-16; depreciation supposed to be felt less by soldiers than by civilians, 17; Pennsylvania to make up to troops for loss by depreciation, 33; depreciation by end of 1780, 34; issue discontinued in March 1780; 37; depreciation values, 37; ceases to have any value, 233

Convicts, enlisted in Pennsylvania Line, 35, 233

Conyngham, David H., on last hours and execution of Mason and Ogden, 156-58; source, 264

Courts martial, of John Williams, 58; of Theophilus Parke, 111; of Mason and Ogden, 154-56; of New Jersey ringleaders, 222; of Pennsylvania soldiers at York, 234-36, 250, 269-70

Cox, John, of Bloomsbury, Trenton, 104

Craig, Thomas, repairs huts at Mount Kemble, 29; 75; threatened by men, 192; 202

Cranberry (Cranbury), N. J., 75, 115, 116, 117

Crofts, William, sentenced and pardoned, 234-36, 250, 256

Crosswicks, N. J., 102

Dagworthy, Mary, sends stockings for New Jersey Line, 208

Dayton, Elias, rumors about in New York, 140; on Caleb Bruen, 171; secret service in New Jersey, 180; knowledge of British emissaries to Pennsylvania mutineers, 183-84; in command at Chatham, 209; 210; preliminary settlement with New Jersey mutineers, 211-12; 218-20; Woodruff carries British offers to, 224-25; 226, 231, 232

Dayton, Jonathan I., double-dealer at Elizabethtown, 174; distrusted by Daniel Coxe and Isaac Ogden, 174, 265

Decker's ferry, Staten Island, 95

Deep Run bridge, N. J., 115

De Lancey, Oliver, chief of Clinton's secret service, 69-70; 71, 92, 93; his Journal of Pennsylvania mutiny, 94, 139-40, 243-49 (in full); to Staten Island with Clinton, 95; on reliability of Gautier, 162; to send proposals to West Point garrison, 164; 168; garbled name in cipher, 174; on Ottendorf as emissary, 176-77; advances to William Thompson, 178; seeking men of property or West Point deserters to send to Pennsylvania mutineers, 178-79; 183, 184; arrangement with Gifford, 185-87; sends emissaries to New Jersey mutineers, 213-14; 225; career, 243

De Lancey family, 42, 67

Denny, Ebenezer, on after-mutiny at York, 251-52

Denyce's ferry, Long Island, 83

Depreciation certificates, withheld from soldiers, 59

Desertions, frequent at Morristown 1779-80, 19; mass execution of deserters at Morristown, 20, 23-25; British invasion of New Jersey intended to encourage, 25-26; 45; of John Williams, 58; 70; to Arnold and William Odell, 93; from West Point, 178-79; deserters formerly with Humphreys, 267

Detachment, of New England troops, to be sent against Pennsylvania mutineers, 189-93; sent against New Jersey mutineers, 215-24

Dewees, Samuel, not a mutineer at Mount Kemble, 53; on after-mutiny at York, 253-57

Dewey, John, 206

Donaldson, John, of Light Horse, carries message from Wayne, 98; meets Reed at Bristol, 101

Donlop, Sergeant, at Stony Point, 18

Doty, Thomas, 206

Dubbs, Leonard, account of after-mutiny at York, 256-57

Ducats, 38

INDEX 275

Earhart, John, 21
Eastern States. *See* New England
Eliot, George, 206
Elizabeth Point, N. J., 68, 94, 165, 224
Elizabethtown, N. J., Pennsylvania mutineers kept from going towards, 14; road to, 47; American advanced post, 66; 69, 71; Andrew Gautier there learns about Pennsylvania mutiny, 82; 102, 107, 115, 117, 141, 161, 166, 168, 170; Dr. Dayton double-dealer in, 174; 180, 181, 183, 184, 210; New Jersey mutineers expected to come to, 213, 214, 224, 267
Enlistments for long and short terms in different States, 16; conflict over at Mount Kemble, 34-35; negotiations over on January 4, 72-74; Pennsylvania mutineers demand discharges, 75-76; ruling by Committee of Congress, 108; conflict among groups of mutineers, 112; 20-dollar and 120-dollar men, 128; charges as to false enlistments, 128-29; 130; soldiers oaths as proofs, 130-31; 148; false swearing, 197-201; disputed in New Jersey Line, 208
Erskine, Mrs. Robert, entertains Howe and officers, 218
Essex County, N. J., Minute Men, 170; 224
Eustis, Benjamin, 234
Evans, Absalom, shoots Tolbert, 44-45; source, 269
Ewing, George, on May Day at Valley Forge, 207-08
Execution, ceremonies at Morristown in May 1780, 21-25; of James Coleman, 24-25; at Pompton, 222-23; at York, 234-36, 250-57

Faithful friend, sent by Gautier to Princeton, 95; probably drops paper and gets away, 119; his return and report, 161, 168; 175, 245, 266
Farman, Jonathan, 206
Fegany (Feguny), guides Mason to South River, 116; afraid of being accused of treachery, 167; 266
Ferry Street, Trenton, 150
Fieldpieces, seized by Pennsylvania mutineers, 45, 48; given up at Trenton and sent to Philadelphia, 200, 202
First Troop Philadelphia City Cavalry. *See* Light Horse, Philadelphia
Fishbourne, Benjamin, carries Wayne's letter to Washington, 14; at Stony Point, 52; arrives at New Windsor, 64; returns to Wayne with answer, 66, 127; 136, 155; in charge of execution of Mason and Ogden, 156; in Wayne's secret service, 180-81; 183
Flower, Benjamin, with artillery artificers at Carlisle, 36
Foreign-born soldiers, in Pennsylvania Line, 43-44; Lafayette on, 137-38; Washington on, 138; in New Jersey Line, 207
Forest of Dean, N. Y., 217
Forlorn Hopes, at Stony Point, 19
Fort De Lancey, refugee post on Bergen Neck, 68
Fort Hill, and road, 28, 29-30, 39, 47
Fort Schuyler, mutiny of New York troops at, 20
Fortescue, John, convicted of mutinous actions and shot, 234-36, 250, 269
Franklin, Benjamin, 238
Franklin, Samuel, tried for exciting mutiny, and pardoned, 234-36, 250, 256, 269
Franklin, William, royal governor of New Jersey, plans to embody loyalists for plunder and revenge, 90
Frelinghuysen, Frederick, commissioner of New Jersey legislature, 210; asked by Washington to use New Jersey militia against New Jersey mutineers, 215-16
Friendly Sons of St. Patrick, Wayne member of, 51
Frink, Nathan, claims to know leader of Pennsylvania mutineers, desires to raise turmoil in Connecticut, 141; sources, 263
Frost, Nathaniel, 206
Fürstner, Andrew, British spy sent towards Trenton, 115-16; report, 267

Gage, Thomas, 42
Gautier, Andrew, Jr., British secret agent in New Jersey, 67-68; 71; first report on Pennsylvania mutiny, 82; proposals to mutineers sent to him to be forwarded, 87, 93-94; has sent faithful friend to Princeton, 95; 140; faithful friend has returned, 160-61; believes mutineers will join British, 161; called by De Lancey most reliable of correspondents in New Jersey, 162; asked for name of Pennsylvania leader, 165; 167; faithful friend, 168; 174; apparently called Mr. A. J., on

Clinton's List of Proposals, 175; distrusts Gould, 183-84; reports on New Jersey mutiny and requests payment, 225; 243, 244, 245, 248; sources, 262, 264, 265, 266; referred to as Mr. J., 268; 269

Gautier, Andrew, Sr., New York loyalist, cabinetmaker, 67

Gautier, Daniel, New York loyalist, through whom Andrew Gautier letters were sent, 67-68

General Orders, on pay of Continental soldiers, 16; announcing execution of deserters, 20; trial of Williams, 58; on character of American soldiers, 110; on suppression of New Jersey mutiny, 226-27

George III, 84, 89, 185

German Regiment, dissolved by new arrangement of 1781, 36; five companies at Mount Kemble, 42

Germantown, battle of, 206

Gibbons, James, at Stony Point, 18

Gibraltar, British mutiny at, 142, 266

Gifford, William Bernard, double-dealing secret agent, 184-87; report of New Jersey discontents, 210; 247, 249; sources, 251, 265, 266, 267, 268

Gillit, Israel, 206

Gilmore (Gilmour), David, leader of later New Jersey revolt, 220; tried and shot, 222-23

Gloucester County, N. J., 98

Goshen, N. Y., 88, 89

Gould, British spy, brings earliest news of Pennsylvania mutiny to British Headquarters, 66; sent to Elizabethtown for further news, 67, 68; 71; returns with information, 82; 86; takes copies of proposals to Gautier, 87; to *Neptune* and ashore, 93-94; does not return with Gautier's answer, brought by somebody else, 95; return delayed, 141, 160-61; possible source of rumor, 162; on Clinton's List of Proposals, 174; 175; possibly double spy, letter to Dayton, 183-84; brings news of New Jersey mutiny, 213; carries note to Gautier, 225; 243, 244, 262-63, 266, 267, 269, 270

Goznall, George, said to have been member of Board of Sergeants, 57; tried and shot for mutiny, 236, 270

Grant, George, leader of New Jersey mutiny, 211; not blamed for later revolt, 220; sentenced in form, but pardoned, 222-23

Gratuity, of 1779, to Continental soldiers, 17; misused as bounty for reenlistment, 111, 128-29, 131; Committee of Congress in error about, 144

Greene, Nathanael, tries and shoots Goznall, 236, 270

Half-carolines, 38

Half-johanneses, 35, 38

Hamilton, James, testifies against Samuel Franklin, 235

Hand, Edward, brigade at Mount Kemble, 30; born in Ireland, 137

Hardenbergh, Abraham, at mutiny of New York troops, 20

Hatfield, Cornelius, loyalist partisan and guide, 69; proposals to send out, 94; on Clinton's List of Proposals, 174; 175; letter to Gifford intercepted, 187; report of New Jersey discontents, 210; 248

Hayes, Colonel, (possibly Lieutenant Colonel Samuel Hay of 7th Pennsylvania), meets Bruen at Trenton, 172

Haynes, mistaken name for Mason, 167, 266

Hayward, Simeon, 206

Heath, William, commander at West Point, 187; suspects Massachusetts troops of disaffection, 190-91; ordered to detach men to march against New Jersey mutineers, 215

Hendricks, John, on double-dealing spies, 180-81

Hessian Grenadiers, Yagers, 68

Highlands, of Hudson River, department of West Point, 64

Hopewell, N. J., 102

Horses, Army, sent off for want of forage, 62; in bad condition, 151

Hospital, Army, at Morristown, 29, 56

Howe, Robert, report on temper of troops at West Point, 191-93; commands detachment sent against New Jersey mutineers, 217; report to Washington from Ringwood, 218-19; suppresses revolt, 220-24; learns from Dayton about British invasion plans, 225; returns to West Point, 226

Howe, Sir William, Clinton's predecessor as British commander-in-chief in North America, 177

Hubley, Adam, 43

Hudibras, tavern at Princeton, 60

Humphreys, David, aide to Washington,

INDEX

leader of party sent to capture Clinton or Knyphausen, 63; failure, 63-64; his attempt reported to British by American deserters, 267

Humpton, Richard, 202

Hunt, Judge Daniel, host to Reed at Maidenhead, 105, 122; conference at his house of Reed and Wayne, 122

Huts, demolished at Mount Kemble, 29; construction and arrangement, 30-31

Hyer, Jacob, keeper of Hudibras tavern at Princeton, 60

Hynds, mistaken name for Mason, 167, 266

Independence Hall, 78
Infelt, Joseph, 21
Irish (Scotch-Irish), in Pennsylvania Line, 43, 51, 74, 109, 137
Iroquois. See Oneida, Six Nations
Irvine, William, born in Ireland, 137; to Princeton, 150; 155; on re-enlistment of Pennsylvania soldiers, 200

Jamaica, West Indies, 92, 93
Jockey Hollow road, Mount Kemble, 28, 29, 30, 44, 47, 49
Johnson, Ithamar, 206
Johnson's bridge, N. J., over South River, 115
Johnston, Francis, Wayne's letter to, 35; 47; to Philadelphia with news of mutiny, 51, 78; insulted by mutineers, 199
Jones, John Paul, 239
Jumel Mansion, formerly Roger Morris house, New York, quarters of Knyphausen, 63

Kemble, Peter, New Jersey loyalist, his house Wayne's quarters at Mount Kemble, 41-42
Kemble, Stephen, son of Peter Kemble, 41
Kennedy, Archibald, his house at 1 Broadway, New York, Clinton's Headquarters, 63
King's College, Andrew Gautier student at, 67
King's Ferry, 217
Kingston, N. J., 167
Kirkbride's wharf, Bordentown, 195
Knox, George, at Stony Point, 18
Knox, Henry, sent by Washington with circular letter to New England governors, 139, 204; report, 268

Knyphausen, Wilhelm von, Washington's plans to capture, 63-64

Lafayette, Marquis de, Philadelphia to Trenton, 79-80; desires to address Pennsylvania mutineers, 80-81; to Princeton, but not permitted to address them, 96-97; to Morristown, 98; 105, 106, 134; letters from Morristown, 135-37; on foreigners in Pennsylvania Line, 137-38; 166, 169; to Ringwood, 219; conclusions about January mutinies, 229-30; 233; joined by Wayne in Virginia, 236; letters to France about mutiny and need of French aid, 238-39

La Luzerne, Chevalier de, French minister at Philadelphia, 80; Lafayette's letters to, 136-38; and ratification of Articles of Confederation by Maryland, 239

Lancaster, Pa., light dragoons at, 36; 202

Land, 100 acres promised to each Continental soldier at end of war, 33; 200 acres to Pennsylvania recruits, 35

Latimer, Henry, on march of Pennsylvania mutineers to Van Nest's mill, 54-56

Laurens, John, aide to Washington, Philadelphia to Trenton, 79; brief visit to Princeton, 97; to Morristown, 97; favors use of force against mutineers, 134; 136; his mission to France, 238-39

Lawrence, Daniel, 206
Lawrence, Elisha, instructions to go as emissary to Pennsylvania mutineers, 177
Lawrenceville, N. J., 79
Lee, Charles, 100
Lee, Henry, on Pennsylvania Line, 236
Legion. See American Legion
Leonard, Jacob, 206
Levering, Jeremiah, boy in artillery at Mount Kemble, 32
Light Horse, Philadelphia, history and character of troop, 98-99; to escort Reed and Committee of Congress to Trenton, 99; not to be used against mutineers, 121; put in charge of Mason and Ogden, 121; 152; at execution of spies, 156-58
Lilly, said to have been shot at York, 253, 255; possible identification, 256
Lincoln, Joseph, 206

Liquor, sold to soldiers by women, 32; special issue to Pennsylvania Line on New Year's Day, 42; regulations at Pompton, 231

List of Proposals Sent out and by Whom Carried, A, in Clinton's handwriting, 173-75

Livingston, William, governor of New Jersey, suggests that Pennsylvania mutineers cross the Delaware, 79; Mason's attempt to capture, 87; 88, 90, 155, 185

Livingston, William Smith, on aftermutiny at York, 250-51

Long Island, 68, 82, 91, 95, 185

Loring, Joshua, on Ottendorf as emissary, 177

Lott, Mr., aids British spy, 115

Louis XVI, King of France, his birthday celebrated in Philadelphia, 37; 89

Louis d'ors, called French guineas, 38

Loyal American Rangers, corps raised by William Odell, 93

Loyalists, raids into New Jersey, 69; desire Clinton to treat Pennsylvania mutineers as enemies, 83; believe rebel leaders are losing hold on people, 84; partisans threaten to hang six rebels for every loyalist hanged, 88-89

Macaroney (Macaroni) Jack, said to have been member of Board of Sergeants, 57; said to have been shot for mutiny at York, 253-57

McClellan, Joseph, on outbreak at Mount Kemble, 42-43; testifies against James Wilson, 235

McClenachan, Blair, of Light Horse, to Princeton, 105; 107; in charge of Mason and Ogden, 121; 123, 124, 145; on commission to settle Pennsylvania claims, 152

McFarlan, British emissary, carries proposals given to Thomas Ward, 141; double-dealing at Princeton and Trenton, 170-73; agrees to counterplot with Wayne, 172-73; on Clinton's List of Proposals, 175; 176, 184; returns to New York, 212; 248, 264, 266, 269

McFarland, Andrew, captured with Gifford at Elizabethtown, possibly same as spy McFarlan, 170, 184

Mackenzie, Frederick, on collapse of American rebellion, 84-85; on William Odell's corps, 93; assistant adjutant general at British headquarters, 95; on difficulty of getting information from New Jersey, 167-68; 243, 251

McPherson, James Frederick, testifies against Samuel Franklin, 235

Magazine, at Mount Kemble, 30

Maidenhead (Lawrenceville), N. J., 79-80, 81; proposed conference of Reed and Wayne at, 104, 107, 121; conference held, 122-24; 126, 150

Maloney, John, said to have been member of Board of Sergeants, 57; said to have been shot for mutiny at York, 256; possible identification, 256-57. See Macaroney Jack

Maryland, German Regiment partly raised in, 36; loyalists there expected to rise against rebels, 84; ratification of Articles of Confederation, 239

Maryland Line, huts at Mount Kemble, 30; threatened by disaffection from Pennsylvania Line, 236

Mason, John, emissary to Pennsylvania mutineers, in prison in New York, 87; history and character, 87-92; his Warning to Rebels, 88-90; his wife in prison, 91; offers himself to Clinton as spy, 92; made sergeant in William Odell's corps, 93; chosen to carry first set of proposals to Pennsylvania mutineers, 93; route to Princeton, 115-17; meets Williams at Nassau Hall, 117; detained by Board of Sergeants, 117; turned over to Wayne, sent under guard to Reed, 117-19; met on road by Reed, 121; returned to charge of Board of Sergeants, 123-24; to Princeton, 126; debate over execution of, 126-27; 132, 144, 146; to Trenton, 148; delivered to Reed and Wayne, then to Committee of Congress, 153-54; trial and conviction, 154-56; tells of alleged plot to capture Washington, 155, 157; last hours, 156; dies bravely, 157; news of him late in reaching New York, 160; 161, 164, 166, 167; his name mistakenly reported as Oglethorpe, Haynes, Murphy, Hynds, 166-67, 168, 169; witnesses of execution, 172; 173; on Clinton's List of Proposals, 174; 175; news about in New York, 187-89; 212, 244, 248; sources, 261, 264, 265, 266

Massachusetts Line, some of soldiers mutiny at West Point in January

INDEX 279

1780, 20; 113; temper of Line at West Point in January 1781, 191-92; voted gratuity and clothing, 204; petition of sergeants of 2nd Massachusetts for redress, 205-06; detachment sent to suppress New Jersey mutiny, 217-18; hardships at West Point, loyalty at Pompton, 221; 226

Mathews, David, royal mayor of New York, offers reward for capture of Governor Livingston of New Jersey, 87-88; 92

Mathews, John, appointed to Committee of Congress, 79; but remains in Philadelphia, 108

May Day, celebrated at Valley Forge, 207-08

Meigs, Return Jonathan, at Connecticut mutiny, 22

Mendham, N. J., 28, 134

Middle Temple, London, Reed at, 99

Middlebrook, N. J., winter quarters of Continental Army 1778-79, Pennsylvania mutineers halt at, 54; 56, 62

Middlebush, N. J., 75, 88

Middlesex County, N. J., 56

Middletown Point, N. J., 177

Militia, New Jersey, 50; at Rocky Hill, 56; 65, 75, 79; vigilant along coasts and roads, 86; posts taken by, 101-02; sympathize with Pennsylvania mutineers, 102, 108; not feared by mutineers, 113; encountered by British spies, 115-17; 137, 152

Militia, Pennsylvania, 65, 79; sympathize with Pennsylvania Line, 108

Millstone, N. J., 56

Minthorn, John, a leader of New Jersey mutiny, 211; not blamed for later revolt, 220

Mitchell, Reuben, 206

Mitchell, Timothy, 206

Moidores, 38

Monmouth, battle of, 206

Monmouth County, N. J., 177, 228

Moore, Thomas, 134

Morgan, George, his farm site of Pennsylvania mutineers' camp at Princeton, 60

Morrill, Amos, 217

Morris, Mr., loyalist between Cranberry and Princeton, 116

Morris, David Hamilton, boy at Mount Kemble, 32

Morris, Gouverneur, Washington's letter to, 38

Morris (Roger) House, now Jumel Mansion, quarters of Knyphausen, 63

Morris, Samuel, of Light Horse, 98; on commission to settle Pennsylvania claims, 152

Morristown, N. J., 13; hardships of Continental Army in winter quarters at, 1779-80, 18-19; execution of deserters, 20, 23-25; Arnold at, 25; 28, 66; jail, Mason escapes from, 87; 89, 101; unidentified British secret agent at, 119, 168-70; officers and troops remaining at, 134-37; 140, 162; 174, 182, 187, 206

Morrisville, Pa., 152

Mount Kemble, part of grand camp at Morristown, outbreak of Pennsylvania mutiny at, 13-14; Plan of camp, 28; citadel at, 28, 30, 39, 182; guard posts at, 28, 30, 39; women at, 31-32; children at, 32; details of outbreak, 42-47; mutineers leave camp, 47-48; 67, 73, 109, 133, 182, 183, 208, 231, 236, 240

Mount Pleasant, Monmouth County, N. J., 177

Moylan, John, 40

Moylan, Stephen, with light dragoons at Lancaster, 36; joins Wayne at Princeton, 74; 97; to Maidenhead with Wayne, 122

Murderer's Creek, New York, Continental artillery park at, 217

Murphy, mistaken name for Mason, 107, 266

Mutiny, threats of at Valley Forge, 15; of Massachusetts soldiers at West Point in January 1780, 20; of New York soldiers at Fort Schuyler in June 1780, 20; of Connecticut regiments at Morristown in May 1780, 22-23; of British at Gilbraltar, 142; in Continental Articles of War, 235. *See also* New Jersey Line, Pennsylvania Line

Nassau Hall, in 1781, Board of Sergeants quartered in, 60-61; 96; Mason goes to, 117

Neptune, British armed schooner in Raritan Bay, 83; lands Gould and Mason, 93-94; 141; puts Woodruff ashore, 165

Nesbitt, Alexander, of Light Horse, sent to Princeton, 105; 107; in charge of Mason and Ogden, 121; 123, 124

280 INDEX

New arrangement, of Continental Army in 1781, 34; in Pennsylvania Line, 34-35, 42, 202, 266; in New Jersey Line, 186, 211

New Brunswick, N. J. *See* Brunswick

New England, bounties to soldiers in 1779, 16, 17; Washington's circular letter to governors of, 102; soldiers chiefly natives, 113; troops at West Point to go against Pennsylvania mutineers, 188; gratuities and clothing to troops, 204-05; detachment sent to suppress New Jersey mutiny, 215-24; trouble with New Jersey troops at Princeton, 232; efforts to quiet grievances of troops, 238

New Hampshire Line, voted gratuity and clothing, 204; detachment to Ringwood, 217-18; at suppression at Pompton, 221-23; 226

New Jersey legislature (Assembly), sends members to Princeton, 75; efforts to quiet New Jersey Line, 209-10; commissioners at Chatham and Pompton, 210, 212, 215, 231

New Jersey Line, bounties paid in 1779 and 1780, 16, 20; deserters sentenced to death, 20; brigade ordered by Wayne from Pompton to Chatham, 50; 64; where posted, 101; sympathizes with Pennsylvania mutineers, 102; not feared by Pennsylvania mutineers, 113; detachment restless at Mount Kemble and marched to Chatham, 135; 137; rumors about in New York, 140, 165; 186; officers try to enlist discharged Pennsylvania soldiers, 200; history before mutiny, 206-10; discontents at Pompton, 208-10; outbreak of mutiny at Pompton, 210; march to Chatham, temporary settlement, and return to Pompton, 211-12; report of mutiny reaches New York, 212-13; New Jersey mutiny compared with Pennsylvania, 216; renewal and suppression of mutiny at Pompton, 221-24; Orderly Book, 230-31; history of Line after mutiny, 230-31; resentment towards New England troops, 231-32; after the war, 237

New Jersey militia. *See* Militia, New Jersey

New Jersey Regiments: 1st, 211, 220; 2nd, 209, 220; 3rd, 184, 207, 209, 211; 4th, 234

New Jersey Volunteers, Provincial (loyalist) corps, 140

New Market, N. J., 160

New Utrecht, Long Island, 185

New Windsor, N. Y., Washington's Headquarters, 13, 62, 66, 82, 97, 102, 187, 189, 215, 217, 219, 225

New York Gazette, on Gifford, 184-85; 187, 267, 268

New York Line, mutiny of 1st Regiment, 20; deserters sentenced to death, 20

Newark, N. J., report of Pennsylvania mutiny from, 66-67; 115, 141; Bruen family in, 170; Isaac Ogden from, 225

Newhall, Ezra, 192

Nicaragua, plan for expedition against, 93

Nichols, Jonathan, a leader of New Jersey mutiny, 211; kinsman of Woodruff, 213; not blamed for later revolt, 220

Nyack, N. Y., 63

Oaths, of soldiers, permitted as proof of Pennsylvania enlistments, 130-31; false swearing at Trenton, 197-99; 200-01, 212, 232, 237; not permitted as proof of New Jersey enlistments, 212

Odell, Jonathan, report of spies detained, 167, 266

Odell, William, raises corps of adventurers in New York, 92-93; 117; sources, 261, 262

Officers, New Jersey, disgruntled, 208

Officers, Pennsylvania, behavior at outbreak of mutiny, 14, 43-47; share soldiers' hardships, 33-34; repressive discipline, 40; ordered to Rocky Hill, 56; not permitted to enter Princeton, 74-75; to Cranberry and Allentown, 75; at Pennington, 108; men's grievances against, 110-12, 128-29; in straits for money, 111-12; feeling about mutineers, 133-34; excluded from Trenton, 196; conflict with commissioners, 197; insulted by men, 199; some of them involved in mutiny of June 1783, 236

Ogden, Benjamin, 116

Ogden, Isaac, 225

Ogden, James, of South River, Mason's guide to Princeton, 116; character and status, 116; detained with Mason, 117; sent to Wayne and

INDEX

Reed, 118-19; met on road by Reed, 121; returned to Board of Sergeants, 123-24; to Princeton, 126; debate on execution of, 126-27; 132, 144, 146; to Trenton, 148; delivered to Committee of Congress, 153-54; trial, sentence, and execution, 154-56; 161, 164; name apparently mistaken as Oglethorpe, 166-67; 168, 169; witnesses of execution, 172; 173, 187-89, 212; sources, 261, 266, 269

Ogden, Nathaniel, 116

Oglethorpe, reported detained by Pennsylvania mutineers, name possibly a mistake for Ogden, 166-67

Old Bridge, N. J., on way to Princeton, 116, 117

Oneida, Indians used to kill New York mutineers, 20

Orange County, N. Y., conflict between Whigs and Tories, 87-88

Orderly Book, of the New Jersey Line, extracts from, 230-31; 258, 266

Oswegatchie (Ogdensburg), N. Y., 20

Ottendorf, Nicholas Baron de, proposed as emissary to Pennsylvania mutineers, 176-77, 264

Pardon, offered by Wayne to Pennsylvania mutineers, 49; questioned by Reed, 105; Board of Sergeants ask for confirmation, 106; confirmed by Committee of Congress, 108; 113-14, 127; made conditional on surrender of spies, 144; 146, 150; form of pardon, offered to New Jersey mutineers, 212; terms held to have been violated by men, 220

Parke, Theophilus, cashiered with infamy for defrauding soldiers, 111

Parkin (Perkins?), information furnished by, 165-66, 265

Parsons, Samuel Holden, on temper of Connecticut troops, 192-93

Passaic, N. J., 67

Paulus Hook, N. J., British garrison at, 67, 68; British spies sent by way of, 141; 267

Pay, of soldiers, considered higher than British pay, 16; actual value at end of 1780, 34; pay of sergeants, 57; Washington asks three months' pay for all Continental soldiers, 139; one month's pay to each Pennsylvania soldier, 197; pay at discharge of Continental Army, 237; pay in arrears, according to *Pierce's Register*, after war, 260

Pennington, N. J., Pennsylvania officers at, 108, 103; Wayne's visit to, 196

Pennsylvania, Council, and State government in general, attempts to buy clothing for troops in Europe, 29; to make up to soldiers for loss by depreciation, 33; new bounty voted in 1780, 35; difficulties in supplying Line, 36-37; subscription to aid soldiers, 37-38; Council sends Potter with money to Mount Kemble, 38; 47; demands of mutineers referred to Council by Wayne, 73; 75; Wayne sends express to Council, 76; Council learns of Pennsylvania mutiny, 78-79; sends Reed and Potter to negotiate with mutineers, 99; not wholly blamed by mutineers, 110; 118, 123, 146, 152; Council thinks Wayne too hasty in offering reward for surrendering spies, 158; 194, 195, 196; difficulties over money and supplies for settlement, 201; has not kept engagements with Pennsylvania mutineers, 233

Pennsylvania Line, regiments of Continental Army enlisted and supplied by Pennsylvania, 13-14, 16; added bounty of 1778, 16; terms of enlistment, 16; special hardships, 17; first to receive gratuity of 1779, 17-18; summer campaign of 1779, against Six Nations and at Stony Point, 18; frequent desertions in 1779-80, 19; deserters sentenced to death, 21; assists in putting down Connecticut mutiny, 23; execution for desertion, 23-25; brigade to West Point, 26; huts at Mount Kemble, 29-31; women and children with at Mount Kemble, 31-32; privations, 32-34; effects of new arrangement on, 34-35, 40; conflict over enlistments, 34-35; convicts enlisted in Line, 35, 233; return of Pennsylvania troops at Mount Kemble and elsewhere in December 1780, 36, 261; arrangement set for New Year's Day, 42; character of troops, 43-44; outbreak of mutiny, 43-47; mutineers leave camp, 47-48; deficiency of soldiers' records of mutiny, 53; first halt at Vealtown, 53-54; good conduct of mutineers on march to Princeton, 57; organization of Board of Sergeants, 57-59; temporary military organization, 57, 96-97; grievances mentioned to Wayne, 59-60; plan to send committee of mutineers to Congress, 59-60; camp on George Morgan's farm at Princeton, 60; demand discharges of 20-dollar men, 75-76; rumor of Arnold's friends and British gold among mutineers, 79-80; mutineers accused of intending to lay country waste, 80; British proposals to mutineers prepared in New York, 85-86; summary of mutineers' position, 109-14; Line called by Reed flower of Continental Army, 113; resolve to be regular and chaste, 114; mutineers refuse to turn Arnolds, 118; not sure Reed has come to Maidenhead, 123-24; negotiations with Reed at Princeton, 125-32; doubt whether rank and file will accept decisions of Board of Sergeants, 130; numbers at Princeton and left at Mount Kemble, 135, 136; mutineers desire Wayne to remain at Princeton, 148; march to Trenton, 150-51; precautions taken there, 151-52; reports of Pennsylvania mutiny in New York, 160-67; St. Clair's plot to deceive mutineers, 168-70; Washington's plan to suppress mutiny by force, 189-93; mutineers restless at Trenton, 195-96; false oaths, 197-98; desire to re-enlist, 200; discharged men to rendezvous after furloughs, 202; new arrangement completed, 202; Pennsylvania example followed in New Jersey mutiny, 208-09; Pennsylvania Line after January 1780, 232-37; settlement completed, 232; difficulties of raising regiments for Southern campaign, 233-34; after-mutiny at York, 234-36, 250-57; mutiny of April 1782, 236, 270; mutiny of June 1783, 236; after the war, 237.

Pennsylvania militia. See Militia, Pennsylvania

Pennsylvania officers. See Officers, Pennsylvania

Pennsylvania Packet, account of executions at York, 235, 250; account of celebration of Articles of Confederation, 239-40; account of mutiny at Mount Kemble, Princeton, Trenton, 267

Pennsylvania Regiments: 1st, 47, 199, 202, 234; 2nd, 46, 47, 56, 199, 202, 234, 236; 3rd, 47, 200, 202, 234; 4th, 46, 47, 112, 202; 5th, 29, 42, 47, 56, 199, 202; 6th, 47, 202; 7th, 47; 8th, at Pittsburgh, 36; 9th, 29, 42, 47, 56; 10th, 42, 47, 53; 11th, 42-44, 47, 57; artillery regiment (4th Continental Artillery), 30, 79, 199, 202, 234

Pennsylvania sergeants. See Sergeants, Board of

Perkins. See Parkin

Perkins, Theodore, 206

Perth Amboy, N. J., British armed party landed at, 77; 162-63

Philadelphia, British armed galley, lands Mason in Raritan River, 94

Philadelphia Light Horse. See Light Horse, Philadelphia

Phillips, William, on difficulty of getting information, 162; doubts Pennsylvania mutineers will join British, 163

Pistoles, Spanish, 38

Pitt, Catharine, married to James Ogden, 116, 156; marriage bond, 261

Pittsburgh, Pa., 8th Pennsylvania at, 36

Playter, George, called Dr. Welding (Wilding), refuses to carry proposals to Pennsylvania mutineers, but goes to William Thompson, 177-78; sources, 263, 265, 269

Pluckemin, N. J., Pennsylvania mutineers march through, 54, 164

Pompton, N. J., New Jersey brigade ordered from to Chatham, 50; 101, 135; New Jersey Line to winter quarters at, 186, 207; discontents at, 208-10; 213, 215, 216, 218, 219; suppression of New Jersey mutiny at, 221-24; 228, 231, 232, 236

Porter, Billy, 191

Potter, James, of Pennsylvania militia, member of Pennsylvania Council, to Mount Kemble with money for Line, 38, 40; to Philadelphia with news of mutiny, 51, 78; sent by Council to negotiate with mutineers, 99; 100; to Maidenhead, 105; 121, 123; at Princeton negotiations, 125-32; 151; appointed to commission to settle Pennsylvania claims, 152; joins with Reed in report to Washington, 260, 267, 268-69

Poughkeepsie, N. Y., 89

Pratt, Ephraim, 206

Primrose Brook, Mount Kemble, 28, 47

Princeton, N. J., Pennsylvania mutineers turn towards, 14, 48; 28; march

INDEX

of mutineers to, 54-56; Princeton in 1781, 60-61; negotiations with mutineers at, 72-78; 79, 80, 82, 86, 93; visit of St. Clair and Lafayette, 96-97; 99, 100, 101, 104, 105, 107, 109, 113, 114, 115, 116; Mason and Ogden arrive at, 117; 118; Reed hesitates to come to, 120-21; Reed to Princeton, 123-24; Reed's negotiations with mutineers at, 125-32; number of mutineers at, 135; 137, 138, 140, 151, 154, 161, 165, 166; British secret agents afraid to be seen near, 168; Gautier's faithful friend at, 168; 169; McFarland and Caleb Bruen at, 170-73; 174, 175, 177, 183, 187, 188, 209, 216; clash of New Jersey and New England troops at, 231-32; 240

Princeton College. *See* College of New Jersey

Proctor, Thomas, 30; Philadelphia to Trenton, 79; 81; excluded by men, 199

Prospect, George Morgan's farm at Princeton, 60

Provisions. *See* Rations

Provost, military prison in New York, 87; Mason in, 91

Putnam, Rufus, 191, 192

Queen (Broad) Street, Trenton, 151
Quibbletown (New Market), N. J., 160

Rabels Defiance, 90
Rations, due Continental soldiers, 15; shortage at Valley Forge, 15; at Morristown in 1779-80, 18-19; in Connecticut Line, 22; complaints over at Mount Kemble, 32-34; shortage at West Point, 62; Washington on needs of Army, 103; number drawn by Pennsylvania mutineers, 145; given discharged mutineers, 201-02; shortage in Massachusetts Line, 205, 221
Rattoon, John, finds guide for Mason to South River, 94; furnishes information, 160; 266
Reading, Pa., 202
Reed, Esther De Berdt, wife of Joseph Reed, heads subscription of Philadelphia ladies for shirts for soldiers of Pennsylvania Line, 37, 99
Reed, Joseph, President of the Supreme Executive Council of Pennsylvania, and so of Pennsylvania, under constitution of 1776, 16, 32; leaves Philadelphia for Trenton, 98; history and character, 99-100; at Bristol, 100; meets Donaldson of Light Horse, 101; at Trenton, 104; proposes conference with Wayne at Maidenhead, 104; to Daniel Hunt's, Maidenhead, 105; invited by Board of Sergeants to Princeton, 106-07; receives oral information and at first declines to go, 107-08; confers with Committee of Congress at Trenton, 108-09; calls Pennsylvania Line the flower of the Army, 114; 119; attempts to draw mutineers to Trenton, 119-20; snubs Bowzar, 120; fears to go to Princeton, 120-21; meets Mason and Ogden on road to Maidenhead, 121; makes more confident proposals to mutineers through Wayne, 122; confers at Maidenhead with Wayne and colonels, 122-24; decides to go to Princeton, 123-24; negotiations at Princeton with mutineers, 125-31; makes final proposals, 130-31; returns to Maidenhead, 131; conflict with Wayne, 132; about Mason and Ogden, 132; St. Clair's letter to, 134-35; 138, 142; 143, 144; on number of mutineers, 145; proposals accepted with counter-proposal, 145-56; refuses counter-proposal, 146; opposed to Wayne's remaining at Princeton, 147; desires to speak to men at Trenton but not permitted, 151; to Bloomsbury, 152; demands surrender of spies, 152-53; spies brought to him but sent to Committee of Congress, 153; afraid mutineers might plunder Philadelphia, 154; avoids paying reward promised by Wayne, 158-59; 161, 162, 190; his plan to please women of Pennsylvania Line, 194; difficulty in carrying out proposals, 195-96; responsibility for hasty settlement, 198; 199; proclamation, 201; his zeal disapproved by Wayne, 203; 234; report to Washington, 260, 268-69

Reeves, Enos, on outbreak at Mount Kemble, 42-43; in Wick's orchard, 45; on conduct of mutineers, 48

Reward, promised by Wayne for surrender of Mason and Ogden, 118; Wayne insists on it, 145; payment avoided by Reed's stratagem, 158-59; 194

Rhode Island Line, bounty of 1780, 20; gratuity of January 1781, 204-05

Richardson, Ebenezer, 206

Richmond, Jonathan, Board of Sergeants quartered at his tavern at Trenton, 152
Ringwood, N. J., Connecticut detachment at, 217; troops from West Point arrive at, 218; Washington and Lafayette at, 219
Robertson, James, royal governor of New York, character, 140; gossip about emissaries sent to Princeton and expected rebel deserters, 163; to Staten Island to encourage New Jersey mutiny, 213; plans to invade New Jersey, 225-26
Rochambeau, Comte de, 229
Rocky Hill, N. J., Pennsylvania officers ordered to, 56; 140
Rogers, William, Pennsylvania chaplain at execution at Morristown, 23-24
Ross, Stewart, of *Neptune*, lands Mason, 94; 165
Ruggles, Isaac, reports hanging of two spies, 166-67, 266
Rum, price of at camp in 1779, 17; allowance due Continental soldiers, 17; shortage at Mount Kemble, 32-33, 39; necessary for troops at West Point, 193; to be kept from Pennsylvania mutineers, 195

St. Clair, Arthur, ranking officer of Pennsylvania Line, disliked by Wayne, 41; from Philadelphia to Trenton, 79-80; 81; to Princeton but rejected by mutineers, 96-97; in command at Morristown, 97; 98, 105, 106; brought British proposals by unidentified emissary, 119; St. Clair's decoy letter to Wayne, 134; 135, 136; arrests mutineer sent to Mount Kemble, 137; born in Scotland, 137; plans to use unidentified emissary in counterplot, 168-70; 171, 175; counterplot discouraged by Washington, 187-88; 190
St. George, Richard, junior deputy adjutant general, 243
Sandy Hook, N. J., 64, 181
Scalps, Indian, taken by Pennsylvanians for bounty, 37
Schuyler, Philip, Washington's letters to, 19, 188
Schuyler family, 42
Scott's tavern, 177
Secret service, American and British compared, 180-81
Sergeants, Board of, Pennsylvania Line, first suggestion of, 14; originate in committee proposed by soldiers and consented to by Wayne, 49; first meeting with Wayne, 54-55; organization and members, 57-59; conference with Wayne on January 3, 59-60; quartered at Nassau Hall, 60; negotiations with Wayne on January 4, 72-74; promise to settle in six days, 73; suspicious of interference from outsiders, 75; notes and apparent threat to Wayne, 75-77; declare they will fight British, 77, 118; reception of St. Clair and Lafayette, 96-97; determined to stay at Princeton till settled with, 97; send soldiers to Philadelphia to correct false rumors about mutiny, 100; conference with Wayne on first letter from Reed, 105; exchange of notes with Wayne on clothing and pardon, 105-06; invite Reed to Princeton, 106-07; some of them regret mutiny, 108; detain Mason and Ogden, 117; Reed avoids answering directly, 120-21; demand return of Mason and Ogden, 123-24; negotiations with Reed at Princeton, 125-32; not sure Reed's proposals will satisfy rank and file, 142-43; agreement to Reed's proposals, with counter-proposal refused by Reed, 145-46; refuse to halt troops at Trenton for Reed to address them, 151; quartered at Richmond's tavern at Trenton, 152; unconditionally surrender spies, and keep promise to settle in six days, 153; send spies to Reed, then to Committee of Congress, 153; refuse to accept reward for surrender of spies, 159; Reed's two comments on refusal, 159; continue in command, 195-96; asked to continue still by commissioners, 200; discontinued and dismissed, 232
Shiell, Hugh, carries message to Committee of Congress, 121
Shreve, Israel, by Washington considered incompetent, 209; at outbreak of New Jersey mutiny, 210; to Chatham, 210; possible understanding with original leaders, 211; return to Pompton, 212; ordered to compel submission if possible, 215; information to Howe, 218-19; absent at time of suppression, 220, 222; retires, 231
Sign of the College, tavern at Princeton, 60-61
Siscoe, Isaac, British spy sent to neigh-

INDEX

borhood of West Point, 95, 264
Six Nations, of Iroquois, expedition against, 18, 24, 206, 211
Skinner, Cortlandt, intelligence received by, 139-41; on Clinton's List of Proposals, 175
Smith, Pennsylvania soldier named, 256
Smith, Claudius, loyalist partisan of Orange County, 88, 91
Smith, Jack, said by Dewees to have been shot at York, 253, 254; possibly referred to by Dubbs, 256
Smith, Philip, tried for mutinous expressions and shot at York, 234-36, 256
Smith, William, royal chief justice of New York, talks with Robertson, 163; writes address to West Point garrison, 164, 265
Smith's Clove, N. Y., 88, 218
Soap, 40
Somerset County, N. J., 56
Somerset Court House (Millstone), N. J., 56
South Amboy, N. J., 68, 71, 77, 94, 102, 160, 165, 166, 167
South River, N. J., Pennsylvania mutineers urged to cross, 86
South River, N. J., village of, 94; bridge at, 115; James Ogden joins Mason at, 116; 166
Spanish Main, 93
Spies, or emissaries, unidentified, British spies carry handbills to Morristown, 21; American spy reports on news of mutiny at British Headquarters, 71, 76-77; further report by possibly a second American spy, 82; admiring spy (actually Yeomans) on good behavior of Pennsylvania mutineers, 56, 265; British spy (actually McFarlan) on Williams, 58, 117, 249, 266; Newark informers (actually Thomas and Abram Ward), about outbreak at Mount Kemble, 66-67, 262; spies as regularly used by British, 70; spies when caught generally hanged by Americans, 86; emissary sent with oral message to Pennsylvania mutineers, 94; Hatfield's messenger, 94, 175; emissary (presumably Gautier's faithful friend) who dropped proposals at Princeton, 119; emissary who carried his proposals to St. Clair at Morristown, 119, 168-70, 175, 188, 264; two trusty men (one Yeomans) to go to West Point, 141, 265; British spy on Gibraltar mutiny, 142, 266; emissaries (possibly others besides McFarlan and Caleb Bruen) who dropped proposals at Trenton, 154; spy (Joseph Clark) from Morristown, 162; gentleman who could be depended on, 165-66, 265; British correspondents fear to go near Princeton, 167-68; 175-76; American spies often unidentified, 180; double-dealing spy mentioned by Hendricks, 181; double-dealing spy employed by Wayne, 181-83; American spy possibly to be identified with Gould, 183-84; three of Dayton's spies captured by British, 184; women as spies, 190-91, 210; unknown informer about New Jersey discontents, 209; emissaries (possibly others besides Blank and Woodruff) to New Jersey mutineers, 224; loyalist from Trenton (actually named Buchanan in Information of Deserters), 228. See also Blank, Faithful friend, Gould
Spotswood, N. J., 115, 116, 117
Sprague, Theodore, 206
Springfield, N. J., 66
Sprout, Ebenezer, 191; petition of sergeants to, 205-06; commands Massachusetts detachment sent against Pennsylvania mutineers, 217, 222-23
Stapleton, John, assistant adjutant general, interview with Mason, 92; 93; at British Headquarters in New York, 95; 243
Staten Island, 64; Gould to, 66; 68; loyalist partisans, 69; 82, 94; Clinton to, 95; 128, 139, 167, 174; Robertson and De Lancey to, 212; invasion expected from, 225
Stewart, Charles, orders mutineers fed at Princeton, 74; carries news of mutiny to Trenton, 78-79; 81
Stewart, Walter, to go with Wayne after mutineers, 14, 51; on Pennsylvania grievances, 16-17; his regiment holds out against mutiny, 46; character, 51; on way to Princeton, 54-56; 72-74, 76, 80, 97; just treatment of soldiers, 111; 118; to Maidenhead, 122; 134; Lafayette's letter to, 135, 136, 145, 155; threatens to prosecute his men for perjury, 199; 202
Stirling, Earl of, said to be hated by Pennsylvania mutineers, 81; orders court martial for Mason and Ogden, 154; concerning New Jersey Line, 209

INDEX

Stony Brook, Princeton, 125
Stony Point, N. Y., capture of, 18, 52; 217
Stuyvesant family, 42
Suffern, N. Y., 42, 207, 217
Sugar, price of at camp, 17
Sugar House, prison in New York, 69; Bruen in, 171, Woodruff in, 225
Sullivan, John, Washington's letter to, 17; against Six Nations, 18, 24; chairman of Committee of Congress, 79; 108; Lafayette's letter to, 136; report to Washington on surrender of Mason and Ogden, 138; on trial of spies, 155; his letter received by Washington, 188-89; 190, 206, 211, 216
Summer Seat, Morrisville, Pa., house of Thomas Barclay, quarters of Committee of Congress, 152; trial of Mason and Ogden at, 154-56, 157, 187
Supreme Executive Council of Pennsylvania. See Pennsylvania, Council
Sussex County, N. J., 89
Sutlers, 32, 192, 231

Tammany, King, 207
Tents, regulations, 60
Thacher, James, on executions at Morristown, 23-25; march to Ringwood, 217-18; trial and executions at Pompton, 222-23
Thompson, William, British advances to, 177-78
Throop, Benjamin, commanding Connecticut troops at Ringwood, 217
Ticonderoga, N. Y., 84
To the Officers and Soldiers of the Continental Army, loyalist verse, 162
Tolbert, Samuel, wounded at Mount Kemble by Absalom Evans, 13, 44-45, 269
Totowa, N. J., Pennsylvania troops at, 27, 29
Trenton, N. J., Continental stores at, 74; New Jersey legislature in session at, 75; suggested conference to be held at, 76; 79, 80, 81, 97, 99; Trent-Cox house (Bloomsbury) at, 104, 115, 119, 152; Reed tries to draw Pennsylvania mutineers to, 119-21; 138, 145, 146, 148; mutineers march to, 150-51; Trenton in 1781, 151-52; 156, 157, 162, 165, 166; McFarlan and Bruen at, 170-73; 175, 187, 193; settlement at, 194-203; 208, 209, 218; settlement completed at, 232; 237, 240

Trescott, Lemuel, 191
Trumbull, Jonathan, governor of Connecticut, efforts in behalf of Connecticut Line, 204-05
Tuttle, John, leader of New Jersey revolt, 220; trial and execution, 222-23
Tyger, Cornelius, on behavior of Pennsylvania mutineers, 54; on rising at West Point, 164; 246; 265

Unidentified loyalist, verses by, 162
Unidentified spies. See Spies, or emissaries, unidentified

Valley Forge, privations at, 15, 18; huts at, 30; New Jersey Line at, 206; May Day celebration at, 207-08
Van Cortlandt family, 42
Van Nest's mill, N. J., 36
Van Rensselaer family, 42
Van Veghten, Derrick, and Van Veghten's Bridge, 54
Vealtown (Bernardsville), N. J., 14, 53
Vermont, reported disaffected, 84
Verse, by John Mason, 90; by unidentified loyalist, 162; by George Grant, 211
Virginia, bounty paid soldiers in 1779, 16; Arnold's raid to, 39, 84, 180; Virginia Line at Vealtown, 53
Voorhies, Nancy, married to Gifford, 185
Vose, Thomas, 191
Vulture, British armed sloop, 83; Fürstner landed from, 115; lands party with flag of truce at South Amboy, 160; lands armed party at Perth Amboy, 162

Waiters, officers' servants in Continental Army, 32
Wallis, Samuel, secret traitor in Philadelphia, on Mason at his execution, 157, 265; proposed as emissary to Pennsylvania mutineers, 265; 267
Ward, Joseph, captured by Mason's band, 91
Ward, Thomas, of Orange County and Bergen Neck, 69, 87; attempts to capture William Livingston, 87, 155; given proposals to send out, 94; these carried by McFarlan, 141; alleged plot to capture Washington, 155
Warning to Rebels, A, by Mason, 88-90
Washington, George, at New Windsor at time of Pennsylvania mutiny, 13; on privations at Valley Forge, 15; on

INDEX

depreciation and common soldiers, 17; on hardships at Morristown in 1779-80, 18; requisitions, 19; on lack of system in Army matters, 19; on Connecticut mutiny, 22-23; on spirit of soldiers in June 1780, 24; Arnold dines with, 25; assigns Pennsylvania troops to Mount Kemble, 29; 31; on prospects for winter, 38; opinion of Wayne, 41; Latimer's letter to, 54, 56; pardons Williams, 58; no money for Washington's table, 62; plans at end of 1780, 62-63; British plans to capture Washington, and Arnold's suggestion, 63; first steps on hearing of Pennsylvania mutiny, 64-65; changes mind about going to Philadelphia, 66; 68; efforts to prevent guerrilla warfare in New Jersey, 69; 70; advised by Wayne not to come to Princeton, 78; 83, 88, 95; on Philadelphia Light Horse, 98-99; 100; circular letter to New England governors, 102-03; 112, 113; his letter of advice reaches Wayne, 127; instructions cited by Wayne, 132; letters to from Morristown, 134-36; on distresses of troops at West Point, 138; on native and foreign-born soldiers, 138; sends Knox to New England, 139; 145, 154; plot to capture Washington according to Mason, 155, 157; 159; reported in New York to have gone to Congress, 161; 163; 164, 167; on St. Clair's projected counterplot, 169; 171, 173; records of Washington's secret service, 180, 181; 182, 185; on Gifford, 186-87; consults his officers about West Point troops, and orders detachment to march if necessary against Pennsylvania mutineers, 187-89; judgment of Pennsylvania mutiny, 189-90; fears letters will be intercepted, 190; disapproves of Heath's investigations, 191; thinks detachment will not be necessary, 194; 200, 202-03; on petition of Massachusetts sergeants, 206; receives news of New Jersey mutiny, 206; 207, 208; opinion of Elias Dayton and Shreve, 209; resolves to suppress New Jersey mutiny, 215-16; goes to West Point, 217; orders to Robert Howe, 217; to Ringwood, 219; reproves Shreve for absence at time of suppression, 222; 226; to Rochambeau and New England governors on suppression, 229; not sanguine about Pennsylvania recruiting, 233; Wayne sends court martial proceedings to, 234; instructions to Laurens, 238

Wayne, Anthony, first letter about Pennsylvania mutiny, 13-14; order of January 2, 14, 49-50; at Stony Point, 18, 52; repairing clothes at Totowa, 27; headquarters at Kemble's house, 28, 30; on shortages at Mount Kemble, 32-34; on depreciation, and land for soldiers, 33; 35; asks money for recruits, 37; plans defenses for camp, 38-39; 40; character of, 41; dislikes St. Clair, 41; declines invitation to Beverwyck, 42; meets officers to settle new arrangement, 42; arrives at scene of mutiny, 45-46; and Irish soldier, 46; stand at cross-roads, 47-48; issues order, 49-50; fear of British landing in concert with mutiny, 50; warns Congress and informs Washington, 51-52; dealings with mutineers on way to Princeton, 54-56; guard ordered for, 55; meets sergeants on January 3, 59-60; quartered probably at tavern at Princeton, 60-61; Washington's first advice to, 65; 66; negotiates with Board of Sergeants on January 4, 72-74; 75; sends express to Pennsylvania Council, 76; asks Council to send member to Princeton, 77; letter to Washington, 77-78; 80; plans laid for Wayne's capture by Mason, 91; 95; Board of Sergeants confer at his quarters with St. Clair and Lafayette, 96-97; instructions to light horseman, 98; 101; invited by Reed to Maidenhead, 104; confers on Reed's letter with Board of Sergeants, 105; two notes from Board of Sergeants, 105-06; message to Reed, 107; 108; just treatment of soldiers, 111; 114; on surrender of Mason and Ogden, 117-18; 119; another letter from Reed, 119-21; confers with Reed at Maidenhead, 122-23; 125; urges execution of Mason and Ogden by mutineers, 126-27; at negotiations between Reed and Board of Sergeants, 125-32; dissatisfied with Reed's proposals, 131-32; conflict with Reed, 132; about Mason and Ogden, 132; 134; St. Clair's decoy letter to, 134; hopes to divide mutineers, 136; 137; 139; unable to learn mutineers' secrets, 143; 145, 146; gets some credit for march to Trenton, 147; mutineers desire him to remain with them, 147-48; to Trenton, 150; at Bloomsbury, 152; spies brought to, 153; presides at court martial of Mason and Ogden, 155; reports Mason's revelations of alleged plot to capture Washington, 155, 157; Wayne to Pennington, 158; reward promised by Wayne to sergeants evaded by Reed, 158-59; 161, 166, 168; unidentified emissary sent to by St. Clair, 169; plans to use McFarlan and Caleb Bruen against Clinton, 172-73; episode of his secret service, 180-83; 188; 189, 190; at Pennington, 196; his quarters fired on at Trenton, 199; on re-enlisting in Pennsylvania Line, 200; summary of settlement on January 21, 202-03; 207, 208; tribute in verse to, 211; reports final settlement, 232; on difficulty of recruiting for Southern expedition, 233; after-mutiny at York, 234-36, 250-57; with Line to South, 236.

Welding (Wilding), Dr., pseudonym for George Playter, 177-78, 263, 265, 269

West Point, N. Y., 13; mutiny of Massachusetts soldiers at, 20; 26; shortages at, 62, 65-66; 83, 95, 113; garrison informed of Pennsylvania mutiny, 138; British secret agents sent towards, 141; 162; rising at reported in New York, 164; address to garrison drafted by William Smith, 164; deserters from refuse to go to Pennsylvania mutineers, 179; 186; temper of troops at, 187-89, 190-93; 215, 217, 226

Westfield, N. J., 224

Whippany, N. J., 42

Whisky, allowance due Continental soldiers, 17; 218, 236

White, Francis, wounded at Mount Kemble, 13, 44, 45

Wick, Temperance, mutineers and her horse, 49

Wick, Thomas, house and orchard at Mount Kemble, 28, 30; magazine in orchard seized by mutineers, 45; 49, 182

Willettstown, N. J., name often given to South River village, 117

Williams, John (?), president of Board of Sergeants, 57-58; probably John Williams of 2nd Pennsylvania, sentenced to death for desertion but pardoned by Washington, 58; 76; reported to be willing to join British, 107; receives Mason and Ogden at Nassau Hall, 177; turns them over to Board of Sergeants and Wayne, 118; shows spies to Line, 126; proposes to send them back to Clinton with taunting message, 126; said to be drunk or illiterate, and incompetent, 129; 153; name still not known to British in New York, 165; 247; sources, 249, 266

Williamson, Sergeant, reported to be a leader of Pennsylvania mutineers, 165-66

Wilson, James, convicted of exciting mutiny and shot, 234-35, 250

Wilson, Thomas, convicted of exciting mutiny and shot, 234-35, 250

Witherspoon, John, President of College of New Jersey, member of Committee of Congress, 79, 108

Women, with Pennsylvania Line at Mount Kemble, 31-32; to Princeton, 109; at West Point, 190-92; Reed's plan to please, 194; women of New Jersey Line disorderly, 208, 231; woman informs Shreve at Pompton of mutiny, 210; at York, 253, 255

Woodbridge, N. J., 107

Woodruff, Isaac, mayor of Elizabethtown, 224

Woodruff, Uzal, of Elizabethtown, British spy, and double-dealer, goes out and back on secret errand, 141; landed from *Neptune*, 165; back from Kingston, 167; on Clinton's List of Proposals, 174; imprisoned by British for treachery, 184; reports unrest in New Jersey Line, 210; brings word of New Jersey mutiny, 213; carries proposals to New Jersey mutineers, 214; reveals himself to Elias Dayton, 224; career, 224-25; 246, 248, 263, 265, 268; sources, 269

Yeomans, Ezekiel, reports rising at West Point, 164, 265

York, Pa. (in eighteenth century commonly called York Town to distinguish it from the County), 202; after-mutiny at, 234-36, 250-57

York (Manhattan) Island, 226

Yorktown, Va., 223, 232, 236